FAIR WINDS OF DEATH

Marcia,

Thanks for coming
on this trip with me!

Fair Winds Always!

Bill Wade

9 May 23

FAIR WINDS

OF

DEATH

B. R. WADE, JR.

A WADE PUBLISHING NOVEL

Wade Publishing LLC
1782 Trinity Road, Belington, West Virginia 26250
www.wadepublishing.com

Copyright © 2021 by Billy R. Wade, Jr.

Library of Congress Control Number:
2021913882

ISBN 978-1-7375461-0-8 (paperbound)
ISBN 978-1-7375461-1-5 (e-book)
ISBN 978-1-7375461-2-2 (hardcover)

Printed in the United States of America

This is a work of fiction. Space and time have been rearranged to suit the convenience of the book, and with the exception of references to historical figures, any resemblance to persons living or dead is coincidental. Certain long-standing and factual institutions, ships, buildings, military facilities and equipment, vehicles, and public places are mentioned, but the characters involved are wholly imaginary and their interaction with these actual entities is pure fantasy.

This work does include some of the author's recollections of serving in the United States Navy while attending Yeoman A School at NTC Bainbridge, and later serving as a Yeoman to the Naval Investigative Service Office Norfolk. Those recollections have been added to honor all the fantastic men and women he knew and served with at the time.

ACKNOWLEDGEMENTS

At first, writing the words you are about to read seemed a lonely task. The screen, the keyboard, and a comfy chair were my only companions—that is, excluding the voices in my head. However, I now realize that this book, and I with it, are products of every person I have met, every place I have been, and everything I have seen and done. I am so very grateful to all of those influences.

There are a few people who actually participated in the creation of this book and I am in their debt:

Alice handled the initial punctuation and grammar editing chores efficiently and with great kindness.

Louise provided a level of professional editing that massaged rough words into a readable story.

Brooks (aka "Rooster"), a retired Navy F-4 pilot, helped keep me straight on the Phantom specifics.

Alice and Dave provided opinions after their beta reads of the manuscript.

Stewart expertly did the formatting of the pages and gave them a very professional look. He also created a cover that is intriguing as well as eye-catching.

I

THE PAIN WAS INTENSE. NO matter how much he tried to give it a rest, the muscle in his lower back was driving him loco. Movements involving his upper body caused pains to shoot throughout his torso and right to his brain. But pain was not allowed to take control, as Raul still had several more hours of digging before he could stop. And with most of the work confined to the tunnel, which was only four feet high, his hunched-over position tweaked that bad muscle every second he was there. Approaching middle age, he felt way too old for this crap.

When Enrique left at the end of his shift, he told the others it looked like there were only about twenty meters of digging left. Enrique was always positive to a fault. "Only a little over twenty meters," he grumbled; but when his back hurt so much, it may as well have been to the end of the damn island. Twenty meters was a long damn way. The rest of the diggers—Carlos, Mario, and Luis—were just as negative, or maybe they were just realists. They still had tons of dirt to move, and all this digging had to be done while keeping the tunnel a total secret.

Vicente kept telling him they needed to hurry; *the big boss wanted this done last week,* he kept yelling. No one on the crew knew who the hell the big boss was. All contact with the big boss had come through Emilio, Vicente's cousin. All they ever heard was that the big boss was a Cuban-American, and ruthless. There were rumors he was related to Jesus Martinez, a friend who'd fled Cuba with his parents several years ago. But no one knew for sure, and no one was stupid enough to ask.

If they had not been paid so well, they would have told Vicente and his cousin to *besame el culo*—but instead they kept digging, hauling out dirt, and installing the track, roof supports, and lights. Their negative attitudes were greatly offset by lots of money, at least in the eyes of the average Cuban citizen. That helped make life more positive.

It was extremely hard to be positive living in Cuba under Castro, and even harder when you had to do almost anything to survive. Legal jobs were hard to find, so to earn money for food, many Cubans turned to illegal jobs. And that often meant drugs. Vicente's crew figured the reason they were digging a hidden tunnel deep under the fence was an illegal one, and probably involved drugs. But the smart—and safest—thing to do was not ask questions or even guess out loud.

So they kept digging, kept loading dirt into the small carts that ran on the track they installed, and kept their mouths shut. Each day saw the tunnel getting deeper, and each day Vicente complained about the lack of speed. Raul currently had the midnight to four a.m. shift. Since there was only room for one person in the tunnel at a time, Raul filled the cart with dirt and, using the continuous rope that looped around pulleys at each end, pulled it back toward the entrance.

When the cart full of dirt arrived at the tunnel entrance, Vicente loaded the dirt into his truck. At least this part of the operation was easy to conceal; the tunnel started at the back of a deserted warehouse, a little over two hundred meters from the fence they were tunneling under. Twice a day, Vicente would drive his truck out the roll-up warehouse door and head to a secluded location. There he would dump the load and head back.

The digging project lasted another three weeks. When it was finally completed, Emilio and Vicente drove them all to a fancy house on the beach, near the town of San Antonio del Sur, for celebratory drinks. It was hinted that the big boss would be there to show his appreciation for all their hard work. A couple of the diggers voiced their hopes for a big bonus.

The rum flowed freely and everyone enjoyed themselves with several young girls who were hired for the evening. Shortly after midnight, the big boss arrived with two other men who both looked unhappy to be there. The girls were sent home. The big boss introduced himself as Paul and said he was pleased with their work. His two friends just stood near the doors, staring back with stone faces.

The boss was all smiles as he sampled the food and drinks that had been laid out for the celebration. He seemed to enjoy chatting with his workers, listening intently to their tales of digging. He smiled as he asked each man to step outside individually to receive his personal thanks and a small bonus. The *small bonus* ended up being a small piece of 9mm copper-covered lead in the back of the skull, courtesy of one of the boss's two friends.

An hour after that was accomplished, a small boat headed straight out, about 2 km, to a spot where the water depth was around 1000 m. Five carefully weighted and wrapped bodies were quietly dropped over the side, and the boat quickly returned to shore.

That next week, the chief of police of Guantanamo was told he was "not being very helpful" by family members of the five men who had failed to come home. People go missing in Cuba all the time, he told several families at different times that week. Perhaps their missing relative tried to get to America. If they were on the wrong side of politics, perhaps Fidel's people had picked them up. "Check back later" was his standard reply when the families of Carlos, Mario, Luis, Raul, and Enrique came for help. None of the families ever found out the truth. Such was life in Fidel's Cuba.

2

"Damn, this big dude is heavy," he muttered to himself as he pulled the body through the underbrush of the wooded area. The Monday morning sun would come up in a few hours, and he had to finish this job before then. He stopped beside a large tree that had a bunch of dead limbs lying under it. *Perfect, dead goes with the dead,* he thought.

After covering the body with as much of the debris as he could quickly haul, he checked the area for anything he might have dropped as he returned to the road. Dumping the car was the next task in the job.

Traveling a few miles farther down the road, he spotted the place he needed in a gas station that had been abandoned for several years now. He parked the car behind the station and poured gas, from a container he'd brought, all over the interior of the Buick. Next, he popped the trunk and made sure its contents were soaked with gas as well.

He set two timers. Funny calling this jury rig—which he'd seen done in an old movie—a real 'timer.' But it would do the trick. He lit two cigarettes and got them going well, then placed one inside a paper matchbook, up near the match heads, and closed the cover. He did the same with the second cig and matchbook.

4

One he placed in the trunk, on top of some crumpled paper he had found in the car. The second was put in the driver's seat, surrounded by more paper. With the trunk and windows open, he wasn't concerned about the gas vapor igniting until the timers started a good flame. He just needed a few minutes to get away from the area.

He walked around the building, checking that no one was around, and started jogging a few hundred yards down the road to where a buddy was waiting with his car. Getting this job done had made for a long weekend and an endless night. Now he needed to hurry back to the base to finish the job and get ready for the day's work. As they drove away, a faint glow rose behind them.

On the way back to the base, he thought: *nothing is easy these days.* He went back over the events to make sure he had not screwed up somewhere. The person he'd originally been instructed to kill had not behaved as expected on Friday morning. He'd gotten to the apartment just in time to see the target close the door and walk toward a waiting Buick that had the big dude in the driver's seat. The same Buick he had just torched.

He followed them to another apartment, where they stayed inside through Saturday afternoon. He had watched them as they went out arm-in-arm to dinner. And he was there watching when they finally got back to the apartment. Guess the guy got lucky several times, as it was late Sunday afternoon when they again came out. This time the big guy carried a pair of suitcases. Fortunately for the watcher, the parking area behind the apartment was empty and not visible from the road.

The target was already in the running car, and the big guy was putting the second suitcase in the trunk. He quietly walked up behind him and slammed the tire iron against the side of his head. The big guy soundlessly fell forward into the trunk, and he quickly lifted his legs and crammed the rest of him in.

After closing the trunk lid, he rushed to the driver's door, opened it, and jumped in. The look of surprise on the victim's face was comical until he wrapped his huge right hand around her throat and started squeezing. She fought a bit and scratched his arms, but in a short time stopped moving.

He still held the tire iron in his left hand and realized he had jammed the pointed end into the target's gut during the struggle. Good news was there was little blood coming out since her heart had already stopped beating.

He loaded the woman's body in the trunk of his Chevy and his buddy—not *really* a buddy but a low-life worker for the big boss—drove it and followed him as he drove the big guy's Buick toward Dam Neck. The big boss had sent him along to make sure it was done.

Now heading back to the base to finish the job, he dropped the buddy off at his car, a few blocks from the main gate, and drove onto the base like nothing was unusual. The guard saw the sticker and waved him through. He drove around, looking for just the right place to carry out the final step of the job, and saw what he needed behind the base exchange.

3

WEATHER AT THE END OF November in the Tidewater area of Virginia can either be fair or nasty. The warmth of the Atlantic and Chesapeake Bay waters keeps the snow to a minimum, but cold weather still arrives and with it frequently comes miserable rain. But from time to time the weather gods play nice, and the eleventh month can be reasonably decent.

Such was the case that early Monday morning, as Naval Investigative Service Office Norfolk special agents John Driscol and Douglas Knox exited their separate vehicles, behind Naval Station Norfolk's base exchange, to face clear skies and temperatures in the low fifties. And to face a crime scene.

The exchange is like a big department store that sells to active duty, retired military, and all their dependents. The discounts gotten there beat the off-the-base stores, which makes it an attractive way to save money. On military pay, saving money is a good thing. The Army has similar stores and calls them 'PX,' short for Post Exchange. Like any large retail store, a lot of trash is created, and the two NIS agents were looking at one dumpster behind the exchange.

"Your turn to search the dumpster, Doug," Driscol said with a big grin. "I'll get the camera. While we wait for the M.E., you interview the employees."

"Maybe we can get the exchange employees to lie out all the trash for us in nice, neat rows," answered Doug with a smile. "At least the medical examiner is the first to go in, since he has to pull the body out before we dig."

One of the early morning stock crew staff had found the body at 0630 hrs when he carried out a load of trash. Once over the panic and shock, he got the manager on duty to take a look. The frantic call from the manager to the Shore Patrol office resulted in the SP Officer of the Day (OOD) placing a call to NIS after dispatching several SPs to the exchange. Two NIS agents were on call and responded within forty-five minutes; Knox got to the scene a few minutes ahead of Driscol.

The SP OOD also called the medical examiner's office at the base hospital, and they dispatched a forensic doctor, assistant, and ambulance to the scene. All the key players were on the scene by 0730 hrs. By then, the SPs had secured the area and sequestered the employees who had knowledge of the find.

While getting the camera from the car, Driscol asked the manager to find several ladders and bring them out. He was shooting photos of the area around the dumpster when the ladders were delivered and set up beside the dumpster, with care taken not to disturb any possible evidence. Driscol pointed his camera down into the dumpster and started taking photos of the body and the inside of the dumpster around the body.

Knox was fast with the interviews, as only one employee had opened the dumpster and seen the body. The other eight staff members on duty had no knowledge of the incident. The manager had only called in the problem after being shown what was in the dumpster. The exchange was closed on Sunday, so no one was around the previous night who might have seen any vehicles behind the building.

Having wrapped up the interviews, Doug started documenting the scene:

Initial finding: Body is that of a female, age yet undetermined. Caucasian. Short, light brown hair. Civilian clothing in disarray. Skirt pulled up to the waist. No underwear visible. Blouse hanging loose on left shoulder. Body is lying face down with left arm under the body. Right arm extended over the head. No jewelry visible.

Left shoe missing. Right shoe is a white tennis shoe. Blood visible on the right side of the body and on the trash below. No coat nor purse seen.

Knox stopped his note taking to brief the M.E., who had just arrived. He and Driscol moved over to the side of the dumpster so they could monitor the scene while giving the M.E. space to climb in. Dr. Sidney Wentworth had been the medical examiner on the base for as long as either agent had been with NIS. He was well respected in both the medical and legal communities for his expertise and ability to find things others missed. The fact that the senior stood 6'3" and spent his free time in the gym only added to that respect.

"I hate bodies in dumpsters. No respect for the dead," grumbled Dr. Wentworth. He looked carefully at the body, felt for movement of the head, and mumbled, "Probably dead for at least twelve hours based on status of rigor and touch check of body temp." The doctor straightened up and grimaced. "Andy, pass me the kit," he yelled to his assistant. "And I'll need four bags for the hands and feet."

After securing bags to preserve any evidence on her hands and feet, then checking the liver temp, the M.E. called Andy to bring a body bag into the dumpster. They carefully rolled the corpse onto the bag, examining its front. John shot more photos of the subject, face side up. They checked the area under the body for any loose clothing items, zipped up the bag, and gently carried it out of the dumpster to the ambulance. Dr. Wentworth stripped off his gloves and walked over to Driscol, shaking his head.

"What a waste. She was a cute girl in her early twenties. John, we have an estimated time of death at 1630 hours yesterday, based on rigor in the neck and liver temp. Strangulation looks to be the cause of death due to the abrasions on the neck and petechial hemorrhaging, but since she also has one small stab wound on the lower right abdomen, the official cause will have to wait until I open her up. From the looks of her hands, she fought the killer. We may have some tissue under the nails. And, yes, I'll check for rape." Sighing, the doctor asked, "Anything else you need from me right now?"

"No, Doc, you've given me enough to get started. Now Doug and I need to spend our turn in your dumpster unless you want to do that part as well."

"No, my medical degree prevents me from entering the same dumpster twice in one day. Just make sure there are no other bodies in there that I missed. I need breakfast. Talk with you later." The doc turned and headed to the ambulance while Doug and John approached the dumpster to start their part of the search.

After removing each piece of cardboard and trash from the dumpster and sorting those with blood from those without, Doug noticed something in the dark corner near where the body laid. He used a small piece of cardboard to move it over into the light and saw that it was a piece of jewelry. He slid it onto another piece of cardboard and held it up. It was a pin in the shape of a bird. And the back had what looked to be blood. He called that info out to his partner.

"Bag it," replied John.

An hour later, nothing else had showed up from the search of the dumpster. Still no purse, no coat, no left shoe had been found. Only a small amount of blood was seen on the dumpster trash, which led John to speculate she was killed elsewhere and dumped there. The autopsy would confirm that, or not. What little evidence was found was bagged and tagged and loaded into the trunk.

"Doug, when you get back to the office, check with base personnel and see if anyone is listed as UA this morning. I'll get this film over to the lab and wait for it to be processed. Hopefully, by then the doc will have some more information for us. You can also check with NPD and PPD for any missing persons' reports, although it might be too early. Ya never know," grumbled John as he turned and walked toward his car, adding: "I need a lot more coffee."

4

NEITHER NORFOLK POLICE DEPARTMENT NOR Portsmouth Police Department had any open missing persons reports that matched the deceased woman. While still a fairly new resource at four years old, the National Crime Information Center (NCIC) had become a great aid to investigations like this, so was notified of the incident in hopes they'd find a match in their missing persons' files.

Knox quickly roughed up a request to be sent to all the NIS Resident Agencies (NISRA) asking them to check with the local units to see if there were any UAs that morning. He gave it to the clerical staff, who ensured it was distributed to the various NISRAs under the control of NISO Norfolk.

Nothing had come back from the Unauthorized Absences lists, but the agent assigned to Naval Air Station Oceana NISRA, located in Virginia Beach about ten miles from Naval Station Norfolk, called in with a report. He had relayed the description to the various squadrons, and one of them remembered seeing someone like her at the NAVSUP (Naval Supply Systems Command) Fleet Logistics Center Norfolk.

When he checked with the supply officer in charge, he was told it might be Ensign Joan Appleton, as she fit the rough description. She hadn't been listed as UA because she had started a week's leave Friday to spend Thanksgiving with her folks in Ohio. The agent brought a copy of her service record to the NISRA office ASAP.

Driscol made it back to the NISRA office about the same time as Agent Bill Collins arrived with Ensign Appleton's service record. The file photos indicated the body was that of Appleton, but the M.E. would have to make it official. Driscol took the service record and drove to the hospital.

The M.E. verified that the body was that of Joan Appleton. The official cause of death was strangulation. The puncture wound from an undetermined half inch diameter round object on her side was not deep enough to cause mortality. It may have occurred during the struggle. There were bruises on her arms and someone's flesh under the fingernails of her right hand.

There had not been a sexual assault, but the body had been made to look as though there had been. After her clothing was bagged and tagged, Driscol drove back to the NISRA offices with that and the preliminary autopsy report. Calls had to be made; the official next-of-kin notification had to be started.

Agents Steve Crosser and Clyde London headed over to the Fleet Logistics Center Norfolk to start questioning co-workers. Their stories were pretty much the same; the Ensign had left duty on Friday and was to be on leave this week visiting her family. No one noticed anything odd about her behavior the last week or two. And no one could understand why anyone would kill such a friendly person. They checked her desk, but nothing of importance showed up there. Cards with the agents' phone numbers were passed out in case anyone remembered something that might help. It didn't look promising.

While the questioning was underway at the Logistics Center, Agents Joe Mabry and Darrell Tasker went to her apartment to interview her roommate and possibly neighbors. Carol Younger, a biology teacher at Norfolk High, had been sharing her apartment for the last six months. She mentioned Joan's trip home and that she'd been glad for her roommate; holiday time at home is important. But she was totally distraught over her death, and the circumstances of it.

Joan had already left on Friday afternoon by the time Carol got home from the afterschool football game. As far as she knew, Joan had planned to take a taxi to the airport. And no, she didn't know the name of the guy Joan had been dating for the last few weeks. He had never come in, always meeting Joan somewhere. Rather mysterious.

The few neighbors who knew Joan didn't offer much more info. No one recalled seeing a taxi that afternoon, but most worked and wouldn't have been home yet. Time to check with the cab companies to see if there were records of a pickup at that address on Friday. More questions than answers.

When Driscol returned to the NISRA office and climbed out of his car, he saw that Supervisory Special Agent Sam Maker was just coming in to work. Maker was running late due to a dental appointment. As they climbed the back stairs to the office, Driscol filled Maker in about the murder. When Driscol told him the name, Maker stopped.

"Are you sure about that, John?"

"Sam, I just left the M.E.'s office where he verified ID using her service record. What's the problem?" asked Driscol.

"Problem is I just had a meeting with her last Friday morning. She was a potential informant I wanted working for me and she was going to gather info about possible fraud at the Logistics Center. You might not remember we got an anonymous call a few weeks ago about theft being covered up over there. I've been looking into it from the recorded financial reports to see if anything looks off. We had planned to sit down after her week of leave and plot out a strategy." Sam looked frustrated as he said that.

Driscol shook his head and replied, "Well, we need to solve her murder now. Her family will want answers, and they deserve them."

5

LATE WEDNESDAY NIGHT

2 DECEMBER 1970

THE BUZZ FROM A COUPLE of beers was starting to ease as David walked back to the transient barracks late that night. Even though it was early December, the weather was nice; it was a clear night, and the temps were still in the fifties. But he hustled, since time had gotten away from him and he had to be back on duty at 0600, just about six hours from now. Dreading it, he hurried along toward the transient barracks.

Having had a nice rack on his last duty station, the aircraft carrier USS Forrestal, spending a week or two in the transient barracks was rough. The barracks were built during the big war and had not been upgraded much since then. Open cubicles, crude shared toilet facilities, thin wood walls, and mediocre heating and air conditioning made it seem more like a boot camp facility designed for torture rather than a place for a seasoned petty officer like him to hang his hat. At least it was bigger than his space in berthing on the carrier.

His assignment to the transient barracks was temporary, starting with his transfer to shore duty in Norfolk, Virginia. The main barracks were full, so he had to use the transient for a while. He could put up with it until a spot opened up in the main enlisted men's barracks, which was much nicer, with four-man rooms and good environmental controls in each one. Since it was shaped like a giant X, the four-story building had great lounge areas in the center of the X featuring comfortable seating, TV, desks, and a constantly changing stack of magazines. It was a much nicer place.

After the day's duty at the Naval Air Station Norfolk, where he worked as an aviation machinist mate (AD), David was tired and frustrated. He was having challenges learning all about this land-based aircraft, after spending two years dealing with carrier planes. It was not a terribly difficult change, and he'd master it shortly, but mastery was needed now, not the near future. He had gotten a short answer when he asked the Chief about something strange he found in the wheel well of one of the P2V Neptune patrol aircraft.

There were a number of Neptunes in the squadron. Designed and built by Lockheed, these beautiful aircraft are powered by two Wright eighteen-cylinder radial piston engines and two Westinghouse J34 turbojet engines, one of each on each wing. Armament can include rockets, free-fail bombs, depth charges, and torpedoes, depending upon the demands of the mission. The aircraft were outfitted with air and surface radar, and sonobuoys and a magnetic anomaly detector to aid in the submarine search. The P2V aircraft are in constant use as they patrol up and down the east coast, watching for Russian subs as well as ships in distress. Those stationed in Virginia would fly down to Guantanamo Bay, Cuba, a base nicknamed Gitmo, as part of their standard patrol.

Maintenance was important to keep these older P2V aircraft flying, and while performing the standard maintenance on one of the aircrafts' landing gear struts, David noticed what looked like a strange access hatch in the wheel well. A quick check of the maintenance manual showed this wasn't a normal feature on the Neptune. But when he asked about it, the Chief got a bit angry, telling him to ignore it and get back to work on the landing gear. It was a strange answer since most chiefs are happy to educate, but being the new guy to the unit, David let it go.

After the duty shift was over, David had joined five shipmates for dinner at the mess hall. He asked the guys about the strange compartment, and no one knew anything about it; none of them wanted to discuss work. "Ask the Chief again tomorrow," one of them said. Dinner was cheap, and the food was just above average, so David focused on that. Having a glass of beer would have been nice, but that was not available in the mess hall.

So to take the edge off the day, David and two of the guys went over to the enlisted men's club for a round or two. It was a lot more fun to spend time there, drinking and listening to music rather than sitting on a bunk in the transient barracks. David didn't notice that the other three guys had been giving him strange glances before they headed off in a different direction after dinner.

Quietly entering the barracks, David laid topside. In civilian terms, he climbed to the second floor and strolled down to the end of the passageway to the head. Might as well take the time to get rid of the beer before falling into the rack, he thought, as he shuffled to the urinal.

Loud snoring was coming from most of the cubicles, and only the night security lights were showing in the passageway. He noticed there were no security lights in the head, but that didn't bother him since he could turn the overhead light on without bothering any other sailors.

As he turned to go into the dark head, he was not at all prepared for a hand to clamp over his mouth and more hands to grab his arms and pin them behind his back. Someone turned on a small flashlight. A sharp pain came to his arm as a needle was inserted, and the last thing David ever saw was a known face smiling at him as the light-force in his head was shut off and death overtook him.

A week later, the officer in charge of housing read the M.E.'s report, provided as the result of the investigation by the two agents of the Naval Investigative Service (NIS). The report clearly stated AD3 David Nelson had died of a drug overdose. All indications were that it was self-administered. He had recent needle marks on his arms. The investigation also showed that the chief petty officer in charge of the transient barracks had found a small stash of drugs tucked in Nelson's bunk the morning the body was discovered, and he turned them over to the investigators.

Testing showed the drugs to be cocaine, and a large quantity was found in his bloodstream. Since the blood alcohol level was also high, it was concluded that David had been too drunk to realize he was giving himself an overdose. The Navy was satisfied with the M.E.'s report but not happy about the cause of death. They were seeing too many drug users, pushers, and fatal overdoses.

His parents were notified of his death, and his body and belongings were shipped home to Selma, Alabama for burial. Despite protests from his parents that he was not a drug user, the case was closed. With no other recourse, the Nelsons continued their complaints with the Navy officials in Washington.

6

NERVOUS HARDLY EXPRESSED HOW WALTER King felt that Thursday, the second week of December. He knew what he did a couple of weeks ago was the right thing, but the bad guys wouldn't have agreed had they known. After all, he'd turned into a confidential informant (CI) to help the Navy get rid of these horrible drug dealers. That they used the military to help push drugs just rubbed him the wrong way—it was so un-American that giving info to that NIS agent seemed to be the right thing to do. But that was before he noticed the frequent glances from many of those he worked with daily at the Logistics Center. How could they know?

Maybe I'm just getting paranoid, he thought. After all, his call to the NIS office had been from a pay phone off the base, and the face-to-face meeting with an agent named Driscol had followed at a small diner over on the West Side of Portsmouth. No familiar faces were seen, and it was the first—and last—time he would be there. At that meeting, he was given a code name, actually a couple of letters and three numbers, that he was to use when contacting Agent Driscol with information.

And if the agent needed to contact him, Driscol said he would make himself visible as a sailor but wouldn't talk with Walter. Walter was to then call in to the NISRA office as soon as he could. So far, the agent had not showed up, and there were only three times that Walter had called him with information. And each time the call was placed from a different pay phone, nowhere near the base or any sailor hangouts. No one could possibly know he was a CI.

Each day was filled with moving boxes from railcars, trucks, or aircraft to storage areas, and from storage areas to trucks waiting to head to the units needing the supplies. Handling all those supplies meant lots of paperwork had to be done—boxes checked in, weights verified, origination and destination checked, double-checked, and then sorted. As a storekeeper rating at the petty officer second class level, Walter did more than just lifting and stacking. He handled inventory control, and as he walked the paperwork through the needed channels, he tried to act natural and not think about the information he had passed on to the NIS.

But something was not right with the shipment just received from an inbound cargo plane. A couple of boxes weren't in the right place, though that happens occasionally. He normally would have the pleasure of reporting these things to that cute Ensign Appleton, but she had recently died, he had been told. What a shame. And the new guy, LTJG Pattalo, said he didn't have time for any of that and to take the problems to the Chief. As he started back to check on the discrepancy, he heard a call on the PA system, by the Chief, to report to the office. He'd check all that later.

The Chief inquired about a problem with a shipment from the previous week, and Walter pulled the information from file. Seemed another storekeeper had misfiled one of the forms. It was nothing serious, but still a frustrating and time-consuming error. Once that was solved, Walter mentioned the problem he was currently facing, and the Chief said he knew Walter could handle it.

After Walter left, the Chief went out to the warehouse floor toward a sailor who was running a forklift. The Chief pulled him aside and had a few words with him. The sailor was seen nodding his head in a positive response, and he left the warehouse early.

The next day was the first in over a week that Walter was not on the duty roster. It was time for a bit of fun, he thought. That night he'd drive over to Suffolk to spend a couple of hours seeing a classic movie, the big feature of a midnight showing at the Chadwick Theater. The Chadwick was a restored historical theater on Main Street in Suffolk. Seeing *Casablanca* with Bogart on the big screen, in such a setting, was a real treat. So what if it was nearly thirty years old; it was still a great movie.

It was sad that no one else in the unit wanted to go, but they spent their time at the Black Knight Inn, a short drive down Hampton Blvd from the base, watching the topless dancers and getting drunk. There was nothing wrong with a drink every now and then, but Walter didn't like the taste of it, so staying clear was easy.

But as that loose translation from the Scottish poet Robert Burns said, the best laid plans of mice and men often go awry. And while Walter's actions had done a great job of keeping his association with NIS under the radar of the bad guys, there were other forces in play. Walter had been exposed.

He was surprised when a pair of bright headlights came quickly up behind him as he drove down Route 460 from Norfolk. As he approached a small bridge outside of town, the idiot with the bright lights sped up and pulled toward the left lane as if to pass. But instead he hit the driver's rear of Walter's car, causing the back end to spin to the left. Walter was shocked and in a panic over the sudden jolt, and rather than hitting the brake, his foot accidently pressed the accelerator. Pointing to the side of the road and with more power going to the rear wheels, the car shot off the road and down a steep embankment toward the water thirty feet below.

Several medium-sized trees slowed, and finally stopped, the speeding car before it hit the water. Walter's head whipped back and forth due to the sudden stop, and he blacked out.

As he came to, pain attacked him from all directions and blood was flowing from his wounded forehead into his eyes. So when a dark figure appeared by his window, Walter couldn't make out who it was. He tried to call for help, but the steering wheel pressing against his chest made breathing hard, and no words came out. Through the side window, which had shattered during the crash, a hand reached in and pulled Walter's head back.

A bright light shined in his eyes, and then someone was pouring a burning liquid into his mouth. It tasted like the whiskey he had tried once. He coughed as he tried to breathe. The hand dropped the bottle onto the seat beside Walter and vanished. The dark figure said "Goodbye, King" and walked away.

Walter never smelled the gasoline that was leaking from the ruptured tank. He was still coughing from the whiskey when the fire started under the back of the car. And by the time the local police arrived and a fire truck was called, the car was fully engulfed in flames.

The county sheriff handled the investigation. When the deputies finished, they passed copies of the case files and evidence to NIS agents Tasker and Mabry. They'd been assigned the follow up and closing of the Navy's side of the case.

7

THE OLDER DARK BLUE PICKUP drove up Hampton Blvd, toward the main gate of the Navy base, at just below the speed limit. Since it was after midnight, there were fewer cars on the road. But there were always a good number of police on patrol. Too many college kids partied heavily every night. And the driver of the pickup didn't want to attract any special attention.

The passenger front bumper of the truck was bent in, and the fender had some damage as well. At least both headlights were still working, so there was less chance of the police pulling him over. Up ahead on the right, the road that led to the old Virginian Railway engine facility provided an easy place to stash the truck. He turned onto the road and ignored the 'no trespassing, railway property' sign on the right.

Located just outside the main gate of the naval station, the rail facility was little used after the merger, about ten years ago, with the larger Norfolk and Western Railway. Both railroads hauled coal from the hills of West Virginia and dumped it into waiting ships at the coal piers owned by the railroads. The older Virginian Railway piers were still being used, and several locomotives were resting there, waiting to face another day of pushing loaded coal cars up the ramp to feed the huge ships.

The pickup drove slowly to the locomotive shop area and down between two of the locomotives. He parked the truck right next to one of them, turned off the engine, and opened the cab windows.

After checking the area and making sure no one was around, the driver removed two gas cans from the back of the pickup. He poured one all over the interior of the cab, and the second one was poured over the hood, truck bed, and cab roof. He lit a match, and ducking down, tossed it into the cab.

The resulting fire was spotted and reported a few minutes later. Two fire trucks responded quickly, but the fire was so intense it totally destroyed the truck and heavily damaged the locomotive right next to it. It also slightly damaged the locomotive on the other side of the truck. No body was found in the truck, and there had been no witnesses in the area.

The firemen working all around the fire, along with the massive amount of water from their hoses, had destroyed any footprints or evidence left behind in the ugly mixture of ballast, dirt, and oil. The Norfolk Police Department handled the crime scene and received the fire chief's report of an accelerant being used.

8

TWO DAYS LATER, THREE ARTICLES appeared in the Virginia Pilot newspaper. One reported on the single-vehicle crash that had occurred on Thursday night, on Route 460 near Suffolk. The accident and resulting fire, which took the life of Petty Officer Walter King, was deemed due to drunk driving. The Navy accepted the local sheriff's report and handled the standard notification of next of kin.

The second article was about a strange car fire in the rail yard near the Navy base. In this incident, an older pickup truck was gutted by fire, and two locomotives were damaged. The NPD investigation showed the pickup had been stolen the previous day. No suspects were found. The damaged truck bumper was not linked to the damage on Walter's car, since the fires had destroyed any paint traces that might have been there. This was destined to become a cold case, as far as the local police were concerned.

Farther back in the paper was the third article. This one reported on finding a decomposing body suspected to be that of a Navy flyer, the subject of a recent search. His car had been found abandoned and burned south of Virginia Beach, near Dam Neck, back in November.

The body was found by a golfer who had hit his ball way into the rough. The corpse was well hidden at the base of a large tree, approximately two miles from where the car had been found before Thanksgiving. The Navy, still performing an autopsy to determine the cause of death, had withheld his name pending notification of next of kin.

9

THE NEW YEAR'S EVE CELEBRATION should have been a great time for GM2 Roger Mobley, since he was getting out of the Navy in a few weeks and heading back home to Chicago. Or he might just re-enlist and become a lifer. He hadn't fully decided yet. The Navy had been good to him, considering his options back in Chicago ... find a two-bit job or join a gang. Neither looked good, so perhaps a career in the service was the right choice. A decision best put off for another day.

He stood near the end of the pier where his ship was docked, leaning against a temporary shed that had been built on the pier. He watched toward the southwest for the first of the fireworks. While waiting, he reflected on all he had done over the last few years.

His six year hitch had taken him from the south Chicago suburbs, to boot camp just north of Chicago at the Naval Training Center Great Lakes, to duty on a destroyer on the West coast. There he'd been assigned to the weapons department, but after excelling in training, he was sent back to Great Lakes for gunner's mate school. This new training led to a promotion, enabling him to remove the three simple stripes of the Seaman and sew to his sleeves a new patch, this one showing an eagle over the crossed cannons of a gunner's mate, with a single red chevron underneath. This patch announced his new rate and rating as a Gunner's Mate Third Class.

His new assignment, after training, was aboard a fighting ship stationed in Norfolk—the USS Newport News. From there, over the last five years, he'd traveled to the coast of Vietnam twice, Subic Bay in the Philippines, over to San Francisco, down through the Panama Canal several times, and finally back to the Navy town of Norfolk, the home port of the heavy cruiser also known as CA-148.

Roger had lost a portion of his hearing while working in the huge, 8⊠ gun mounts of the Newport News. Those huge guns made a lot of noise when firing, and even with ear protection, some damage happened. The Newport News had three main turrets: two forward and one aft, each holding three of the 8"/55 guns. The naval terminology of 8"/55 means the internal diameter of the barrel is 8" and the length is the diameter times the second number—55—resulting in a barrel that is 440", or 36.6' long.

Into each barrel, the gun crew would load a projectile weighing up to 335 lbs, followed by a powder charge of 78 lbs, and go through the firing sequence. This would result in the projectile leaving the barrel at 2,500 feet per second and allow it to travel a maximum of just over twenty-seven miles! During the cruise to Vietnam in 1967–68, Roger helped send, from these guns, nearly 60,000 rounds of high explosives toward the enemy.

He worked hard, studied harder, and passed the test for his next promotion. Getting the second chevron of a second class petty officer put him in charge of one of the crews that operated the main gun turrets. He was a tough but fair supervisor who had the respect of his crew, and he made sure they were efficient in all tasks. He was proud that his efforts had led to several other promotions of the men under his care.

But events over the last few months had been worrisome. He had spotted some of his gun crew using drugs. That cannot be allowed to happen in the military, especially when dealing with ammunition. There are too many chances for deadly mistakes. After talking to each one individually, Roger realized that tactic wasn't doing any good. But he hated to be a snitch, and knew that going to his chief or the division officer would simply result in a Captain's Mast for the guilty—they would probably be reprimanded, lightly punished, and returned to duty. And since he'd have to testify at the mast, he would suddenly become the enemy. Secretly calling the NIS agent he'd met during a different investigation on the ship, last spring, seemed the solution.

So he had called the agent earlier in December, reminded him of their previous contact, and described the problems he was having with some of his crew. He explained why he didn't want to go through the normal chain of command, and hoped it wouldn't cause him any trouble. The NIS agent told him his information would be kept confidential, and that NIS was initiating an investigation.

And they did. A few days after that phone call, a new gunner's mate reported on board and was assigned to Roger's crew. He was a hard worker and friendly with the rest of the crew, so it was a bit of a surprise to discover, last week, that he was an undercover NIS agent and that several members of Roger's crew were now in the base brig charged with drug use and distribution. Roger had not been implicated. And he hoped it would stay that way.

With his hearing loss, Roger did not notice the sailor that walked up behind him on the left as he stood in the shadow of the shed. Another sailor approached from the right at the same time, and that got Roger's attention. Roger greeted him and asked if he was going to watch the fireworks.

Before he could hear the response, the pipe hit the side of Roger's skull. As he started to fall, the two men grabbed him and pushed him over the edge of the pier. They watched the body for a couple of minutes, as it floated face down between the pier and the hull of the cruiser, to make sure he was not coming back up.

On the morning of New Year's Day, a body was recovered from the water and moved to the medical examiner's office. The autopsy showed blunt force trauma to his skull and sea water in his lungs. The conclusion of the M.E. was that he'd slipped and fell, hitting his head against the pier on the way down and subsequently drowning. NIS Special Agent Joe Mabry was called to the scene, but didn't find anything suspicious. It looked to be a sad ending to an otherwise stellar career.

However, a few days later the agent was called back to the pier when a piece of pipe was found inside the shed that looked to have blood on it. Analysis showed it was blood—and a match to that of GM2 Mobley. The case was changed from accidental drowning to murder, and reopened.

10

THE TUESDAY MORNING SHORE PATROL shift noticed a car in the back corner of the officers' club parking lot. Usually this area was the parking for the club staff, and they wouldn't be on duty for several more hours.

Parking behind it, the SP petty officer radioed in at 0730 hrs that he was leaving his vehicle and checking on a possible abandoned car. This car was memorable since it was decked out in bright gold paint with a black roof. Dark charcoal-colored mag wheels and a reversed cowl hood scoop added the look of power and speed to an already sleek design.

He approached the 1969 Chevrolet Chevelle Malibu S/S from the rear driver's side and looked in the back window. Rear seat clear. But when he looked into the front seat, he realized it was more than just an abandoned car; it held a body lying down across the two bucket seats.

The NIS agent arrived in nearly record time. He'd just walked into the office when the call for an agent came in from the SP OOD. Knowing the SP OOD would also make the call for the medical examiner, Special Agent Steve Crosser ran back to his car and raced to the club. Another agent was in route, but Crosser beat him to the scene.

After securing the area around the car, the SP circumvented the door locks, opened the doors, and verified the man was dead. At least with both doors open, the smell would dissipate somewhat. Good thing it was late January … if this were summer, the inside of the car would be nauseating. Nothing would be moved until the M.E. did his magic with the body. No touching, no moving, but looking was fine.

SA Clyde London pulled in and grabbed his camera from the back seat. He said hello to Crosser and started shooting photos of the area, the car, and the body. Crosser finished interviewing the SP who had found the body and chatted with several other SPs to get their input. Nothing of interest there, but he had to check. Still waiting for the M.E. to arrive, Crosser walked over to the car.

Looking inside, Crosser saw that the body was dressed in casual civilian clothing. He looked to be in his mid-twenties, Hispanic, short military haircut, and very dead. White powder was on the victim's hand and the floor of the car, indicating a possible drug-related case.

The car had a base sticker that showed it was owned by an enlisted man, so the question of what it was doing in the officers' club parking lot came to Crosser. He might be a part-time employee at the club. But checking with the club management would have to wait until the victim's identity was verified.

The keys were in the ignition, so Crosser gloved up and removed them. Finding the right key, he opened the trunk and quickly surveyed what was there. Nothing there seemed exciting … the expected tools, car jack, tire iron, some dirty clothing, a white tennis shoe, beach towels, a fishing tackle. London took the time to shoot photos of the trunk and contents. They were still looking at the trunk when the medical examiner arrived.

"Wish you guys would stop finding dead bodies," grumbled Dr. Sidney Wentworth as he approached the car. He looked carefully at the body and yelled, "Andy, get me the kit. And I'll need two bags for the hands."

After securing bags to preserve any evidence on the hands and then checking the liver temp, the M.E. called Andy to bring a body bag. They carefully maneuvered the body from the car and onto the bag, allowing them a quick examination of the front of the body. Clyde shot more photos of the body face up and a detail photo of the face, then went back to the car to take more of the interior as it looked without the body.

Dr. Wentworth pulled the wallet from the dead man's back pocket and passed it to Steve Crosser. Texas driver's license said this was Peter Rodriquez of Brownsville, Texas. Age twenty-three. The enlisted military

ID card provided more pertinent information, letting Crosser know this was Storekeeper Third Class Peter Rodriquez, to be exact. Forty-three dollars, a ticket stub to a concert from earlier in the year, a condom, two gasoline credit cards, and a photo of a cute dark-haired girl were the only other contents of the wallet.

The doctor's liver thermometer allowed him to place the time of death at approximately six hours ago, shortly after midnight. Rigor had started but hadn't completely spread throughout the body, somewhat confirming TOD. Cause of death would have to wait until the doc got him on the table, but the white powder on his hands and face indicated probable cause as another drug overdose.

Doc and Andy loaded the body and headed off to the hospital. Crosser asked the SP to have the car towed to the secured lot, where he could remove all the evidence in a more controlled environment.

Before the end of the day, NIS had found that SK3 Peter Rodriquez was listed as UA from the Fleet Logistics Center. He had not reported in on Monday for duty. Crosser and London spent the afternoon clearing the car and doing the "bag and tag" on all the contents. The trunk was a mess, and that took the longest.

It would take until Wednesday for Dr. Wentworth to call Crosser with the final autopsy results. They were inconclusive. While the COD was probably a drug overdose, it was easy to do since the cocaine in his nose was nearly pure. Chemical analysis showed the cocaine also contained a large quantity of the poison sodium cyanide. It was impossible to tell which of these stopped his heart first.

Blood was found on some items in the truck and was being processed. The case was reclassified from a drug overdose death to murder.

II

MARCUS

IT WAS A LONG DRIVE from my parents' home in Florida to the new assignment in Virginia, as I recall that day six heady months ago. Being early March, there had been a possibility of snow, but I lucked out and had clear skies all the way. Driving through Georgia was a pain as the new Interstate Highway 95 was still under construction, so there was a lot of jumping off and on as I went north through the state. The worst part was Savannah, where it seemed the locals sent traffic on a winding path around some of the worst parts of town. The Department of Transportation said they'd finish the highway next year, but they never gave an actual date: "next year" just kept being pushed off.

My 1965 Plymouth Barracuda was a dream to drive. A Formula S package put a 4-barrel carb on top of the 273 cubic inch V-8 for extra power. Better suspension and larger wheels and tires were featured under the beast, and a black racing stripe running down the center of the car, front to back, accented the exterior. The 'Cuda came from the factory painted Barracuda

Silver with black interior, but an expensive trip to a local paint shop had changed that to a nice bright yellow that made the black racing stripe pop. The exhaust hummed nicely as I cruised up the new interstate highway.

I had a lot of time to think about this new chapter in my life. Well, I had the same old job, only with a new location and some interesting undercover work, but I just started a big new chapter in my personal life. Here I was—Naval Investigator Marcus James Colt—heading to the Norfolk Naval Station, on the Virginia coast, for the new assignment. While I needed to focus on the multiple problems at hand on the base, I was looking forward to getting this next assignment completed and behind me. But all this was right then being overshadowed by the fact I'd just dumped the girl of my dreams. A relationship of almost two and a half years was gone, and I was bouncing between depression and relief. Mostly relief, it seemed. It had been a rocky start to 1971.

Sandy Cane came into my life while I was home after college graduation, before I started my Navy career, back in the late summer of 1968. My civilian wardrobe needed some new additions, so I drove to the big mall in Clearwater, Florida, just a few miles from the folks' house. I dedicated a morning to picking up a couple of new shirts and jeans at the Sears store there. The young lady working in the men's department got my attention as soon as I walked in to look around.

Miss Cane, according to her name tag, had short, dirty-blonde hair, a pleasant body shape, and twinkling blue eyes. Her looks reminded me a lot of the crazy girl on the TV show *Laugh-In*, but Miss Cane had more of the 'girl next door' look about her. Her laugh was infectious, and it immediately eased the stress I usually feel shopping. And for the next hour, I had her full attention.

It was surprising that such a good-looking girl would show me any attention. Granted, I stood six feet tall and was somewhat athletic, but my weight of 150 gave me a very slender look. My face wasn't Hollywood quality and my ears stuck out a bit too much, in my opinion. Add to that the fact I looked younger than I really was. At least my brown hair cooperated when I combed it. Well, usually.

I have to admit that I left the store with more than expected. In addition to acquiring several bags of shirts, ties, jeans, and trousers, I'd also acquired a date with Sandy for the upcoming weekend. Being only Tuesday, Saturday seemed to be a long way off.

That Saturday night finally arrived, and the first date with Sandy went well. I picked her up at her parents' house, and after doing the obligatory meeting of the parents, we had dinner at the local Steak and Ale restaurant. We had a lot of ground to cover in getting to know each other, so dinner lasted longer than the wait staff would have preferred. Since we ordered dessert and coffee, they didn't rush us out. Leaving a decent tip helped soothe their attitudes a bit.

Sandy had graduated from high school just over a month ago and was surprised that I'd just graduated from Georgia Tech with two degrees. She'd assumed I was just a year or so out of high school. I explained that I'd finished high school a year early and was able to squeeze two four-year-degrees in just over three years by not goofing off, and working hard. At that point, I felt it was best to not mention that I'd also finished my master's degree, and on my last birthday, June 14th, I had said goodbye to the age of twenty-three.

Since my early teens, I'd been frustrated that I looked so much younger than I actually was. Adults told me that in later years I'd greatly appreciate that physical attribute, but as a teen, it limited my social life as I looked several years younger than my classmates. It was a great way to limit dating, as most high school girls didn't want to be seen with a guy that looked like their kid brother.

Now having Sandy, who just turned eighteen, think I was around twenty-one worked in my favor. Not that I was intending on taking advantage of her; I just wanted to spend some time with a girl that made me smile a lot without the complication of her parents thinking I was a cradle robber due to being six years older. If things got serious later, there was always time to admit my 'old age.'

After dinner we went for a long walk along the pier at Clearwater Beach, continuing the stories of our lives and enjoying each other's company. I explained that I was only going to be in the area for the next few weeks since I was going on active duty with the Navy. She didn't think I looked much like a warrior, and we had a friendly laugh over that. I explained that I expected to be mostly doing office work. That satisfied her.

We spent a lot of time together over the next few weeks, but decided that the distance and my military service would work against any more permanent relationship. Not mentioned was the number of deaths in Vietnam that was plastered on the evening news every day.

We agreed that, when I got time to come home, I'd call to see if she was free and we could share time together. Naturally, letter writing and the occasional phone call would help keep the fires burning. But neither of us would be tied down, and both were free to date others.

Well, that agreement lasted until the night before I was to head north to my duty station in Washington D.C. Sandy didn't want to let me go, and even whispered in my ear that we should get married, eloping that night, so she could go with me. That didn't look like a good plan as far as I was concerned, and I knew her parents would have a fit if it was said out loud. So I promised I'd get back as soon as I could, but a lot depended upon the whims of the Navy.

We corresponded frequently, and I did get back to Florida fairly often. Our time together was great, and we both could see a wonderful future together. So it was natural that just over a year later, at Christmas 1969, I gave her a ring and we planned on setting a wedding date for some time in the summer of 1970. Sandy was happy, all the parents were thrilled, and we had lots of time to work the wedding planning around my Navy activities.

12

MY NAVY ACTIVITIES WERE RATHER mundane in my first sixteen months of being assigned to the headquarters of the NIS, located in the Navy Yard in Washington D.C. From this office space, investigations were managed all over the world, at every Navy and Marine base and on every ship. Every type of crime was handled by the NIS agents, as well as security background investigations. In civilian terms, think of the Shore Patrol members as the beat cops and the NIS agents as the detectives of the police force.

I had been assigned to a division of NIS that acted like the police department internal affairs unit. We looked into any possible problems, crimes, bad behavior, etc., within the NIS personnel, including civilian agents, to make sure that we all were the good guys. We had full authority over all the agents and military personnel. And all this made us pariahs to most of the staff. The four of us who did the investigations also did most of our own paperwork, since it was very sensitive.

True, it was not the easiest job, but I knew it had to be done. And it did involve more than a bit of travel, but since there are about a dozen Navy and Marine bases in Florida, I'd been able to get home to visit Sandy more often than we ever expected. The other guys knew I was in love, and if an assignment was in Florida, they passed it to me. Life was good for this Lieutenant.

But the one thing that can be counted on is that the Navy is not concerned about anyone's social life. In early January 1970, I was called into the Admiral's office; Vice Admiral John Chance was the commanding office of NIS. He was one of the few three-star admirals who was an all-around good guy, and well respected in all circles. I thought he was a great CO until he told me that I was going TAD to beautiful downtown Saigon. The temporary additional duty (TAD) assignment was extremely sensitive and I'd be leaving in two days. And no, I could not tell anyone where I was heading. No one … period.

After he explained the situation, I had a better understanding about it all, and agreed that it had to be done on the down-low. I headed to the BOQ, Bachelor Officer Quarters, to pack my seabag, as the saying goes. I put most of my gear in storage since I didn't know the length of this assignment. No need to hold on to a much needed room.

All I could do was call Sandy and tell her I was on an assignment that would take me out of the country for a while, and no, I would not be calling often, and even letter writing might be delayed. She wasn't happy about this, but understood that the Navy was in charge: I go where I am sent. I promised to call as soon as I could. Before the call was over, she cried, and I lied. I said not to worry, as I'd be in a safe place.

The assignment was not in a safe place. Saigon had too many little guys in black pajamas on bicycles, throwing hand grenades into buildings, for it to be called safe. No matter, the job had to be done. It is still highly classified to this day, but I did get it done and at least I came home. Some others didn't.

I wrote Sandy as often as I could while I was over there and got a few letters from her. Most of them said how much she missed me and what she was doing with the wedding planning. With this assignment so vague, we had not set a wedding date, which resulted in much of what she wanted to do being put on hold until I got back to the states. That was frustrating for her.

I did have the opportunity to call a couple of times. Those were a big disappointment, as her mother, Marie, told me each time that Sandy and a girlfriend had gone out for some fun. "Sorry," she said, "no idea when she will get home. I'll tell her you called." I couldn't help but wonder what kind of fun she was having. I knew I wasn't having any fun where I was!

Nothing lasts forever in the military. Such was true with that assignment, as it finally ended in mid-August 1970. I'd spent over five months in Vietnam and almost a month in sickbay afterward. One day they will probably make a movie out of the incident. It would be a great action flick.

I survived it, and my scars from the wounds would eventually fade. The sealed records go into great detail about the case, the awards—too many posthumously—that were issued, and my early promotion to Lieutenant Commander. I got to trade my railroad tracks for a gold leaf, but at a high price. They were right: war is hell.

When I reported back to NISHQ, my new rank came with more responsibility, as the division officer over internal affairs had been transferred. I took his place.

But before I had to take the reins of the position, I could take a couple of weeks' convalescence leave, so I left immediately to Florida and to Sandy. When our team was on the mission, we didn't have a lot of time to shave, so most of us had beards. The team had embraced the relaxed facial hair regulations put in place by the previous CNO. So like the other guys, I came back to the USA sporting a full mustache and a goatee. Neatly trimmed per Navy regs, of course.

My kid sister, Elle—well, she was no longer a kid since she was in the tenth grade at Clearwater High—had arranged for Sandy to be at the folks' house when I arrived. When I pulled into the driveway, everyone came out of the house and the family surrounded me with hugs and kisses. Sandy gave me a brief hug and announced that if I expected any kisses from her, I needed to shave "that mess" off my face. Sis and the folks liked it, but my fiancée had greater power at that moment in time, so I headed to the bathroom for a date with the razor. At least it wouldn't remind me of being over there anymore.

Even after I shaved there was some awkwardness and tension with Sandy. I hoped it would fade like my scars after we spent more time together. And it mostly did. After a few days, it was almost like old times again, and there were many happy moments, including seeing Elvis live at Tampa's Curtis Hixon Hall convention center in early September. I told her we'd need to put off the wedding until the spring since my new assignment at HQ would initially take more of my time. She reluctantly agreed, and we talked in detail about a June wedding the next year.

After my leave was over and I got back to HQ, the new job took all of my time and then some. I bought a townhouse in Alexandria to try to look the part of a more settled Navy officer. The BOQ is fine for a while, but there's nothing like having your own place to put all the stuff that accumulates with life.

Work was consuming and before I knew it, Christmas was coming. I had Sandy fly up to D.C. and I put her up in the Willard Hotel on Pennsylvania Ave., right down from the White House. We had a wonderful Christmas, sharing all the sights and soaking up the power that the capitol exudes. Sandy liked the townhouse, she said, but immediately started planning furniture and wall color changes to be made as soon as we were married.

The NIS Christmas party was a great time, and Sandy was the hit of the party in her simple black dress accented with a string of pearls I'd picked up in Hawaii on the way back home. Everyone told me how lucky I was to have her on my arm. I agreed.

Saying goodbye at the National Airport was difficult for us both. The long time apart, followed by the great time together those last two weeks, made us both realize we needed to be together all the time to feel complete and be happy. And we promised to talk about, and complete, the wedding plans very soon.

But again, the Navy had other ideas for my life. It was early on Monday, the second week in January 1971, when the Admiral called me into his office. He told me I again was going TAD, but this time just down the road to the Chief of Naval Operations' office in the Pentagon. No, it was not open to debate and no, he couldn't tell me why I was requested. The request had come directly from the CNO, and I was to report only to him. Immediately.

That left little time for clearing my desk at NIS, so I passed the buck to my assistant in the division, gave the staff my regrets, grabbed my cover—the military term for hat—and hit the door.

As I checked the rearview mirror in the 'Cuda, after finally finding a parking spot at the Pentagon, I wished I'd taken the time over the weekend to get a haircut. At NIS, we are allowed a more relaxed look with longer hair since we frequently did undercover work. And to help hide some of the scars, I had let my hair grow even longer. But now, working for the CNO, even temporarily, I felt I looked like a bum. Oh well, too late now.

13

GETTING IN TO SEE MY new boss in the Pentagon, later that Monday morning, was an expected challenge. I knew I was required to surrender my sidearm, so after approaching the sign-in desk, I provided the Marine guard with my ID, told them I was armed, and asked if they had a safe storage for my weapon. They answered in the affirmative and I unbuttoned my jacket.

After I removed my Colt 1911 .45 from the shoulder holster, I dropped the magazine into my left hand and laid it on the desk. I then worked the slide to extract the round from the chamber, catching it in mid-air before locking the slide open and laying the weapon and extra round on the desk beside the magazine. The Marines were surprised that I carried with a round in the chamber.

I smiled and told them, "Remember, if you need a weapon, you need it ready to use." They returned the smiles and said they appreciated the truth that many others failed to recognize.

My time spent previously in the Pentagon had been extremely limited, so I relied on one of the Marines on watch to escort me to the Office of the Chief of Naval Operations. I thanked the corporal for his assistance and asked that he leave a bread crumb trail so I could find my way out. He smiled, did a precise about face, and departed.

Opening the office door—it was way too fancy to be called a hatch, as naval terminology demanded—I was surprised that there were only two desks in the outer office. Thick, dark blue carpet covered the deck, and dark wood paneling covered the bulkheads. The proper amount of naval artwork covered the walls and a set of double doors were in the back bulkhead, between the desks. There were a few chairs placed around for those who had to wait.

A second-class Yeoman was on the phone at the desk on the left, and a Master Chief Yeoman, whose name plate on his desk identified him as David F. Bartow, stood beside the other desk. The Master Chief had a John Wayne look about him that conveyed the image of high intelligence and a massive 'do not mess with me' attitude. His uniform was perfect, his "fruit salad," the ribbons on his left chest that indicated medals earned and areas served, was immense, and the gold "hash marks" on his left sleeve, each representing four years of service, added up to twenty-eight years plus. As he looked me up and down, I was sure that I had not passed muster in his opinion.

"How may I help you, Lieutenant Commander?" inquired the Master Chief. He pronounced "Commander" as if it were a sour taste in his mouth. Then after a brief pause, a light obviously came on in his head and he continued, "You must be Mr. Colt. The Admiral is expecting you." Then he paused again, giving me another strange look.

"OK, Master Chief, what's the problem? Lay it on me," I said. *Here it comes: he thinks my hair is too long and I'm not squared away.*

"Sir, no offense, but I think I have tee-shirts older than you." And he gave a look of constipation as he realized what he'd said out loud. The Yeoman, who was still on the phone, gave a slight smile.

"No offense taken, Master Chief. As a senior citizen, you probably do. Next time I visit my grandfather in the retirement home I'll ask if he remembers serving under you when he was in the Great White Fleet before the Great War." I responded with a big smile that bordered on being a smirk. The Yeoman on the phone couldn't hold back a chuckle.

The Great White Fleet was the nickname for the sixteen-month journey around the globe accomplished by sixteen of our battleships, all in white paint, back in 1907–09. That event happened nearly ten years before we got involved in the Great War, World War I. President Roosevelt—Teddy, not Franklin—had ordered it to impress upon Japan that we were a world power and could move our forces from the Atlantic to the Pacific with ease. The Master Chief was old, but not that old.

The Master Chief broke into a huge grin and extended his hand. "A genuine pleasure to meet you, Mr. Colt. Please follow me." And he turned and walked toward the doors in the center of the back wall. Two sharp knocks received an "enter" in response. He opened the right door, stuck his head in and said, "Admiral, Lieutenant Commander Colt has arrived."

A rough voice responded, "Send him in. You come back with your pad, and have Cummings get the coffee."

Admiral William Gallagher was the epitome of what comes to mind when someone says Navy Admiral. Standing just under six feet and with just a small amount of fat on his body, the thing that immediately caught my eyes was the weathered look of his face. Crow's feet beside each eye and a permanent tan on aged skin—skin that had seen too many hours on the bridge wing of a naval vessel—grabbed my attention first. Then I noticed the receding hair line and the gray that was working toward over-coming the brown in the crew-cut hair. His mouth was compressed in a straight line as he looked me over. The four stars on his collar gleamed with power.

I marched over and stood at attention in front of the CNO's desk. "Lieutenant Commander Colt reporting as ordered, sir," I said.

Like the outer office, the Admiral's office featured thick, dark blue carpet, and his huge wood desk centered on the main wall. The Admiral's flag, a US flag, and the CNO's flag were positioned behind his desk. Two sofas faced each other over a highly polished coffee table over to the left side of the room, near the windows. The wall to the right side of the Admiral's desk featured the expected "I was there" plaques and photos; it was a perfect place for a photo-op with the Navy's highest-ranking Admiral.

After what seemed like forever, the Admiral extended his hand and finally said, "At ease, Colt, and have a seat on the sofa. Admiral Chance highly recommended you for this assignment, but I admit you are not what I expected." The Admiral sat across from me on the other sofa.

"I get that a lot, sir," I answered. He didn't seem pleased with my response. I really needed to hold the sarcasm inside my head. Before I could say anything else, the Master Chief returned with his pad and took a seat on the other sofa.

"Admiral," said the Master Chief, "Mr. Colt can handle himself quite well. From what I have read in his files, both his standard service record and the closed file on his last assignment, and especially the way he came back to me just now, he can hold his own, and he has my vote."

"Thank you, Master Chief," said the Admiral with a sarcastic smile. "Glad he has your approval. Americans can now sleep safer tonight." And he turned back to me with a serious look and said, "Colt, we have a lot to discuss. Now that you have approval of both your CO and the Master Chief here, a man who has been near my side for most of our thirty-year careers, my concerns about you are hereby dismissed. And I hope you put as much trust in Bartow as I do. He has saved my ass too many times."

YN2 Cummings opened the door that moment and pushed in a rolling coffee service, complete with white mugs carrying the USN anchor and chain logo. The Admiral gave a quick nod and said, "Thank you, Cummings. That will be all. Hold all calls except from the President, SECNAV, or my wife."

"Aye, aye, sir. Can do." And with that, Cummings exited and closed the door.

Bartow stood and approached the coffee service. He poured a mug of black and passed it to the Admiral. He looked at me with a question on his face, and I responded, "One sugar and a dash of cream, please." As he prepared my coffee and a mug of black for himself, he turned to the Admiral and asked, "How much of this will be on the record, sir?"

"David, with the exception of the TAD paperwork, nothing else about Mr. Colt will be documented. Log him in as a security officer reporting directly to me and note that he is working off-site. Assign him a phone code." The Admiral turned to me and said, "Colt, you will notice that the Master Chief and I have a much laid-back and close relationship. I call him David in private and he calls me Admiral or sir, his preference."

"I understand completely, sir, I can only hope the Master Chief will allow me that honor one day." I smiled at the Chief as he handed me the mug of coffee and returned to his seat across from me.

The Chief smiled and said, "Sir, that depends on how our competition at the pistol range works out. The Admiral and I have been shipmates more times than he wants to recall so he gets a pass, but you will have to earn the privilege."

I laughed and said, "You're on, Chief."

The Admiral grunted and pulled us back to the subject at hand. "Colt, you have seen the reports on increased drug use and sales. And you may be aware that there has been a rash of unsolved deaths in the Fifth Naval District. Especially in the Norfolk area. Sadly, confidential informants who have been helping fight the drug problems have also turned up dead."

"Admiral Chance and I talked about the problem last week and we decided an investigation must be initiated, but it needs to be done quietly." He grunted, took another sip of coffee and continued. "There was another suspicious overdose death yesterday down there. This has to stop. So in addition to doing the investigation quietly, it needs to be done quickly."

Setting my coffee mug on the table, I looked at the Admiral and said, "Yes sir, I am aware of the problems. But since the overviews of the deaths I have seen do not show any obvious connections needing the touch of internal affairs, I have not spent any time looking into it. I assume the consensus you and the Admiral reached on the deaths of the CIs is that there is a leak in NIS and/or, perhaps, other places. And that an investigation from internal affairs will cause the leaker to crawl back into his hole."

The Admiral smiled and reached for his coffee. "Congratulations, you just gave a short synopsis of your next assignment. The important question is how are you going to handle the investigation and fix the problem?"

There's nothing like being blindsided by the leader of the US Navy to kick up the stress level. I knew I was getting a new assignment, and since I was reporting to the CNO I knew it was a high level and important one, but not having a clue what it was about left me wishing I was invisible. Nothing generates pressure like having to prepare a staff briefing in thirty seconds or less.

But when under pressure, go with your gut. I looked at the Admiral and said, "Since it cannot be an active IA investigation, I will need to go undercover. And the deeper under I go, the better the chance I'll have."

The Admiral nodded and sipped more coffee as he waited for me to go on with the "plan" that I was trying to formulate immediately.

"I need to go into NISO Norfolk as a junior petty officer—a just-out-of-school third class Yeoman would be best. One who is new to the intelligence field. From that position, I will be able to ask a lot of questions without causing suspicion. And I should be able to find a way to view all the case files and evidence discreetly, to compare them with the HQ file copies to see if there are any discrepancies. And that should give me time and opportunity to evaluate the military and civilian personnel."

I took another sip of coffee and continued. "I will need a copy of everyone's records, including security clearance BIs, before I go—and copies of the unsolved case files. I will call Admiral Chance and ask him to have copies of the unsolved case files made and sent to me here. But I can't go through regular channels at NISHQ to get the personnel records, so that will have to be done some other way. And I will need to get some training as a Yeoman ... faking it won't work in a small operation like a NISO." I looked over at the Chief and asked, "I assume we can quietly work with someone at BUPERS to gen up a service record for this Yeoman."

"Yes sir, Mr. Colt. I know just the guy," said the Chief with a smile. That smile told me he knew a Master Chief in the Bureau of Naval Personnel (BUPERS) that he called by his first name and, like Bartow, he had hash marks all the way down the sleeve.

"As soon as I get the NISO and NISRA personnel files, I will verify that no one there knows who I am. Since I have been out of the USA for most of last year, and spent most of the year before that in the NISHQ office spaces or at NISOs down south, I don't think my face is well known in the Norfolk NISO. I just need those records and some Yeoman training to get going," I explained and took another sip of coffee. "I hate to delay the investigation, but I need a good cover story and a few weeks delay is needed so I can get some Yeoman A School experience."

The Admiral smiled and said, "Chance, and David here, were right. You are what we need." He reached over to hit the intercom button and Yeoman Cummings immediately responded.

"Cummings, get the CO of NTC Bainbridge on the line and ask him when the next Yeoman A School class starts. Get that info, ask him to hold, and let me know yesterday."

"Aye, aye, Admiral."

"Colt, do you have a name you want to use for this Yeoman?" asked the Admiral.

"Williams, Mark John. DOB 05-14-50. That will work," I said. The Chief wrote that on his pad, laid it on the Admiral's desk, and exited the room quietly.

"Admiral, I have NTC Bainbridge CO Captain Jason Anderson on line three. The current Yeoman class started today, sir, the next one is six weeks off," said Cummings on the intercom.

"Good morning, Captain. Admiral Gallagher here with a special request for the Naval Training Center," said the Admiral after punching the button for line three. "I am doing well, thank you … And I appreciate that, Jason. Uh, huh … Yes, that's true. Jason, I'm pressed for time so here is what I need; I hope you can help me. Can you find room in the Yeoman A School class that started today for a young man I have working here? He's sharp and it is time for him to get some formal training. And you know we have very few Seamen running around here in the Pentagon so he needs his crow."

The Admiral rolled his eyes as he listened to Anderson ramble on. I figured there might be a class limit, but then again, the CNO can make things happen. He smiled and said, after listening to Anderson for a full minute, "How about this, Jason. Put him on this current class roster and he will be there next Monday. Like I said, he is sharp and can catch up the first week's lessons in his spare time. Will that work for you?"

The Admiral finally said "thank you" and rattled off the name I'd just given him. Then he closed the call saying, "I appreciate your extra efforts, Captain. Williams will be there bright and early Monday morning. Good day." He hung up the phone and smiled at me. "I do hope you know how to act like an enlisted man, because as of Sunday afternoon, you are a Seaman, Yeoman Striker."

"The good news, Admiral, is that I spent two painful weeks going through the reserve basic training course at NTC Orlando the first of last year. We thought it might be needed with the project I had upcoming that was sidelined. I still have my seabag packed and will pick up the quills I need," I responded.

The rating of Yeoman is designated on the enlisted man's sleeve with an insignia of crossed quills. It dates back to the quill and ink writing the Yeoman did back in the day. A Seaman has three stripes on his upper left sleeve. When pursuing a Yeoman rating, the Yeoman insignia is applied above them and he's then referred to as a Seaman, Yeoman Striker.

Right then, Chief Bartow returned and said, "Admiral, if you are finished with Mr. Colt, I need to get his photo shot for the new enlisted ID card. His enlisted record is being set up right now showing boot camp in Orlando, and him being assigned here right after the first of last year. And do you want him to have the 'get out of jail free card,' also?"

"Good plan, David. Stick with Colt this week and make sure everything he needs is handled. Colt, keep in touch. I won't bother you, but if you need me, you know where to call. Get it done. Quickly and quietly. Dismissed," ordered the Admiral. The Chief and I popped to attention and left his office.

14

THE REST OF THE WEEK was a blurry mess. Monday afternoon I was borrowed a dress jumper from Cummings for my enlisted ID photo and new enlisted service record. Master Chief Bartow called in several favors and got friends to make copies of all the NISO and NISRA staff records that I'd need to study. They'd be hand delivered on Wednesday to the CNO's office.

I called Vice Admiral Chance and requested copies of the suspicious case files from NISO Norfolk. He would get them copied without fanfare and bring them to the CNO's office by Thursday.

Cummings made a trip to the Navy Yard and picked up the yeoman insignias that I needed to sew to my own enlisted uniforms. I just needed to make sure they still fit, since I'd lost a bit of weight in Vietnam the previous year. And they probably needed to be cleaned and pressed. That was an agreeable task for Tuesday, I decided.

The sun was well "over the yardarm," as the saying goes, hours ago. As we prepared to call it a day, I asked Bartow about his plans for the evening.

"Easy answer, Mr. Colt. Not a damn thing," he said. He went on to tell me his wife had passed away a few years ago, and until he was forced to retire, the Navy was his life.

"Tell ya what, Master Chief. How about joining me for dinner?" I asked. He first balked at the idea, but after I bugged him a bit more he agreed. We decided to head to our individual homes to change into civilian clothing. I told him to meet me at the Old Ebbitt Grill on 15th Street NW at 2000 hrs.

Dinner was splendid. It always is there. But the best part was it gave us a chance to get to know one another without the uniforms and rank getting in the way. I insisted that at times like these, first names were mandatory. In no time, it felt like we'd known each other for years. And the pistol range was calling us for a match.

Sitting at a table in a back corner allowed us to talk about the upcoming investigation and what could go wrong. Having his twenty extra years of Navy experience to draw from was a remarkable asset. We went over my plan, tweaked it a bit, and decided it probably had a better chance of working than any other plan we'd considered. It was a good ending to an interesting day.

15

TUESDAY I GOT TO THE Pentagon just after noon. I'd spent the morning in my townhouse, checking every piece of clothing in my seabag, sewing the quills in place, and putting another shine on the shoes. Everything still fit fairly well, but I had to adjust the web belt for my dungarees about an inch, since much of the weight I lost last year had been in my gut. I dropped off all the uniforms, including dungarees, at the cleaners and was promised they'd be ready by Wednesday afternoon.

Bartow, Cummings, and I spent the afternoon going over my new service record. After they were sure everything looked good and proper, they questioned me multiple times on everything in the dang thing. Marcus Colt was being pushed to the back of my mind, and Mark Williams was taking over.

Wednesday, Master Chief Bartow and I met at the pistol range at Marine Corps Base Quantico at 0900 hrs for a bit of fun. A quick call the day before from the CNO's office ensured we had space at the range. Amazing how powerful those three letters can be. Yep, just say CNO and many doors open! We decided to focus on combat shooting at ten yards. After a couple of hours and about 1,000 rounds through our 1911 Colt pistols, we agreed that we were almost equal in shooting skills. On each set, one of us would edge out the other by only a point or two.

However, I did have the edge on David—I earned the right to call him by his first name even when in uniform that day—when shooting with the non-dominant hand. David had never practiced that so I outscored him greatly each time. It was a splendid morning and a wonderful chance to blow off some of the stress that had been building. I suspected I wouldn't have an opportunity to do that again for a while.

Thursday morning I walked into the CNO's office suite wearing my enlisted dress blues, complete with my crossed quills over my Seaman's stripes. I had changed the way I was combing my hair, had a few days growth on a new mustache, and was now wearing black framed glasses, so when Cummings looked up, he didn't recognize me. His jaw dropped when I introduced myself as Seaman Williams, reporting for duty. Guess clothes do make the man.

Interestingly, my fresh look also fooled both Master Chief Bartow and Admiral Gallagher, for at least a minute or so, when they arrived. For the rest of the day, I was allowed to answer the phone and do normal office work under the watchful eyes of both Cummings and Bartow. They corrected me when I messed up, and offered suggestions on better ways to act to keep in character. The hardest part of the day was getting Cummings to quit calling me "sir."

But all good things must come to an end and so it was with my time—a very long week—in the CNO's office. I'd decided to spend Friday taking care of personal things like paying my house payment and utilities, etc., six months in advance, and dumping the leftovers from the fridge. Little things like that are never seen in the spy movies, but they must be done.

As I prepared to leave the office, David passed me the "get out of jail free" card the Admiral had mentioned on Monday. Frankly, with all the other stuff going on, I'd forgotten about it. It was a standard ID-sized card that was laminated. On one side was my head shot with no uniform showing, my real name, rank, etc. I turned it over and read the back.

> Lieutenant Commander Marcus James Colt is working directly for, and with the full authority of, the Office of the Chief of Naval Operations. All requests he may have should be considered as coming directly from me and be fulfilled without question or delay.
> Signed, William M. Gallagher
> Chief of Naval Operations.

"Well, that should work, I suppose," I said with a smile as I slid the card into my wallet behind my ID card.

"It has not failed yet, Mr. Colt," answered Master Chief Bartow. "Just you take care of yourself and always watch your back. You know the number to call if you need us and when you do, no matter who answers the phone, say 'SA268 calling for the Admiral' and that will cut through the bull. Good luck, sir."

I shook David's hand and thanked him. We'd built a strong working relationship and friendship in just a matter of days. I could see why the Admiral relied on him so much.

Turning to Cummings, I saluted him and thanked him for taking me under his wing that week. I also said, "Lester, it has been a real honor to work with you on this project. I truly appreciate your patience with me." He wished me luck, and I headed out the door. It had been such an intense week, I felt like I was leaving family.

16

SUDDENLY IT WAS SATURDAY AFTERNOON, and I knew I had one more important task to handle before heading to Maryland the next day. I had to call Sandy. I hadn't tried to call her that week, and she hadn't put forth the effort to call, either.

After several rings the phone was answered, and much to my surprise, it was Sandy on the end of the line and not her mother. Her voice sounded as nice as ever.

"Hello, Beautiful. How are you?" I asked.

"Oh, hi, hon. I wasn't expecting to hear from you today. What's going on up there? Everything okay?"

I took a breath, held it for a sec, and started. "Sandy, it's been another rough week up here and I needed to hear your sexy voice to recharge my battery. I feel better now. You doin' okay?"

"Yea, doing fine down here. Carol and I are heading out to a club in just a bit for some dancing." She seemed to say something under her breath, but I couldn't understand it. So I asked.

"I just know what you are going to say about my dancing. You don't like it. But with you gone all the time, it's the only fun I can have. And

51

remember, it's just a dance. It's not like I'm sleeping with anyone. It's only a dance," she whined.

"I understand your frustration, Sandy. Same here. But the Navy has the higher priority right now. That's why I'm calling. The Admiral gave me a new assignment and I'll be gone from the office and my townhouse for about two or three months. I'll be calling you when I can, but there is no number I can give you in case you need to call me. My mail will be forwarded, so that option is open to you. If there's an emergency, call my office and they will get a message to me as soon as they can."

"Great," she said with a voice filled with a mixture of frustration and anger. Mostly anger. "Call me if you ever get back from this assignment. I have to get ready to meet Carol. Talk with you later. Bye." And the line went dead.

That went well, I thought. *No, it really did not, and I need to stop the sarcasm, even with myself.*

So I spent the rest of Saturday afternoon going over that call in my mind—wondering what I could have said, or should have said, that I hadn't. Perhaps I took my oath too seriously or put more work into my job than I did my relationship. We had nearly two and one-half years invested in this relationship. It had been a great time for us both, yet also a source of frustration for us both, with the frustration coming from different directions.

Maybe if we'd married over a year ago things would be different. Or maybe we'd now be heading to divorce court. Hard to say. I just knew there wasn't enough bourbon available in the house to handle the stress of the situation, so I went out to get a bite to eat.

As I sat in the restaurant, I realized why I usually just get take-out or cook at home. Eating in a restaurant alone is a depressing thing to do. All around are couples enjoying their meals, laughing together, holding hands, sharing stories, and just enjoying each other's company. I had not enjoyed that for weeks now, and it looked like it would be many weeks or months before I could enjoy it again. I finished my meal quickly and headed back to my townhouse feeling rather depressed.

Entering my place and seeing the phone in the hall reminded me of the disastrous call with Sandy. There was no need for me to call her since I knew she was out having fun ... again.

I decided to lose myself in education, so for the umpteenth time I read the Yeoman's Handbook I'd borrowed from Lester Cummings. In two days, I was going to be a full week behind in my class studies, and I needed to learn all this stuff quickly. I was determined to be the best dang Yeoman that NTC Bainbridge had ever created.

17

BAINBRIDGE NAVAL TRAINING CENTER WAS built in 1942 as an additional boot camp to handle the need for many more sailors to fight World War II. In these boot camps, civilians would learn the Navy way and eleven weeks later emerge ready to be sent to the fleet. It was named after Commodore William Bainbridge, who commanded the frigate Constitution when it defeated the British HMS Java during the War of 1812.

Now it handles non-recruit training in several different schools, including radioman, yeoman, and nuclear power. Barracks and school buildings were all wood-frame structures and by 1971, many had seen better days. A couple were thought to be haunted. But they served their purpose and produced the trained personnel the Navy needs.

In addition, it was the boot camp for the WAVES ... women in the Navy. Formed in 1942 to free up men for sea duty, the Women Accepted for Volunteer Emergency Service, henceforth known as WAVES, was officially disbanded in 1946 when women were allowed to join the Navy just the same as men. The name continued due to its popularity, even though the official unit was gone.

For me, it was a simple seventy-five-mile drive up to Port Deposit, Maryland from D.C. that Sunday afternoon. Then a few more miles up a side road to the base. Students' personal vehicles were not allowed on the base, so I parked the 'Cuda in the designated parking area just outside the main gate. I hoisted my seabag on my left shoulder, tucked my service record and orders under my arm, and headed to check in at the main gate.

The weeks in Bainbridge went by quickly. The class work was interesting and I picked it up quickly. In short, the job of a Yeoman was to run the ship's office and take care of the officers' service records. Every document in the jacket had to be done just so, with zero errors and filed in a specific order. At some other NTC, a bunch of men and women were learning to do the same thing with enlisted service records; they would soon wear the insignia of a Personnelman. Even with all the women's lib stuff and bra burning, the names of Navy specialties had not changed. Face it, Yeoperson or Personnel-person just don't have the same savoir faire.

In addition to learning to be a Yeoman, I used this time to learn how to act like a twenty-year-old enlisted man. I hung out with a guy named Chuck whom I'd found out was also from Florida. He was a year or two older than the rest of the class, and married, so we felt comfortable together since I was engaged—and often felt as though I were married to Sandy. Observing the other, younger students in the off hours proved to be the most informative. I focused on current slang and music selections since songs from my favorite group, the Beach Boys, were considered golden oldies now.

Most evenings, after chow and a bit of studying, were spent in Fiddler's Green, the enlisted men's club. WAVES were attending several of the schools, including the Yeoman A School, so there were always members of the opposite sex available to share the time in the Green talking, drinking, and dancing.

My education was going great, but not so much my personal life. Sandy was not at all happy with my new assignment since it was cutting into the wedding planning again. Hard to plan a big wedding when you can't nail down the wedding date.

It was no surprise that every time I called to chat with her, her mom again told me she was either working or out with girlfriends. I'd never expected her to sit at home and pine, but her being out all the time was frustrating. Guess she was upset with me over things I couldn't control. I spent a lot of time humming the song "I wonder what she's doing tonight" by Barry and the Tamerlanes, from 1963.

The more I thought about it, I realized the thing that bothered me the most about the whole mess was that her being out "having fun" didn't bother me much at all anymore. Maybe I no longer cared enough. Maybe we'd just drifted apart like in that song "You've Lost That Lovin' Feelin'";

the wedding might be the only thing holding us together. That was a perfect recipe for a disastrous life.

After the phone call that afternoon and another talk with Marie, who was supposed to be my future mother-in-law, instead of Sandy, I decided a big distraction was needed and well deserved. It was Valentine's Day and I had really wanted to hear Sandy's voice and get some reassurance about our relationship. But that didn't happen.

So I proceeded over to Fiddler's Green to escape my life that Sunday night. I'd selected a table in the back to get away from everyone for a bit, with the hope the loud music and bourbon on the rocks or two would take my mind off the negative thoughts about Sandy running around in my head.

Several of my classmates entered the Green, including Patricia Newton, who had to be the best-looking gal attending the Yeoman A School. Standing 5'7", she had medium length brown hair and hazel eyes topping off a figure that most of the other WAVES wished they had. She had enlisted to get out of Seattle, Washington, where the two options open to her were getting married or working for Boeing. For now, she wanted neither and had been somewhat standoffish with the men in the class. So it was a surprise to look up and see her taking a seat next to me.

"You look down, Mark. What's wrong?" she asked. "Your Valentine dump you?"

She was close. I hated to spill my guts, but I needed someone to talk with about it all. So I gave her the quick overview about Sandy. Especially the way Sandy was always out dancing all the time even though she said nothing was going on with those guys she danced with at the clubs. Sandy kept telling me it was "only a dance."

Was she cheating and should we split up? I was not completely sure and feared making a big mistake. Pat said she wouldn't offer advice, but knew the feeling as she'd been in a similar situation right before joining the Navy. A good friend had given her a test that helped clear up her feelings.

"Do you want to try the test?" Pat asked.

"At this point, I'm willing to even try hypnosis if it'll help," I responded. She laughed.

Claudine Longet started singing "I Love How You Love Me" on the jukebox. Pat stood, grabbed my hand, and said, "Come. Dance with me."

The dance floor of the Green was not huge, so it was impossible to hide in a crowd. Knowing other members of the class were watching made me nervous. Pat pulled me close and laid her head on my shoulder. She moved my hand from her back down to rest on the top of her near-perfect butt. I gave her a quizzical look, but kept my hand there. We moved with the music for a bit and then she whispered, "Let's start the test. Close your eyes and keep them closed. Do not say a word no matter what."

After another moment or two, she pulled my head down to meet hers and gave me the most erotic kiss. It started slow, with just a brush of our lips, and then as our lips parted the kiss became deeper and her tongue explored mine as her right hand started slowly massaging the back of my neck. She pulled our bodies even closer together as we swayed to the music and held the kiss.

When our lips finally parted, she breathlessly whispered, "Now tell me the first thoughts you just had. And no, I don't mean surprise or being sexually aroused. That is an expected non-controllable physical reaction unless you're a queer or I'm losing my appeal." She softly giggled and looked deeply into my eyes, "What emotions are you feeling, Mark?"

My mind was like the eye wall of a hurricane, with all kinds of stuff whirling around at high speed. I no longer thought about where we were. I didn't want to be analytical at that moment. I just wanted to be right there, right now. Finally, I was able to whisper back through heavy breaths, "Desire, excitement, confusion, and oh, yea, more than a few sexual thoughts."

"Keep those thoughts, shut up, and keep dancing. Hold me tighter. But remember, it's 'only a dance,' right?"

At times I'm a bit slow, but I picked up on the "only a dance" comment and smiled. We finished that dance but realized it was a different song that was ending, and we hadn't even noticed. I wanted it to go on for a few more hours. We returned to our table hand in hand. We were both flushed and still out of breath. We just sat there and looked at each other for an unknown amount of time. Finally, I asked her to tell me about that test.

"My ex-boyfriend taught it to me. He was majoring in psychology and specializing in human behavior. At a party where things got a bit carried away, he saw me kissing his roommate. He pulled me aside and asked what emotions I was feeling during the kiss. And my answers were similar to yours. He then told me that if my first, or even second, reaction had been guilt or regret, then my love for him was foremost in my mind. Otherwise … well, I think you now know. We broke up that same night."

She squeezed my hand and continued, "I've wanted to kiss you for weeks. Now I'm sorry I waited until the class is nearly over. Let's get out of here." We got up and headed to the door and walked out into the night.

18

THE LAST TWO WEEKS OF class went by too quickly. While the class work and testing got much more intense, my small amount of free time was spent with Pat. We studied together and always hit the mess hall at the same time. We shared many more dances and good times at Fiddler's Green. Pat and I had a bond that time would never erase.

The following weekend we didn't have any watch duty, so we grabbed Chuck, jumped into my 'Cuda, and spent Saturday in Washington D.C., taking in all the monuments and museums. The three of us even danced down the Capitol steps like Debbie Reynolds, Gene Kelly, and Donald O'Connor in *Singing in the Rain*.

Then Sunday we took in the sights of Baltimore and finished the day with dinner at a fantastic old seafood restaurant. It had been a great weekend with friends. Friendships and memories are some of the best parts of military life.

Thursday night before graduation was spent in the usual way. Patricia and I were together for dinner and ended up at Fiddler's Green for our last night of dancing together. It was fitting that the last song we shared that night was a slow one … Andy Williams singing "And We Were Lovers," the theme song from *The Sand Pebbles*. That had been a great love story set in the Navy, with Steve McQueen playing a petty officer in love with Candice Bergen. All the words of the song were appropriate for us, since we had no regrets.

After the graduation ceremonies on Friday morning, I headed south with Pat and Chuck and all our gear crammed in the 'Cuda. I gave Pat a ride to D.C.'s Dulles International Airport so she could catch a flight home to Seattle, where she'd spend a week or so before heading to her new duty station in Pearl Harbor, Hawaii. We both promised to write, but I doubted either of us would. It was what it was, and things change. We shared a warm smile, a quick hug, a chaste kiss, and that was the extent of our goodbye. She turned and walked away.

Back to the 'Cuda, I revved the engine, and without a glance in the rearview mirror turned it due south. To save him from wasting a couple of days on a slow bus, I'd offered to drive Chuck all the way to Orlando and to the waiting arms of his wife, Norma. Like me, he had only ten days travel to his new duty station—a carrier based out of Mayport, Florida— and the bus took another day and half to get there. It was on my way anyway, and he could help drive. Plus he was good company and even picked up the food costs on the trip, since I refused his gas money.

We made great time heading south, and even with a stop in to meet Norma when I dropped Chuck off at his apartment, I got back to Clearwater late Saturday afternoon. I had over a week of leave left before I had to report to Norfolk, so it looked like there was plenty of time to study the NISO personnel files and to take care of things with Sandy. I knew what had to be done, and I believed it was the best thing for both of us. That still didn't make it easy. So I decided to put it off for a day and spent the rest of Saturday sleeping.

Sunday afternoon I called Sandy's house and found her home. That had to be the first time in over five weeks! She was surprised to know I was home, as she thought she wouldn't see me for at least another week. I told her I'd pick her up at three p.m. And yea, we could run out to Clearwater Beach for a bite to eat like she wanted.

When I got to her place, only Sandy was at the house, as everyone else had gone to a relative's house for the afternoon. After only two months apart, her hugs and kisses seemed more strained even in the quiet of an empty house. Nothing like we were back in December for those two wonderful weeks. Or maybe she was fine, but I was the different one; hard to say. Anyway, we chatted for a few minutes and then headed to the beach.

Pier 60 is a Clearwater landmark. Jutting out into the Gulf of Mexico hundreds of feet, it got its name from the east-to-west state highway called SR 60 that, depending upon your point of view, either starts or ends there at the pier. It's a great place to fish, and a popular place for couples to stroll along while enjoying each other and the gorgeous views of the Gulf and the beach. It held a special place in our hearts, as our first date two and a half years ago had ended with a late night stroll along the pier.

So it was fitting that our relationship came to an end on Pier 60. After an early dinner, we ended up on the pier and talked for hours, watching the sun set into the Gulf. We both shared our frustrations with everything that had gotten in the way of our lives together. For Sandy, it was always the Navy getting in the way of our marriage, and for me, it was her always partying and not showing full support for my career. It was perhaps the most honest talk we'd ever had.

With the sun fully set, the evening turned into night before I finally came to the hardest part of the conversation. Holding both her hands in mine, I told her we needed to end the engagement so she would be free to make up her mind about what she wanted. She cried, disagreed, and told me all she wanted was us together. I told her she needed to be totally free for a while to think things over. If in a couple of months she still felt there was a chance for us, then we could get back together when my current assignment should be behind me. She slid the diamond off her finger and placed it in my hand. We hugged and, as if on cue to make things more depressing, a light rain started to fall as we stood there embracing.

It was fitting, and I guess some would call it a sign, that as I parked in her driveway Ray Price started singing "For the Good Times" on the radio. I shut off the engine and we listened to the entire song in silence. We just sat there in the dark car watching the rain blur the windshield. She laid her head on my shoulder as we held hands while the song played out. There was nothing left to say as Ray sang.

I think we both knew, deep down, this was our last time together. The last time to feel at least a small part of the love that had burned bright inside us for years. The love that had burned out due to circumstances of life beyond our control. Probably no one was at fault. Bad things happen to good people. And all that other crap people say to make themselves feel better.

With the song over, we ran through the rain to her front door. Both of us were crying as I lightly kissed her damp cheek and whispered, "Goodbye, Sandy." She just stood there. I turned away and walked slowly back to the car. By the time I got into the 'Cuda and looked back at the porch, Sandy had already gone into the house. No parting words, no wave goodbye. Driving home was very difficult with rain rolling down the windshield and tears rolling down my cheeks.

19

As I DROVE PAST THE Norfolk city limits sign, my wallowing in memories stopped and my mind came back to the present. Bridges had been burned and some good times were in the past. Some great people had recently entered my life, made some changes to it, and now they too were gone. *May you all have Fair Winds and Following Seas, shipmates.*

Life is a collection of people and events that turn into memories as we age, and they eventually become the faded photographs in our minds. Over time, the pain subsides and the remaining memories are mostly good. If we are lucky, those mental photo albums will be chock full when our lives come to an end.

I just hoped that recent pains that had yet to subside would not take my mind off the job I had to face. Maybe I just needed to stay away from women for a while. As for Sandy, I couldn't get past the feeling that she had not been honest with me about all her dancing. Those feelings left too many open wounds that needed time to heal.

There was a lot to get done before reporting in at the base on Tuesday as Yeoman Petty Officer Third Class Williams. Seemed like at least a hundred items were on the list of things to do before I'd be ready for duty on

Wednesday morning. Now it was time to find the real estate office and get down to business.

Getting into Norfolk by noon on Friday was perfect. That allowed time to meet the lead real estate agent at JT Reality and see the house he'd found for me. My demands to him earlier in the week were simple: a quiet neighborhood not near the base, utilities included, and a two-car garage had to be part of this furnished, ready-to-move-in rental. And he said that he had the perfect place.

Finding his office was easy. I just followed the directions printed on the signs that seemed to be all over town. The owner greeted me at the door of the office. "Call me JT," he said. He was a slightly overweight, middle-aged fellow who was happy to take good care of a Navy officer who didn't ask the price and didn't flinch when told the first and last month's rent were due on signing, as well as a two-month security deposit. Good thing I didn't have a dog, as that would have meant another deposit.

I followed him the three-mile drive to the house and was pleasantly surprised. It was a two-story frame house, probably built in the early part of the century. The front porch even had a swing. While not as fancy as the Painted Ladies in San Francisco, it came close.

We did a walk through and I asked the expected questions. JT gave the expected answers. So I signed the rental agreement and handed over the check, getting the keys in return. JT left and I spent an hour unloading the 'Cuda and stashing my stuff in the right places. The garage was detached, but large. I made sure the powered garage doors worked.

A quick look around the neighborhood was encouraging: lots of trees and shrubs would block the view and not many neighbors were around. There were multiple ways to get out of the area in case a quick egress was needed. Having anyone there at the house was not in the plan, but it's good to be ready for anything. I drove around the neighborhood as I made a quick run to the local grocery for some basic food stuff to get me through the night. While there, I picked up a newspaper and headed back to the house for the next step in the plan.

Setting down in the living room with a cold glass of iced tea, I perused the classified ads looking for the right car—the car that a low-level enlisted man would drive. It had to be something not too new, flashy or memorable, a dark color to help it blend in with the night, and it had to be at least ten years old. Getting one with a decent-sized V-8 would be a big plus. You never know when you might need to get out of somewhere quickly. So I looked for any pre-1960 sedan with a V-8, dark blue or black in color.

Then I saw it in the second column of the classified ads. While it didn't fit all the criteria because it was a classic, my gut said this was the right car. It was a 1956 Chevy Bel Air four-door hardtop with a 265 cu in V-8. A Super Power Pack option added a four-barrel carb, giving 33 more horsepower, and it had a manual three-speed transmission, Harbor Blue body with two-tone blue interior, and only 45,000 miles. Asking price was only $1,450. I drove back to the grocery store and used the pay phone in the parking lot to call the owner. Yes, it was available, and they provided instructions to their house.

The car looked fine, and according to the owner, all maintenance was up to date and there were no known issues. I gave it a good look over and a lengthy test drive and was pleased. And the owner quickly accepted the $1,250 cash I offered. He signed over the title and passed me the keys. I told him I'd be back to get the car in about an hour, and returned to the grocery store.

I needed to get the phone in the house turned on. Running to the grocery store parking lot had gotten old after just a few trips. I called a taxi and asked them to pick me up from my house in fifteen minutes. That gave me time to get back to the house and stash the 'Cuda in the garage.

After picking up the Chevy, I headed to the gas station for a fill-up, then back to the house for the evening. I sat down and made a list of things I needed to get done on Monday ... car registration, phone activation, and whatever other ugly thing might jump up in my way. With that done, I turned off the lights and went upstairs for some much needed sleep.

20

SATURDAY AND SUNDAY WERE BOTH a mess as I unpacked my civilian and officer clothing, got things situated around the house, and set up an office in one of the upstairs bedrooms. I checked with the local post office; they'd received the large boxes I mailed to my post office box that the realtor had set up for me. The boxes contained the hand tools and office equipment I needed but didn't have room in the 'Cuda to transport. In addition, they had a package from D.C. that contained more files I needed to study.

I'd purchased a small document safe at a local office supply store, and after slowly and carefully getting that heavy thing up the stairs, got it bolted to the floor inside the 'office' bedroom closet. *There goes the security deposit*, I thought as I drilled holes through the wood flooring into the floor joists. Might be cheaper to just leave the safe there when I moved out.

At the second trip to the office supply store, I purchased two metal two-drawer filing cabinets. They were hauled up the stairs to the new office. Then a quick trip to the big lumber yard/hardware store saw two 30" hollow-core doors loaded into the back of the 'Cuda. The store also had twelve-inch squares of cork, so I added twenty-four of them and a can of contact cement to the stash of stuff needed to finish the office.

One of the doors was placed on top of the two filing cabinets to form a crude but effective desk. I covered one side of the other door with contact cement, then applied a sheet of cork. After the edges were trimmed, the new corkboard was leaned against the wall, setting on two of the dining room chairs. The new pieces of 'furniture' were arranged so I could sit at my new desk and study the suspect board right in front of me. But right now it was as blank as my mind.

I'd also found a machine shop, on Saturday afternoon, that was able to fabricate and install a steel box in the trunk of the Chevy. It was a simple design, and I already had the combination lock, which they quickly installed. Like the one in the back of the 'Cuda, this would allow me to safely store sensitive materials, and my weapon, out of sight and inaccessible to the bad guys—yet handy for me.

After better stocking the fridge and pantry Saturday night, I knew it was time to get to work. I had goofed off enough getting my background established for this investigation. So Saturday night and the rest of the day Sunday, after worship services, were spent reviewing the personnel files and security background check files of everyone at NIS. The leaker, if there was one, had to be in that group. But I was just not seeing it. They all looked clean. Well, all except for two civilians and one sailor who concerned me.

Petty Office Dexter Wilson was the sailor. Granted, he was nearly as new as I was to the unit, but he had transferred in from the Philippines, a haven for drug users and sellers. Could he be a go-between from over there who had worked out a way to get here to take care of some issues? Namely getting rid of confidential informants? Seemed like a stretch, a very big stretch since one of them had died before he got here, but I'd seen more farfetched things become true. I needed to spend some time getting to know Dexter Wilson.

As for the two civilians, I needed to meet them and look them in the eye before I could even start to eliminate them. Rereading the files drummed their info into my head, and laid the groundwork for the real work of this next week. Both were special agents of NISRA Norfolk. There was absolutely nothing in their files that would normally throw any doubt or suspicion their way. "Squeaky clean" is the usual way to phrase it.

But they were the agents of record on five of the eight concerning cases. Sure, it could be a coincidence. Coincidences really do happen, but not that often when dealing with criminals. And to make matters worse, these two guys were the agents handling two of the dead CIs.

21

FIRST TASK FOR THE DAY saw me driving to a nearby phone booth and calling the phone company about my service installation. They verified the work order had been issued, but it would be at least a few more days until they got to it. Maybe next week it would be working. Ugh, what an inconvenience a dead phone could be: causing me to dash to a phone booth like Clark Kent. Reminded of dead things, I headed back to the house to go over the suspicious files.

Looking at the unsolved files for the dead sailors didn't immediately give me connections. I had copies of the investigations for those that died before I was assigned to the CNO's office. There was one female supply officer who was strangled, and three male petty officers: one in aviation, one in supply, and one in gunnery. One died of a drug overdose, one was killed in a car crash, and one fell off a pier and drowned. And the car crash guy's file was not even an NIS investigation; the local police had taken care of it. Aside from them all being assigned to the same base, all being unsolved cases, and all being dead, there was not a hard link.

Then there were the four files Master Chief Bartow had sent me. Three were also drug overdoses that had suspicious qualities. "Suspicious" since the drug used to kill one of them was cocaine. One was a shooting with the body dumped on the base. Again, the weak link was drugs, but nothing else connected them.

Except for one other connection, four had called NIS and shared information. A fifth had been ready to cooperate. And the information the four shared was all drug related.

Three of the dead worked in supply. Okay, the link might be there. Or it might be coincidental. I needed to look into each of the current and previous duty stations for the deceased, as well as their private lives. A firm link might pop up there. At this point, I'd even accept a weak link such as the drug connections.

And it probably was a very weak link. Drug use was climbing everywhere in America, including in the military. Sad to see it. In the stats from NIS for 1970, about fifty percent of the case load was doing background information checks for security clearances. Of the remaining fifty percent, around sixty percent of that was drug related. The next highest category was sex crimes—rape, homosexuality, child abuse, pornography, indecent exposure, etc.—at around twenty percent. All the other crimes—murder, fraud, theft, suicide, sabotage, etc.—took up the last twenty percent. So finding a link with drugs was about as common a thing as finding a sailor who wanted a beer with his burger. Pretty dang common.

And I needed to look into the NIS procedures on securing the identities of the CIs. Who had access to their information and how were the CI files stored? The two civilian agents that concerned me both worked for the NISRA. Might they be leaking the information? If so, why? What about other CIs; were they in danger? I hoped to quickly determine the answers to these questions when I started work on Wednesday.

It was time for lunch, so I dashed out to grab a burger, and while out I took care of the auto tag for the Blue Beast. The '56 Chevy needed a name and that was an obvious choice. And it fit well since, in comparison to the 'Cuda, it was a beast to drive. Now the Blue Beast had a Virginia auto tag and inspection sticker. At least it looked more like a local vehicle than the bright yellow 'Cuda with a Florida tag and officer's base sticker. That might come in handy.

22

ALL THE PREP WORK WAS done and now it was time to get fully into my role as a new twenty-one-year-old Yeoman heading to a new duty station. Time to start watching my back. Time to find the bad guys.

I slowed to approach the main gate of Naval Station Norfolk around 1500 hrs on Tuesday afternoon, with a copy of my orders ready to show the guard. He directed me to pull over at a small building, where I was given a temporary pass for my private auto, a map of the base, and directions to the transient barracks.

The chief petty officer in charge explained what I needed to do, within the next few days, to get a permanent sticker for my Chevy. He welcomed me to Norfolk and "invited" me to leave his office. At least he was polite about it all.

After checking in with the watch desk at the transient barracks, I was assigned a bunk and, for a small fee, a combination lock for the locker in my cubical. I didn't get much sleep that first night as sailors were coming and going, and most were not careful about noise. Those who were not moving around snored loudly. But eventually, I acclimated and drifted off to sleep.

Having set the travel clock for 0600 hrs for the Wednesday wakeup, I was brought back to life by the chimes to find a sailor in undress blues sitting on the empty bunk across the cubicle. His sandy-colored hair was parted in the middle. His face sported a mustache that matched his hair color, and a friendly smile. It was difficult to determine his height, but his lack of body bulk told me he didn't spend time in the gym.

He asked, "Are you Williams?" Well, that was a bit of a shock—to have a stranger know who I was after being on the base only a few hours. After I shook the cobwebs out of my head I realized he was not a total stranger, as I recognized him from the photo in his service record. I tried not to let that show on my face.

I jokingly asked if he was a mind reader, but knew in reality this fellow was assigned to the unit I was joining, and the Chief probably told him to be on the lookout for me. Shaking the extended hand of second class petty officer Dexter Wilson, I did the formal introduction thing and started the expected quizzing about him, the base, and the new job. Dexter had transferred in a few weeks earlier and was still housed in the transient barracks. His cube was two down from mine, but not for much longer, he hoped. He was looking forward to getting into the newer barracks.

Frankly, I knew a lot about YN2 Dexter Wilson. Nothing exciting was found in his files. He was born in Kansas City in 1946 and his family lived on a farm outside of town. He had nearly two years of college under his belt before joining the Navy in 1966. Boot camp in San Diego was followed by an assignment to a destroyer home ported in Japan. He went to Yeoman A School after spending eighteen months on the tin can, and then was transferred to Naval Station Subic Bay in the Philippines for duty with the 7th Fleet.

There he excelled as a Yeoman, working in the office of the NAVSUP (Naval Supply Systems Command). His evaluations contained nothing but praise for his work, from all the previous duty stations. There were no weak spots in his record. And his six-year hitch was ending late next year unless he re-enlisted. So unless he slipped up and said something weird, there was nothing, absolutely nothing, which linked him to the dead CIs or drugs.

Being new to Naval Station Norfolk, it was a great momentary stress reliever to have Dexter there as a tour guide. I had enough on my mind without having to constantly look at a map of the base to find places I needed to be. I just hoped I could ditch Dex when the time came to do other things.

After a quick breakfast in the mess hall, an experience best forgotten since greasy eggs and stress do not mix, we walked a couple of blocks down the main drag of the Naval Station to the office. The office complex was on the second floor of the headquarters building for the Fifth Naval District.

Dexter insisted on throwing out some history and technical information as we ate, and he continued now as we walked on to the office. Most of it I already knew, but my cover persona did not, so I let him ramble on and on. The man sure liked to talk.

As Dex told it, the Navy breaks up the world into districts, with a large Navy base as the headquarters (HQ) for each district. Norfolk is the 5th Naval District, extending from northern Virginia down through much of North Carolina. Multiple ships, Navy and Marine bases, and all units therein are assigned to the 5th Naval District.

At Norfolk, one large old multi-story, multi-wing brick building on the main street of the base is designated as the HQ. Viewing the building from the air, it would look like two capital E letters back to back. The center of the front E was the entrance. This building houses the admiral in charge of the district and his staff, on the third floor, with a few other units on the first and second floors.

NISO Norfolk was housed in the entire western wing of the second floor, with the front half of the wing dedicated to the military and civilian staff that was the NISO and the back half used by the agents and clerical staff that made up NISRA Norfolk. Thinking I was a total novice, Dexter explained that our organization was made up of three layers.

In Washington D.C. was the NIS headquarters, where the admiral in charge hung his hat. Under NIS were multiple offices, NISOs, which coordinated the work in a geographic area, such as we did for the 5th Naval District. And under each NISO were a number of Resident Agencies, NISRAs, which housed the agents who did the actual investigative work at various locations around the district.

23

NISO NORFOLK WAS MY NEW duty station. Well, it was the new duty station for Mark Williams, who I happened to be at that moment. We climbed the stairs to the second floor and walk toward a closed door. The upper part of the door was frosted glass, which had painted upon it in black block letters: Naval Investigative Service Office. Dex opened the door and we entered to face a desk with a stern-looking sailor sitting behind it. One side of the desk was against the right wall of the passageway, and a low, gated wood railing connected the left wall to the desk.

Dexter smiled and said, "GM2 Jimmy Kincade, meet the new guy, YN3 Mark Williams." Dexter turned to me and continued, "Mark, Jimmy, and two other of his associates handle the physical security for us. Everyone checks in with them. And if he likes you, he buzzes you in."

Jimmy stood and welcomed me to the unit. GM2 Kincade looked the part of a security guard, with his flattop haircut, well-developed upper body, and a stature of well over six feet. I had to look up at him. He reached under the edge of the desk and pressed a button, which caused a buzz as it unlatched the gate. We walked through and into the NISO world.

I dumped my service record, orders, and cover on a desk in the AUTOVON room, which Dex said would be my work station. Then I shadowed him as he did his morning ritual of a dozen tasks to get the office ready for the day. Most important was to put on two large urns of coffee. Other tasks included picking up the overnight radio traffic from the building across the street, getting the skipper's newspapers from the reception area on the first floor, and putting them and a carafe of coffee on the skipper's desk before he arrived.

We'd just finished all he said needed to be done, and had just sat down with a fresh cup of coffee, when a chief petty officer entered the AUTOVON room. Dexter spoke first and said, "Perfect timing, Chief. I just finished showing Williams all the things to do upon arrival." Dex continued and shifted his attention to me, "Mark Williams, this is Chief Paul Giatano."

I stood and extended my hand. "Good morning, Chief." Having spent days reading and rereading all the personnel files, and listening for a few hours to Dex describe all the traits of the NIS crew, I had a good idea who Chief Giatano was. Chief Yeoman Paul Giatano joined the Navy in 1951 right after graduating from high school in South Philadelphia. His enlistment had been just in time to ship out on the USS English, DD-696, a destroyer home ported in Norfolk, VA, for duty off the coast of Korea. He graduated from Yeoman A School a year later and excelled at every duty station over the last two decades. Looking at him, you might not see a warrior, as he stood at 5'6" and suffered from early baldness. But he could spot a typing mistake at ten yards and could give an ass-chewing like a Marine drill instructor.

The Chief's handshake was firm and quick. "Good to meet you, Williams," he said. "Grab your record and orders and let's move to my office."

We exited the AUTOVON room, turned left and went down two doors to the office area where the Chief and another Yeoman hung their hats. It was currently empty, but we'd just taken a seat, and the Chief had just started reading over my orders, when the door opened and two men entered. Interestingly, one was an Air Force officer.

We both stood when Lt Col J. Scott Tiller, USAF, entered the room—he waved us back down, but we remained standing. "Colonel, this is our new Yeoman, Petty Officer Williams. Williams, this is Lt Col Tiller who has been appointed to head this area's office of the new Defense Investigative Service. They will soon take over doing all the BIs we currently handle," offered the Chief as part of the introductions. "And this tall guy is YN1 James Henderson. He spends most of his time in here with me."

I shook both of their hands and we talked a minute or two exchanging the standard meeting pleasantries. Then they wished me luck, grabbed their coffee mugs, and headed to the door.

The Chief seemed happy with what he read in my service record and put it in his 'out' basket. "Henderson will file that later," he said. Then he started a lecture on security, running through the list of things I was to do and of what was expected from me. It was the standard spiel I'd given so many new guys at the NISHQ over the years, but I put on my best 'I am anxious to learn' face and suffered through it.

In short, I'd be working for Dexter and taking over his early morning rituals while spending most of my time in the AUTOVON room, sending and receiving traffic from NISOs and NISRAs everywhere. And oh, yea, I was now in charge of the coffee mess and we'd better never run out!

The Chief stood and said, "Let's go meet the rest of the people."

We walked back past the AUTOVON room and continued to the door at the end of the hall. It opened into a reasonably sized office where a YN2 sat at a desk. Doors led off each side of the office.

The Yeoman stood and the Chief did the introductions. "Frost, this is Williams, who will be working with Wilson. Is the skipper in yet?"

"No, Chief. But the XO is here. Nice to meet ya, Williams," said YN2 Sidney Frost as we shook hands.

"Ditto, Frost," I replied.

The Chief knocked twice on the door on the left side of the office and pushed it open. "Commander, I have the new guy Williams here if you have time to meet with him."

"Great! Get in here," boomed a voice from the office. We entered and I came face to face with a man I knew only by his record.

Commander Karl Peterson, age thirty-eight, was the executive officer (XO) of NISO Norfolk. He could easily be the poster boy for the Navy, as he sported a square jaw, stood 6'1" and had little body fat. He still wore the flattop haircut of his days at Texas A&M, where he excelled in football and majored in business. He possessed a booming voice that all old quarterbacks had, and a strong handshake. He was hoping that his next assignment would be commanding officer of a NISO, and based upon the recommendations in his service record, that would probably happen.

"Welcome aboard, Williams," he boomed out so strong I expected the photos on the wall to rattle a bit. He tried to crush my hand but I put up enough resistance that no bones were damaged.

Much like the Chief, Peterson gave a canned welcome speech. Then he wanted to know if I played football. Before I could answer, he went on to tell me that every fall, the military and agents squared off against each other in a friendly football game. He said it was similar to the funny game from the movie *MASH* except we were not as good as they were. He chuckled at his joke. The last game was so bad that the guy I was replacing dubbed it the annual Toilet Bowl Game: everyone played like shit. But everyone had good fun and a great cookout afterwards. I told him I looked forward to playing in it later that year.

At that time, voices were coming from the Yeoman's office, and the Chief excused us. We came out just in time to see the commanding officer, Captain Humphrey H. Miller, walk into his office.

"Captain, have you got a minute?" Chief asked the CO before he could close his door.

"Always for you, Chief. Come on in."

We entered the office and I came to attention. The Chief did the introductions and the CO ordered me "at ease" and told us both to take a seat. I immediately liked this guy.

His service record read like a movie script that famous screenwriter Frank "Spig" Wead would have penned back in the late 1930s about a true Navy hero. Miller graduated near the top of his class from the United States Naval Academy in 1942, where his roommate was the guy who was now the CNO. They had remained best friends since those plebe days. Service in WWII saw then-lieutenant Miller as gunnery officer on a destroyer in the south Pacific, and by the end of the war as XO of a cruiser, as LCDR Miller.

He was under fire most of the war and successfully led his ship and crew through multiple Kamikaze attacks. The Korea conflict saw LCDR Miller as captain of his own destroyer, where he received many commendations for saving flyers who parachuted into the sea, from damaged aircraft, on their way back to their carriers. His ship also did its fair share of shelling the shore in support of the troops on the ground.

The war in Vietnam gave him an opportunity, around 1960, to move from fleet operations to intelligence, where he also excelled. He spent many years in various intelligence posts around the world and was now serving in his sunset posting. He was well respected by all those who served with him and would retire next year as the Commanding Officer of NISO Norfolk after thirty years of excellent service.

I liked the CO's welcome speech: "Listen to the Chief and don't screw up. Welcome aboard." And we left his office.

Up the hall from the CO's suite was the office of LT Gregory Kensey. According to his record, Mr. Kensey was a decent lawyer and served as the legal assistant for NISO. His job was to review case files before they were passed to JAG, the Judge Advocate General's office, for prosecution in a court martial. Dex had told me that Kensey wasn't well liked by the other sailors in the unit, as he had a tendency to talk down to everyone. Looked like the Juris Doctorate might have gone to his head a bit.

Still, Kensey seemed nice and his welcome speech was short. He tried to impress upon me the importance of doing everything 'just so' in hopes that it wouldn't be kicked back by the JAG staff for a re-do. I promised to do my best.

Leaving the LT's office, the Chief told me that the intros to the NISRA staff would have to wait. He had things to do, and the agents were all out in the field. So I made my way to the AUTOVON room to start my new career as a Yeoman in NISO.

Before I opened the door to rejoin Dex, a funny feeling came over me—more of that paranoia stuff. I glanced down the hall toward the NISRA office space. There was a lady standing in the hall, staring at me. I waved, and she immediately turned and headed into an office. *Interesting,* I thought; *interesting, but strange.*

24

DEXTER WAS ALREADY AHEAD OF the morning ritual in the AUTOVON room. This was the place where a couple of ASR-35 teletype machines kept us in contact with NISOs and NISRAs all over the country, and our HQ in D.C., via the AUTOVON network. The room also contained two standard issue gray metal desks, two gray filing cabinets, a supply storage cabinet—also gray, a large darker gray metal cabinet that housed the AUTOVON switching equipment, and the high-speed tape transfer. This piece of equipment looked like a reel-to-reel tape deck using pale yellow paper tape instead of brown recording tape. It too was gray.

AUTOVON, the Automatic Voice Network, was a worldwide American military telephone system with high-speed switching centers. Sending a teletype message required voice calling to the target location, voice verification that they were ready to receive, and performing a machine handshake by pressing several buttons on the ASR-35. If the electronic handshake was accepted, the paper tape started running through the reader. On the other end, their machine was punching tape and printing the report at the same time.

The first thing to do each morning was print the teletype traffic that had been received overnight. The quantity of traffic from headquarters was so large that it justified a download, via a high-speed system, that spit out a ton of paper tape featuring multiple reports. The crew at headquarters in D.C. sent the traffic overnight. Most of the time, the take-up reel caught the tape, but on occasion, like that morning, the reel failed and the yards of punched paper tape ended up on the deck.

Our first task was to run it through one of the teletype machines to generate the printouts. After each report ended, we cut that report's tape from the download tape—a quick snip with scissors took care of that—and paper clipped it to the printout. Then we distributed it to the correct office. Most of the traffic was simply carried down the hall to NISRA Norfolk for the agents to take some action. Some of the reports needed to go to one of our remote NISRAs, so we transmitted the report to that NISRA and filed the office copy. Dex was finishing up the sorting of those overnight reports when I came in.

"What is with the redhead down the hall?" I asked Dex after closing the AUTOVON room door. "I looked down the hall just now and she was just staring at me. I waved, but she disappeared into an office."

"Oh, you saw her, eh?" He smiled, responding, "She was probably just checking out the new guy. Red's name is Laura Scott, one of the NISRA secretaries, and she is a real piece of work, I tell ya. The first week I was here she tried to set me up with her daughter. Something is not right there, but I have no idea what. I told her I was too old for her girl and that I focused on older college girls only." He snickered and turned back to typing a response on the ASR-35.

"What is she … a high school girl?" I asked. "Or just butt ugly?"

"Neither one, Mark. She graduated about a year ago from Norfolk High and frankly is actually close to being a true knockout. Red hair, just like her mother … she has a pretty face and a decent body from what I could tell. Of course, she keeps her clothes on while visiting the office so it's hard to really say," he responded, laughing at his joke. "But her mother freaks me out and the little voices in my head keep yelling 'stay away.' And I always listen to those voices."

"Interesting," I mumbled.

About that time the second ASR-35 rang. We went through the answering process and the keys started flying, typing the incoming report. A stream of punched paper tape crawled out of the unit on the side. Dexter showed me the proper way to fold the tape and attach it to the report. Then we went over the distribution of the report and its copies. He left to carry it to the proper location.

That gave me a moment to survey his desktop and do a quick check of the drawers. I wasn't expecting to find anything incriminating, but it never hurts to look. Now both machines had incoming traffic, so I was sidetracked by work for a few minutes. I had them ready for distribution when Dex returned from his delivery run. He seemed impressed that I had not screwed them up. *Oh, good, I get a gold star for my efforts!*

The machines sat quiet for a bit, so I had time to get to know Dexter better. I asked about his previous duty station and what he did in his spare time. We talked about his education, hometown, and plans for his post-Navy days. Good news for me was that he loved to talk about himself. All of his comments and answers led me to believe that the uncertainty I'd felt about him was misplaced. The things I thought might be issues turned out to be just coincidences. But I would reread his files that night and pull more info from him the next day, since I didn't believe in coincidences.

The day went by quickly and it was time to do the shutdown routine. Dex explained all the procedures I needed to follow to get the high-speed download machine ready to receive the overnight traffic from HQ. And the tasks for closing down the coffee mess. I told him to head on out and that I'd finish up for him.

Hanging around late gave me a chance to talk with Jimmy at the security desk before he bugged out for the night. On the pretense of wondering when I might need to keep the coffee hot in the evenings, I asked him who would normally hang around late at night, who came in early, etc., so I'd know what to expect.

He was open and friendly, and provided info about two agents who frequently stayed late. The military staff rarely hung around after hours. And the secretarial staff of the NISRA were punctual about leaving on time. And no, there were no security personnel on site during the evenings and weekends. All of the doors were locked and only the agents, officers and a select few enlisted had the keys. And agents didn't have keys to the military offices. The CO and XO had full sets of keys to all areas in NISO and the NISRA, but my set of keys would only open doors in the NISO.

I thanked Jimmy for his help and headed out the door. I left the base and grabbed a take-out burger on my way to the house. Day one at NISO Norfolk was done. The one sailor that concerned me on paper seemed to be clear. And now I had a secretary from the NISRA to add to the shrinking list of suspects. Well, it wasn't yet shrinking: I'd removed one and added one, so it was a wash.

I choked down the burger as I reread Dexter's files. While it was a great way to get indigestion, it was also a great time saver. The little things that bugged me in his file were explained by his comments that day. So it looked like they really were coincidences. Go figure.

I still needed to review the NISRA personnel records that night to see if anything popped there, especially with Laura Scott. Then I'd return to the base for some sleep in my rack at the barracks.

I started with Laura's file. Her personnel record was clean. Scott, Laura MacKenzie. Female, age thirty-nine, widow, some college, but no degree. Born in Bath, NY. Family moved to Norfolk when WWII started and her father joined the Navy. Husband was a Marine Gunnery Sergeant killed in Vietnam four years ago. One daughter, Karen Marie Scott, age nineteen. Laura started working at NISRA Cherry Point, located on the Marine Corps Air Station Cherry Point in North Carolina, over six years ago, while her husband was stationed there.

After his death, she wanted to move back to Norfolk and requested a transfer to NISRA Norfolk. Laura scored high on all of her testing and every evaluation had been positive. Well-liked by her co-workers.

Latest BI update flagged a large deposit in her account last July. It was determined to be an insurance payoff for a life insurance policy. No record of the deceased was in the file. Wonder who died. I might have to get close to Laura to get more info. Could she be taking money to divulge CI names, claiming it was an insurance thing? Nothing else looked out of place in her file so that didn't seem likely. But what about Dexter's comment about her pushing her daughter on him? Interesting.

The other two NISRA files I needed to reread belonged to Joe Mabry and his partner, Darrell Tasker. It would probably work out to be like Dexter's case when I got a chance to softly interrogate the agents. But it bothered me that these guys were also the agents Jimmy said stayed late frequently. Too many questions and too few answers.

Enough research for the evening. It was time to head back to the base so Dex would find me in my rack in the morning.

25

THURSDAY MORNING STARTED ABOUT THE same as Wednesday, except I set the alarm for an hour earlier and skipped the mess hall. I figured I'd pick up a quick snack at the cafeteria in our building later in the morning.

Getting all the morning tasks done before the rest of the crew arrived allowed me the opportunity to spend a few minutes hanging around the coffee mess and chatting up individuals as they got their morning brew. Most folks would just think I was being friendly, but it gave me an opportunity to pull more info from everyone. I had hoped Laura would show, but that didn't happen.

Dexter arrived and was surprised I had everything done already. We grabbed more coffee and headed to face the noise of the teletypes, picking up where we left off in our conversation yesterday. I got more info about Dex. Like I said, he did love talking about himself. And his comments reassured me that cutting him off the suspect list was the right move.

I again asked about Laura. He repeated some of the same info from the previous day, and kept telling me to use caution. He had no specifics, but his "little voices were never wrong." We had a good laugh at that one.

Even with the ringing bells and typing noises of the two AR-35 tele-types and Dex sharing his sexual exploits from the previous evening, I was able to set up a plan in my mind to deal with Laura. I told him I'd be right back, and walked down the passageway to the NISRA office spaces.

As the great Chinese general and military strategist Sun Tzu wrote in his military treatise nearly 2,500 years ago, one must keep his friends close, and his enemies closer. While I was not sure she was an enemy, she sure was a person of interest in my investigation. It was time to get closer to her and determine if she was an enemy.

Luck was on my side. Laura Scott was the only one in the office. When I entered, she looked up and asked, "What do you want?" She held a cold, deadpan expression, but her voice had a slight Scottish accent. It went well with her red hair. And it was very easy on the ears.

On her desk was a nice brass name plate, so I looked down at it and re-plied, "Good morning. Laura Scott, I presume. I am Mark Williams, the newest addition to the NISO crew. Just wondering, do any of y'all back here like hot tea?" I hoped my smile might break through the cold look I was getting. It didn't.

"Why?"

"I now handle the coffee mess, and if there is any interest in hot tea, then I'll get a small pot to keep hot water handy. I like a good cup of tea every now and then. It helps clear my mind. But I'm not going to waste the effort if no one else will use it," I responded. And as I did so, I took the time to look over the photos on the wall beside her desk. One showed Laura leaning against a Marine with a young teenage girl in front of them. "Your family?" I asked.

"Yea. That photo was taken a year before Ben died in Vietnam. It's just my daughter and me for now," she responded quietly, her face softening.

"So sorry for your loss. We have lost too many good people in that hellhole." Silence overtook us for a moment, then I said, "Look, I have to get back to help Dexter. Check with the other folks back here for me and see if the tea water pot is something desired. Let me know." As I turned to leave, Laura gave me a small smile.

"I will, Mark. Thanks for thinking of us," she answered and gave an-other smile.

Ah, progress with the Ice Queen. It just might turn out to be a good day.

When I got back to my desk, Dex was wondering where I went. I told him about my plan for tea, and he thought it was "too British" for him. We chuckled over that one, but then he got quiet.

"Mark, just be careful around that woman."

I agreed. She might be trouble, but she was interesting.

The rest of the day was a rerun of Wednesday. I tried to hang out in the coffee mess in hopes of talking up some of the agents, but they dashed in and out quickly. They hardly said two words to this lowly sailor except for bitching about the poor quality of the coffee.

Later in the afternoon, Laura stuck her head in our office and softly said that tea would be a nice change. With a softer voice, her accent became stronger. Before I could respond, she pulled the door closed. Dex just shook his head and said, "Trouble with a capital 'T' that one is."

He was probably right, so I just shrugged my shoulders and went back to typing.

After shutting down for the day, I made a quick stop at the local grocery on my way to the house. There I picked up a few boxes of different tea bags, index cards, a good-sized electric coffee pot, a couple of kitchen racks, and a few spices. Friday morning was going to see a new look to the NISO coffee mess.

26

"WHAT THE HELL IS THIS?" The Chief's loud voice rolled down the hall from the coffee mess as I left the CO's office after placing his carafe and newspapers in the proper spots.

"Good morning, Chief," I smiled as I entered the coffee mess. "How are you this fine Friday morning?"

"Williams, are you responsible for this?" he demanded.

I looked at the counter where the two coffee urns rested. Over to the side was a new, smaller coffeepot that had a small sign in front reading "Hot Water for Tea." Beside it was a neat rack holding a variety of individually wrapped tea bags. To the front of the coffee urns, small index card signs were attached: one read "Standard Brew" and the other "Special Brew."

"Guilty, Chief. I figured a couple of small changes to the mess might be appreciated. Your standard coffee is on the right and a slightly different one is on the left. You might want to give it a try." I dropped a quarter in the money can and poured myself a mug of the special brew, enjoying the pleasing aroma of cardamom and cinnamon that was released.

"No, thanks!" he grumbled. "I'll stick to my standard black cup of joe." As he took a sip, a strange look came over his face. "Damn, this is good. What the hell did you put in here?"

I couldn't stop the laugh from coming out. The Chief gave me his best evil look, but I just shook my head and told him. "Chief, I did the unthinkable … I completely cleaned the coffee urns this morning. The gunk in the bottom of the urns was disgusting. And when I brewed that standard urn, I added a good portion of sea salt. It's much more flavorful than the table salt that has been used in the past. And in the second urn, in addition to the sea salt, I've added cardamom and cinnamon. You might want to try that for your second cup. Unless you prefer tea; it does have calming qualities you might need," I added with a big grin.

He shook his head, dropped a quarter in the money can, and as he left the mess I heard him mumble, "What is this man's Navy coming to? Tea of all things!"

Before heading to my desk, I strolled down the hall to the NISRA area. No one had yet arrived, so I left a note on Laura's door announcing that tea and flavored coffee were now available in the mess.

The morning went by quickly and with no excitement. A few heads popped around our office door and complimented us on the 'new' coffee and the tea selection, and even the Chief was seen heading in for additional cups with a smile on his face. Dexter was surprised by it all.

Great, I thought. I'd made life better for the NISO and NISRA staff, but my frustration was building as I was getting nowhere fast trying to access the NISRA agents. I had to come up with a way and soon.

Dexter returned from lunch and announced that I was free to go 'put on the feed bag.' "Once a Kansas country boy always a Kansas country boy," I said. So I took him up on the offer and went down to the cafeteria. I'd just found a table in the corner and set my tray down when a soft voice interrupted me. Looking up, I found two redheads holding trays.

"May we join you, Mark?" asked Laura.

I quickly stood and said, "Yes, of course. Nice to see you again, Laura." And I turned to what looked like a younger version of Laura and said, "Hi, I'm Mark Williams."

"Mark, this is my daughter, Karen. She recently started working in the JAG offices next door, and occasionally we get to share lunch." Karen smiled as her mother provided the pertinent info.

"Pleased to meet you, Mark. Mother said you were the new guy here. How do you like it so far?" Karen asked with a soft voice similar to her mother's but with just a bit more authority to it. Seems she was the stronger of the two women.

Karen had a cute face. It was not one that would qualify her for modeling school, but it had a freshness that held your eyes. Looking at this young lady with green eyes and glowing red hair, and just a hint of freckles around her nose, I decided that I so liked being here right that minute. Of course, I couldn't say that exactly in those words so I responded with the standard line: it was a nice duty station and the people I worked with had been welcoming.

Karen told me she was a clerk in the JAG office and really liked that work. She and I chatted about the challenges of our new jobs and of being the new person in the office, and the fun I faced being new in town and getting lost. Laura didn't add much to the conversation until we were getting ready to leave.

Laura turned to Karen and asked, "If you can find the time, why don't you and Mark plan on getting together this next week so you can show him around town. I know he would appreciate that, right Mark?"

"That would be nice, but I hate to impose on Karen's time."

Karen glanced down and softly said, "I would be happy to be your tour guide, Mark. How does Tuesday or Wednesday after work sound to you?"

I didn't want to seem too anxious, so I suggested I pick her up at home after work on Wednesday. We could grab a bite to eat and she could show me all the interesting things about Norfolk. Karen agreed, and Laura had that 'cat who ate the canary' look on her face. *Interesting*, I thought.

We talked a bit more and then left the cafeteria. Karen headed back to the JAG offices. I walked with Laura back up to the NIS spaces. She was still quiet so I started talking.

"Karen must fill you with pride. She is a beautiful lady, and working with JAG is a real accomplishment."

"She does, for sure. I'm glad you two are getting together. She hasn't been dating much. Not sure why. You two just have some fun. Okay?"

I promised to do just that and got directions to her house. She seemed relieved, but since she was a strange one, I was not sure I was reading her correctly. Time would tell. Then the thoughts turned to Karen and her position with JAG. There she could have access to sensitive information about the CIs, so I had to do more digging there, as well. Now there were two redheads causing concern and another name to add to the suspect board.

As I returned to my office, I decided that Dexter didn't have the 'need to know' about my upcoming date with Karen. Nor did he need to hear about the lunch with Karen and Laura. I didn't want to get another lecture from those little voices in his head.

Finally at 1600 hrs, the day was over, the coffee urns were dumped and washed, and I headed out the door. I needed the weekend to get deeper into research on this case, and I really needed to finalize the strategy I'd formed for getting to know the agents.

27

EARLIER THAT DAY, I'D HIT upon an idea for getting agent access and needed to contact the boss for help. Although I was reluctant to suggest it since it showed what I considered a failure on my part, there comes a time when pride takes a back seat to getting the job done. I needed access to the agents, and the fact was I couldn't do that alone.

Since I was still waiting for the phone at my house to get connected, I cruised into downtown Norfolk to find an isolated phone booth for making the call. I tried to select the right words that would quickly convey to the Admiral my needs. He preferred conciseness.

I drove past a booth in a quiet part of town, rounded the next corner and stopped. No pedestrians were in sight, and there were no additional vehicles making the turn, so I did a quick turnaround in a driveway and headed back toward the phone booth. Parking about half a block away was prudent. I could stroll past the booth, look for any tails, and then circle back. Precautions can be a time-consuming pain, but better that than the pain of a bullet or knife.

The area was clear. After all, it was still a half hour before the five o'clock rush. And this part of town is filled with student housing for those attending Old Dominion University, and with that the normal group of pubs and hangouts that are part of college life. The bulk of these kids don't come out until after dark, which was still over an hour away. So I checked the phone to make sure the wires were still connected, and dropped the change into the slot. The operator demanded more coins after I dialed the number, so more went in.

"Office of the Chief of Naval Operations, Master Chief Bartow speaking, how may I be of assistance, sir?" barked the man who was the gate keeper to seeing the boss. If the Chief didn't like you, you went to the bottom of the visitor list. Fortunately for me, the Chief and I worked well together. Probably had something to do with our shared time at the firing range and that we were about equal at pistol competitions. Competition builds respect.

"Good afternoon, Master Chief. SA268 calling for the boss."

"Right away, sir. Hope all is well with you today. He is in a meeting, but I know he wants to hear from you, so hold one moment."

There were only a couple of us who work undercover for the CNO, and with the constant threat of disclosure and the constant changing of cover names, using a code name makes things much better. I lobbied for '007' but that was not allowed for some reason.

I glanced around while waiting to make sure no one seemed interested in my call. The coast was clear, as they said in the old movies. In less than thirty seconds, Admiral Gallagher was on the line. The day must have been a rough one for him, as his usual light attitude was hidden behind a gruff response: "What's wrong?"

Wasting no time on pleasantries, I dove right in. "Things are going fairly well, sir, all things considered for three days. Looking at the NISO, I have eliminated all the military. However, I'm concerned about a couple of the civilian staff members, with two being agents who give me a funny feeling … at least on paper. I will need a bit more time to wrap up those ends. But right now, I feel I could move faster if I bring Captain Miller up to speed and get his help."

"I trust your plans. What can I do to help? I gather that is why you called."

It was frustrating when the Admiral was one step ahead of me. Guess that came with all the gold on his sleeve and twenty plus years more experience than I had on my resume. "Admiral, I am aware of your personal connection to the NISO CO, so I would appreciate you giving him a quick phone call and letting him know that a man will be stopping by his house later tonight to share some important info. Just tell him that. Nothing else is needed." The 'personal connection' was that they'd been roommates at the Naval Academy.

Keeping the Admiral as far away from the investigation as possible would help me in the long run, and also protect the Admiral in case I messed it up. But there are times when a higher authority can do more. "I'll base the amount of disclosure to him by judging his responses to my initial comments. I will do all I can to keep him safe during all this."

"No problem. I'll make the call no later than 1800 hours today. Will that work?"

"Perfect, sir. Greatly appreciated."

"Take care of yourself," replied the Admiral right before he hung up. No time for pleasantries.

Well, that had gone better than expected. Now came the difficult part: sharing part of the operation with Captain Miller, and doing my best to keep the rest of it out of his hands and away from the staff at NISO Norfolk … especially those staff members that my gut still hadn't cleared of suspicion.

So I returned to the base to change into my dress uniform before heading to the Captain's house. Traffic was picking up, which made checking for a tail harder, but everything still looked clear. Perhaps my paranoia was running wild. Probably not; I have found personal security a good thing to worry about on more than one occasion in my life.

28

DUE TO HIS LENGTH OF service and being in charge of the 5th Naval District's crime investigators, Captain Miller was highly respected, and as such rated one of the smaller houses on Dillingham Blvd, nicknamed Admiral's Row. In this section of the Norfolk Naval Station, both sides of the street are lined with beautiful homes that had been built right after the turn of the century.

Those living in these houses over the years had seen two world wars, Korea, and now the problems caused by Vietnam; lots of history to tell if the walls could talk. Many of the trees surrounding the homes were planted about the same time the houses were built, and had grown to provide an elegant, shady lane look to the street during the summer. But with spring still a few weeks away, the trees now provided a skeletal, spooky look to the street. Hoped that wasn't a sign about my investigation.

All of the houses are well maintained. That's because those serving time in the brig for minor infractions of the Uniform Code of Military Justice get the pleasure of doing yard work around the base, under the watchful eyes of several Shore Patrol members. Each house features a two-car driveway that ends behind the house, at a garage. There are several larger homes that house the top brass.

Since entertaining is a standard for these leaders, in addition to the two-car driveway, there is a circular drive in front of the houses so visiting guests don't have far to walk. And in case of emergencies, the Admiral's aides always have the car by the front door, ready for the Admiral to jump in and go fight the good fight.

The Captain's house, while smaller and newer, was nothing to look down on. The red brick was offset nicely with white trim, dark green shutters, and an ample supply of rose bushes in beds that had been lined with the same brick used to build the house. No oil stains on the driveway. No grass clippings or leaves on the sidewalks. I noticed that the slate roof didn't have any bird droppings, making me wonder if the maintenance crew polished the roof, too. "Squared away" and "shipshape" were the only terms appropriate for the place. The spotless white door was adorned with a brass knocker in the shape of an anchor.

I parked in the driveway and headed to the door. The sun was setting and the porch light was already turned on. Shifting my briefcase to my left hand, just in case I needed to quickly salute, I used the brass anchor to announce my arrival with two loud bangs, and waited.

It was a short wait. Expecting to see either the Captain or his wife, I was a bit taken aback when the door was opened by a lovely young lady. It was one of those moments when you feel like you're meeting a fashion model on her day off. No, not a model; she looked like Grace Kelly in the movie *High Society* except her hair was longer and she was much prettier.

She had a laid-back look, with long legs encased in blue jeans, white deck shoes, a sweatshirt bearing the ODU logo, sand-colored hair pulled back in a ponytail, and a beautiful face with the brightest smile I had ever seen. There was no evidence of makeup and it was not needed on that face. Standing around 5'6", she had to look up at me. Trying to keep from grinning too much, I found my voice and said, "Hi. I'm Petty Officer Williams and Captain Miller is expecting me. Is he available?"

This lovely vision just stood there for a few seconds. "Sure," she finally stammered. "He's in the study. Follow me, please."

"Thank you, Miss," was all I could get out before she turned and led me to the Captain. I removed my cover and took a deep breath to get ready for the challenges I'd soon face.

She opened a door off the hall and said, "Uncle Humphrey, there's a sailor here to see you."

Before I got to the study door, I heard the Captain say, "Thanks, Kelly. Send him in, and please ask your aunt to join us." Watching Kelly walk away was the best pleasure of the day, but I quickly put that aside to walk into the study and come to attention. Captain Miller was sitting at a beautifully carved wood desk. He rose and walked around it, slowed to give me a look up and down, and said, "At ease, Williams. I must admit you are not what I expected."

"I understand, sir. I hope I can clear up some of your confusion quickly. But I do need to speak with you in private, sir." I hoped my facial expression hid most of my frustration of doing a family meet and greet. But I suppose it didn't.

The Captain smiled and slightly nodded his head, extended his hand, and said, "That we can do. But first you need to meet my wife, Dorothy. When my best friend, who happens to be the Chief of Naval Operations, calls and says a man he completely respects and who basically speaks with his voice is coming to see me tonight, I assumed it was someone from my past. I was not expecting my newest Yeoman to appear. Naturally, expecting an old shipmate, Dorothy wanted to meet you. It won't take much time."

After shaking his hand, I returned the smile and was getting ready to respond when Dorothy and Kelly entered the room. I could see the family resemblance as Dorothy looked to be a fifty-ish version of Kelly. Same smile, same sparkling gray eyes, same slender figure and oozing enough charm to make anyone feel welcome in her home.

"Dorothy and Kelly," said the Captain, "this is Mark Williams. He is the newest Yeoman to join NISO. Mark, this is my wife Dorothy and niece Kelly Anne. Ladies, based on a call I received earlier today, he and I have some things to discuss that might be awkward in the office. Does that sum it up, Williams?"

"Yes, sir, it does. Mrs. Miller, Miss Kelly, it is a pleasure to meet you both, and I hope that my visit will not disturb any plans you might have for the evening. I'll try to be brief with the Captain's time," I said as I shook their hands. Seemed that Kelly was a bit slow releasing mine, but probably that was just wishful thinking on my part. I noticed the skipper glancing over at her.

Mrs. Miller's smile was welcoming, and she said she would return shortly with coffee. With that, she and Kelly departed and closed the study door.

"Have a seat, Williams."

I selected a place on the sofa and he sat in a chair across the coffee table from me. The ticking of the clock on the mantel was extremely loud as the skipper waited to hear what I had to say. Time to get the difficult part over, well, at least the easiest difficult part. "Sir, it sounds like the Admiral went into more detail than I had asked of him. May I ask what all he told you?"

Again, the skipper smiled, but this time it was a grin that a shark has right before it attacks. Years of being a naval officer had honed that talent well for him. After a second or two delay, which seemed to me to last several minutes, he said, "I am not used to being interrogated, especially by a junior enlisted man, but considering the strange situation, I'll let it pass."

The Captain shook his head and continued. "Admiral Gallagher told me that a man working for him would visit shortly and one—ask for my help with a situation, and two—provide as much information about the situation as he felt was needed to accomplish his mission. He then added that when you speak I should consider any requests you have as coming from him and that he has utmost respect for you and your abilities. We then shared some personal stuff which I assure you was not related to your visit. Good enough?"

I took a deep breath. "Yes, sir, thank you. Captain, I basically work directly for Admiral Chance ..."

"What?" exclaimed the Captain. His eyes narrowed and his jaw seemed to clench as he barked, "Explain that."

"Sir, if you can hold all your questions, I think I can provide the answers quickly and in a less confusing way."

"OK, carry on."

At that time, a gentle knock on the door interrupted us and Mrs. Miller brought in a tray of coffee and cookies. Looked like the cookies were fresh home-baked and the coffee was steaming. "Hope I'm not intruding, but coffee always makes meetings better, right Humphrey?" she said with that warm smile. She placed the tray on the coffee table and asked if there was anything else we needed.

"Thank you, dear," replied the Captain, "we are fine." Again, Mrs. Miller smiled that warming smile and left the room, silently closing the door behind her. The Captain filled two mugs that had the NIS logo, and spent a quiet moment adding sugar and cream to his. I added a bit of sugar to mine and took a sip. Nice brew with just a hint of cinnamon.

"And you were saying, Williams?" asked the Captain as he sat back in the chair. The coffee cup at his lips hid whether he was smiling or frowning.

I took another deep breath and started over. "Captain, I work directly for Admiral Chance and have been assigned to NISHQ for several years as a special investigator for internal affairs. First of the year the Admiral responded to a request from the CNO and I was sent TAD to the CNO's office. There I had a private off-the-record meeting with Admiral Gallagher, and he explained that he needed a special investigator to look into some sensitive issues. He did not want any of the usual NIS agents on this nor did he want me to use the standard investigating methods or reporting conduits."

I took another sip of coffee and continued. "The recent deaths of several confidential informants here in the Norfolk area have caused some concerns in D.C. The short version is that the CNO believes we have a leak or two in the system down here and I have the task of finding and plugging them."

"So, you are not really a Yeoman?" The frown on the skipper's face conveyed his frustration with things so far. "And you are here to spy on my command."

"Yes, I certainly am a Yeoman; at least for this assignment. Before getting here, I graduated academic honor man at the Yeoman A School in Bainbridge, Maryland. I can see by your look that more information is needed about that." Another quick sip of coffee gave me a few seconds to gather my thoughts.

I took a deep breath and tried to change the subject. "But my concern, sir, is that the more you know about me the greater opportunity that you might accidently let something slip in conversation. And the less you know about what I'm doing, the less likely you could get tainted if something goes awry." I could tell that was not going to be enough to keep the skipper happy. Now the hard part would be trying to determine how little I could say and still keep him happy.

The Captain leaned forward in his chair, placed his coffee mug on the table with a bit more force than needed, and looked me right in the eye with a look that I was reluctantly prepared to receive. His voice lowered as he said, "Let's get something straight, Williams. My trust of the CNO is just about limitless, and he vouches for you, but, and this is a very big but, I will not have you running around my command doing things that I do not know about. Is that clear?"

"Yes, sir." I responded. It was obvious that he was on a roll and more was coming.

"And to make things extremely clear for you, know that I can be a rather nasty enemy, and an extremely good friend. Based on Bill's, excuse me, the CNO's recommendation, I ask that you read me in as much as you feel comfortable knowing that I have been in this man's Navy since before you were born. I know how to keep secrets, and know how to keep my coat tails clean. Bottom line, tell me how I can help you," he said softly and retrieved his mug for another sip of coffee.

Bottom line was right; I needed his help and I trusted him. And having a powerful man as a local backup might come in handy. It was time to bring him most of the way into the tent.

"Captain, take a look at this. It might help ease your mind a bit," I said as I opened my briefcase, moved out the normal stack of paperwork, and opened the hidden compartment in the bottom. I extracted my real Navy ID card and passed it to him.

"While the one I carry in my wallet is a valid enlisted ID issued specifically for this assignment, the one in your hand is my actual ID."

"You are a Lieutenant Commander? Hell, you barely look old enough to be a petty officer much less an O-4!" he said with more than a bit of surprise in his voice. With a smile, he looked again at my ID and handed it back, asking, "So should I be calling you Marcus?"

"It would probably be best to stay with Mark, or better yet just Williams. No need to complicate things or get out of the roles we need to play," I said with a smile. "As for the current rank, I just received that promotion a couple of months before starting this assignment, so if anyone called out 'commander' I'd be the first to look around for one. I spent four years in ROTC at Georgia Tech so after I graduated with double majors—mechanical engineering and criminal justice—and came on active duty, I was sworn in as an O-2. After over nine months of working with Admiral Chance, an O-3 position came available in his organization. Since I already held my master's degree in criminal justice, and was already doing the specialized work of the departing O-3, the selection board decided my qualifications overshadowed the time in rank deficit, so I went from Lieutenant Junior Grade to Lieutenant."

"And what about the time in service and time in grade needed for the Lt. Commander slot? How did you get past that?" he inquired.

"Sorry, sir, I cannot get into that. The CNO might share that info with you if he desires, but I am not at liberty to say," I responded.

"Okay, now what about you being an actual Yeoman. What is that all about?"

"Captain, the only way I can do my job is to make sure that no one knows what my real assignment is, and to do that I must actually be the person you and all the others in the unit expect to see. I have to fit in. To accomplish that I did spend a couple of weeks in enlisted boot camp over a year ago, and from the third week of January until two weeks ago I was attending the Yeoman A School in Bainbridge, MD. And my service record, at least the one created for this investigation, shows I am a real Yeoman. So if the Chief or any of the other Yeomen ask me a question I can give a correct answer. The extra training on using a manual typewriter at a minimum of sixty-five wpm will be an asset to me in the future, I suspect," I said with a grin.

"Anyway, my assignment is to find the leak, if one exists, and end it. The fact that at least four confidential informants have died in the last few months has raised some big concerns. No other NISO has this CI problem."

The Captain grunted, and I continued.

"While I have already cleared the military, there are three civilian employees I need to look at deeper, and I am sorry to say that two of them are agents. And, no, I don't have any specifics on any of them; just more of a gut feeling based on all I've read. There are two ways you can help me." I took another sip of coffee as I prepared to get into the specifics.

He gave the standard "continue" hand signal and I pushed onward.

"First off, Chief Giatano is doing a great job bugging the housing people to get me moved from the transient barracks over to the main barracks. Problem is I can get more done right now and stay under the enlisted staff radar by remaining in the transient barracks. There are some sailors there that I want to look at, and frankly, coming and going from there will attract a lot less attention to my movements. What I was thinking is that you could tell the Chief that you might transfer me to the NISRA in Saigon. I saw the radio message asking for a replacement yeoman. You could tell him you are considering it and will let him know in about a week. That should give me time to wrap up things in the transient barracks."

"That would work," replied the skipper. "I'll talk with him on Monday morning. What else?"

"Second, and most important, I need to dig into more of NISRA Norfolk and get to know the agents. I want to see if I can find something there. And I know that usually we are not allowed that access," I said as I refilled my mug. I tried one of the cookies while stirring the coffee and found them to be excellent. I told the skipper that. "I need to watch and listen to the agents to see if I can pick up on anything."

"I was thinking I would ask Admiral Chance to send out a directive asking that select NISOs do an evaluation of the NISRA record keeping. We would be one of those selected. And since I'm the 'new guy' in the unit who has taken a few criminal justice college courses, I would be the logical choice to spend countless hours reading boring case files to make sure they are complete, and for efficiency, I would be doing it right there in the agents' area of NISRA Norfolk. Do you think that would work?" I asked.

The skipper also grabbed a cookie and leaned back in his chair. A look of inspiration came over his face and he answered, "That would work. Also, I can talk with Supervising Agent Maker ... have you met Sam yet?"

"No, sir. When the Chief took me around for the 'meet and greet' on my first day, all the agents were out of the office. I've only met one of the secretaries in the NISRA."

"OK, Marcus, see if this scenario will work for you. We set up the evaluation of the case files. But I do not need any higher authority to do that. I'll just tell Sam it needs to be done, and there will not be any need to go into any justification. To help with your cover, you will probably need to visit some or all of the other NISRAs to check their files as well."

"Yes, Captain, that will work," I agreed. "Fact is, there might be something at one of the NISRAs that helps connect the dots. Just have to look and see."

The Captain rubbed his hands together like a gambler ready to throw the dice, and said, "And I'll have a private meeting with Sam where I explain to him my concern about the leaks and mention that you have criminal justice education. I'll tell him it would be a good idea to allow you to ride along with the agents to get a feel of things."

"Sir, it is probably not a good idea to let him know that I'm looking. Based on all I've read about him, and what little I've overheard at the office, I don't suspect him of having anything to do with the leaks, but he might inadvertently let the cat out of the bag," I responded. "Let me work my way in based on what I hear and see. Often there is a door ready to be opened if you just look for it."

The Captain poured another mug of coffee and grabbed a second cookie. His eyes focused on the ceiling as he pondered my modification of his suggestion. You could almost hear the gears turning as he ran all we'd discussed around in his mind, and after he finished that cookie, I knew he was ready to fill me in.

"You're right," he said. "Sam is a damn good man, but there is too great a chance something might slip or he might look at you in a way others would pick up on. We will go with the evaluation of files this next week, and I'll let you have free rein on everything else. Agreed?" he asked.

"Perfect. I will await orders from the Chief on Monday," I responded.

"Marcus ... uh, I'd better stop that right now ... Williams, unless there are some other work-related issues to cover, I do have a personal question for you."

I thought we'd covered enough of the personal stuff and I was happy with the work problems we may have fixed, so I was taken back a bit by his question. But I figured as the skipper he had the right to ask, so I said, "We are good with the work issues. What is the question?"

"Are you now, or have you ever been, married? Or are you in a relationship?" he asked with a smile.

"No to all, sir."

"Good. As an experienced investigator I assume you saw the look in my niece's eyes when you were introduced," he said, shaking his head. "Kelly lives here with us while she is in school at Old Dominion—she's graduating this year—and she is her own woman with her own thoughts. She may start to show up at the office more than she has in the past now that you are working there, so be forewarned. She is a strong-willed woman and I think you are in her sights." His grin got big with that thought.

"Yes, sir, I noticed, Captain, and I will be on my best behavior," I replied with a grin that matched the skipper's.

"I expect nothing less from an officer and a gentleman ... even when he is undercover. By the way, you look good as a petty officer. You might want to keep that Yeoman career path open if the 'commander' thing doesn't work out," he said, laughing.

We shook hands and I departed the study. On the way to the door, I could see Kelly reading a text book in the living room, so I stuck my head in and said, "Goodnight, Miss Kelly." I was rewarded with that smile again, followed by a soft voice saying goodnight in return. Nice.

29

I DROVE BACK TO THE transient barracks after locking my briefcase securely in the trunk safe of the Blue Beast while still in the Captain's driveway; the trunk safe made me feel much better. Since it was early for a Friday night, there weren't many guys hanging around the barracks. I decided to look around again, so I strolled up and down the main passageway glancing into each cubicle. I figured if anyone questioned me I'd tell them I was looking for a buddy who was supposed to be meeting me.

Each cubicle looked squared away. Nothing was out of place and all the racks were neatly made. I knew that one of the sailors to meet a strange death, PO3 David Nelson, had been bunking in cubicle 225, the twenty-fifth cube on the second deck of the building, at the time of his death, so I went that way next. I slowly walked by his cubicle, but didn't see anything of interest.

Since the Captain's coffee was nearly through my system, I hit the head for some bladder relief where Nelson died, then took my time washing my hands. That gave me the opportunity to look around the area where his body was found. I was not expecting to find anything, since it had been several months, but it didn't cost me anything to have another look.

I had to admit that the self-inflicted overdose seemed valid since any kind of struggle should have been noticed by others in the area. I'd need to check with the chief in charge of the barracks to see if anyone had been assigned to cubicles #224–227 that night. Yea, it was a long shot.

I went back down the passageway and lingered at the opening to what had been Nelson's cubicle. Again, I didn't expect to see anything not covered in the investigation file, but at least seeing the scene of the crime gave me a better feel for it all.

The look around did kick off one thought; had there been other ODs here? If so, there would be NIS case files. I needed to check on that as soon as I got access to the NISRA area.

And thinking about the chief in charge of the barracks, I realized I should look into him and his staff as well. Perhaps there was a link there. Next time I talked with Bartow, I'd get him to send me a copy of their personnel records.

Heading to my cubicle, I changed out of my dress blues and put on the standard weekend garb consisting of blue jeans, tee-shirt, long-sleeved flannel shirt, and work boots. I left the barracks, jumped in the Blue Beast, and headed to the house for some rest and a lot of file review.

30

NICE THING ABOUT WORKING AT NISO Norfolk was that we usually had the weekends off. Agents were always on call, but our clerical tasks could wait for a day or two to be handled. The skipper had told the 5th Naval District admin office that his military staff was on call 24/7 and wouldn't have time to take part in the rotating duty roster of the building. We had other things to do rather than stand fire watches at the front door all night long. While infrequently, we did come into the office at irregular hours, so he was being factual to a degree. And as the new guy, my day started at least an hour before everyone else, so that counted as irregular hours.

So with a free weekend, I was able to spend Saturday going back over all the data I'd acquired so far. Spread out on my improvised desk, it was an unimpressive grouping of information. Lots of holes still had to be filled. But at least there was a small stack of personnel records—copies provided by BUPERS for this investigation—of the military staff that had all been cleared.

But there was still something about the liaison Air Force officer that bothered me. At some point in the future, there was to be a consolidation of handling the background investigations needed for security clearances. Currently, each branch of the service did their own, resulting in multiple agents covering the same geographic area—a classic example of government waste. Not sure who'd decided to combine the efforts, but it seemed like a great idea. And from that the Defense Intelligence Service (DIS) was born.

In the future, a DIS agent would visit neighbors, co-workers, teachers, and anyone else they could find to ask about the loyalty of a service member needing access to classified information. The ability to see, touch, and work with classified material labeled 'secret' or higher depends on the comments received from people you've known in the past. And of course, there's a check to see if you subscribe to any subversive publications or have been seen in the company of anyone considered not worthy. Yea, your past can come back to haunt you.

Our liaison officer, J. Scott Tiller, Lieutenant Colonel, USAF, would eventually be in charge of the DIS office covering most of Virginia, Maryland, and North Carolina. He was sent to us to get him acquainted with what all goes into a background check. He frequently looked over the shoulders of those of us doing the clerical work, and had spent most of his time with the agents going into the field. While he still had a hollow kingdom—no office space, no workers—that didn't prevent him from maintaining a lofty air while in the NISO office area.

I drained my second cup of coffee for the morning and pondered what it was about Tiller that bugged me. His service record was clean and it was filled with plenty of positives that would make him a good leader with the new DIS organization. I started thinking about the interactions we'd had at the office. Not much there either. He asked questions and we provided the answers. Just doing what he was being paid to do.

Maybe what bothered me was that he used his middle name, a fairly common practice, but there was always something annoying the way he introduced himself as 'J. Scott Tiller.' Nothing wrong with his first name of Jonathan, but the way he said 'J. Scott' came across as puffing himself up. Why not just use *Scott*? Oh well, it was his name and his problem.

Half way through the third cup of coffee, I had an epiphany. And it was triggered by the coffee. Every morning when Tiller arrived, he made a beeline for the coffee mess. And since I was the one now making the coffee and getting all the accoutrements ready, we usually met there every morning. When he said, "Good morning, Seaman," it bothered me since I was wearing the insignia of a petty officer, which is at least one pay grade above Seaman. And I'd heard him call other petty officers 'Seaman' and I'd seen the negative looks on their faces.

Enlisted personnel in the military are not paid very much. Sailors take a lot of pride in their assignments, their rating (occupation specialty), and their rate (pay grade). Civilians usually just call it all 'rank,' but only officers are referred to as having rank, while enlisted have their rates and ratings. I understood the resentment of being called a rate lower than the one you had earned. I suspected the colonel would not appreciate being called a lieutenant or major. Perhaps he didn't realize he was insulting the men. Maybe there was a way to fix this without offending him.

I looked at the clock and realized the morning was history. It felt like I was just going in circles as I returned, again and again, to the same personnel files in hopes that a different answer would appear. The reality of the situation was that the military personnel were clear. The issue with 'J. Scott' was just a personal thing. I needed to focus on the three civilian employees—a secretary and two agents.

It was time for me to break for lunch, fill the stomach, and hopefully clear the head. I grabbed the old Chevy keys, my Virginia state map, a map for Norfolk, and headed to the door. It seemed like a good time for a drive around the area.

31

THE NEAREST GROCERY STORE IS a huge facility called the Giant Open Air Market. Nothing is really open to the weather, but the ceiling of the place is so high you feel like you're outside. In addition to groceries, they sell records and tapes, car accessories, clothing, and a few other things. It's where I'd bought the coffee pot for the mess. But one of the best features is a restaurant inside the store that's open 24/7.

At the Giant restaurant, you pick your choice of meat from the refrigerated case, pay the restaurant clerk for the meat and your selection of sides to go with it, and sit down. A short time later your meal, centered around the piece of meat you had selected, is served to you on china plates. Nice service. But that day, I wanted to get out and drive around to get a better understanding of the area, so I asked the deli clerk to prepare two special sandwiches to go. I gave him specific instructions, and after a short wait he handed them over the counter. I picked up a cold six-pack of soda to go with my lunch and dinner and proceeded to the checkout line.

Like everything else in the Giant, the checkout area is huge and features many registers. So the wait in line was unusually short for a Saturday. As I laid my stash of chow on the counter and reached for my wallet, a tap came to my left shoulder. A soft voice asked, "Who's joining you for lunch?" I turned and found myself staring into the gorgeous gray eyes of Kelly Anne.

"Is everyone in Norfolk concerned about the business of others?" I asked sternly, then smiled.

She was not caught off guard one bit by that, and quickly responded, "Just think of me as part of the informal Welcome Wagon group." Then she broke up laughing.

The cashier was not enjoying our exchange and again asked for payment. I pulled out a twenty and received the change all while trying to decide between asking Kelly to join me for lunch or to just get on with my business and not get sidetracked. As I grabbed the bag, Kelly said, "Well, answer me, Mark. I saw two sandwiches—who is joining you for lunch?"

"I would be most honored to have the pleasure of your company, Miss Kelly," I answered with an accent that would have worked well in the movie *Gone with the Wind*.

"Right answer, Mark. Now I won't have to tell my uncle that you were mean to me," she shot back with a sweet smile. We both had a friendly laugh at that one.

As we started toward the door, I stopped and asked, "But what about your groceries?"

"I probably shouldn't admit this," she said, "but I don't have any. I was driving by and saw you walk in. And I stopped to follow you." Her mouth twisted up to the left with one of those "I just got caught" looks. "My uncle was not able to give me much info about you, so I just started my own investigation on this new guy named Petty Officer Mark Williams."

"Interesting," I replied. "So is it proper for me to start a similar investigation on one Miss Kelly Anne?"

She punched my empty arm, then latched on to it, and said, "You had better!"

As we walked toward my car, Kelly said she had the perfect spot to enjoy our lunch. I drove and she navigated, giving what seemed to be endless directions while showing points of interest. We finally ended up on the east side of Norfolk and were driving down Oceanview Avenue, past small two-story houses, when Kelly pointed to a parking lot on the waterfront side of the road.

"Pull in there and park down to the right end," she ordered. After I fed the parking meter, I grabbed the lunch bag and Kelly led me to a short wall that separated the parking lot from Oceanview Beach. Since spring was still a week or so away, the beach was deserted. Small waves rolled in, and the seagulls dropped onto the wet sand, also looking for lunch. A slight breeze blew in from the bay, bringing the taste of the salt water with it.

We sat on the wall facing the water and Kelly immediately pointed to the right. "That is the Chesapeake Bay Bridge Tunnel. It's seventeen-and-a-half miles of road that features two one-mile-long tunnels to allow the Navy easy access, with its big ships, without disturbing the vehicle traffic. It opened seven years ago and replaced the auto ferry service that had been here for decades."

"Wow, are you a part-time tour guide?" I asked.

"Not officially, but I like to know about the area where I live. It does bother me that they call this Oceanview Beach when it actually is on the Chesapeake Bay waters and not the ocean. I suppose who ever named it was not as picky as I am."

I offered a blessing on our lunch and passed her a sandwich and soda. Fortunately, I'd grabbed a handful of napkins when I picked up the sandwiches, so we were prepared for anything. She unwrapped one end and took a bite.

"Well, that is different. Nice crunch," she quipped. "I was expecting a standard sub. What is this thing?" And then she took a bigger bite and smiled.

"Welcome to a taste of Tampa, Florida. There's a section of Tampa that's called Ybor City. It's the place where many Cubans settled years ago, and it's famous for hand-rolled cigars and Cuban food. *Eso, querida señora, esun sandwich Cubano* ... in English ... that, dear lady, is a Cuban sandwich. Locals down there call it a Cubano. I think the clerk at the Giant thought I'd lost my mind when I told him to put both ham and sliced roast pork on the sandwich, add Swiss cheese and mustard, hold the mayo, and include a slice of dill pickle. This French bread is the closest thing to real Cuban bread they had, not perfect, but it will do. The pressing and grilling finishes it off nicely."

Kelly gave a quick laugh and said, "Great flavor. While I'm not a tour guide, you sure sound like a talented, multi-lingual chef." After a swig of soda, she said, "I could get used to eating these. What other culinary or linguistic surprises do you have for me?"

"If I told you, then they wouldn't be surprises," I responded with a smile.

We finished eating in silence, watching the waves and the gulls. The silence felt comfortable. After stuffing the wrappers and napkins in the bag and depositing it in the trash can, I felt the time was right for the big question. As we walked along the water's edge, I turned to her and asked, "Kelly, what will your boyfriend think about us having lunch together?"

"I see you are about a subtle as a sledge hammer," she said as she tossed her head to the side and gave me a quizzical look. "I like that. But since a boyfriend does not exist, I don't know. Probably the comments would be the same as from your wife."

"Sounds like subtlety is one of your super powers too. For the record, there is no wife or girlfriend. And the fiancée that was to have been the wife by now is history. But really, I can't understand how you are unattached. There are lots of choices for you here in this college-slash-Navy town."

She had a faraway look in her eyes, and a shadow seemed to cross her face. Then it was gone and she looked happy again. She took a deep breath and said, "I had a wonderful relationship a couple of years ago. Richard and I would have been married for about a year by now, but the draft got him first. And Vietnam kept him. He died there almost two years ago when an enemy tunnel he was checking out blew up. They were not able to recover his body, or those of a couple of other soldiers who died with him, due the intensity of the blast."

"Sorry is such a weak word for a time like this. Just know that I sort of understand as I also lost some close friends over there this past year. Granted, none of those guys were as close to me as Richard was to you, but the pain of all the loss was still intense—and Sandy is out of my life now, too. It creates a pain and emptiness combined. I am so sorry for your loss and suffering. No one should have to go through it." I felt my throat tightening and my eyes starting to water as the hurt of our losses washed over me.

She stopped, reached over and took my hand in hers. She looked up at me and smiled, and then she frowned and hesitated just a bit before she said, "Of all the condolences I have gotten since then, yours is the most sincere and comforting. I see you really do understand what is going on inside my head. That is a nice feeling."

An automatic reaction caused me to release her hand and pull her into a gentle hug. Not any sort of a sexual embrace, but the type that's the sharing of mutual pain and suffering. We stood that way for an unknown amount of time, then separated and started walking again. No words were needed.

As we walked she finally spoke. She looked at me and said, "I tried dating again about six months after his death, but just couldn't feel comfortable. It seemed like I was cheating on Richard. So, for most of the last two years I have focused on my education. I will soon have my master's in psychology and be able to start working as a clinical psychologist. I plan to specialize with those coming home from Vietnam with what was called 'battle fatigue' in the past and is now known as Post-Vietnam Syndrome."

"From what I've seen, you will never be without work. Too many troops are coming back with those mental issues as well as drug problems. Not a pretty sight. I bet you will be a good one."

She sighed and said, "Now that info is out there, I guess your next question is why an older woman is chasing after a young sailor. As you probably have guessed I'm almost twenty-four, but since my birthday is later this year, you could consider it twenty-three and one-half if it makes you feel better." Her mouth again twisted up to the left with the 'I just got caught' look.

That look shattered my somber feelings and I started to laugh. I realized I couldn't lie to this woman. And I didn't want to lie to her. I took a deep breath and responded, "Not a problem, young lady, since I'll hit twenty-seven in just over two months. You won't be charged with cradle robbing."

"Really? Come on, you look so young even with that cute mustache," she said with a look of honest surprise. "Do you have a painting aging in an attic somewhere, like in Oscar Wilde's *The Picture of Dorian Gray*, that is keeping you young?"

"For sure, I turn twenty-seven in June. I know I look like I'm around twenty and that's a problem I have lived with for some time, but it comes in handy at times like now. And no paintings are hidden in any attics. Can I trust your confidence?" I asked.

"I know the obvious answer is 'of course' but I want you to know that I overheard my uncle and aunt talking last night after you left. I didn't hear all they said about you, but did catch a comment that you aren't who you're portraying. And I could tell Uncle Humphrey is impressed with you. Therefore I know that whatever you are doing here is important, and as a Navy brat, I know how to keep my mouth shut. I guess I have no shame, as I admit I was interested in you from the moment I opened the door yesterday. I do hope you feel you can trust me." She had a very serious look on her face as she spoke.

I nodded a positive response. "Remember, trust is a two-way street. I trust you with the information I'll tell you, and you have to trust me when I don't tell you everything. Agreed?"

"Agreed. And I promise to try to keep my natural curiosity under control and not ask too many questions that might put you in an awkward position. Note that the key word there is 'try,' so be patient with me. But who are you really?"

"Kelly, my given name is Marcus, so calling me Mark is fine, and truthful. My last name isn't Williams, but stick with that for now. I'm here on an investigation from the NIS headquarters in D.C., which is my normal duty station. And what I need from you is to continue to think of me as just a junior Yeoman in your uncle's office. That should be the easy part."

I looked in her eyes as I said the next thing. "The hard part is that if you see me outside the office—at any place, at any time—do not acknowledge that you know me unless I initiate the contact. There is some undercover work I'll be doing. And you may see me with another girl or two as part of the investigation, but trust me when I tell you that's just part of the job, because your interest in me is intensely reciprocal. And I do not say that lightly. There is something special here."

"Okay," she said quietly.

I think between what she overheard at her house and the things I just said, her mind was overloaded a bit. Hell, my mind was overloaded at that moment! I suspected there would be other questions coming soon. Maybe she was surprised that I had a strong interest in her. But for now, I put all of those thoughts aside and simply took her hand in mine as we strolled down the beach.

We walked along in silence for some time, found some interesting shells, watched the ships in the bay, laughed at the gulls, and finally headed back to the car as the sun was starting to set.

She pointed out various restaurants and stores as we drove back to the Giant. As I dropped her off at her car—a 1965, bright red, two-door Mustang convertible—in the Giant parking lot, she leaned back into my car and asked, "When can I expect the call about our second date?"

"You count a sandwich and a tour of the beach as a date?" I asked jokingly.

"You betcha, sailor. And it was a good one in my book. By the way, I never kiss on the first date, so I'm looking forward to number two. Call me! Soon!" And she turned to get into her car.

"Soon. Very soon!" I yelled back with a grin as she waved goodbye. I waited and watched until she drove off, thinking that the second date could not come soon enough. Then reality slapped me across the face and the job at hand filled my mind, pushing thoughts of Kelly aside for now. I returned to the house and the pile of work waiting for me there.

32

MONDAY MORNING

15 MARCH 1971

MONDAY MORNING WAS RATHER BORING. After the stress of getting close to Laura and Karen at lunch on Friday, talking with the CO on Friday night, the excitement of spending the afternoon with Kelly on Saturday, and the intense work of rereading all the NISRA personnel files on Sunday, the office just didn't have that same level of excitement. Just as well: my brain needed some down time.

I'd driven back to the base late Sunday night to spend the few hours of sleep in my rack in the transient barracks. I ran into Dexter when I walked in the barracks and he asked where I'd been; he mentioned noticing my empty rack Saturday night. I told him I'd driven around to see some of the sights, spending the night on the road when it got too late to get back to the barracks. He told me he'd be moving to the new barracks on Monday so I'd be on my own next week. "Don't oversleep."

I got to the office early and started the two vats of coffee and the tea water, ran over to the radio shack to pick up the daily traffic, and picked up the CO's short stack of newspapers from the distribution desk downstairs. After a quick look at the Washington Post's and Wall Street Journal's headlines, I placed the newspapers on the Captain's desk. I ran his carafe to his office as soon as the standard brew was done perking.

And before all that was finished, the ASR-35s start ringing and traffic started arriving from all over the US. Fortunately, by that time Dexter had usually arrived to handle one of the machines. The noise level wasn't too bad in the small office space, but it was best not to have a headache while working. Add to that noise the constant talking by Dexter; he always had a story or two about some girl he met last night or a rerun of his conquests the previous weekend. Because he was self-centered, I rarely had to answer any questions about my off time.

I was in the process of sending one of the downloaded reports to the NISRA in Charlottesville when the Chief came in. "Williams," he said, "the skipper wants to meet with you and me on the double. Let's go."

"What's up, Chief?"

"No idea, but we will soon find out." With that, he turned and headed back out the door. I jumped up and followed right behind him.

After the Chief knocked on the skipper's door, we heard "enter" and walked to his desk, popped to attention, and the Chief said, "Reporting as ordered, sir."

"At ease," the Captain said. "Have a seat."

Standing by the Captain's desk was the XO. He sat down in a chair that was at the right end of the desk. The Chief and I selected chairs directly against the wall facing the two of them. Nothing was said for at least a minute as the Captain continued reading something on his desk. He finally looked up and said, "Chief, I know it has only been a few days, but is Williams doing okay?"

"Yes sir, Captain. This Yeoman has caught on to the way we do things here quickly. And he fits in well with the rest of the crew," responded the Chief. "And I think you will agree he knows how to make coffee right."

"Good," the Captain said with a smile. "I have a different task I need someone to address. It's a bit of a boring one that might look to be a waste of time, so the new guy would be a natural. But in this case, I think Williams' education will be helpful. I don't know if you noticed in his service record, Chief, but Williams had more than a few college courses on criminal justice. Right, Williams?"

"Yes sir. I have completed most of the core courses at Georgia Tech in criminology," I answered quickly.

The Captain continued, "So we have the round peg we need for a round hole. Chief, I want Williams to start an evaluation of case files at each of our NISRAs. He needs to read through each file to determine if every report is complete. Get with Sam and have him introduce Williams around, show him the NISRA setup, give him full access, and then turn him loose. Also tell Sam to provide access to all the agents, in case he finds something in a file that needs more info from the reporting agent. I don't expect him to look for problems with the casework, just to make sure that all the reports are there and in proper order. This task needs to be finished as quickly as possible. But be complete, understand?"

"Aye, sir. We will get right on it. Is there anything else?" asked the Chief.

"Just one other thing. He needs to get to the other NISRAs, so schedule your workload expecting him to be gone frequently. Carry on, Williams. Chief, stay for a minute."

I stood, came to attention, and left the CO's office, closing the door behind me. I decided this was a good time to make a head call and lose the morning coffee.

Back in the CO's office, as he later told me, the Captain looked at the Chief and asked, "Has Williams been moved from the transient barracks yet?"

"No, sir. No space for him in the permanent barracks yet, but I check with the housing office daily. I did get Wilson a spot and he will move there later today," replied the Chief.

"Tell them to hold off on Williams for at least another week. We might need to move some personnel around as there have been some developments in Vietnam that require more staff. Williams might have to be transferred over there. I will let you know my decision soon. Until then, keep this to yourself, Chief."

"Aye aye, sir. Anything else, Captain?"

"No, dismissed."

After the Chief left the office, the XO got up and closed the door. He looked at Captain Miller and asked, "I'm not sure I can see what good Williams can do. We think we have a leak, but having a new kid digging through the files looks a bit ridiculous, sir."

"XO, the good news is that if we have a problem with any of the agents, they won't suspect this 'new kid' has the ability to find anything in the files, much less something that could incriminate them. But I think Williams can use his education here to possibly uncover any problems. Bad news or a worst case scenario would be that we've wasted his time for a couple of weeks and in the process burnt a bit of gas when he runs out to the other NISRAs. Just be ready to back him up if it comes to that." With that the Captain looked back to the file on his desk and the XO returned to his office.

33

AFTER CATCHING UP WITH THE Chief as he was leaving the CO's office, we headed down the hall to the NISRA Norfolk office space. The Chief told me the code for the door keypad and demonstrated how it worked. It was a simple four-code sequence that unlocked the door to the agents' office space. I asked how often the code was changed, and the Chief said whenever someone got transferred out. Seemed to be a weak system, I thought, but held my comments.

The office space was rather ordinary. Desks were set in groups of two, with the two facing each other. Standard paraphernalia covered the desks ... telephone, desk blotter, lamp, in and out baskets, calendar, etc. Most of the desks were in use, and the Chief led me to the back of the room where there were two offices closed off from the big area. A couple of the agents looked up as we walked toward Sam Maker's office. The Chief knocked and stepped inside. I followed and we waited until Sam got off the phone.

"Mornin' Chief ... what ya need?" asked Sam as he hung up the phone and looked directly at me. "And I have seen you around, but haven't been introduced. I'm Sam Maker, the senior agent of this NISRA. By the way, you make great coffee."

"Thank you, Agent Maker. Mark Williams." I extended my hand and Sam stood and shook it. Sam had a firm handshake. He looked his age, a man in his mid-forties starting to go gray around the edges of his short haircut. His shoulder holster contained a snub-nose revolver, probably the standard .38 caliber. And he came across as an easy-going guy, but I knew his record said otherwise.

"Call me Sam. After all, we are on the same team here. And again, Chief, what ya need from me?"

The Chief cleared his throat and explained the task the Captain had outlined and the role Sam needed to play: providing me with a quick introduction to the paperwork and introducing me around to the other agents. "OK, Williams, get to it," said the Chief as he turned and left the area.

Sam smiled and we chatted a bit. I suspected his job as an agent was the reason he asked a ton of questions, but then again, he could just be curious about a new guy, one he was somewhat stuck with having in his office space, looking over his shoulder. I asked if there was a desk available I could use for the duration of this assignment, and I promised to try to keep out of everyone's way.

"Use the desk over by the radiator. Everyone ignores it due to the excess heat. But I suppose you can handle it for a week or so." Sam paused, and his face twisted into a grimace as he said, "Mark, I'm not sure what the Captain expects to find, but I can guarantee you that all of our files are complete and concise. I check each one before it's considered closed." Sam stood and pointed me out the door.

"I understand completely, Agent Maker, but the skipper has assigned this task and it must be done. One of these days he might share his reasons with me," I responded with a grin, as one would expect.

"Last time I'll tell ya, call me Sam. Don't get on my bad side." He returned the grin. "I'm not one who is big on formality around the office; I leave that up to the Navy brass. But I do expect everyone to do the job right," he said as he shook his head and walked out of his office.

"I hear ya loud and clear, Sam. I'll try to stay on your good side, and I appreciate all the help."

Sam took me around, introducing me to all the agents who were in the office, and the clerical staff. Joe Mabry and Darrell Tasker were a team; they used the desks closest to mine. Both were in their early thirties and seemed friendly enough. Both fit the look of ex-FBI, which I knew they were, as each sported a clean-shaven face, well-trimmed hair, white shirts, and dark suits.

No one was sitting at the next set of desks where Sam pointed, telling me Stephen Crosser and Clyde London sat there; they were at a conference on changes regarding drug evidence collection and testing procedures. Every agent needed to attend, so they went in teams to reduce the negative impact on open cases.

Looking down the middle of the office, the two desks next to the radiator were empty, and the last set of two, next to them, would normally be occupied by John Driscol and Douglas Knox. They were at the range that morning undergoing re-qualification with their pistols. A large conference table, a photocopier, and more filing cabinets filled the rest of the office space.

Sam spent a moment explaining my job to the two agents present and told them to pass the info on to the others when they showed up. He also told them that my security clearance was high enough that I could be privy to everything said.

Agent Tasker smiled and said, "Williams, I don't envy you that task. Reading Joe's chicken scratch will be a real challenge." Joe Mabry laughed and threw a paperclip at Darrell.

"You guys need to be nice to Mark—he's responsible for the coffee you like so much. He has full access to our entire area, and you may find him here after hours. Give him whatever he needs and try not to shoot him." Sam winked at me and we walked out of the agents' office area and across the passageway to another office.

34

THE NOISE COMING FROM THE office was a clear indicator that this was where the secretaries took the agents' notes and rough reports, turning them into something readable. The noise of the IBM Selectric typewriters was familiar. And it was easy to tell they used an offline ASR-35 to cut the paper tapes needed to forward the reports and requests on to other NIS offices. Lots of chatter came from those devices as they did their magic.

The lady in charge of the office, Mrs. Ruby Judge, reminded me of the actress Elsa Lancaster as the somewhat strange aunt in *Bell, Book and Candle* with Jimmy Stewart. Short, a bit overweight, early fifties, married, glasses perched on the end of her nose, and a big smile that looked like the grin of a tiger.

As she started to introduce me to her staff, I said hello to Laura and explained to Ruby that I'd introduced myself to her the previous week. The third secretary was a woman in her mid-fifties, married, with a pleasant voice. Laura seemed to be looking me over as if trying to look into my soul. But I was always a bit paranoid.

Sam explained my job to them and asked that they cooperate with anything I needed. They all agreed and welcomed me to the Norfolk office.

But as we walked out, I glanced back to find Laura Scott still staring right at me. Huh. She wasn't a bad looking gal … a dozen years older than me, but still nice on the eyes. My thoughts jumped to scenes from the movie *The Graduate*, featuring that Hoffman guy chasing both Mrs. Robinson and her daughter, and alarm bells started sounding in my brain. *Don't go there!*

We re-entered the agents' area, where Sam showed me that behind a locked door on the back wall was the file room, a place where the case files were stored in cabinets. Closed files were kept on site for a year, then moved to a storage warehouse on base; after five more years they were shipped to another warehouse somewhere around D.C. Files were stored in NIS case number sequence in all locations.

Here, the boxes containing the case files all had clear labeling on the ends. Some boxes contained several different case files, others held only one. A lot depended upon the amount of paper in each file.

There was a card catalog system, similar to those found in libraries, which allowed someone to find the NIS case number by searching for victim or suspect names, locations, case category, etc. The catalog case and all file cabinets were locked until needed. Each agent had a key, as did Mrs. Ruby Judge, the head secretary for the NISRA.

"Sam, the Chief gave me the door combination. Can I get a set of keys to the file room and the various cabinets? Since I'm a new guy here in Norfolk, and don't have a lot of outside activities or friends, I'll be spending a few late evenings and weekends here to wrap this project up as quickly as possible. Gotta make a good impression on the skipper."

"I'll dig up a spare set. Nice to see some enthusiasm around here. Maybe it'll rub off on some of these agents. Anything else?"

"What's in the vault in the back of the file room?" I asked. Sam had seemed to ignore it on the tour.

"We keep extra weapons and ammo there. And it's the storage for all the evidence. In addition, there are some files that fall into the Top Secret category and they're stored in a safe inside the vault. None of that data is anything you'll need to be evaluating."

I nodded my understanding and asked, "Who has the combination to the vault and to the safe?"

"Why do you care?" Sam asked with a frown on his face. "Nothing in there is part of your project."

"Like I said, I'm the new guy and need to impress the skipper. I plan to do a security write up about each of the NISRAs. When I get out of the

Navy and head back to school to finish my degree, I've decided to focus my engineering studies on plant security, and this will be a great practice run for me. And who knows: fresh eyes often notice weak areas that everyone has accepted as gold for a long time." I paused. "Don't worry; I plan to share it with you before turning it in to the boss."

"Do you have experience in that area?" Sam inquired. "Work with the police or a security firm?"

"No, just common sense coupled with a ton of college courses in engineering, which kicks up my analytical thought processes, and a few courses in criminology, which helps me to think like a bad guy at times."

"Okay, you do your write up, but make damn sure I see it before anyone else. And if I like what I read, I'll let you read the security analysis I prepared last year that no one read. Then maybe we can share methodologies and whine about the inadequacies of government service and budgeting over a beer or two. As for access to the vault, all agents have the combination. Only Ruby and I have the combination to the safe."

Sam turned, went back into the file room, and approached the vault. He spun the dial several times and after hitting at least four numbers, he pulled the handle and the door opened. "Come on, you might as well also see this. Since you might need access to the evidence boxes, I'll give you the combination too."

I stepped into a vault that was only about six feet wide but at least twenty feet deep. Half of one side was lined with racks holding everything from Smith and Wesson revolvers and Colt 1911 pistols to pump shotguns, M-14 rifles, and even a couple of Winchester Model 70 bolt action rifles with scopes. Obviously, these last ones were for sniper work.

Boxes of ammunition for each weapon were stacked on the shelves below the racks. The rest of the walls were covered with shelving and contained many boxes of evidence, each with the proper case label on the end identifying the case number. Against the back wall of the vault stood the safe.

Sam walked to the safe and worked the combination. He pulled open the door and stepped aside so I could see the interior. There was nothing exciting to see in there; just a few ledger books and a couple of stacks of files. But he did reach inside and pull out a set of keys. He also pulled out a logbook, into which he entered the keys' serial numbers along with the date and time when he gave me a copy of these keys to the file room and cabinets. I signed the receipt and made a mental note of who had received keys in the past.

He also pulled out one of the hardback ledger books and tucked it under his arm before securing the safe. I couldn't see any writing on the exterior of the book, so I had no idea what it contained.

I thanked Sam for showing me the vault and giving me the keys. We secured the doors and exited the file room. Sam checked his watch and said, "Mark, I'm just about late for a meeting with chief of detectives of the Norfolk Police Department. We get together every week or so to look over cases that might have impact on the base. We've built a trusting, working relationship since he was appointed last summer, and it's helped us both. So, you know what to do and where everything is. By the way, we usually have 600–900 cases per year, so have fun." And he left.

I went to the supply room and grabbed a couple of legal pads and a few pens. The Chief was nowhere to be seen, so I opened the door to the AUTOVON room and gave Dexter a run down on my project, and why I wouldn't be helping him for a while. He was not too happy about it, but was glad I was stuck with a boring job and not him. I left him mumbling about the lack of fairness in the world and headed back down the hall to NISRA Norfolk.

When I got back to my new desk, I called Dex in the AUTOVON room and gave him my new phone extension. He was still mumbling about the injustice in the world. I offered to trade jobs, which he refused, then told him to go get a cup of tea and calm down. He quickly hung up.

35

To keep things looking normal, I started with the last file closed, with the intent of working backwards. I didn't want anyone seeing me pull the specific files about the dead CIs. When no one else was around, I could focus on those cases, but going directly to them first would cause too much attention.

The last file had a case number ending in 409, so I knew there were that many files ahead of me just to get to the first of the year. And I needed to be on the lookout for any new ODs from this year that looked strange. Then I could dive into the specific cases of interest from last year. I probably needed to spend more hours there late at night when no one was around—then I could get through them much faster. *Who needs a life outside the office anyway,* I thought with a sigh.

The 409th closed file for 1971 was rather boring. A Seaman apprentice had been caught smoking weed. The division officer thought he might be selling the stuff, so he called us to investigate. It didn't take long to check out. The NIS investigation showed the kid was stupid for smoking marijuana on base, but he was not a dealer.

The thin file included the proper paperwork: an NIR or Naval Investigative Request that starts in the investigation, a couple of ROIs, the

Report of Investigation, and the final piece, the RUC, or Referred Upon Closing report. That one documents what was done with the bad guy and the evidence. In this case, Seaman Apprentice "Stupid" was referred back to the commanding office for punishment. All documents were complete and in the proper order. I initialed the lower corner of the case label on the outside of the file with the day's date. Back into the box and on to the next one.

I did start a log of drug cases, with locations, dates and times of buys, and type of drug entered. This type of information could help create a profile of the dealer habits in the future.

The morning quickly turned into mid-afternoon, and I was so wrapped up with getting through the files that I failed to stop for lunch. Driscol and Knox returned from the pistol range and bragged about their great shooting. I introduced myself, and Darrell gave them a brief rundown on my assignment. Both offered their condolences on the boring task. They seemed like nice guys. We chatted about shooting a bit, and John offered to take me to the range one Saturday afternoon when we weren't too busy.

I kept my nose in the files as the four agents discussed the events of the day and status of several cases that were underway. It was easy not to show interest as most of my career had been spent putting on a blank face and seemingly ignoring what was going on around me. It helped, as it allowed me to hear things that intense questioning wouldn't bring forth.

As 1600 hrs approached, the agents started closing file drawers and getting their desks in order. They drifted out and left me alone with my task. Planning to work into the early evening, I continued for a few more minutes, but hunger was taking over. I was losing focus. Time for me to call it a day, too.

I locked the files, secured the file room door, double checked that nothing was left on my desk, grabbed my cover, and headed to the door, then stopped. A small delay wouldn't be a problem, I thought, so I quickly glanced at each of the agents' desks. Nothing obviously out of place, but it never hurts to look. I hit the light switch and exited the area.

As I walked toward the crossover passageway where I'd exit the NIS secured area, I saw Captain Miller leaving his office, and Kelly with him. I slowed down to time the meet at the crossover and was rewarded with a smile from Kelly. Wearing a light blue Madras shirt over a medium gray skirt, Kelly looked radiant and ready for a relaxed evening.

"Williams, I'm surprised to see you still here," said the Captain.

"Afternoon, sir, ma'am. I got wrapped up in my new assignment and lost track of time. Heading out shortly, sir." We were the only staff members left in the NIS spaces, and Petty Officer Jimmy Kincade, who manned the security desk at the crossover door, was packing up for the evening, getting ready to lock all the doors.

"I don't believe you have met my niece. Kelly Anne, this is our newest member of the NIS group, Mark Williams," said the skipper with just a hint of a smile as he stayed in character with the undercover operation. No one was to know I'd been at his house the previous week.

I extended my hand, and Kelly shook it. "Very pleased to meet you, Miss Kelly," I said.

She again seemed to be holding my hand just a moment longer than normal, and smiled when she said, "My pleasure. Hope you can help keep Uncle Humphrey out of trouble around here." I chuckled as expected and returned the smile.

"I need a small favor, Williams, if it would not be too much to ask. Kelly's car won't start and she needs to get to ODU campus. And I need to meet Mrs. Miller, who is waiting for me right now at the officer's club. Would you be able to drive Kelly to school?" he asked. "Kelly, you can find a ride home later, right?" She nodded a quick yes.

"Always happy to be of assistance, sir," I responded. "I'll be just a moment as I secure the coffee mess and double check the AUTOVON room. Be right back."

And with that I headed down the passageway to the coffee mess and just unplugged the two urns; clean up could wait until morning. The AUTOVON room was quiet and all set for the overnight download, so I locked the door and returned to the crossover. The Captain was walking away, and Kelly stood there waiting, alone and quiet.

"All set, Miss Kelly. Let's go, I'm parked out back." I said goodnight to Jimmy on the security desk and we headed down the crossover. I was not sure if his wink and smile indicated I was lucky or I just had another job dumped on me by the skipper.

After we cleared the NIS area, Kelly laughed and said, "Hurry up, we have places to go!" We left the building and walked over to the enlisted parking area. I held the passenger door for her, then fired up the Blue Beast and headed toward the main gate. ODU was a few miles down Hampton Blvd, but I didn't know exactly where she was heading, so I asked for directions.

"We, and I do mean *we*, are going to the campus bookstore. I am going to buy you a dictionary and put a paperclip on a specific page," she said rather harshly.

Not sure what had happened since Saturday evening, I looked over at her with surprise and weakly smiled. "Okay, what is that all about?" I asked.

She pointed to the small gold watch on her left arm and said, "Mark, it has been nearly forty-eight hours since we parted at the Giant. You told me, in no uncertain terms I might add, that you would be calling 'soon.' Fact is, I recall hearing you say 'very soon,' so obviously you do not know what the word 'soon' means, nor the modifier of 'very,' since I haven't heard from you in nearly forty-eight hours. We will fix that lack of knowledge right now when I mark the dictionary page containing the definition of 'soon' with a paperclip." With that, we both started laughing.

"Okay, guilty as charged," I said. "But save your money and I promise to not let it happen again. Here's that 'trust' thing coming up already. I was busy with work all day Sunday, and stuff at the office today was hectic. Am I forgiven?"

"Only if you buy me dinner right now so we can call this our second date," she quickly said. She smiled and reached over, took my hand off the wheel and gave it a quick squeeze.

Dinner at a local seafood restaurant Kelly recommended was good. We spent a lot of time sharing information about each other, and found we had many similar interests in music, books, and old movies. It was a nice dinner, lasting into the early evening.

Then it hit me that I'd never been this comfortable with any other woman I had dated. Even time spent with Sandy seemed a bit stiffer or more awkward than the relaxed feeling I now had with Kelly. It was exciting and scary. People just don't fall deeply in love in a matter of hours, do they? All I knew was that I was having feelings I'd never had before. Yea, it was scary.

It was time to call it an evening, and as we walked back to my car I wasn't sure how to get Kelly home without my car being seen at the Captain's house again. When I mentioned it, Kelly said no problem since she'd left her car at the base exchange parking lot and we would just go there. "I thought it wouldn't start," I said.

She giggled. "If I had turned the key, it probably would have! The car is fine. I left it there and walked to your office in hopes of spending the evening with you."

I sat behind the wheel and didn't yet start my car. I stared straight ahead and quietly asked, "How will you explain your car to the Captain, Kelly?" I really didn't need any complications with an angry skipper while trying to solve my assignment.

"Don't be mad. I guess it's time for more honesty," she replied. "Mark, Uncle Humphrey and I have a special close relationship. I feel closer to him than I do my own father at times. So Sunday afternoon while Aunt Dorothy was off to a bridge club meeting, he and I had a nice long talk about you. And you and me."

"Okay," I responded slowly. "I'm not angry, just concerned. How extensive was this talk? I need to stay on the Captain's good side." I didn't know what to expect next from her.

"I gave him the facts. Just the facts. The fact that I was drawn to you the moment I opened the door on Friday and saw you standing there. I explained to him the facts of how I found you Saturday and convinced you to spend the afternoon with me. An afternoon which reignited feelings I'd thought were gone forever. And I told him the fact that I plan to spend as much time with you as I possibly can while you're here. And that in two months after I graduate, if you're no longer here, the fact I will be moving to D.C. to be near you."

She took a deep breath and continued, "By the way, the dead car excuse was his plan as a way for me to 'officially' meet you at the office without anyone knowing about last Friday. So he knows my car is fine." And with that, her mouth again twisted up to the left with that cute 'I just got caught' look.

I was left speechless. Unbelievable that anything like this could happen so fast! The only thing that felt right at that instant was to reach over, gently touch her cheek, and softly kiss her waiting lips. One kiss led to another and the passion grew. We finally stopped just before the car windows fogged over and started laughing at the happiness and excitement we both were feeling.

I regained my voice first and said, "Well, this is one hell of a second date!" We continued to laugh until all the passion energy was gone. Then Kelly leaned over and gave me a kiss that would have made Scarlett and Rhett envious.

Getting my breath back after that one was a challenge. But once I did I asked, "And what exactly did the Captain say after hearing all of your facts and plans you have with a guy you've known for just over forty-eight hours?"

"Are you sure you want to know?" she asked with a big grin on her face.

"No, not really, but I need to know so I can hopefully keep my job," I responded with a laugh.

"He had a hard time expressing all his feeling in detail because I think he was afraid he might let out too many secrets about you. But he told me he knew you to be a man of honor, integrity, and extreme intelligence. And that he was happy I'd found you. But he warned me not to get in your way since you have an important job to do."

She leaned over, gave me another kiss, and continued, "I also think getting the positive comments from my Dad helped him see what a good guy you are. Dad called Saturday afternoon while I was out with you, and my uncle said they had a nice long talk about you. So the 'Captain' is happy with us being together and your job is safe," she explained. "And it looks like Daddy is happy with you as well."

"Comments from Dad?" I asked in total surprise. "What have you told your father about me?"

"Not a thing. I haven't talked with Dad in about two weeks," she continued with the twisted-up mouth. "Mark, if you had the time to get to know my family better before I fell in love with you, then you would have discovered my Aunt Dorothy's maiden name is Gallagher. She is the CNO's little sister. I am his daughter."

Oh, boy. I sure did not see that one coming. *This investigator hasn't seen much of anything coming when dealing with one special lady named Kelly Anne Gallagher. Great investigative work there, Marcus.* I laid my head on the steering wheel and closed my eyes. Oh, boy, indeed.

After a short while I got over my surprise and we shared a laugh about the situation. I told her I knew I had a lot to learn about her, and she'd better go easy on me with all these new facts.

We agreed to meet at the Giant market on Thursday, right after I got off work, for another interesting evening of getting to know one another over dinner. She had classes on Tuesday and Wednesday evenings.

I dropped her off at her car at the exchange, and watched her drive away. Kelly, and all that she said, was spinning around in my mind. And there was no way I could stop thinking about the kisses and the feelings I had as I headed back to the barracks.

Or the fact I was now dating the CNO's daughter. Nothing like a few complications to mess up the brain.

The rest of late Monday night, after dinner with Kelly, was a total waste of time as far as the investigation was concerned.

36

TUESDAY MORNING WENT WELL, THOUGH I was still trying to fully understand what had happened with Kelly the night before. I had to admit—she'd captured my heart in a way I'd never known. She was something. I was just not sure what! Beautiful, smart, intriguing, witty, and most definitely on my mind all the time.

But dating the daughter of my boss was bad, and at least 100 times worse since my boss was the dang Chief of Naval Operations. You cannot get any higher than that in this man's Navy. If it went bad with Kelly and me, my Navy career was history.

My heart was telling me to hold on to her tight and never let go, and my head was still going in circles—no help at all. No, that was not completely true. Somewhere in the back of my head a little voice kept telling me *watch out because you are in a rebound relationship.* Decisions of the heart are best not made while rebounding.

Guess the real question I needed to answer was whether or not I was in a rebound relationship with Kelly. Sandy and I had been drifting apart for some time and, looking back on it with that great 20/20 hindsight, it's easy to see that we were so wrapped up in getting through the wedding that we failed to see our love had pulled an "Elvis." That is, it had left the building.

I admit that I missed her some—our relationship had become comfortable—but I must also admit that I felt a great sense of relief now that it was all over. No more stress, wondering what she was doing or who she was doing it with. And no more hearing grief after she was told I had a new work assignment. Rebounding … no, not at all.

As for Pat, that was one of those rare, beautiful events that Longfellow defined as "ships that pass in the night" in his poem. A rather humorous yet perfect way to describe the relationship between a man and a woman who both wore Navy uniforms. I'd never forget Patricia, but there were no rebound issues there either.

I was up early—actually I didn't get much sleep due to thinking and probably overthinking the Kelly issue—and made it into the office early enough to have all morning tasks completed an hour ahead of time. That allowed me the opportunity to check out the NISRA agents' desks again. Still nothing worth writing home about lying around there. So I pulled the next closed case and started digging.

More coffee was needed to help focus on the files, so I headed back to the coffee mess for another cup. The rest of the staff was starting to arrive, and as I approached the coffee urn, I saw a familiar light blue uniform. "Good morning, Seaman," said Lieutenant Colonel J. Scott Tiller.

I had a flash of inspiration along with my frustration of hearing the incorrect rating, and quickly replied, "Good morning, Commander." Using his equivalent Navy rank might just subtly get the point across.

He frowned and started to respond when we noticed the Captain standing at the door. The CO looked at me and said, "Petty Officer, you look like you need more sleep. And did I hear you calling our favorite 'flyboy' by a naval rank? Wake up, sailor!"

"Sorry, sir. Not enough coffee to be thinking clearly yet." I turned to Tiller and said, "Sorry, Colonel, it won't happen again."

The CO smiled and turned to J. Scott and continued, "Colonel, I suspect we all have challenges at times with the different branches' personnel structures and nomenclature. I remember an Army officer at the war college who insisted on calling any Navy enlisted man who wore a 'Dixie Cup'—you know, the round white hat—a 'Seaman.' And he did so even when the man's arm was clearly displaying the eagle and chevrons of a Non-Commissioned Officer, a Navy petty officer, like Williams here. I had to explain to him that petty officers worked damn hard to get that 'crow,' and calling them a 'Seaman' would be the same as calling an Army sergeant a 'private' or you calling an Air Force sergeant an 'airman,' which we know you would never do."

Tiller looked like he wanted to turn invisible, and hastily replied, "Very true, Captain. No one ever wants to insult any member of our fighting forces. Petty Officer Williams, please accept my apology."

I think my tongue was starting to bleed: I'd bitten it hard to keep from laughing when the skipper put J. Scott in his place. "Not necessary, but thank you, Colonel," I said quickly before excusing myself to head back to work. Suddenly my day had gotten just a bit better with a small victory under my belt. And again, I owed the skipper. I was so thankful I told him all I did that Friday night.

When I finally got behind the locked door of the agents' area, I let loose with a huge laugh. I felt a bit sorry for J. Scott, but in the long run, Captain Miller did him a favor by correcting a mistake that had caused some hard feelings with the current staff and would be a problem for him in future commands with joint forces. Things would be better for all as we went forward.

37

WITH THE J. SCOTT PROJECT behind me, I was back to reading the files in hopes of uncovering a nugget of interest to help the situation at hand. After a while the files started to blur together. You can only read so many reports of security clearances, drug abuse, and sex, mixed with a few other crimes, before it becomes a total bore.

But I had to focus on determining if there were any other incidents that could link to the cases I was following. Someone somewhere had to see something at some time. Sadly, this someone had not seen anything linking them in the case files.

Sam Maker was the first agent to arrive, and he came over to my desk. "Morning. Find anything interesting, Mark?" he asked.

"Sorry, Sam. Nothing earthshaking yet. So far, all the i's are dotted and the t's are crossed. Your crew is doing the paperwork job right. Will let ya know when I find something evil."

"Keep having fun," he said as he walked away to his office and closed the door.

That day, Clyde London and Steve Crosser were still out at the drug conference. Driscol and Knox had called in. They were already at the site of a possible break-in on the base. They'd be in as soon as they gathered all the evidence and interviews.

Darrell Tasker and Joe Mabry strolled back in after getting their morning coffee. They were talking about a basketball game they watched last night. They asked me how the job was progressing and I gave the stock answer of how much fun I was having.

Before I could start a decent conversation with them about their jobs, Sam called them into his office. Shortly, they both emerged and were gone, out the door. Guess another case came up. Another day was going by without the chance to chat with the two possible leakers.

The rest of the morning was spent going through case file after case file. Checking the files for the specific reports, as my cover story required, was quick and easy. Logging in the info I gleaned from each case took a bit longer, but I was starting to see a pattern with the drug cases. It might lead somewhere, but too soon to tell. A lot of number crunching had to be done first.

I skipped lunch since my stomach was too nervous to eat, due to the excitement of the previous night. I can survive on coffee for a while. But I did break the file reading routine and headed to the AUTOVON room to give Dexter a lunch break. And even with that hour stop, by the normal end of the day I'd finished all the files for 1971 up to the end of January.

I had wanted to leave the office at normal time, but I decided it was a good day to stay late and do more digging. Nothing going on that night with Kelly, and I really needed to get this mess under control. It had already been a long day of reading files, so a few more hours of the same would not kill me.

But three hours later, things got a bit more exciting as I read what I thought would be the last file for the day. Around 1900 hrs, Agents Tasker and Mabry came back into the office. They'd left earlier on a case and were not expected back that day. It was interesting that they looked a bit shocked when they saw me.

"Good evening, gents. Everything okay?" I asked.

"Hey, Mark. We didn't expect to see you here this late. Did the Captain put you on report and assign you extra duty?" asked Joe Mabry laughingly.

"No, just trying to get this boring task done. As I told Sam, since I'm new in town I don't have a lot of activities outside of work to fill my time. May as well get this job done and get out of your hair," I replied. "What brings you in so late?"

"This is the only quiet place where I can help Joe cram for his next advancement exam coming up in June. Too many children in either of our houses for quality study time. We get together a couple of times a week to go over policies and procedures which might be on the exam," answered Darrell.

"That's great. I'll get out of your way. This was the last file I had planned to go through tonight anyway. The eyes are starting to cross."

After I came back out of the storage area and locked the door, I turned to the agents and asked, "Hey, my curiosity is getting the best of me and I have a quick question about procedures around here. If you don't mind."

They both nodded 'okay' so I continued, "I see both of your names popping up on drug files frequently in these closed cases, and the other agents not so much. Is there a reason for that or just luck of the draw?" I queried.

"Mostly it's due to the extra training on drug issues that Darrell and I have taken. Sam keeps trying to get time for everyone to go through that course, but the caseload keeps getting in the way. Steve and Clyde finally got their training finished today. Before that, if Darrell and I were free, then we got the first crack at the drug cases," Joe said as he pulled a couple of books from his desk drawer. "Now Steve and Clyde can help more."

"That makes sense. Thanks for the info. I'm out of here, so you guys have a great time. See ya in the morning."

38

AFTER A QUICK CHANGE INTO civvies at the transient barracks, I headed off to the house for a quiet night of case study and planning. The lack of lunch was the highest priority in my mind as I pulled into the Giant parking lot.

After a quick scan of the meat and seafood cases, a large piece of fresh salmon got my attention. A dash down several aisles added rice, green onions, red onions, teriyaki sauce, zucchini, and a very nice bottle of Chablis to my hand-carried basket. At the checkout I halfway expected Kelly to show up, but I was not that lucky. The only smile I found there was a fast one from Darlene the cashier as she handed me the change.

Dinner was easy to prepare and tasted great. Considering how hungry I was, I suspect a simple peanut butter and jelly sandwich would have received my rave reviews. And the time spent cooking was also spent on the case.

The few minutes needed to chop the red onions and zucchini for sautéing and cut the green onions to add to the rice, and the twenty minutes needed to watch the rice cook, allowed me time to sit at the breakfast bar with a glass of Chablis and ponder the new info from Joe and Darrell.

Their justification for being in the office late sounded legitimate. As did the reason for having their hands on most all of the drug cases. Looked like my two somewhat solid suspects were off the list.

So there I was, seven days into the investigation, and the only suspects still on the list were a pair of good-looking redheaded women who just happened to act somewhat strange. Hell, if acting strange were enough to get you arrested, the jails would have been full and overflowing for decades, especially during the hippie-filled 1960s. But you play the hand you're dealt. Time to focus on a pair of red queens I got.

After finishing dinner and cleaning up the kitchen, I headed up to my office. I started to use a marker to "X" off the two agents who were no longer under consideration, but I stopped. I'd still need to confirm their stories before they got the big "X" across the face. Sam should be able to confirm or deny all they'd told me about the test and the reason for frequent drug case assignments. I just needed to get it into a conversation without being too obvious about it.

My mind wandered back to the two redheads. I admit it was a pleasant place for my mind to linger awhile. Laura was a very nice-looking widow. And it had been several years since her husband died. But there were no indicators around her desk that she had been seeing anyone. Perhaps she was holding back on romance to avoid upsetting Karen who, like most daughters, greatly loved her father. Then again, it could be that Laura's strange behavior was sexual frustration. Or, back to the initial thought: she might be selling confidential information. But I couldn't see her getting the access to the information that resulted in dead CIs. The sex issue seemed more valid.

And as for Karen, here was another nice-looking woman, but her mother seemed to be pushing her on just about anyone ... including me. Girls that looked as good as she did usually didn't have trouble getting dates. Why was she not dating more? And an extremely big question was: how much access did she have at JAG to our CI information? And how was I going to determine that? Wonderful—a lot more questions had come forward instead of the needed answers.

On considering both women and their relationship, it might be that Laura's desire for Karen to date was a way to justify her own dating. If Karen was in a good loving relationship, then she might not have the desire to dump on Laura for wanting the same thing.

Rereading Laura's files did nothing to help the situation. And I came to the conclusion that the next night's date would be the time and place to get a few answers to way too many questions. Perhaps seeing Laura in a non-work setting might help answer a few.

I'd had enough for the night, so I dropped the cover over the board, turned out the office light, and headed to bed. I would get up early enough to stop by the transient barracks and change back into my uniform before heading to the office.

39

AFTER GETTING ALL THE USUAL morning tasks accomplished, I headed to my desk in the agents' room. It had been a quiet morning, with none of the excitement of Tuesday morning. J. Scott was nowhere to be seen, and the rest of the NISO crew was subdued when they arrived. Not every day is exciting in the world of intelligence and investigations.

I was going over my notes on cases that included the use of confidential informants when the agents started drifting in to work. Mabry and Tasker were doing their pistol quals that day, so they checked in and darted back out the door. We wouldn't see them until later in the day.

London and Crosser checked in and immediately left to continue the follow-up on the drug case that Tasker and Mabry started working the day before. Driscol and Knox were busy with paperwork from the rape case and the break-in over in base housing.

Sam Maker came in, and after brief 'hellos' he closed his office door and grabbed the phone. His head was down and notes were being taken for a good while. When he finally hung up, he grabbed his coat and headed to the vault. Soon he came back out carrying the same hardback ledger book I saw him with the previous week. He made a general announcement to no one in particular as he headed out the door: "I'll be at NPD if ya need me."

Having spent hours reading the case files for the dead CIs, the next step was to go through the evidence in hopes that something there would open a door to the answers I needed. Heading into the vault with my note pad, I was filled with a ton of determination to find something somewhere.

Time to start with the oldest case first, that of Ensign Joan Appleton. She died on 22 November 1970 and death was by strangulation. Not a pleasant way to go. This case was plagued with problems, starting with: where was she from Friday afternoon, when she left her apartment on leave, until Monday morning when her body was found back on base in a dumpster.

The evidence box for her case contained the clothes she was wearing when her body was found. Some articles of clothing were missing from the crime scene and had yet to turn up. No purse was found and nothing was in her pockets. The only piece of jewelry discovered was a small pin in the shape of a strange bird; it was lying next to the body. The victim's blood was found on the pin.

Blood and tissue samples from under her fingernails were still in storage at the hospital. The blood type was B positive, giving the attacker a greater likelihood of being either Asian or Black; Caucasians and Hispanics have only a nine percent chance of having B positive blood. Skin samples ruled out the suspect being Black. Not very concrete, but at least a start.

Nothing turned up in her apartment that could shed light on her activities over that weekend. The roommate knew there was a boyfriend, but no contact info was available.

The bird pin kept grabbing my attention. Maybe it would lead to a link. It was unusual in its shape. Nice colors similar to a seagull, but it had more black on the wings and an orange head. I'd seen gulls with black, gray, and white heads, but I didn't recall orange. Interesting. I decided it needed further study, so I signed the evidence log for the case to show I was removing it. Perhaps Kelly knew someone at ODU in the science department who knew their bird stuff. Yea, I needed a bird guy … ornithologist, that's the word!

The next CI case was Storekeeper Third Class Walter King. He died on 10 December 1970 in a single-vehicle auto accident that resulted in a horrific fire. The evidence box contained little, due to his body and the interior of the car being consumed by the fire. One bag held samples of the burnt car seat, which testing had showed contained an accelerant. The other bag held the burnt whiskey bottle. The bottle was interesting, since comments in the file stated King was not a heavy drinker—so why the whiskey bottle. Was he set up?

As I continued looking into the cases of the other dead CIs—GM2 Roger Mobley, SN Paul Wayne, and PN3 Elliott Abbott—I was surprised to find very little helpful evidence. Mobley had drowned, perhaps after being hit in the head. Wayne had died of a drug overdose at a local bar. His body was found in the alley behind the bar and it was not considered a suspicious death. Abbott's death was very suspicious: his body was found behind one of the many warehouses near the piers; a small caliber round had entered the back of his skull.

These cases were all too random, and the only connections that linked them together were the fact they were CIs for NISRA Norfolk. And I'd pretty much cleared the entire NISRA staff except for the two redheads.

And thinking of which, I needed to head out for my date with them; well, I'd be seeing both, but dating only one.

40

IT WAS SURPRISING HOW QUICKLY Wednesday evening and my first date with Karen came. Not knowing what she had planned for dinner, I dressed in dark blue jeans, a light yellow button-down Oxford shirt, and a navy blue sports coat. That look should keep me in good standing at most eateries. I grabbed an appropriate tie to stash in the car in case she decided on some place more upscale. 'Always be ready for whatever comes your way' is the best motto for survival.

I fired up the Blue Beast and headed out. Using the directions Laura had provided, I easily found her house. It was located on a cul-de-sac in a suburban neighborhood on the south side of Norfolk. Most of the homes there were two-story brick that were probably built in the 1950s. All had been well maintained, and the streets were clean. All around, this was a nice place. I parked on the street and headed to the door.

Laura opened the door before I could ring the bell. Her smile, as she looked me up and down while holding the door open, indicated she was pleased with my attire. "Hello, Mark, come on in. Karen will be down shortly. Have a seat. Care for a drink?"

"No thanks, Laura. With all the driving we are going to do on this Norfolk tour, I don't need a DUI on my record."

She chuckled. I walked over to the mantel to survey the photos displayed there. The large one in the center featured an older gent standing by a barn.

Laura walked up behind me and placed a hand on my shoulder. She pointed to the center photo and said, "That was my great-uncle Thaddeus, a wonderful guy who never married. He really helped us after Ben was killed. He passed away last year, and left us his farm in Maryland and a nice insurance policy. The money paid off both this house and farm."

She pointed to another photo at the end of the mantle that showed a white farm house with wooded mountains in the background. "We've hired a man to run the place, but we don't get to visit it much. It's in western Maryland over by Cumberland. It might turn out to be a good retirement place for me, or part of Karen's dowry."

"Great that you had family to be with you during your difficult times. He looks like he was a great guy to be around. He has that carefree look," I responded. But I was thinking: *who the hell says 'dowry' anymore, and especially to a guy on the first date with her daughter. And her hand is still resting on my shoulder.* Dex's little voices were invading my mind!

"Hi, Mark. Ready for an adventure?" Karen had quietly entered the room and was standing right behind us. Her mother quickly pulled her hand off my shoulder and we turned to face Karen.

"Always ready for an adventure with a beauty contest winner," I said as I looked at Karen and smiled my best smile. She did look nice, and blushed slightly at the compliment. Her glowing red hair was pulled back behind her shoulders, falling free, and the plaid skirt and white blouse with a pewter Celtic knot enhanced her Irish look. She just needed the slight accent to be a true colleen from the old sod. "What do you have planned for us this evening?"

"Nothing dangerous. At least for the first date." She grinned. "How about a tour of some of the fun places to spend time, followed by a meal at my favorite spot?"

"Outstanding plan. Let's go!" I said. I promised Laura we wouldn't be out too late, and we headed out for the adventure. Karen was an excellent navigator, and in no time I had seen a good selection of restaurants and places for young adults to hang out. Many were the types of places that attracted the college crowd, which Mark Williams would normally be drawn to for their services. So I logged most into memory in case I needed them again.

We ended up at a place just off Hampton Blvd, a few miles south of the main gate of the base. The parking spot was about a block away from a restaurant called the Red Mule Inn. Fittingly, the sign over the door was a caricature of a big red mule as seen from the back, his head looking back at us, flashing a huge grin. Music drifting out of the door was not too loud and featured a male singer with an acoustic guitar. A sign in the window said that Groove was playing there that week.

We were able to get a table near the back of the place. At least it was a bit quieter there, since Groove was near the front door. Karen went over all of her favorites on the menu and we placed the order she suggested. I was impressed by the quality of the Reuben. And Groove was actually good; he sounded like Simon without the Garfunkel guy. Easy to see why this was Karen's favorite place.

We had a good chance to talk about ourselves and share likes and dislikes. My early impression was accurate: she was more assertive than her mother. We talked about how she was affected by the loss of her father and that it had caused her mother to have fits of depression for a couple of years. It was only with the help of her great-uncle in Maryland that her mom had gotten past the grief.

I told her I'd seen his photo on the mantle. I asked her about the farm, and she openly told me about the insurance policy her mom had received. Karen loved the farm and hoped to move there someday. But for now, she felt she needed to hang around near her mother just in case she had a depression relapse … even though she really wanted to head to the farm. She felt guilty that she wanted to leave her mother, who might need her.

Getting down to a question that was bugging me, I asked Karen what her mother meant about her not dating much. Obviously, a cutie such as her should have a line of guys outside the house. I could see I hit a nerve with that question, but Karen seemed comfortable talking about the differences between her and her mother.

Just like Karen felt guilty about hanging around for her mother, her mother felt guilty about hanging around. Laura kept hoping Karen would get serious with someone, get married, and move out. And Laura hated thinking she was holding Karen back from a happy life. Both had major guilt issues.

I told her about the dowry comment and she rolled her eyes and laughed. "At least you were strong enough to hang around after that. I tried to date a guy last year and he told me he felt the flu coming on and bolted out the door right after Mom said that."

"His loss," I replied, and we shared a pleasant laugh.

As we finished our meal and listened to the music, I realized that guilt was eating at the back of my mind. I wondered what Kelly was doing, and wanted her here right now. But I had to focus on the case.

It seemed too early to push the real questions I had about these two, so I just stuck to the standard first date topics. We talked more about the farm and other things. Conversation was easy with Karen, and it was a challenge to keep reminding myself that I was looking into the actions of her and her mother and wasn't just on a date with a cute, sweet girl.

Fortunately, it quickly became time to get her back home, so I could pull back from those inviting green eyes. As we walked out of the Mule and headed to the car, Karen locked arms with me. And when we reached the car, she stretched up and kissed my cheek.

"I hope we can get together again soon, Mark. You are probably not the kind of guy I want to marry any time soon, much to my Mom's disappointment, but you sure are fun to be around."

"Ditto, Karen, on the fun part, but I think the first date is rushing the marriage decisions a bit, don't you?" And that one earned a good laugh and a punch in my arm from Karen.

As we drove back to her house, we discussed a possible date the next weekend when there was a special Irish festival event going on at ODU campus. We'd talk about it at lunch next week—perhaps on Monday. And I considered that the Monday lunch might be a good place to bring up what she was doing at JAG and get her comfortable talking about it. Sometimes opening the door is the hardest part of any interrogation.

I walked her to the door and thanked her for a great night. As I turned to leave, Karen wrapped her arms around me and softly kissed my lips. "Thanks for a great evening, Mark. I look forward to seeing you again soon," she whispered, then released her hold on me and went into the house. Yep, she was an assertive one. But she wasn't Kelly. And Pat's kiss test just proved it.

41

AFTER THE NORMAL MORNING ROUTINE, I headed back to the agents' area for more file reading and hopefully some important clue finding. Granted, it had only been three days, but I'd expected to uncover a lot more by now. Of course, having the agents out of the office in pairs for the last three days, doing their firearm quals, taking training, and working cases cut into the amount of info I could pick up from them.

Now that the pistol quals were done, there was an opportunity to get more info. Sam Maker mentioned the previous afternoon that they'd planned a meeting for that morning, since everyone would finally be back in the office. The agenda was to cover all open case files and get everyone up to speed on their statuses. From my position across the room, reading files, I had a great chance to learn what was happening in the field.

They got started a bit later than expected, since Tasker and Mabry had been called out early to pick up a suspected drug user from the SPs. As soon as they got back into the office, Sam called the meeting and they all headed over to the conference table.

There was one open rape case from Monday night that Driscol and Knox were working. A WAVE had been attacked after leaving the enlisted men's club. She was hospitalized for a day with a few cuts and bruises, and the physical exam showed she had been raped. Several suspects were being investigated and they felt a line-up would be helpful. They scheduled it for Friday afternoon.

The bulk of the open caseload were drug cases. Most of these cases were low-end users who stupidly got caught using and/or possessing. Most of the time it was easy to catch the users; getting the dealers was the problem. And too few of them were being locked up.

As I listened to the discussion, I decided there was information I needed to share that might help the agents get their jobs done. And get more of the drugs off the base. I just had to be careful not to put too many cards on the table and reveal I was more than an entry-level Yeoman. So I grabbed my coffee mug as if heading to the mess, and as I walked by the conference table, I slowed and looked at Sam.

"Got something to add, Mark? Or just nosey?"

"Probably a little of both. Sam, you know about my education at Georgia Tech. Do the rest of the guys know?"

"No, I never shared that with them. They liked your coffee so much I didn't want them to be afraid of you because of your vast knowledge," Sam answered in a friendly sarcastic way. "Troops, Yeoman Mark 'Coffeeman' Williams had completed most of the criminal justice courses at Georgia Tech before signing up for Uncle Sam's Seagoing Country Club. So he has a lot of book knowledge about evil people, as well as a great coffee recipe. What's on your mind, Mark?"

"I am the NISO 'fly on the wall' around here, so I couldn't help but notice that most of the cases you're discussing today, and many of those in the files I've been reading, are on the low-end drug users and not the middle dealers or the high-end dealers."

Tasker jumped in, "Thanks for stating the obvious, college boy."

"Darrell, you have to establish a baseline in any discussion, all right?" I continued on before he could respond. "Most all of the closed cases mention y'all staking out the area where the druggie told you he bought the drug, but no success from the stakeout, right?"

Maker spoke before anyone else could. "True, Mark. No one is ever around. So?"

"One of the case studies I read in school talked about the dealers using as small as a two-week and up to a thirty-day rotating schedule for locations. They tell the 'buyer of the day' where they'll be tomorrow, but no other info is passed on. So if the buyer skips 'tomorrow' he has to hunt around for a dealer. That forces the buyer to make daily buys so he will know where the dealer will be the next day. And it keeps the amount of drugs the user has on hand way down, in case they're arrested. Have you considered that?"

Everyone was looking at each other around the table. Faces showed quizzical looks and shoulders were shrugged. Knox was the first to speak and offered his thoughts. "I gotta admit, we never considered that. It just seemed logical that random buys were the standard, or the buyer knew the seller and would talk with him about where he would be later. Interesting theory."

"Look at this chart I prepared from the cases I've reviewed." I picked up one of the pads from my desk and laid it in the middle of the table. "It plots drug buy dates and locations, and you can see that the same spots are used frequently, but while the date pattern looks random, you can see that there is a schedule. It's just kicked off balance by switching week two and week four back and forth every five weeks. So a quick glance will not show a pattern."

I pulled out a chair after Sam pointed to it and joined the table. "Joe, you and Darrell were discussing a drug user you had picked up from his command this morning. Where is he now?"

"In interrogation. Figured we'd let him sweat a little before going after him. Why?" answered Joe.

"Where did he buy his drugs?" I asked.

Joe told me the location and I circled a different location on the plot I had dumped on the table. "Based upon this data, I suspect there will be a dealer at this location tomorrow."

"Yea, right," responded Doug as he pushed the legal pad back at me in disgust.

"How about a test of the theory? When you talk with Seaman Stupid, tell him you know the dealer he bought from and that this dealer is wanted for murder. Then tell him you plan to charge him with murder since they are 'friends.' But if he will tell you where this dealer is going to be tomorrow ... uh, scratch that. Better yet, just ask him to tell you the location where he was going to make his buy tomorrow, and then if he does, say you would tell JAG that he had cooperated and was probably not involved with the dead sailor." I shrugged and continued, "What do you have to lose?"

Joe shook his head and said, "We already read him his Article Thirty-One rights. I doubt he'll give us that info."

Again, I shrugged and said, "He isn't the sharpest knife in the drawer, so he'll probably be more concerned about a murder charge. But again, what do you have to lose?"

Sam stood up and said, "Not a damn thing, Mark. Joe and Darrell, go give it a try right now."

They left to go have some fun with Seaman Stupid and the other five kicked my idea around while looking at the data plot. I took that time to head to the coffee mess for a refill and give them a chance to say things they might not say with me present. I looked in on Dex and things were going well in the AUTOVON room.

Heading back to the agents' area, I saw Laura coming out of her office, heading my way. And for the first time in the office, she was actually smiling. "Good morning, Laura. Things going well so far today?"

"Mark, absolutely. Karen told me that she had the best time last night. Thank you so much."

"It was a true pleasure, Laura. She is such a sweet gal. We'll try to get together again next weekend if our schedules will allow. Excuse me, but I have to get back to work. Talk more later."

Opening the door, I saw seven sets of eyes staring at me. Tasker stood up, saluted, and said, "About time you got back here, Mr. College Boy, sir." The other agents broke out in laughter.

"Mark, the good news is that Clarke, or Seaman Stupid as you called him, was more than happy to avoid a murder charge and shared the location of his dealer for tomorrow. Right where your plot said he would be. Job well done on this research," announced Sam.

"Super. Now what's the bad news that usually follows the good?" I sat down and took a sip of my special brew.

Sam nodded and pointed to the data plot. "From what we understand about this, and from what we just saw with it in operation, we can figure out where the bad guys are going to be. But we need a firm starting place. We have the one guy in custody who gave us his dealer, but what about all the other dealers?"

"Since you guys get paid the big bucks, you get to do the hard work," I chuckled. "Now if I was a special agent, I'd look at the locations that have the greatest number of hits, and place undercover agents there to see who shows up the most. If a sailor is there frequently, then there's a good chance he's the dealer."

"Granted, it's a hit–miss situation and will cost some man hours, but unless you can bust additional Seaman Stupids, then that's the best option," I continued. "Perhaps the SP units can kick in some additional manpower for a short term. Or call in some of the agents from the other NISRAs. But either way it'll have to be a quiet project 'cause if the bad guys hear about any surveillance, they'll change their routine and we will be back to square one."

Everyone nodded in agreement with that last statement. They knew this was a one-time chance to put the hurt on the druggies. I had given them a plan and now they had to put it to work. Time to head back to the files and look for more info and leads on the targeting of the CIs.

42

SAM KEPT GLANCING OVER AT me after the morning meeting was over. It was beginning to feel like I might have blown my cover. Keeping my nose in the files, I hoped to convey the low-level Yeoman look. Check the reports, note anything that might help with my investigation or help the unit, sign off, and grab the next case. Repeat.

While Sam stayed in his office on the phone most of the morning, probably getting the extra manpower lined up, the other agents were busy working out a plan to thwart the druggies. Occasionally when I looked up, one would give me a thumbs-up sign for my input to the morning meeting. At least they liked something besides my coffee. The Captain might have been right: perhaps this Yeoman thing was the right career path for me.

As I was finishing up another file and contemplating a lunch break, Sam walked over to my desk. He smiled and asked, "Mark, do you have time to join me for lunch?"

"Sure, Sam. I was just heading down to the cafeteria," I replied. "Will that work for you?"

"I have a better plan. Come on." And we walked out of the office.

Rather than the crowded cafeteria, Sam drove us off base to a small family restaurant over in Oceanview. He obviously was a regular since everyone working there either waved or called his name when we entered. The décor was typical for a place near a beach, complete with gray and blue paint, fishnets hanging from the roof, and plenty of line—a nautical term for rope—used to edge the tables, counters, and even the posts holding up the roof.

We headed to a booth in the back, near the kitchen door, and took a seat. "Order whatever you want, Mark. Lunch is my treat as a 'thank you' for your input at today's meeting. Your analysis of the drug data points was first rate. It got the guys excited, since your input was the first solid thing we've had to go on in months. I really appreciate it," Sam said as he looked around. He seemed to be checking out the other diners, looking for problems.

"Glad I was able to help, Sam. Working with raw data is a fun thing for me. A lot more fun than reading all those files, I'll tell ya. But thanks, your comments are greatly appreciated. You and your crew would have figured it out without me."

"Okay, now that we have the mutual admiration BS out of the way. My question is simple: who the hell are you and what the hell are you doing here? I don't care what college you attended, that analysis is not something a 'college boy' could have worked out in … what, three days of studying the files?"

He took a drink of his coffee and continued. "And in the fifteen years I've been here, the CO has never, and I mean never, asked any of his people to look over my files. I like you, and I'm in your debt for this morning, but I have to know who the hell are you?"

Like Captain Miller had told me, Sam Maker was a good man, and a damn good agent. The Supervisory Special Agent title fit him well. Like all great seasoned agents, he'd been able to see something that shouldn't have been there and knew how and when to address the issue. My only challenge was to determine how much of the truth to tell him, because I knew he was just like Captain Miller and would know BS when he heard it.

"You're good, Agent Maker," I said with a big smile. My gut was saying this was the time to trust Sam. I hoped my gut was still right. "Sam, I'm here from NISHQ to determine if there's a leak in the NISO or NISRA that's resulting in the deaths of the CIs."

"That makes sense. It's been a thorn in my side for months now, and I was surprised HQ hadn't started an internal affairs inquiry already. But what's with the Yeoman uniform? And who are you really?"

"The less you know, the better things will be, Sam. Just stick with calling me Mark and thinking of me as just a Yeoman. By the way, I did become a Yeoman so I could fit in here and basically be ignored by most everyone. I asked the skipper to initiate the file review so I could get closer to the agents. When we looked over the problem in D.C. we figured there had to be a leak with the agents or the NISRA secretarial staff. But the NISO members do not have access to the CI list so that eliminated them. By the way, Captain Miller is aware of who I am and what I'm doing here."

"Okay. No one will get any info about you from me. What have you determined about the CI issue, 'Just a Yeoman' Mark?"

"Before I get into that, there are a couple of questions. First question … is Joe Mabry up for a promotion? I was working late Tuesday and both he and Tasker came back to the office. When I asked what they were doing, Darrell said he was coaching Joe for the next exam. He said their houses are too noisy to concentrate with the kids and all. This true?" I asked Sam.

"Very true. Joe is a great agent but he has challenges taking tests. Kinda freezes up. So Darrell is helping him cram. It's been going on for weeks now. Why?"

"Hold that thought. Second question, why do they get assigned to more drug cases than the other four guys?" I asked.

"Easy answer for that one. Until this week, they were the only agents I had that have completed the training on the new regs regarding drug evidence collection and testing procedures. So, yes, they get assigned to drug cases more than the other agents. Steve and Clyde finished the training this week, and I hope to get Doug and John in sometime in the near future. It's so hard to find the time with the caseload we have to process," he answered.

"Sam, I was concerned about Joe and Darrell before I got here. Looking at them on paper, they look like possible suspects since they handled most of the suspicious cases, and several of the CIs were under their control. They had a great amount of access to the information. But after talking with them, doing some snooping around, and seeing the rigorous control you have over the CI lists, I'm no longer concerned about them."

Sam shook his head in frustration. "Hell, I could have told you that."

"True, but I have to make sure myself. You would have done the same," I replied.

Sam nodded in agreement and I continued, "I'm also looking at Laura Scott's daughter. She works at JAG and might have access to the CI info through the cases. And there is something just a bit off with her and her mother. After I check her out completely, the unit is cleared."

Sam smiled and picked up the check. "Good to know. Let's get back to the office and see whatever other problems we can fix before the sun sets."

43

THE AGENTS WERE STILL BUSY working on a battle plan for snagging the drug dealers when Sam and I got back to the office. I decided to stay out of their way in order to keep in my role as "just a Yeoman" and avoid getting too much attention. I knew Sam would want my input on their plan once it was finalized.

Hate to admit it, but I felt relieved knowing there were two good men who had my back in the office. Sam and Captain Miller now knew what I was really doing there. While Sam wasn't as read-in as the Captain, he was aware of the cases I was investigating and why, so he could help direct pertinent new info my way as it came in from the current investigations.

Keeping my nose to the grindstone back at my desk, by day's end I'd reviewed closed cases back to September 1970. More drug data was mined from the files as well as more information about unusual deaths of military personnel. Like with the drug information, I started gathering the data points on those cases.

Faint connecting lines were starting to appear in my mind. There were still too many holes, but things were looking good for it all to fall into place soon. I just needed one or two more pieces to show themselves. The best way to solve any problem, of course, is to go back to the beginning. Too often the obvious is overlooked, as are little things that at first seem immaterial. So as it was necessary to get back to studying the suspect board and files, I closed down the office on time and headed to the house.

As I pulled into my driveway, I suddenly remembered I was to meet Kelly at the Giant market after work. How could I forget that! My mind had been too wrapped up in case files to remember anything else that day. Good news was, it only took a few minutes to get there from the house, so I headed that way immediately. I was just a few minutes late so there was no need to panic.

Kelly was sitting in her car near the same spot she used on Saturday. I pulled in beside her car. She just sat there, so I walked over to her car. I opened the passenger door, got in, and said, "Hello, beautiful lady."

She just sat there, staring straight ahead.

"Sorry I'm late, Kelly. The work load at the office was intense and I just ran late getting out of there. Forgive me?"

"For working late, I forgive you. For the other thing, not so much," she quietly said.

"Okay, I give up. What's the 'other thing' that has you upset?" I asked. I was at a total loss.

"As I was leaving class last night, I saw you and that redhead leaving the Red Mule Inn. Looked like you two were having a great time together." With that, she started to cry softly.

The clicking of the clock on her dashboard seemed extremely loud as I sat there gathering my thoughts. Just as I had decided on Saturday, I couldn't lie to this woman about this. And I no longer wanted to keep things from her. Time to cross the Rubicon.

"Let's go, lock your car, and come with me." She started to refuse, but I continued, "Look, Kelly, words will not relieve your pain right now. I need to show you something, and it won't take long. If after seeing it, and listening to my explanation, you still want to be upset with me, then so be it. Come on." And I got out of her car and walked to mine.

Fortunately, she followed and slid into the passenger side of the Blue Beast. We drove off toward my house with Kelly sitting as close to the passenger door as she could get.

"Why are we here?" she asked as I pulled into my driveway. "Who lives here? That girl?" That was the first she had spoken since getting in the car.

"Come on" was all I said as I led her to the front door and unlocked it. "This is my house, and I need to show you something upstairs in my office."

"Your house? But you live on base. What's going on?" she said while I was hanging her coat on the hall tree. I saw her staring at what hung there: my blue officer's jacket with the LCDR gold stripes on the sleeves and my combination cover. Her face now held a dazed look. She did a quick look around the living room and glanced into the kitchen. Still confused, she asked, "Who else lives here?"

Heading to the stairs, I turned to her and said, "No one. Time for full disclosure. Come on." And I started walking up.

"Mark, stop," she said softly. "You told me the other day that I needed to trust you and I tried. I'll do better, I promise. But I was weak and jealous when I saw you with that girl last night. You do not need to prove anything. Let's leave."

"No. Your trust, your approval, and your love are too important to me. Come on." And we climbed the stairs together.

It took over an hour to explain the mission I was on, what I'd done, who I was looking into, and what my next steps would be. Seeing 'Red' on the suspect board, along with her mother and my list of concerns about them, erased most of the jealousy she held.

I warned her that there would be at least another date with 'Red' soon, as I still had concerns about her and her mother. Kelly smiled at me and nodded an okay. When I told her she now knew more than her uncle and her father, her eyes got round like saucers.

However, the biggest shock she got was me opening up about being an officer and not needing glasses. She laughed, saying she was just getting used to the idea of marrying an enlisted man with ugly glasses. Now she had to readjust all her thoughts.

I let the marriage comment go by without a follow up remark. There were still a lot of things in my life to open up about, but they would wait until the shock of that evening settled down. But that talk would be had soon.

We headed downstairs after she was completely versed about the case and walked into the kitchen. Both of us were starving after that long stressful discussion. I took some leftover rice, a few veggies, an egg, and some sliced ham from the fridge, and with the help of a few spices, did a quick batch of fried rice for our dinner. She was impressed with the quick, but tasty dinner, and even helped wash the dishes.

We moved to the living room and sat next to each other on the sofa. She laid her head on my shoulder and gave out a huge sigh. "Mark, I am so sorry I didn't trust you. It just hurt so much to see you with another woman. You warned me about her, but I didn't know how much it was going to hurt."

"I know," I replied. "The guilt of being with someone else last night was making it hard to maintain my cover and look like I was having a good time. I wanted to be with you."

We continued talking for hours. She said sitting next to me just felt right and felt like home. I agreed and gave her a soft kiss. All the stress and sadness of the early evening was completely gone, and we were at total ease with each other. Guess real love had a lot to do with that.

It was quickly approaching eleven PM, so I drove her to her car so she could get home. I followed her to the base, and after seeing her safely turn onto her street, the Blue Beast and I headed to the transient barracks.

44

I WAS HAVING ANOTHER SLEEPLESS night, as all the things Kelly and I had said tumbled around in my mind. I hadn't said anything about the marriage comment she dropped. Wondered if she noticed. The funny thing was, I felt totally comfortable with Kelly, even if she was thinking of marriage already. I just wanted to sit with her on the sofa from now on. But that was a worry for another day.

Right now I needed to worry about the fact that I just spilled my guts about a classified assignment to a woman I'd known for less than a week. And she wasn't even a member of the military. Okay, she was the CNO's daughter, and I had to admit that it was extremely doubtful she was a Russian spy or a member of a South American drug family, but I'd just broken a basic security rule.

Tossing and turning, I started thinking about all she told me Monday night. Just as I do with any case analysis, I went back to the beginning and played it all over again in my mind. Kelly came into the picture on Friday night. After meeting me, she'd overheard her uncle and aunt talking about me and possibly the mission. So the Captain broke a security rule by telling his wife things about the mission and me. Why not, I thought, he'd known her for years; he trusts his spouse completely.

While Kelly was not yet my wife, my brain seemed to have already placed her in that position. That was a fact, since I was having this discussion with myself and trying to justify my actions. Worst case scenario was that we, as a couple, didn't work out and, by the time that occurred, this mission would be over. So no harm done except to my feelings, since I cared deeply for this woman. I knew more about her after just six days than I did about Sandy, who I'd dated for over two years—and she'd worn my engagement ring for over a year of that time. I had to admit to myself that I really wanted to be with Kelly. And I trusted her with my career and my life. Sharing some secret information with someone you know and completely trust shouldn't be a problem.

"That's it!" I said out loud. *Thanks to Kelly*, I thought, *I just solved half the problem cases; I just need to figure out how to prove it.* My excitement couldn't be contained, so there was no need to stay in my rack. I shut off the alarm, dressed, and left for the NISO office at 0445 hrs.

45

I NEEDED A CHANGE OF scenery to get the creative juices flowing. Seeing the same dark gray desk and light gray walls did not help me think along different lines. So I quickly performed all the standard morning tasks, then left a note on Dexter's desk to tell the Chief I'd run out to check on a couple of issues I found in a case file. I hoped to be back in time to relieve him for lunch.

I drove over to Pier 12 and parked where I could look at the USS *Forrestal*, CV-59. This beautiful aircraft carrier makes you want to start singing the National Anthem. While I have never served on her, I knew men who had, and this ship has a ton of history. "The FID"—the *Forrestal*'s nickname, standing for First In Defense—had just returned from nine months in the Mediterranean, where it was relieved by the USS *John F Kennedy*, CV-67—known as "Big John"—out of Mayport, Florida.

Since he was assigned to the USS *John F Kennedy*, my 'A School' buddy Chuck was now on his first Med Cruise. I envied him the simplicity of his duty station. Not to make light of his important assignment as a Yeoman, but unlike me at that time, he had the pleasure of knowing, usually, what each day would bring. And I did miss our chats. It had only been a few weeks since I dropped him off in Orlando, but it seemed much longer.

Thinking of the 'Big John' brought up another memory. I met John Kennedy about a month after the election in 1960. It was a most memorable day for this teenager, filled with the pleasure of meeting the new President and anticipation for the excitement coming the next four years. Those feelings caused the pain of 22 November 1963 to be so much worse for me. He was not a perfect man, but he was a decent President. And since he was Navy in WWII, that gives him a few extra "good guy" points in my book. It is fitting that a carrier bears his name.

With this beautiful sight in front of me, it was easy to clear my mind and get down to business. So much information was pushing to get attention in my mind. It was amazing how much I'd crammed into my head that week. Events over the last couple of days had led me directly to the only obvious answer for the dead CI problem. And I realized that my epiphany a few hours ago was not only a valid answer; it was the only answer.

The time went by quickly as I worked out in my mind the best way to approach Sam about it and how to proceed after breaking the news. I needed to have a firm, workable plan to offer, or I'd end up looking like a total fool. So I ran scenario after scenario in my head until I hit upon one that should provide the evidence needed. It was not something I looked forward to doing, but there was no other way.

It was time to head back to the NIS office and get the plan in motion. I was surprised only a couple of hours had passed; it was just a few minutes after 0900 hrs. It seemed like I'd been there all morning.

As I left the parking area, it hit me that maybe, just maybe, Kelly might be at home right now. The reason I didn't know her full school schedule was that our relationship had progressed so far, and so fast, many things were falling through the cracks. I didn't even know the phone number there at the Captain's house. And now that my house phone was working and she knew all about the house, I had yet to give her that number. Not enough sleep to be thinking clearly, and that could be deadly.

I drove down the street to the Captain's house and figured I'd take a chance. Using the anchor doorknocker again, I waited less than a minute before hearing the door lock being thrown.

Mrs. Miller opened the door, gave me her welcoming smile, and said, "Well, hello Petty Officer Williams. How nice to see you. Come on in."

"Mrs. Miller, please forgive this unannounced visit. But I was hoping Kelly was available for a quick question. I have an issue at work that her contacts at ODU might help me solve. Is she around?"

"Mark, this house is open to you at any time. You are always welcome here. Humphrey should have made that clear to you by now, but I suppose he is doing his best to keep secrets secret," she said with a big knowing smile, a wink, and a nod. "Kelly is in the kitchen. Follow me, dear."

Just as I'd suspected last Friday evening, this lady was the ultimate hostess and could make anyone feel at home in an instant. I felt totally at ease in her presence, even though she knew some of my secrets. And who knew what all Kelly had shared with her about us by now.

When we entered the kitchen, Kelly was sitting at the table with a cup of coffee and the newspaper. Hair pulled back in a ponytail, she was wearing her favorite ODU sweatshirt, and her face formed a quizzical look as she studied an article in the paper.

"Good morning," I offered. Her look of surprise was close to the one from the previous night as she jumped up and gave me a hug and kiss. Seeing my surprised look, Mrs. Miller failed to hold in a chuckle and quietly vanished from the kitchen. Guess Kelly had shared some info with her aunt. And the first kiss led to an even better second one.

Kelly finally released me and purred, "Good morning, Mark. What a wonderful way to start the day." Then her face clouded over with concern and she quickly added "What's wrong? Why are you here?"

"Wrong? After that kiss, nothing could be wrong, Kelly," I replied softly. "But I am working and have a need for an ODU tour guide. Do you have time for a quick run to the campus? I want to find an ornithologist."

"What do you need a bird guy for?" she inquired.

"There was a lapel pin in the shape of a bird at one of the crime scenes, and my gut is telling me it's important. I need to know what kind of bird it is. Looks like a seagull, but has different coloring." I pulled the bagged pin from my pocket.

"No need to travel anywhere. I know a bird guru." She smiled and walked to the kitchen door. "Aunt Dorothy, can you come here a moment please?" Kelly called out.

Mrs. Miller returned to the kitchen. "What do you need, dear?"

"Mark has a bird pin he needs identified. Do you recognize this bird?"

I held the bag out to Mrs. Miller. She looked at it and quickly smiled and said, "Oh, of course. That is a seabird called the Northern Gannet. It's a big bird that is nearly as large as an albatross. Here on the pin you can see it has a sharp bill, pointed tail, and long slender wings. I'll be right back." And she left the kitchen in a hurry, heading down the hall to the study.

"Aunt Dorothy is a long-standing member of the National Audubon Society, and I bet she'll be right back with one of her bird books," added Kelly.

"That saves us a trip to the ODU. Which is good since I need to get back to the office. Some important things are coming together," I said as I took Kelly's hand into mine.

"I understand. Just know I wish I could be spending the next few hours with you, Mark. You complete me," Kelly softly said as she kissed my cheek.

Mrs. Miller returned with a large book and placed it on the counter. "Here we go, here are a couple of photos of the Gannet. What a gorgeous bird with its beautiful orange head." She then read some of the text describing the bird. "*Hunting fish is done by plunge-diving from heights. Most plunge-dives are relatively shallow, but the Northern Gannet can dive as deep as seventy-five feet since it uses its wings and feet to swim deeper in pursuit of fish. They have excellent vision, enabling them to move quickly to reach prey. Their sharp eyes also allow them to detect prey underwater.*"

I jotted down a few notes about the bird. "Mrs. Miller, thank you so much for that identification and info. It really helps with the case I'm working right now. But you ladies need to excuse me as I need to get back to the office and put this information to use," I said as I turned to leave the kitchen.

"Mark," responded Mrs. Miller, "You had better get used to calling me 'Dorothy.' Kelly and I have had several long talks and I know how important you are to her ... to ALL of us in this family. Just be careful out there." And with that, she planted a kiss on my cheek and left us alone in the kitchen.

"That 'careful' comment goes double from me, Mark. Go do what you have to do and hurry back to me. I love you, Mark," whispered Kelly as she leaned against my chest.

I could not find my voice for a moment after that show of love from these two beautiful ladies. I held Kelly closer and pressed her head against my chest. "Love ya." I leaned down and kissed the top of her head. She leaned her head back and our lips connected in a kiss that was a pure sharing of love. With that, I headed back to NISRA Norfolk.

46

WHEN I ENTERED THE NISRA agents' area, I was surprised to see all the agents there at their desks. Sam was leaning against Doug Knox's desk and seemed to be holding court with the group. All eyes turned to me as I closed the door and turned to face them.

"Mark, glad you could join us today," quipped Sam. His smile helped reduce the sting of his reproach. "Hope you had a good morning off."

"Sorry to be late getting to a meeting, Sam. I don't recall getting the memo about this one," I retorted. And with that, some of the agents broke into laughter. "What did I miss?"

"Mark, we were going over plans to identify and arrest as many drug sellers as we can in the immediate future. Your data plots provided the best starting place we've ever had, and I'm looking forward to filling the brig with these low-life scum," explained Sam. "We plan to task the SP with much of the surveillance and move as quickly as possible when they tag the bad guys."

"I suggest you keep the SP out of the loop until all the plans are made here in this office. We really don't need anyone talking about it where the bad guys can overhear," I offered. "But before we get into that, Sam, I need to talk with you about another issue. Can we use your office?"

As Sam closed the door, with all the agents looking in our direction, I knew I had a challenge ahead of me. Good news was that as an internal affairs investigator, I was used to sharing bad news with NIS agents. But my respect for Sam made this one that much harder. He sat behind his desk, and I parked in one of the chairs in front.

"Sam, I need you to keep an open mind and hold your comments for a moment, please," I started. He frowned, but nodded yes and gave the hand signal for me to carry on. "I have spent hours going over all the files associated with the dead CIs. And I think I have reached a conclusion on how the names got out there. I'm still working on the 'why' component of this problem, but I think you and I can figure that out once you hear my 'how' conclusion."

"Well, quit beating around the bush, Mark. Since we're sequestered here and not out with the agents, I suspect you think it is one of us."

"Not one of the agents, Sam. You."

"You have got to be kidding me, right?" yelled Sam as he stood up and leaned over his desk. "No way in hell would I compromise this office!"

"Sit down, Sam. You did not do anything intentional, but I do believe you have been used. Why, I don't know yet, but we can figure it out if you calm down a bit," I said softly and smiled the warmest smile I had in hopes it would defuse the situation.

"Okay, Mark. Sorry I yelled at you. But what the hell are you talking about?"

"The day I arrived back here, you took a ledger from the safe in the vault and said you had a meeting with an NPD detective. You did the same earlier this week. Correct me if I'm wrong, but I suspect that ledger contains names and information about our confidential informants. And in the spirit of agency cooperation, you shared some or all of that information with the chief of detectives of the NPD. And perhaps he shared some similar info with you. After all, you both want the bad guys off the streets and you trust each other. Right?" And with that, I folded my hands in my lap and looked down to give Sam time to gather his thoughts without a condemning look from me.

Sam lowered his head, held a fist to his mouth, and muttered. "Oh, crap. That has to be it. No agent has access to any other agents' CIs. So no one here—but me—knows them all. And yes, I did share that info with Detective Royal. But why would he want to kill our CIs?"

"The 'why' is the next thing to figure out. But step one, we need to keep this between us. I do mean you and me, for now. I hate to keep the guys in the dark, but until we come up with a plan, there's just too much of an opportunity for the guys to say the wrong thing while out in the field. Especially true if we end up working with NPD folks during the druggie crackdown."

I paused for a moment, gathering my thoughts. "Fact is, we might want to hold off arresting any of the druggies until we figure out what to do with this CI mess. For some reason, my gut is telling me they are connected. Just don't know how—or why?"

Sam let out a huge sigh and said, "You know, I so hate it when a lowly Yeoman hands me my head on a platter. Just kidding! But you are right in all respects. We need to keep this quiet, and we need to let the guys spend more time building cases against the druggies. While they do, you and I need to figure out what the hell to do with the NPD. After all this, I need more coffee. Come on." And with that Sam stood and grabbed his coffee mug.

47

ALL THE AGENTS STARED AT us as we walked toward the door with mugs in hand. John asked, "Okay, Sam, what is going on behind closed doors?"

Sam smiled and responded, "Keep your noses to the grindstone planning those drug busts, boys. Will let you know more later, I promise. We have a few more bugs to work out." And we headed to the coffee mess.

I noticed the special brew urn was low, so after filling my mug, I made a new batch. Sam shook his head, watching me add the spices to the coffee basket and fill his mug from the standard brew pot. We just stood there for a moment, enjoying the taste of the coffee and allowing the silence in the mess to let our minds go over all that had been said back in Sam's office.

Perhaps the spices in the coffee kicked my brain into higher gear, or the caffeine overcame some of the sleep deprivation, but whatever caused it, a thought ran across my mind. As the old saying goes, a light bulb clicked on. It was another one of those *eureka* moments.

"Let's go get the big gun involved," I said as I walked out of the coffee mess, took a left turn, and continued down the hall to the Captain's office area.

"What ya got on your mind? Care to share?"

"Sam, I'll be happy to share just as soon as I figure it all out myself. When you have little to go on, you go with what ya got. So here goes." I held open the door to the office of YN2 Sidney Frost—the guardian of the CO and XO—and followed Sam in.

"Sidney, has the skipper got a moment or two, and I mean right now?" I asked.

"Hi, Sam. Hold one and I'll check." He picked up the phone and pressed an intercom button. "Sir, I have Sam Maker and Petty Officer Williams asking for a few minutes of your time." He nodded and said, "Yes, sir. Right away."

After hanging up, Sidney pointed to the door and said, "He's all yours. Have fun."

The Captain was standing behind his desk when we entered. I walked to the desk and came to attention. Captain Miller said, "At ease. Have a seat. What is on your mind, Sam, or should I be asking Williams?"

Sam shook his head and replied, "Captain, Mark will have to take the lead. I've been following him for two days now and I just can't keep up."

The Captain looked at me and smiled. "Guess you have the floor, Williams. Proceed."

As concisely as I could, I let the skipper know that Sam was up to speed on what I was really doing there, and some, but not all, of my background. In addition, I gave a synopsis of my theory and that we'd just agreed that the deadly CI leak was coming from NPD and not any NIS office or personnel.

"Agreed is not the right word, Captain; he is being too kind," offered Sam. "Mark figured it out by himself and then gently let me know his findings. I am truly sorry that my mistake has cost so many lives. You can have my resignation."

"Sam, no resignations will be accepted. Based on Mark's analysis, you were doing your job and a low-life at the NPD is the guilty party here," the Captain replied, then turned to me. "Mark, I assume you have worked out a possible way to prove your accusations. Care to elaborate?"

"Sir, I'm hoping that between your experience and Sam's, y'all will be able to find any problems with my plan." And with that intro, I laid out the plan that had grown in my mind as I walked from the coffee mess to the skipper's office. The bad news was that the plan was still growing as I started to speak.

The Captain listened carefully; his somewhat blank face was partially hidden by his hands, steepled in front of his chin. Sam just kept shaking his head from side to side as I laid out the rough plan. Since the plan was just birthed, it was still small and it didn't take long to get the high points out.

Both of the men I had the utmost respect for just sat there after I finished. I suspect they were torn between thinking it was a good plan and that I was a total nut case. I kept hoping for more of the former. The silence was horrible.

The Captain finally spoke. "Mark, you know this is a dangerous plan. And there are a growing number of people who would be upset if you were injured or killed. But I think it would work. Your thoughts, Sam?"

"Yea, it will work. But I agree it is dangerous."

"Gentlemen," said the Captain as he stood, "Please join me for lunch. There we can clean our minds by talking about golf, the President's latest decision about Vietnam, or the upcoming baseball season. Anything but the subject we just discussed. The cafeteria has fried fish as today's special. My treat."

"Sidney, we will be back in about an hour or so," the Captain passed to his Yeoman as the three of us headed out the door.

48

AT LUNCH, WE DECIDED THAT the best option would be to keep all discussions and planning out of the NISO and NISRA office spaces. It wouldn't look normal for the Captain, the senior special agent, and the newest lowly Yeoman to be seen huddling around a conference table for hours.

So I offered my house as the location for all the planning. Both the Captain and Sam agreed that would be best, so I gave them the address and new phone number. I asked the Captain to pass that number on to Kelly. We decided to meet Saturday morning to put some meat on the bones of the plan.

I returned to the NISRA spaces and spent another couple of hours in the vault, going over evidence boxes from the other dead CI cases. The agents had done a great job with the cases, and nothing there provided me with any information not in the case file. The link had to be the NPD detective.

Since the agents had departed to work on cases, and Sam was nowhere to be seen, I used this quiet time to call Master Chief Bartow with an urgent request. I needed copies of all the service records of the personnel assigned to the Fleet Logistics Center Norfolk, and I needed them there by Tuesday morning. There was nothing like dumping stress on a good friend. But he said he was up to the task and would ship them overnight to my house. Great to have him as a resource.

Again, time got the best of me and by the time I closed the vault, all agents were gone. And I was the last military dude left behind. I cleaned the coffee mess and left for the barracks to quickly change into my civvies. Then the Blue Beast and I were off to the house for another weekend of work.

As I approached my house, it was impossible to ignore the red Mustang sitting in my driveway. A quick glance toward the porch showed the swing moving slowly back and forth. Kelly was waiting for me there. As I reached the porch and looked at the beauty sitting on the porch swing, warmth flowed over me. So much had happened in just a week. I couldn't resist temptation and said, "Hi honey, I'm home."

"About time, sailor," she replied as she left the comfort of the swing and hugged my neck. "I have missed you all day."

"What do you mean by that 'all day' comment? We were together at your house just over seven hours ago," I said as I checked my watch.

She snuggled my neck and whispered, "Love does not watch the clock." She released the hug and gave me a quick kiss.

"Care to join me for dinner?" I asked as I unlocked the door and held it open for her. "There has to be makings for a cold cheese sandwich on moldy bread in the kitchen somewhere."

"That will be perfect just as long as you're sitting next to me."

Once inside with the door closed and locked, we embraced and kissed properly. That kiss was something that wouldn't have been appropriate on the front porch. And like Kelly had said the previous night, it felt like home. It was a very nice feeling.

I was able to find a bit more than moldy bread and cheese in the kitchen. Dinner turned out to be penne pasta with a creamy Alfredo sauce, antipasto featuring ham, olives, cherry tomatoes, crackers, and sharp cheese, and the rest of the bottle of Chablis left over from Tuesday night. Not a huge feast, but much better than a cold cheese sandwich. With a laugh, Kelly said she was disappointed that I did not speak Italian while I was serving. I promised to work on that.

After dinner, we moved to our special spot on the sofa. We talked about the events of the day. Her aunt was excited that she could help with an investigation even if it was just providing bird information.

I asked if her uncle had passed on the house phone number and she nodded. She was surprised he now knew about the house. I explained to her that we were going to use it as a planning location for a sensitive project. And that he and Sam Maker would be here in the morning.

Like the previous night, we used this sofa time to get to know each other better. That evening we shared childhood memories. Laughter filled the room as we learned about each other and divulged all of our embarrassing stories from childhood. As an only child, she'd missed out on all the adventures and wild times of having siblings. She was anxious to meet my sister and share time with her.

We also discussed our schedules for the next week. I reminded Kelly that I'd be seeing 'Red' again that next Saturday, unless things changed. She stuck her tongue out when I mentioned 'Red,' then laughed. And I did not know how long the Saturday morning planning session was going to last, so it was hard to make firm plans for Saturday afternoon and evening.

Kelly gave me the Captain's house phone number and filled me in on her college schedule so I'd know when she was available. Right now, her class schedule was not heavy, but she was spending a huge amount of time finishing up her master's degree thesis. It was due to be submitted in a couple of weeks. In addition, she was a teaching assistant two nights a week, Tuesdays and Wednesdays.

The evening was over faster than either of us wanted it to be. As Kelly was starting to leave, I pulled a key from my pocket and laid it in her hand. "Don't read too much into this. I'm not asking you to move in or anything along those lines. But I don't want you to be left sitting on the porch swing if I'm not here. If you need time away from the Miller house, you can always hide out here. I want you to consider this your house too."

"Oh, Mark, thank you! This will make things so much easier."

"What things?" I asked. Then I noticed her smile had taken the upturn to the left—a look I now think of as the 'left hook'—indicating she'd just been caught or was up to something. "Guess I'll find out later, right?"

She just winked and kissed me goodnight.

I escorted her to her car. I felt extremely lonely as I watched the taillights of the Mustang turn the corner and disappear. Walking back into the empty house, I realized just how empty it really was without Kelly. It was the same with my personal life: empty without Kelly.

49

COFFEE WAS BREWED AND I'D made an early run to the Giant to pick up some fresh donuts and pastries, as well as orange juice. Napoleon was only half right when he said an army marches on its stomach. Of course, food is critical, even for a planning session. But Napoleon missed the other important thing that keeps any military unit going—paperwork. Pens, pencils, and legal pads were now in place on the kitchen table.

I'd brought down the copies of the files on all the dead CIs and had them ready on the table. And I'd asked Sam to bring his CI logbook and any records he'd kept on his meetings with the NPD detective. At this point, even notes on his desk calendar could help establish a time line and show possible links.

The ringing of the doorbell announced the first arrival. The Captain was there, dressed like he was ready for the golf course. Amazing how little the demeanor of a senior Navy officer changes when out of uniform: he still looked intimidating.

"Good morning, sir. Come on in. Coffee and pastries are in the kitchen right down the hall," I said as I shook the extended hand. "I thought the kitchen table there would be best for our planning."

"Nice place, Mark. I can see why Kelly feels so comfortable here," offered the Captain as he looked around. "I hope the CNO provided you with sufficient operating funds to cover it."

"Actually, sir, I am saving receipts in probably worthless hopes of some reimbursement," I chuckled. "Money is not really a problem for me right now since I do not have a family, and while on TAD last year out of the country, all of my pay went right into savings."

As we walked into the kitchen, the Captain gave out a sigh and let go of what was on his mind. "Mark, I warned you about Kelly last week. She has told me how she feels about you, and she tells me those feelings are returned. I'm not going to ask for confirmation, but I will tell you that if you do not feel the same toward her, you had better be honest with her right now."

He paused as if wondering if he should continue, then he did. "Frankly, I think she will ask you to marry her in the next week or so. That girl is a unique piece of work and a force of nature. She is her father's daughter."

"Captain Miller, I'm having a hard time believing my good fortune in meeting and falling in love with Kelly. This is happening extremely fast, I admit that, and it continues to throw me a bit off balance. But it is happening, and I'm ready for whatever our relationship creates. She has my utmost respect and all of my love." As I was saying that, the voice in my head was wondering where it came from! But I knew it came from the heart and not the head.

"Good. Best of luck, son," he said with a smile.

Before anything else was said, I was literally saved by the bell: the doorbell rang. Sam finally arrived and his timing was perfect. I wasn't sure what else I could say to the Captain, and I hoped the subject would be closed now that Sam was here.

"Nice place you have here, 'Just a Yeoman' Mark," he said with a laugh. Then he noticed the LCDR jacket hanging on the hall tree and got a puzzled look on his face. "Who all is here?"

"Just the Captain and me. Let's head to the kitchen." And I led him down the hall.

After the usual greetings and getting cups of coffee, we sat down and started into the subject at hand. Sam had brought a list of the dates when he'd met with the NPD and had discussed the confidential informants. In return, we'd been given info about those working for the police. It was all part of the mutual respect and cooperation.

We cross-checked the dates of the meetings and the CIs discussed at those times against the dates of their demises. True to our expectations, most of them died within ten days of their names being shared with the detective. But that could have been a coincidence. That is, if you believe in those things.

I asked Sam to tell me about his contact. The Captain and I needed to better know who we were accusing.

"NPD Detective Collin Royal was promoted to captain, Chief of Detectives, in late summer 1970. He'd been with the force for about eight years, and before that he was with a small-town department in South Carolina. From all indications, he has been a good cop and played by the rules. Nothing seems off about him or his actions," Sam said. "He's married. Age is around forty-five. Medium build with just the start of a gut showing. Graying black hair. Slight southern accent. Not a bad looking guy, but not movie star material."

"After his promotion, I was in his office to discuss a case where we both wanted the same guy, an ex-sailor who had committed crimes both on and off base. It was then, around the end of October, when he suggested we get together frequently to share case info and work together. He said he wanted to keep Norfolk safe." And with that, Sam shrugged.

"And a couple of weeks later an Ensign, who was ready to become an informant, is murdered," I interjected.

"Right. And that was the first of the unsolved cases."

The Captain finished a pastry and took a sip of coffee. He'd been quiet as he listened to all Sam had to say, but now he jumped directly to the hard part. "Mark, there has to be another way to draw this man out besides putting yourself out there as bait. If he is the one, so far he's done a great job of killing without leaving any trail."

"Wish there was, Skipper. But I sure cannot think of one. No way will I allow any more of our CIs to become targets. We need to know if he's the guy targeting them, and if he is, we need to find out why."

Sam continued, "Besides, Captain, Royal knows all of our agents by sight, so we cannot use one of them undercover."

"And if we work this right, we can hopefully arrest him and one or two associates, before they can pull the trigger on me," I said. "Too bad we do not have enough to get a wiretap warrant, so the best we can do is surveil him from the time Sam gives him my name until he acts."

"And hope he doesn't handle it over the phone," Sam added.

We continued on for another hour, working out the details of the trap. Sam and I seemed to be finishing each other's sentences, though the Captain was the judge we needed to convince that our plan was solid.

It came together quickly, but it was probably as solid a plan as we could bring forth under the circumstances.

But the Captain had one other suggestion. He wanted to bring in an agent from one of the NISRA offices in the Midwest. Maybe find a new agent that had a youthful look about him so he could disguise as a low-level enlisted man. Since no one local would know him, he could be planted as a CI, the same as me. That way, there would be two targets to entice the bad guys to come out, and there would be two guys to watch each other's backs on the inside.

And we decided to put the plan into action toward the end of that next week, with Sam starting the ball rolling by approaching Royal with info about his new CI: me. He would tell him I was going to be inserted into the Fleet Logistics Center office to snoop around for possible drug connections. Since I was new to the base, very few people would know about my association with NIS. And Sam would make sure Royal was aware I slept in the transient barracks.

Then early the following week, Sam would do the same thing with the unknown agent. Assuming we could find one willing to take the risks. Before we could shoot holes in that plan, the Captain walked to the phone and dialed a number from memory.

"Good morning, Admiral Chance. Hump Miller here. Hope I have not caught you at a bad time." And after a short pause to listen to the Admiral in charge of NIS, the Captain continued on to explain to the Admiral where he was, who he was with, what we had planned, and what we needed. "Thank you, sir. Yes, I will be at this number for the next two hours." He gave the Admiral my number and hung up.

"I think that went well," said the Captain. "Mark, the Admiral sends his best regards and is happy that progress is being made here."

After Sam and I recovered from the surprise of the Captain's quick action on his idea, we decided to not do any drug busts the upcoming week. Since it looked like the dead CIs were connected by drugs, we might spook Royal with our busts. Royal had the priority right now.

Our work was interrupted by the doorbell. An overnight delivery service had a package I needed to sign for that had come from D.C. David had come through for me better than expected, and I now had the records of all those in the Logistics Center to read and memorize.

After we went over everything at least two more times, we all sat back to give it one last quiet contemplation. It was at this time that Sam brought up something on his mind that was bothering him.

"What is with the Lieutenant Commander's jacket and cap in the foyer? Someone else live here?" he asked me.

The skipper laughed and said, "I told you, Mark, that Sam is sharp. I think it is time to let him into the tent."

I nodded and signaled the Captain to take the lead.

"It's hard to believe when you look at him, but Mark is actually a Lieutenant Commander who works at the NISHQ. He is in charge of the internal affairs division. And yes, he is years older than he looks."

Sam sat up straight, and looked at me. "Are you telling me you are *the* Marcus Colt? I've heard about you, but never wanted to meet since that would imply an IA investigation is underway. Crap, no wonder you're three steps ahead of me all the time. Your reputation precedes you and, from what I have seen this week, you really are that good."

I nodded again and smiled. "Thanks, Sam. If your crew had all the free hours I used to analyze all that old data, they would have come to the same conclusions. But too many active cases got in their way."

I sipped some coffee and continued, "I am sorry for the subterfuge, but I needed to be in your office space with the least amount of disruption. I cooked up the file check project as a way to hang around and get to know your agents. Face it, your guys were okay talking shop around 'just a Yeoman' but they would have been as quiet as a tomb if I was there as an internal affairs investigator."

"That's true," he responded. "But I'm glad you are here, and because of that, we are finally making progress on this case, and on the drug pusher issues. More great work with that data plot you generated." Sam went on to explain to the Captain the research I'd shared with the agents and how they could now focus on the dealers instead of just the users.

Since noon was fast approaching, I got up to do a quick check of the refrigerator to start planning some lunch while they went over the drug plans. I hadn't expected to be sitting around for a couple of hours waiting for the Admiral to call back. But these things happen. Worst case, I could run to the Giant while the skipper and Sam waited for the call. But before I could check the fridge, I heard the lock on the front door click, and the door opened.

I walked down the hall just in time to see Kelly stumble in, juggling her car keys, purse, several large pizza boxes, and also carrying a couple of six-packs of beer under one arm. I ran over and grabbed the beer right before she dropped it.

She smiled, winked, and said, "Hi honey, I'm home."

We carried the pizza and beer to the kitchen, laughing all the way.

"Hi, Uncle Humphrey. Hey, Sam, how are you?" asked Kelly as she sat the pizza boxes on the counter. "Anyone ready for lunch?" Then she got hit with another bout of laughter when she looked at Sam.

Sam sat there with a totally flabbergasted look on his face. The Captain was chuckling, and I said, "Guess all the horses are out of the barn now, Captain."

"Are you calling me a horse, sailor?" she demanded to know as we all, except Sam, laughed uncontrollably.

50

LUNCH WENT WELL AFTER SAM finally recovered from the shock of seeing Kelly stroll into the house and give me a kiss. Fact is, I was having trouble believing it myself, so I know he was totally confused. But as a professional agent, he rolled with the flow and was soon acting like our relationship had been a thing for months. I could tell the Captain was slightly enjoying Sam's discomfort, and I knew Dorothy would know all about it in a few hours.

After a morning of intense thinking and planning, it was nice to have friendly chatter over a good lunch. The pizza was hot and the beer was cold: a perfect combination. Kelly had been bouncing around the kitchen grabbing plates and napkins from cabinets like she'd lived there for years, which seemed to amaze her uncle and shock Sam anew. I just sat there and smiled. *Life is really good.*

As we were wrapping up lunch, the phone rang and the Captain was right there to answer it. It was the Admiral returning his call and, from the look on the skipper's face, all was going according to his plan. They chatted for a few moments and ended the call after sharing some family information, including the fact that Kelly and I were now dating.

Kelly was grinning ear to ear hearing that. I guess you could call what we'd been doing dating. I just hoped Admiral Chance didn't think I was down here goofing off chasing skirts. The Captain was smiling as he hung up the phone.

"Okay, we have our new volunteer: Roger Robinson. He will fly in from NISRA Chicago on Wednesday afternoon, so I think we should sequester him here and use this place to bring him up to speed that night. That all right with you, Mark?" asked the Captain.

"Certainly, sir. I'll pick him up from the airport and bring him straight here. After Sam and I do the brief, I can run him over to the transient barracks to get settled. Then it will be up to Sam to get him integrated into the command. At least he and I will have a chance to get to know one another before the fun starts."

Now it was Kelly's turn to look confused. "Who is this and what has he volunteered to do?" The silence was deafening.

Sam and the skipper simultaneously decided it was time for them to head home and salvage the rest of their Saturday. I thanked them for their time and planning, and promised to call each of them if I thought of anything else before Monday. It felt a bit strange for Kelly and me to stand on the porch and wave goodbye to her uncle. I had officially followed Alice through the looking glass into a new world.

Heading back inside to clean up the kitchen, Kelly said, "Except for Sam being ready to pass out, I think our first entertaining as a couple went well, don't you?"

"Oh, yea! Surprises can be fun, but now I suspect Sam really hates them," I offered with a giggle. I told her about Sam getting the news about who I was, and how that revelation had also surprised him. Poor guy had a rough day of shocks and surprises.

Cleaning went quick with the two of us attacking it. And as we wrapped up the remaining pizza and stuffed it into the fridge, she finally approached the elephant in the room. "Please tell me what's going on. Who is Roger and what has he volunteered to do? Are you involved also?"

I'd known this question was coming. I took a second to answer while I considered how much I should tell her.

"Kelly, he and I will be doing some undercover work starting the end of next week. It might be dangerous, but probably not. It has to be done, and I'll be part of it. I'll let you know my schedule as soon as I get it finalized, but there will be many nights where I'll be staying on base at the transient barracks. We won't be able to see each other during this assignment. Can we leave it there?" I asked.

"Here is that 'hard part' again, right? Lots of trust and now lots of worry."

I held her close and agreed, "Yea, this is the hard part. The good news is that I'm not heading overseas for a nine-month tour on a carrier or heading up the rivers of Vietnam. This is not that bad; you can handle it."

Kelly pulled away from me and stood with hands on hips in a defiant position. "Lieutenant Commander Colt, know this. My uncle and father are great men because of the Navy. I am who I am because of those two great men and having been raised as a Navy brat. As your girlfriend, and soon to be your wife, I expect you to do your duty as the Navy requires, and I'll do mine as a Navy spouse. Just remember I am here, waiting for your safe return no matter the length of deployment. Always. Got it?"

"Yes, ma'am, message received loud and clear," I said as I took her hands in mine. "And I did hear the 'wife' part of your message. Is that a marriage proposal?"

Her mouth turned up with the left hook again, and she said, "Not yet, but I am building up to it. Think you can handle it, sailor?"

"I'll let ya know. But it's looking positive so far," I answered as I pulled her into my arms again. "Now you remember we have this evening, all day tomorrow, then Monday and Thursday nights before I vanish for a short while."

"I'll make the most of those hours, Mark."

51

THE COFFEE URNS WERE PERKED and the water was hot for the tea drinkers. Running over to the radio shack for the stack of traffic and down to the front desk for the skipper's newspapers didn't take long. The overnight download from HQ was running through the Teletype machines when Dexter arrived and took over the AUTOVON room tasks.

"Have a good weekend?" Dexter asked as he separated strips of paper tape for the incoming files.

"Just another day in paradise," I grinned and headed out the door to start work with the NISRA agents. Most of my weekend *was* time spent in paradise. Just wish there had been a few more days sandwiched between Saturday and Sunday.

Sam had decided he would brief his guys that morning and he wanted me there. The plan was to continue gathering data from the undercover SPs about the druggies, but not make any arrests just yet. But the hard part would be to design surveillance for a potentially dirty city cop, and while doing that, keep eyes on two undercover CIs to keep them safe from the bad guys.

The Norfolk agents would take the lead on this task force since they knew the area better; they'd be called the Core Unit. With Sam in overall command, the other six Norfolk agents forming the Core would keep their regular partners and take eight-hour slots as shift leaders, with one group in charge of following the dirty cop and the other group in charge of protecting the undercover CIs.

Sam made the assignment decisions and appointed Driscol, Tasker, and London to cover Detective Royal. He decided that Knox, Mabry, and Crosser would be in charge of the protection details.

But the key to a successful task force is manpower. NISRA Norfolk did not have enough people, so Captain Miller was on the phone that morning calling in agents from the various NISRAs under NISO Norfolk. He couldn't strip those NISRAs bare, but could move a good percentage to Norfolk for the big planning session on Tuesday afternoon. When things started for real, probably the next weekend, the agents would be scheduled to help out the Norfolk Core Unit on rotating shifts so no NISRA would be too short of staff.

He also planned on calling in a few favors from the COs of a couple other NISOs, to see if they could spare an agent or two. Add to that a few warm and highly trained bodies from the SEAL units stationed at Little Creek, and that should round out a competent protection group for the two dummy Cis, called *operatives* by the agents. I guess the word 'fake' would have been a better choice than 'dummy,' but that morning I was thinking I was a dummy for coming up with this plan. So I would stick with that term.

The Norfolk crew had been briefed and their hundreds of questions asked and answered—when possible. So much wouldn't be known until the plan was in play. Winging it would be dangerous, but there were no other options.

But for now, the Core had to start laying out surveillance schedules, focusing on both the Fleet Logistic Center and the transient barracks as possible places for the attempted assassinations. That is, assuming our speculation was accurate and Royal was the guilty party.

52

WHILE THE CORE UNIT WAS doing its magic with scheduling and prep, I asked Sam if I could use his office for a private call to D.C. He agreed and walked out, closing the door. He was heading over to the officers' club to meet with the commanding officer of the Fleet Logistics Center. They needed to coordinate the placement of the two operatives into the system without raising suspicions. I picked up his phone and dialed a special number.

"Office of the Chief of Naval Operations, Master Chief Bartow speaking, how may I be of assistance, sir?" barked the gatekeeper to the CNO.

"Good morning, Master Chief. SA268 calling; got time to take a few notes to pass to the boss? He needs to know the status ASAP."

"For you, always, Mr. Colt. How are things in the beautiful Tidewater area?"

"There are too many adjectives needed to fully describe it, Master Chief. Just know it is never boring. You can make the decision on how well things are after I give you my report. It has been a hell of a week." I proceeded to give him an update in concise language and in chronological order. I could hear his IBM Selectric clacking away, so I knew he was typing my comments rather than taking shorthand. This was a much faster way to get the info to the Admiral.

When I finished, David said, "I'll get this to the Admiral immediately. Sounds like you have some of this mess under control. At least you have a potential target and a plan of attack. Anything else I can do for you?"

"Now comes the fun part. I need to speak with the Admiral about a personal matter. Is he available? Guess I'll need about five minutes."

"Anything I can help you with, Marcus? You know I'm here for you," asked the Chief with concern in his voice.

"No, David, this is strictly between the big guy and me. Nothing bad, at least I don't think so. He might think it is, so have the fire extinguisher handy just in case."

"Can do. I'll connect you now. Good luck!"

In less than thirty seconds, the Admiral answered. "Gallagher. What do you need, Colt."

"Good morning, Admiral. I will get right to the point, sir. I am requesting your permission to ask your daughter to marry me. I have completely fallen for Kelly and I need to know that you will accept and approve it, sir."

The silence was deafening as I held the phone to my ear. I didn't dare look at my watch because I didn't want to know how long it was before the Admiral responded. I should have done this in person, but time and distance were not on my side.

"Granted," he said with a chuckle. "I have to tell you that based on the comments I have gotten from her uncle this past week, I half expected you to be telling me about your elopement that she planned over this past weekend. Seems that some very interesting things have happened in Norfolk and you have had a most unusual week. David just laid your report on my desk. Tell him your good news while I give it a quick read."

"Bartow here. What's up, Mr. Colt?"

"David, I just asked for, and received, permission to ask the Admiral's daughter to marry me. He seems okay with it. What do you think?"

"As her godfather, I think you need my permission also, Mr. Colt."

I sure did not see that roadblock coming. Knowing the relationship between the CNO and David, I should have expected it. "Is that a problem for you, Master Chief?"

"Mr. Colt, if I may borrow the word I just heard from the Admiral, 'granted.' You two are a perfect match, and I am surprised I did not notice it until now. I promise you that your life from this moment forward will be extremely interesting!" said the Chief with a laugh in his voice. "Here is the Admiral, sir."

"Colt, I like this report. I will call Captain Miller and see if there are any more personnel or other support he needs. I might be able to find one or two folks to help out," said the Admiral formally.

Then he switched to a more friendly, fatherly tone. "Ask Kelly to give me a call soon after you ask her. I know her mother will be thrilled, and I want Kelly to hear my feelings about it all directly from me. Take care of yourself, Marcus, and be careful."

And with that, the line went dead as the CNO is not one for extending small talk. I never had the chance to thank either one of them for their blessing. Interesting.

53

SITTING AT SAM'S DESK AND looking at the phone, my head was spinning and my emotions were a total disaster. Happiness, excitement, fear, concern, joy, worry, and a few others were all vying for control over my body. I needed to handle a few personal things so I could hopefully clear my mind and get back to getting the bad guys off the street.

I picked up the phone and called the Captain's Yeoman, Sidney Frost. "Hey, Sidney, Williams here. Does the skipper have a minute for me?"

Sidney explained that the Captain had already left for lunch at the Officer's Club with the CO of the Shore Patrol Office. He would let me know when the skipper returns. I thanked him and hung up. Might as well grab some lunch too.

As I walked into the cafeteria I saw a flash of red hair: Karen was leaving the cashier and heading to a table. Laura was nowhere to be seen. I quickly grabbed a prepared sandwich and a can of soda then walked toward her.

"Nice to see you again, Karen. May I join you?"

Her smile was encouraging and she replied, "Of course, Mark. Wonderful to see you remembered we had discussed meeting for lunch today." There was not a hint of sarcasm in her voice. "I probably should have called you earlier today with a reminder."

"You are hard to forget, lady. Although I admit getting away from the office today was a challenge—it's so hectic up there today—but glad I made it. How go things in the JAG offices; anything exciting you can talk about?"

While it looked like the city cop was the leaker, I still hoped to open a door for a line of indirect questions that could shine light on her access to our CIs. As the saying goes, it ain't over until it's over. And who knows, there might be multiple leakers. At least that was a consideration I had before arriving in Norfolk.

"Nothing as exciting as what you do at NISO ever happens at JAG. By the time we see the cases, your agents have had all the fun and we just get the boring legal stuff," she replied between bites. "My job is doing the boring paperwork for all the witnesses. I set up their orders to get them here if they are military, and get the subpoenas ready for signature and distribution."

"Well, it might be boring, but it is critical for the legal process," I offered. "Do you get to see any info about the witnesses? You know, what they know, or anything like that? I bet that would make it more exciting."

"No, I just get their names, addresses, and case numbers. From that, I dig up the date of the trial and then spend time typing the paperwork. Like I said, it is downright boring. I bet you see the juicy stuff there at NISO. I tried to get Mom to talk about it, but she hates talking shop."

"Some of what we see is downright disgusting. It's amazing what people will do to other people—or even themselves. The other day, one of the files contained a complete set of autopsy photographs from a suicide case. Eight-by-ten inch glossy photos with way too much detail. The stuff nightmares are made of, I tell ya."

She grimaced and said, "Time to change the subject. Do things still look good for us to attend the festival this next Saturday?"

In my mind, the answer was: *only if you want to be a target*, since by then Royal would know I was a threat to him and whoever he worked with. Fortunately my lips had the right answer for her: "Sorry, but it's not looking good. I've been tasked with helping the NISRA agents on a case. They need a low-level enlisted man to go undercover. They are trying to flush out a bad guy and I volunteered to help. So I'll be working over the weekend."

I could tell that was not the answer she expected or wanted, so I decided to try something. "I do have a backup plan. Have you met my fellow

Teletype guru, Dexter? He is a Second Class Yeoman who transferred in from the Philippines a couple of months ago."

"No, I have not. Why?"

"Well, Karen, you and Dex have a lot in common, especially when it comes to the love of farming. You want to move to your farm in Maryland and Dex was raised on a farm in Missouri. Let me see what I can work out. Okay?"

"Sure, Mark. Like I said the other night, you are fun to be around, but I can't see us being serious. Can you?"

"No, and it is time for honesty. My heart belongs to a lady named Kelly. Being with you has been a great time and you are downright adorable, but it has also made me realize how much I miss Kelly. Can you forgive me?"

"Nothing to forgive, Mark. I just hope that one day I'll find a guy that makes me feel that way and feels that way about me as well. I have only the best wishes for you and Kelly. She is one lucky lady."

We finished lunch talking about the upcoming festival and Scottish music. I realized that our friendship was strong, and that the concern I'd had about Karen being a leaker was no longer valid. She didn't have access to the CI names. And there was no reason for her to be a leaker. Another name marked off the suspect board.

54

WHEN I ARRIVED BACK IN the NISRA agents' room, my phone was ringing. Sidney was calling to let me know the Captain had returned from lunch and was available to talk, if I hurried.

I hung up the phone and dashed down the hall to the other end of the building. When I reached Sid I thanked him again for his help, and he told me to go right in. I knocked twice and awaited the 'enter' call before opening the door.

I walked to the desk, came to attention, and said, "Thank you for seeing me, Captain."

"At ease, Mark. Have a seat please," the Captain said as he pointed to a chair. "I was hoping to chat with you before I returned a call to the CNO that came in while I was having a lunch meeting. At lunch, I met with the CO of the base SP unit. We will get all the help we need from them."

"Great news, sir. I tried to reach you earlier about the CNO, but you had already left. Glad we have the chance to talk before you call him back." I felt like I was squirming in my seat even though I knew I was sitting completely still. Nerves will do that to you.

"Captain, I called the CNO earlier today to give him an update on the progress with this investigation as he'd requested from the onset. In addition, I asked for, and received, his permission to marry Kelly if she will have me." And I waited for the reaction.

"Wonderful! I suspected she would be asking you before the weekend was over," he exclaimed.

"Well, she came damn close, but did not say the actual words. And the CNO thought I was calling him to tell about our elopement over the weekend," I said with a laugh.

And then I became serious. "Sir, I'm a bit old fashioned and believe getting her father's blessing is critical. Now, I am hoping I have yours too. I know the love and respect that Kelly has for you and Dorothy, and I will never do anything that compromises that now or in the future."

The Captain looked down at his desk and slowly shook his head from side to side. I feared that there was a negative reply coming, something like *let's wait to see if you get killed this next week*, so I stiffened up when he started to speak.

"Mark, you have just reinforced the CNO's earlier comment about you being a man of great integrity. While some might ask the father for permission, I don't believe anyone other than you would consider asking an uncle. I told Dorothy Saturday night that this was coming. Dorothy and I are extremely happy to wish you both the greatest happiness in your marriage."

"Thank you, Captain. That means a lot to us both."

"Now back to work. What does the CNO want? Give me a head start before I make the return call, Mark."

"I believe he will be offering more personnel to help with the surveillance, and just about any other support you think we might need."

"Great. Sit there while I make the call."

55

I FIGURED IT WOULD PROBABLY take a while for the Captain and CNO to get past the personal greetings before digging into the support needed for the upcoming task. So as they started their conversation, I stepped out to Sidney's desk and called Sam. I figured he needed to be in on this conversation. He agreed, showing up almost immediately.

When we went back into the Captain's office, he gave Sam a thumbs up and pointed to the chairs in front of his desk. "Yes, Admiral, Marcus just pulled Supervisory Agent Sam Maker into the office to join the conversation. I'm switching to speaker phone so we can all be up to date at once."

In the short period I was out of the office, the Captain had spoken with the CNO, who had routed the call to his admiral in charge of logistics and planning. The CNO had instructed that admiral to avail us of whatever assets we'd need. It's very nice to have multiple friends in high places. This admiral also set up a conference call with Admiral Chance at NIS HQ.

So for the next two hours, the five of us worked out a plan where additional agents would be brought in from other NISOs starting the next week. We felt that by that time, our available NISO Norfolk agents and SP support, who started late this week, would need extra relief from the 24/7 surveillance.

After the call, I asked the Captain to brief Chief Giatano on the highlights of the mission to let him know that, starting Wednesday, he would need to assign the morning duties to someone else.

"Marcus, perhaps now is the time for Lieutenant Commander Colt to be in proper uniform around here."

"Not yet, Captain. We are getting enough sideways looks with the three of us meeting behind closed doors and going to lunch," I answered. "I'm keeping that down to a minimum by telling them we're discussing my evaluation of the NISRA records. Since there is a modicum of truth to that, it keeps them happy and reduces the questions."

I continued, "I would like to keep people around here thinking I'm just a Yeoman for a while longer. Releasing my true identity might generate too much talk, which could get outside these office walls way too quickly. That might jinx things with the mission."

"My agents know you are more than 'just a Yeoman' but not how much more. I'll instruct them to keep even that under their hats for now. I don't foresee a problem with them," said Sam.

"So be it," ordered the Captain and with that, the meeting was over.

As I walked back up the hall toward the NISRA office spaces, I ran the general plan over in my head. I was to be inserted into the office staff of the Logistics Center on Friday morning. Their chief Yeoman had been briefed by Sam and the logistics CO, and they'd provide the cover I needed with the rest of the office staff. I'd be working in the same spaces as Ensign Appleton before she was killed.

Then their chief Yeoman would be doing the same thing with Robinson when he reported on Monday, posing as a seaman working in the shipping/receiving area. He would be in the area where SK3 Walter King worked before his demise. We figured these were likely spots for us to observe anything unorthodox going on.

The Core agents were figuring out where and when to place the watchers, who hopefully would be keeping Roger and me alive. I *really* wanted that part of the mission to succeed. They'd be sharing that info at the meeting the next day.

We still had several days to put the final touches on all the plans, so when 1600 hrs rolled around, I decided my day was over and started the usual shutdown procedures. But I paused when shutting down the

AUTOVON room and, using the phone at my desk, called the Captain's house in hopes of finding Kelly there.

A lovely female voice answered. "Hello, Mrs. Miller. This is Mark. May I speak with Kelly if she is available?"

"And a very good afternoon to you, Yeoman Third Class Williams. If you insist on being formal with me, even after I told you to call me 'Dorothy,' then I must be just as formal in return," she said with a laugh in her voice.

"Touché, Dorothy. Well played. Sorry, I'll strive to do better." And we shared a good laugh.

"Sorry, Mark. She left earlier today and said she'd much to accomplish before the sun sets, but that is all she shared. No idea where she is right now. She normally does not have classes on Mondays."

"I suspect I have an idea where she is. But first, I need to run something by you. Earlier today I asked for, and thankfully received, permission to ask Kelly to marry me from both her father and her uncle. As I explained to the Captain, knowing your relationship with Kelly, I cannot do so without your blessing, as well. Do I have it, Dorothy?"

"Of course you do, Mark! I am so excited. I told Humphrey, after you left here that first Friday night, that this was coming. Now go find her and get busy asking!" she replied with happiness in her voice. And I followed orders and headed out.

Performing my usual ritual, I changed clothes at the transient barracks before driving to my house. However, this time I left the plaid shirt hanging and grabbed a dress shirt and sports jacket.

56

My hunch was right. As I rounded the corner onto my street there was the bright red Mustang sitting in my driveway. Yep, she was making good use of that key I gave her. Big smile time.

As I walked up the porch steps, it hit me just how drained I was from all the emotions, phone calls, and meetings of the day. Hard to believe it had just been ten hours … it felt like a couple of days. Oh, well, at least no one was shooting at me … yet. And before I could rest, there was still an important thing to do.

As I started to unlock the door, Kelly pulled it open. I was so overwhelmed by the sight of her there that all I could do was smile. Words could not cover how I was feeling. And based on the smile I was getting back from her, she felt the same. If this was a glimpse into the future, it was going to be outstanding.

"Wow, you look nice in that sports coat. Do we have plans for this evening?" she asked with a big grin.

"I plan on making plans just as soon as I build up enough energy. It's been a long, tiring day," I said as I closed the door and pulled her into my arms. "This hug is already recharging my system. You look perfect. What say we head to a special store I need to visit, and then we have dinner at your favorite seafood place?"

"Okay. But what kind of 'special store' are you looking to find, sailor?"

"I was thinking, and that usually gets me in trouble, that we might find a nice jewelry store and pick up a one-week anniversary gift for you. Something along the lines of a huge round medallion with a heavy chain to go around your neck and on the medallion it reads 'Back Off, Boys' on one side, and 'Property of Marcus Colt' on the other. What ya think?"

She must like the idea since we were both laughing by the time I got to the end of the description. "I hope you aren't serious about that, Mark. While I like the idea of celebrating our seven days together, I'm not quite sure I want to wear a saucer. Can I pick out something a little bit smaller?"

"Of course. Your input is critical. That's why I didn't go buy something that important on my own. We are a team and from now on we work together." And with that I gave her a kiss and another hug.

She grabbed her jacket and we headed out the door. I stopped at the trunk of the Blue Beast and traded my enlisted ID card for the officer's version, then slid my American Express card in next to it. These would be coming in handy real soon.

Kelly knew a nice jewelry store in the new mall, so we started there. All the way to the store she kept talking about getting a bracelet with her birthstone and mine, and I agreed it was a better choice than the medallion. We found exactly what she'd been describing, but the jeweler would need to install the correct birthstones. He would have it ready to pick up the next afternoon. Perfect. I told them to write it up and handed him my card.

As they wrote up the invoice and special instructions, I steered Kelly over to the ring section of the store. "Which one is your favorite?" I asked softly.

She stared down at the engagement rings and looked at me with that cute left hook smile. "You do know a girl gives a lot of thought to the ring she'll be wearing for the rest of her life. It's not an easy choice. But the good news is I already know what I want. It must be yellow gold, have a plain band with a built-in setting, and feature a single one-carat diamond. Just like that one," she said as her hand directed my attention to the second ring from the left on the third row back.

I called the clerk over and asked to see that specific ring. It really was a thing of beauty. I handed it to Kelly and asked, "Are you sure this is the one you want to wear the rest of your life? Don't you want a bigger stone or multiples?"

She placed the ring on her right hand ring finger and smiled at how well it looked and fit. "Marcus, when the time comes, this is the one. It's perfect. And it seems to even be the right size." And she handed the ring back to me.

I took it back from Kelly and was about to hand it back to the clerk. My plan had been to pick it up the next day when I came to get the bracelet, then propose to her in the quiet privacy of our house. I hesitated when I saw her face sadden just a bit as she released the ring into my hand.

Probably not fitting for this situation, but an old military adage flashed in my head right that moment—no plan survives the first contact with the enemy. Looks like the same principle applies in love. I turned to face Kelly and got down on one knee per the custom.

I held her hand and looked up to say, "Kelly, we may have just met last week, but we have been searching for each other for such a long time. We need each other, we make each other better, and neither of us can afford to lose the other. Marry me and make it permanent."

"Oh, you betcha, sailor!" she cried, kneeling down beside me and giving me a huge kiss. She held out her left hand and I placed the ring on the ring finger to make it a done deal. It was a perfect fit. We kissed again while receiving a round of applause from the store clerks and customers.

A light flashed and I looked up to see the clerk with a camera in his hand. He smiled and asked, "I suspect you want me to add this ring to the bracelet invoice, right, sir?"

Once the emotions of the proposal were past, I finished up the paperwork and we tried to make an escape from the jewelry store. But we couldn't get out of there until we'd received another big round of applause. It was embarrassing. It was also greatly appreciated, and it made our special moment even better. And we were delayed again as we posed for a photo with the manager, to add to his wall of happy couples.

We returned to the seafood restaurant where we'd enjoyed a great meal together a lifetime ago, or in normal time factors, just that past Monday. On the way, I told Kelly about the call to her father and getting his permission, as well as that of David Bartow and her aunt and uncle. She said she hadn't expected anything less from me.

I don't think either of us remembers the quality of the food we had for dinner. Our euphoria was still so high the food didn't matter. After we finished dinner, which was a challenge since we were holding hands most of the time as we tried to eat, we decided it was proper to go share our news with her aunt and uncle.

Both Dorothy and the Captain—I hadn't yet been able to call him by his Christian name when we were away from the office—were thrilled with our announcement. We didn't hang around with them for very long, as we needed to get Kelly home so she could call her parents to share the news with them. It was amazing how easily the phrase 'get Kelly home' rolled off my tongue even though she would be heading back there to the Captain's house later that night for sleep.

The call to her parents went very well. The Admiral was happy for us, and Kelly was beyond thrilled to hear her father share his feelings about the news. Her mother was over the moon with excitement and already talking about wedding planning. I enjoyed chatting with my future mother-in-law and we looked forward to meeting soon. After we finished the call, Kelly and I retired to our spot on the sofa for an hour of talk before she needed to leave. It was a perfect ending to a wonderful day.

57

I WAS EXHAUSTED MONDAY NIGHT so, rather than drive back to the base, I stayed at the house. The quiet of the house let me get a better night's sleep than was ever possible at the barracks. I left for the transient barracks early enough to change into my uniform before heading to the NISO office space. The startup tasks had to be done or the world would fall apart. On most days, coffee outranked secret missions.

When Dexter arrived, I asked him what he had planned for Saturday. He said nothing, so I planted the seed about him going to the festival with Karen. I broke down and told him about the date I'd had with her the week before.

"Man, you survived a trip to their house? Ya got guts, Mark. Not a lot of brains, but a ton of guts!"

Then I explained why I thought her mother came across as a bit strange, and finished it off with some facts. "Oh, go easy, Dex. They both have had some rough, sad days with the loss of Laura's husband, Ben, a few years ago. He was a Marine and died in Nam. And add to that the passing last year of a great-uncle who helped fill the void after Ben's death."

Dex shook his head and a somber look covered his face. "Damn, I didn't know all that. No wonder Laura acts strange. You're right, Mark. Sorry."

"Give some serious thought to Saturday. I will tell you that Karen is a true pleasure to be around. She's cute, intelligent, and just downright fun. Truth is, if I were not involved with someone else, you would never get this chance."

I put on my best Scottish accent and continued, "Her maternal grandparents came over from Scotland right after they married. So her Scottish looks—the red hair, the green eyes, and a few cute freckles—are natural and just one of the many fine assets of this wee bonnie lass, and aye, she's also a great kisser."

After that, I quickly went for more coffee and gave Dex a chance to ponder the situation. He would be an idiot to pass on this opportunity. But some people are stupid, so go figure.

Dashing into the coffee mess, I almost ran over Sam as he turned to leave. He said a quiet greeting and nodded his head down the hall towards the NISRA office space. I got the hint and nodded back. After a quick refill, I stuck my head in the AUTOVON room and told Dex I'd be in NISRA for a while. And I mentioned Karen wanted to live on her farm in Maryland. With his love of farming, that might clinch the deal.

Following Sam into his office, I dropped into the chair that faced his desk but would still allow me to see the agents' area. They were dragging in one by one and each looked as tired as I felt. Must have been a long night for them with their prep work and scheduling.

Sam started the discussion. "Okay, we have a decent plan to cover you two guys both at the Logistics Center and at the barracks. You and Roger will need to limit your activities outside of work so the teams can keep up with you."

"I planned to tell him we would limit our travels to work, mess hall, and barracks. And to keep in character of wild and crazy young sailors, we will need to spend some time at the enlisted men's club. We just have to avoid drinking too much, which would possibly help the bad guys. Will that work?"

"That should. I know the SP and SEAL team troops will appreciate a beer while they keep you under close watch. Problem will be limiting them to just one beer," he chuckled.

We continued the talk for about another hour and reached a point of going in circles, so it was time to stop. You can only beat the ins and outs of the plan so much. It was so well defined it was hard to shoot holes in it. Sam had things lined up perfectly for that afternoon's rollout.

The big meeting would be held in the auditorium in the JAG building next door starting at 1400 hrs. Security was tight for the meeting. People from outside NISRA Norfolk had been told different arrival times to eliminate large groups standing around outside.

With things under control here, I excused myself and went back down the hall to the AUTOVON room. Time to see if Dexter had come to his senses or not. He said he was still discussing things with the voices in his head. I told him not to be a fool and to get Karen's number from Laura right now! Then I told him I was going to lunch.

58

I GRABBED A QUICK SANDWICH and soda from the cafeteria and left by the back door of the building. Across the street from the back of the 5th Naval District HQ is an open field used for parade reviews, athletic events, and just about anything needing a large, open, grass-covered space. There are a few trees around the edges, so I strolled over to the nearest one and sat in the shade to eat. Nearly two hours until the meeting: plenty of time for chow and reflection.

While there were too many noises from the auto traffic in the nearby parking lot, it was more relaxing than sitting in the noisy cafeteria or back in the AUTOVON room. It was nice having a quiet lunch without planning, interrogating, or file reading going on at the same time.

After the sandwich was gone, I leaned back against the tree. It was time for a moment of relaxation. I pulled off the glasses, lowered my white hat down across my forehead, and closed my eyes for a moment. Or two. Perhaps I drifted off for a bit longer.

"Looks like he died. What ya think?"

"At least he looks happy for a change. And he doesn't smell as bad as he did last time we saw him."

"And he ain't bleeding either."

Two gruff voices invaded my quiet respite and I started to get angry about the interruption. At least until I opened my eyes. Two hulking chief petty officers were standing over me. They grabbed my arms and pulled me up.

"Mr. Colt, you are way out of uniform. What are you doing here dressed like that, sir?" asked the older one on the right with a GM insignia under his Chief's crow.

And for the umpteenth time over the last two weeks, I was totally surprised by the unexpected. Two men who'd helped get me out of Nam were standing right here. More proof that life was never boring here in the Tidewater area.

Gunner's Mate (Guns) Chief Petty Officer (GMGC) William "Bill" McCoy and Boatswains' Mate Chief Petty Officer (BMC) Joseph Devland were the senior enlisted men in two different SEAL teams that had accepted me as one of their own and kept me alive during the end of my Vietnam adventure last year. I'd thought they were still stationed in Pearl Harbor.

Once the shock wore off and proper handshakes and back slaps were behind us, they filled me in on how the other men of our crazy crew were doing. Our small group had picked up the nickname "Colt's Crazies," due to the wild things we did to complete the mission.

It was good to hear that Doc had recovered and was back to full duty. Casey was still in therapy for his leg, but expected to return to the unit in about a month. It was sad that Dave had been medically retired and was still in Hawaii, coping as best he could.

Debbie was getting back to normal after losing Leroy; she stayed in contact with Joe. They said she'd been grateful for my call when I got out of the hospital. Johnny's parents would probably never get over his loss, but they were thankful we brought him home for burial and that most of the teams made it home safe.

The happiness of seeing these two men was diminished by the sad memories we shared. The pain was still too raw and my guilt was still intense. I apologized for not staying in touch since getting back to the States, but Bill shook it off perfectly.

"Hell, Marcus, the phone works both ways. If you were only half as busy as we have been, then you were way overworked. We know you care."

"As soon as this mess is over, we'll find time for a reunion before I head back to D.C. That is a promise!"

Then I explained that I was now YN3 Mark Williams, and that I suspected they were here that day for a security meeting at 1400 hrs that was part of my mission. They acknowledged that was true, and explained that their units had been moved to Little Creek just a month ago. I spent a couple of minutes briefing the highlights of the upcoming meeting.

Bill was the first to speak. "Marcus, you've gotten yourself into another fine mess. Obviously we cannot leave you alone, can we?"

"So true, Bill, I need a lot of adult supervision."

Joe chuckled and agreed, "Looks like we get to save the day, and your ugly butt, again. The only easy day was yesterday, so let's get this show on the road, Marcus."

"Okay, guys, remember the name is Williams and we have not yet met. Please stick with that because of all the people you will be meeting shortly. Only Captain Miller, the NISO CO, and Sam Maker, the SSA of NISRA Norfolk, really know who I am. And those two don't even know about our adventure last year. Everyone else believes me to be just another junior Yeoman assigned to the NISO, and one stupid enough to volunteer to be a target. Well, everyone else except my fiancée, Kelly."

Joe looked confused. "Kelly? What happened to Sandy?"

Bill punched him in the shoulder and shook his head. "Obviously, Joe, the man wised up and finally got tired of Sandy never being home when he called. You remember how miserable he was over there."

"You guys just have too good a memory. Some things are best left in the past. But, Bill's right, again. Like he usually is," I answered with a smile and a slap on Bill's back. "I'll find time to fill you in on my good fortune soon."

And Joe was right too ... about time to get the show on the road. We headed back across the street to do just that and get them involved with Operation Vipers.

59

THE AUDITORIUM WAS OVER HALF full when we entered. With so many individuals involved, I prayed they'd all be able to keep it quiet. At least with my SEAL big brothers involved I felt there was a decent chance I'd get through all this without too many new scars.

I grabbed a seat down on the front row and had a legal pad ready to take notes. While I doubted it would be necessary, any real Yeoman would be ready for that. I saw Bill and Joe talking with Captain Miller and Sam, and glancing over my way. And the CO of the SP unit was nearby. In addition to our six NISRA Norfolk agents, there were around twenty-five other men who fit the 'agent' look. About half of them were our NISO Norfolk agents from the other NISRAs.

With the cooperation of Admiral Chance, we'd been augmented with an additional twelve agents from outside NISO Norfolk. They would be here until the operation was completed.

Captain Miller called the meeting to order. He told them the operation was named "Vipers" because we had a poisonous snake, or multiples, in our midst. It had the highest priority over all other cases. He stressed the importance of keeping it all quiet, and introduced those in command of the various participating. Then he turned the floor over to Sam Maker, who outlined the problems and potential solutions perfectly.

Sam went over the physical areas that would be surveilled, and put photos of Roger and me on the overhead projector. They were told to memorize our faces and ensure the bad guys were stopped before they got to us. I liked that order.

Then Sam put a photo of Detective Royal on the screen. He went on to explain that this 'deadly snake was the probable source of leaks that had led to multiple deaths. And while we had to stop Royal, we needed to find out who he was working for and stop them as well. Therefore it was important that the bad guys, who we'd now call 'vipers,' were captured and not killed. We needed them to talk.

SEAL Team Leader GMGC Bill McCoy stood and suggested that the two SEAL teams be assigned to personal protection for the two dummy CIs. The teams were specially trained for that type of work, and with them wearing standard Navy uniforms without their SEAL identifiers, they'd blend in easier than agents acting like sailors. Sam thought that would be a good thing and asked Bill to get with him as soon as the meeting was over.

Two office spaces had been set up for working and planning areas: one in a building next to the transient barracks, and the other in a warehouse across the street from the Logistics Center. Both would reduce the chance of anyone noticing a large group of people coming and going from the NISO offices, and give fast backup access, if needed, at the two primary locations. These working spaces were designated as "Remote B" for the barracks and "Remote L" for the Logistics Center. They were quickly shortened to RB and RL.

Everyone needed to digest all they'd just heard, so the next phase of the plan was for everyone to meet at their designated work space at 0800 Wednesday. The discussion, questions, and answers lasted a total of an hour and a half before winding down.

At 1545 hrs the meeting was finally adjourned. Naturally, the last item was Captain Miller issuing stern warnings about talking to anyone about anything associated with this task force.

I was able to get Sam, Bill, and Joe alone for a few moments as others filtered out of the auditorium. I gave the SEALs the address of my house and told them that Roger and I'd be there the next afternoon and evening. I wanted them to stop by so they could meet with Roger. We could discuss the do's and don'ts the SEAL team members wanted from us to help them handle the security. They agreed and proceeded out the door in different directions: Bill went with Sam for more discussion back at NISRA, and Joe headed back to brief the teams.

The Captain and the Core Unit members were the last ones hanging around. When I walked over to them after the SEALs left, they all turned to me when the skipper asked, "How do you think it went, Williams? Feel confident about it all?"

I was caught off guard by the way the Captain put so much importance on my opinion, but it had happened and time to go with it. I said, "Captain, right now we are at the 'as good as it gets' point in this operation. We can hope that everyone will think about all this overnight. Perhaps their fresh eyes will hit on something our hours of work have missed."

"I suspect you're right. Anything else you want to add before calling it a day?"

I noticed the six agents looking between themselves and a couple giving slight shrugs; a standard sign of either confusion or frustration. My gut was telling me it was frustration, as they'd guessed they were in the dark about aspects of this operation and the Captain's questions to me just proved it. Not a good thing.

"Yes, sir, there is one more thing. But first, we need to retire to the agents' office space for a little more privacy."

And I turned and headed out.

60

As THE AGENTS FILED INTO the office, most of them leaned against their desks and just looked at me. I understood their feelings. The skipper was the last one in; he closed the door and leaned against it. Sam and Bill came out of Sam's office to see what was going on.

"Okay, gents, 'mushroom time' is over. You've been kept in the dark and fed bullshit long enough. First off, know this is all on me. The Captain and Sam have both suggested you be brought up to speed before today, but I nixed that suggestion."

That got the muttering and angry looks going. John Driscol had the most anger in his face as he leaned against his desk with arms crossed. "And just who the hell are you to override SSA Maker and Captain Miller?" he demanded.

I pulled my get-out-of-jail free card from my wallet and passed it to John. "Read it and pass it around, John." As he was reading I continued, "I normally work at NISHQ and am usually in charge of the internal affairs branch, but right now I'm assigned to work directly for the CNO."

That got the muttering going strong, so Sam jumped in. "Shut up, all of you! Mark came here to do a job and he has succeeded. Granted, some in D.C. thought we might have a problem in this office, but the work this man has done, by himself, in just under two weeks, proved them wrong. In addition, he probably solved several of our dead-end cases."

"Thank you, Sam." Turning back to the agents, I continued, "I kept you guys in the dark for the obvious reason; the more people who know a secret, the easier and faster it will get out. That's the justification behind the old 'need to know' requirement the military has used forever. And now you have the need to know. I won't apologize for my deceit, and don't expect your forgiveness, but I do expect your understanding, cooperation, and silence about my identity."

As they passed my card back to me, the anger seemed to leave their faces a small amount until Darrell sarcastically quipped, "Hell, Mark, we knew last Friday that you were more than the low-level Yeoman. Just didn't expect you to be a low-life desk jockey from Internal Affairs." The last part came out a lot less friendly than the first.

Before I could continue, Bill walked up beside me. "Gentlemen, BMC Devland and I had the honor of fighting beside this man last year in Vietnam. You best get any negative thoughts you have about my brother out of your minds before the rest of our SEAL team members find out about those thoughts. Far as the SEALs are concerned, he's one of us."

It was hard to find my voice after that. The agents looked surprised and all nodded in agreement with Bill. And, for the first time, the skipper had a look of shock on his usually stoic face.

I took a deep breath and carried on in a soft voice, "Thanks, Bill. I was not expecting that card to be dealt here today." I cleared my throat and spoke louder. "Okay, moving on and back to Operation Vipers. Sam, can you and these six guys be at my house tomorrow afternoon for a security briefing with the SEAL team leaders and our other crazy CI volunteer, Roger? I'm to pick him up at the airport around 1400 hours, so any time after that will work."

"That will be fine, Mark. Right, guys?" Heads nodded all around and things got quiet. "We will be there no later than 1700. My turn to bring the pizza and beer," Sam replied with an honest grin.

I nodded in approval.

"Mark, I believe I can speak for the other agents when I tell you that you can have a desk here as a special agent anytime. We were pissed, but I understand your actions and appreciate the position you've been in for the last two weeks. Thanks for being open with us about this. Sorry for our initial anger and frustration," Driscol said as he approached me to shake hands.

I thanked them all for their hard work and decided it was time to fold my tent and leave on a positive note. The skipper was still leaning against the door, and stepped aside to open it when I neared. "Got a minute to join me in my office?" he asked.

"Of course, sir."

61

SO MUCH FOR THE POSITIVE note. As we walked down the hall back to the skipper's office, a few thousand things were running around my mind. Foremost I suspected he would want more information about Bill's comment on Vietnam. Something I was still not authorized to disclose.

"Have a seat, Marcus." Closing his office door, the Captain chose the chair next to me rather than the one behind his desk. "Well, that went better than I thought it would."

He shifted position, and continued, "Sorry I put you in an awkward position when I asked you those questions in front of the agents. The simple truth is that Sam and I have realized this is your operation, even though you were controlling it through us. I was not thinking clearly and should have waited until we were alone."

"Not a problem, sir. It needed to come out, and it probably should have sooner. But with all that's going on around here and so quickly, it's hard to have perfect timing. I just hope there are no lingering hard feelings."

The Captain chuckled and said, "After that statement from your SEAL brother, I believe all of them now have complete respect for you. I know it gave me another positive view of a man who already has mine. Getting an award from higher ups in the Pentagon is one thing, but earning the respect of warriors such as that chief is quite another."

He continued, "When I talked with my brother-in-law about you … when was that, less than ten days ago? Seems a lot longer than that. Anyway, he told me you spent some time in Vietnam on a highly classified mission last year. He didn't share mission parameters, but did tell me about your awards. Guess my question is why didn't I see your Navy Cross, Purple Hearts, Vietnam Service ribbons, and that SEAL Trident on your Commander jacket hanging in your hallway?"

"Captain, I did not earn a Trident; never went through BUD/S. I was greatly helped on my mission over there by the two SEAL teams, and I am honored that they felt I did good enough to be considered a friend, and much more honored to be thought of as a brother. I must say that Bill's comments today caught me off guard."

"According to the CNO, you have been authorized to wear the Trident by the Commander of the SEALs after multiple strong recommendations from both of those two SEAL teams. I'm surprised the CNO and Admiral Chance allow you to be out of uniform when not undercover."

"The time spent with the CNO at the start of this mission was so short he did not have the time to bother about it. As for Admiral Chance, he knows I have done a better job in IA than the last few officers, so he doesn't want to rock the boat. Fact is, until the first of last November, those awards were considered Top Secret and I was not to wear them in order to keep the mission out of sight. Not sure why they changed their minds on that."

"Doesn't matter. You should be wearing those. There are two key points in military leadership that are too often overlooked, Marcus. Both of your favorite admirals tell me you have mastered the first: you make sure the men and women serving under you are given full credit for their work. They both told me that on the Vietnam mission, your after-action report credited all of the heroic actions to the SEALs that worked with you. However, the after-action reports from both SEAL team leaders, as well as letters from individual team members, stated that you had done much of that yourself. Your 'confusion' was attributed to your multiple wounds and you were not accused of submitting a false report. So the truth won out and you should wear that Navy Cross," said the Captain.

And while the skipper had the floor, he continued, "Second point of leadership, one that is harder to do than the first, is to humbly accept the deserved praise from those working with you. The SEALs who survived that mission, down to the last man, sent letters to the Commander of the SEALs. Each one stating that, while you have not been through BUD/S, your actions and leadership displayed the character, determination, honor, and guts of a SEAL."

"Marcus, every one of them said they would be honored to serve on any team you lead at any time. They told the Admiral you deserved to be a SEAL and he agreed with them. Your men honored you with that Trident and not wearing it is disrespectful to those sailors who care for you so much."

Emotion was overcoming me, but that couldn't be faced right now. "I appreciate your input, sir, but none of that applies to the situation today. YN3 Williams is not authorized to wear them. Unless there is anything else, I would like to finish up for the day and head on out."

The Captain did not look happy, but he knew I'd blocked his move, and he was out of options. "Dismissed. Will we see you in the morning?"

"Yes, sir. I will be here first thing, then head out to check in with both RB and RL later in the morning. I'll see you then, sir. Good night."

62

DEX HAD ALREADY SECURED THE coffee mess and prepped the AUTOVON room for the night. All I had to do was turn out the lights. I quickly changed clothing at the barracks and drove to the house in record time.

Rest was high on my list of things to do that evening. I'd spent so much time, and so many late nights on this case, that I needed to back away and clear my mind. It was past time to put some music on, cook a nice meal, and then do nothing for a few hours.

It was somewhat of a depressing sight to see an empty driveway. No red Mustang was parked there, but that night was a school night, and at least I knew where she was. But when approaching the porch steps, it hit me that I didn't recall leaving lights on in the back of the house. I pulled my weapon and quietly walked around to the back of the property.

The kitchen windows were high, but a person was visible, standing at the sink. Looked like I needed more curtains on that window because Kelly was easy to spot. I quietly walked to the back door and glanced around the kitchen through the door window; no one else was there.

Unlocking the door as silently as possible, I slid the pistol into my waistband, pulled down my shirt, and walked into the kitchen.

A look of shock was on her face as she turned to see me come in. "What are you doing using the back door?"

"I wasn't expecting anyone to be here, Kelly. So when I saw the light on back here I assumed the worse and came around back to check things out. I thought you had class tonight?"

She came to me and wrapped her arms around me. The kiss that followed was warm and welcoming. "When I told my professor I just got engaged and that you were deploying on Friday, he gave me tonight and tomorrow night off. No class, so I came home."

"Love the way you say 'home.' It is good to see and hold you, Love. Excuse me a second." As I pulled away from her arms, I removed the pistol from my waistband and pulled the two extra magazines from my front left pocket.

"You really are ready for just about anything," she said as I laid the weaponry on the counter.

"That's always the plan. Except I'm never ready for the 'anything' from you, lady. You just keep throwing out surprise after surprise. And I like it!"

She gave me the "left hook" smile and pointed to the dining room. There the table was perfectly set for two, right down to the candles. Then she pointed to the stove that held several pots and a covered pan. "Ready for another surprise? Time to test my cooking, Mark. After you do, you might want to renege on that engagement thing."

Dinner was great on two counts. Not only did I not have to cook it, but Kelly prepared pork chops, fried potatoes and onions, and fresh spinach perfectly. Placing my silverware on the cleaned plate, I gave her the answer. "Guess you get to keep the ring. That dinner was outstanding!"

We'd enjoyed a nice "family time" meal and now it was time to just sit a few minutes and let it settle. But as I started to give her a rundown on the day's events at the office, it dawned on me I'd forgotten to ask about her car.

"I found the extra garage remote and put my car in the garage so it would have time to get to know your 'Cude. Fact is, I didn't want it sitting out in the dew overnight. By the way, those two cars look good together; just like us." With that, she winked.

Again, she floored me. I was not expecting that 'overnight' comment. "Overnight?"

"You betcha, Sailor. I told Uncle Humphrey and Aunt Dorothy this morning that since you were being 'deployed' on Friday for an unknown period, I was going to spend as much time with you as possible. No need to waste time driving back and forth. I've moved into the third bedroom upstairs." And with that, she got up and started clearing the table. The die was cast and the Rubicon had again been crossed, by Kelly this time.

I couldn't think of a thing to say, so I just walked up behind her and wrapped her in my arms. This was some lady. When I finally found my voice, I told her how much I loved her spontaneity and everything else about her.

I then told her the 'good' news: she didn't need to cook Wednesday night. Bad news was, she had to be ready for a small invasion. Sam was bringing pizza and beer for dinner. He'd bring enough for a few, over a dozen, close friends who would be here around 1700 hrs for another planning session. And I was picking up Roger at the airport to bring him here too. She might want to throw together a salad, I suggested.

After getting the kitchen squared away, we retired to the living room, where we spent the rest of the evening on our sofa, discussing things and loving each other. I gave her a brief rundown on Bill and Joe, and what they'd be doing here the next day. As for Roger, I didn't know much about him, but I shared what I knew. Kelly said she would clear out a space for the suspect board to be moved down from the office.

Once all the words were said, we just snuggled, held hands, and enjoyed each other as the perfect way to end the day.

63

KELLY HAD ALREADY TURNED IN, so I decided to visit the upstairs office. I'd escorted her to her door and kissed her goodnight. If sensuality was ever given a rating number, that kiss had to be around a twenty-one out of a possible ten.

Although I was tired, my mind refused to shut down and I needed to do something. Might as well clean off the suspect board and get it ready for the next day's planning session. I decided to wait until the morning to get Kelly's help moving it downstairs.

It was a simple task to place scale shapes representing the transient barracks, Logistics Center, surveillance buildings RB and RL, NISO HQ, and major connecting roads on the board. It would make too much noise that night, so I'd wait until the next day to type up personnel lists to place near each location. It was a crude picture of the areas of concern, but it beat not having one. If anyone had a negative comment, I'd just say this picture was only worth 750 words and not the usual 1,000. Sue me.

Leaving this mission alone and going to bed was the correct action to take right then, but my mind kept running the operation from front to back and then from back to front. Discovering ahead of time what to expect is the best way to keep the bullet wounds to a minimum. I hoped that Roger and I could add a few names to the new suspect list after spending a bit of time at the Logistics Center. That is, assuming the vipers didn't kill us first. I'd really hate for that to happen.

I kept looking at the board, maybe hoping something interesting would appear by itself. There had been so many surprises in this case that I half expected some otherworldly specter to bring something forward. After a few minutes, it did.

Well, it didn't appear exactly, but what hit me was the fact that there were no connections to the real world, also known as the world outside the base, shown on the board. Nor were there any such connections in the case files. Where was it? What tied a local detective to murders of sailors? And why?

Back to one of my standard methods: skip the unknowns and go back over the knowns. So what were the known entities? Detective Royal was dirty—a probable, but very highly likely. Navy personnel helping NIS were dead—a definite. Royal getting their names right before they were killed—a definite fact. Was Royal responsible for their deaths—maybe; hell, highly likely. Drugs were in too many places on the base—a definite fact. Several of the dead were from the Logistics Center—a definite fact. Somewhere there was a link. Where was the one missing piece of this deadly puzzle?

Ultimately, Roger and I still needed to add possible suspects to the board. It stunk that it was going to take more time, and time was never on our side when dealing with vipers. Royal had to have connections on the base. And the most likely place to find his connections was probably the place with the largest number of deaths. The Logistics Center had to be the key location.

Leaning back in the chair, the view of the board did not get any better. It needed names and photos. But none existed just yet. And the hour was getting much later. I just needed a few minutes more to push things around in my mind.

64

"ARE YOU GOING TO WORK today?" Kelly's sweet voice pushed through the dark fog in my mind. "Hello, are you in there?"

My neck hurt. My head ached. Something was rubbing my head. And I was not sure where I was for a second before jumping up from the chair. Kelly was standing there in the office holding out a cup of coffee. Her hair was hanging down across the shoulders of her dark red bathrobe, accenting the shape of her fantastic body as well as highlighting her hair color. Some might say she looked beautiful, but that was wrong. She didn't just look beautiful, she truly was beautiful. There is a difference.

"You have a little over an hour to get ready and get out the door, sailor. Otherwise you will be UA. And that is not acceptable in this house. I'm working on breakfast so hurry up!"

"Guess I fell asleep while working. So glad you are here for so many reasons. But right now, being a great alarm clock is high on that list. Thanks for the coffee, Darling. Gotta shower and shave." I gave her a kiss on the cheek, grabbed the coffee, and headed to my bedroom.

Some people prefer a cold shower to get going. For me, it has to be hot: just a few degrees shy of causing burn damage. The heat helped remove the neck and head pains and prepped my face for a quick shave. Just wished I'd kept a set of undress blues here at the house; that would have saved a stop at the barracks.

Kelly's breakfast was just as great as the previous night's dinner. Eggs scrambled with sautéed bell pepper and onion, a rasher of bacon, and an English muffin with orange marmalade. The best part was it was all topped off with a hug and sweet kiss as I started to dash out the door.

"*Addio, mia bellissima amore*," I said as I took advantage of a second kiss.

"What's that all about?" she asked with a grin.

"I told you last week I was going to work on my Italian. See ya in a few hours, goodbye my beautiful love." And I was out the door. This was going to be a great life!

Light traffic worked in my favor and the quick stop at the barracks for a uniform change didn't take long. I walked into the NISRA agents' office just a few minutes before 0730 hrs. No one was around, so I grabbed my coffee mug and went down to the mess.

Dex was right on top of things; the two urns were done and the tea water was hot. My fuzzy brain needed the caffeine, so I grabbed a mug of the 'special' blend. The spices helped as well. I stuck my head in the AUTOVON room and said. "Well done, Dex, coffee is perfect!" He responded with a vulgar hand signal. He was not impressed being back on coffee duty while I was goofing off in the NISRA. Oh well, he would survive. Then I headed back to the NISRA.

Sam and the agents were flowing in as I went over the notes I'd made on the evidence of the dead CIs, and a few other deaths over the last five months that seemed strange. These cases were so convoluted it felt like trying to push an octopus into a small bucket, with legs going in every direction and changing positions every few seconds.

Everyone was smiling and nodding at me when they arrived, which indicated 'all is good' after Tuesday's disclosures—that or they were sucking up to the guy in charge of Internal Affairs. I preferred the former, but would accept the latter. We just needed to get the vipers.

Sam came over and explained that they'd be having a short meeting to go over the highlights one more time, before the agents set out to the RB and RL locations to set things up there. Sam also planned to call Detective Royal later that day and set up a meeting with him on Friday afternoon. That was when he would "share" the info on the two new CIs. That was when the real fun would begin.

And I went back to the cold cases I was analyzing. Rather than continuing to look at a single sheet of paper with a list for each case, I utilized index cards. Writing each item of evidence on a separate card in bold letters, I took the cards into the file room and laid them out on the worktables.

Creating a row of cards for each case, I then sorted them alphabetically. It probably sounds strange, but looking at things from a different angle or direction is the easiest way to see something that is there, but hidden in the usual format.

Then I created a second set of cards for each case: cause of death was listed on one card, location of the body on a second one, and category of information being supplied as a CI on a third. These also went into the file room and were placed on the table in rows separated by category.

I stood there looking at the cards for a few moments, read down each row one time, and then decided more coffee was needed. Sam mentioned on my way out that their meeting would start in about five minutes and he wanted me there. I told him I'd be back in time.

After getting more coffee down, the brain started to come alive. Seeing the pieces of the puzzle isolated caused me to focus more on each one. Nothing was coming together yet, but my method helped file each one away in the back of my mind, so the electronic gerbils in my brain could work on them while I worked on other issues.

Sam started his meeting with the agents, and I stepped out of the file room to participate. Nothing new was mentioned, but he reinforced the critical parts of the plan and made sure every agent was aware of their job. I mentioned I'd be picking up Roger in a couple of hours and we'd see everyone at my house later that afternoon.

After the meeting, I stopped in the AUTOVON room to talk with Dexter. He was his usual self, letting me know his disappointment in my assignment, which had left him alone. I apologized and handed him a piece of paper.

"This is Karen's office number and her home number. Don't miss this opportunity, buddy."

He just grunted and laid the paper by his phone. As I closed the door on the way out, I saw him start to dial. That was a good sign.

65

I CALLED THE CAPTAIN AND asked if he wanted to visit sites RB and RL with me. He declined. Said he had a list of people to call about additional support. He also mentioned that he hoped Kelly wouldn't be too much of a distraction at the house. I told him that would not be a problem. Oh, boy, just what I needed; a bit more stress.

There was a slight change of plan. Since these sites were near the buildings where I'd be a potential target and where we might find some of the vipers, I decided it was time for a visual change before heading over for the walk through. I had run this thought by the skipper and he'd agreed.

I checked out with the Chief and told him I didn't know when I'd be back in the office. He'd already talked with the Captain and understood the situation. At least he knew the part about me going undercover. He hadn't been brought up to speed on the rest of the details about who I was. Fine for now.

Getting back to the house was the easy part; getting used to wearing my regular uniform was harder. It had been a while since I'd been who I really was. I parked the Blue Beast so I could pull the 'Cuda out and drive it the rest of the day, then entered the house.

Kelly was thrilled to have me home so soon and surprised when I told her why. She'd never seen me as Lieutenant Commander Colt, so I hoped she liked the look. I combed my hair back to the way I normally wore it—the mustache would stay for now. I left the fake glasses on the vanity and straightened my tie before stepping out of the bedroom. Kelly was waiting in the hall and I took her big grin and wolf whistle as a positive reaction.

I smiled back and said, "You must now call me 'sir' whenever I am dressed this way." Her hands immediately went to her hips and a fake frown replaced her smile. "Just kidding. Call me whatever you want, babe," I chuckled.

"Can't wait to see you with your jacket and cover. But I truly like what I see right here, Commander. Yum!"

I gave a run down on my schedule for the rest of the day, and said if all went well, I'd be back with Roger about an hour before the rest of the guests arrived later. Then I'd run him over to the base after our meeting.

Stopping in the hall before heading out the door, I put on the jacket and cover and struck a recruiting poster pose. I got two thumbs up and a wonderful kiss goodbye, so it looked like she might keep me around. The 'Cude fired right up, as always, and sounded great. As I pulled away in the direction of the base, Kelly was already maneuvering the Blue Beast into the garage so it could spend quality time with her Mustang.

I decided, after talking with the Captain about wearing awards the day before, that he was right—of course he was right, he was the skipper—and made a quick stop on base to pick up the ribbons and Trident my uniform was missing. Since I'd be meeting my SEAL brothers later in the day, I added the Trident to my uniform immediately. The other ribbons would be added when I had more time to get them in the correct order.

Walking back to my car, I realized I was a bit slow returning salutes. Since I'd been the one to initiate the salute to any officer the last couple of months, my brain hadn't rewired to be the one receiving the majority of salutes. Back through Alice's looking glass … at least for a few hours.

Site RB was closest, so it was my first stop. The building Sam had acquired gave us easy access, without the doors being visible from the barracks. And it provided an excellent view of the barracks. Off-hours comings and goings wouldn't be noticed if the vipers had the barracks under any form of surveillance.

The agents who were there were really surprised to see me in my officer's uniform. They noticed the Trident and smiled. I told them to keep calling me "Mark Williams" so there wouldn't be any confusion in critical times. All looked good at RB, so I headed over to RL.

Site RL had similar access, where the vipers could not see us. Everything was in place there, too. The teams had established well-stocked stakeout spots and from what I observed, they were ready. I just hoped Roger and I were just as ready.

It was time to head to the Norfolk airport and pick up the last piece needed to make this play ready for a Broadway opening. Well, an off-Broadway opening—that is, way off Broadway.

66

BEING IT WAS BOTH MIDWEEK and midafternoon, the Norfolk airport was not extremely busy. That was the good news. Bad news was, the "arrival" board showed the Chicago flight running late. Like two hours late. I checked with the airline agents and they confirmed there'd been a mechanical issue right before takeoff that caused the delay.

As much as I hated waiting in airports, the drive home was forty minutes long, so I'd arrive there just in time to head back to the airport. Not a lot of brainpower was needed to reach the right decision: walk over to the bar to order a burger and a beer. Lunch had been missed due to the site visits, so it was past time for chow.

But first I found a payphone and gave Kelly a quick update on the schedule. She said she had things well in hand there at the house and not to worry about time. I suggested she head to the Giant and pick up more beer and to check the fridge and cabinets to see if there were any items we might need. Naturally, she was way ahead of me and told me she'd done that in the morning, right after I left for the second time. She was well versed at being an officer's wife.

I aimed for a booth near the back of the bar and sat where I could see people coming into the eatery and get a glimpse of those walking by outside. Some might call that positioning paranoia, but I call it personal security. The waitress took my order quickly and returned with it shortly. The food was decent and the beer cold: excellent combination that provided for another positive for the day. It almost offset the frustration of the delay.

As I munched on the last couple of onion rings, I noticed a gentleman stroll in and sit at a table near the front. He faced the bar where the TVs were mounted and seemed interested in the news program. From my position, I was looking at his left side, so it was easy to observe without too much risk of exposure.

There was nothing about him that caused warning lights to go off in my head, but he seemed familiar. Caucasian, maybe half Hispanic, early to mid-thirties, medium length dark brown hair hanging over his ears, average dress in jeans, dress shirt, no tie, gold watch, no wedding ring, and light-brown corduroy jacket. Slender build, and wearing a pencil-thin mustache similar to the 1930s movie stars. He reminded me of a slightly sloppier David Niven, the actor in *Around the World in 80 Days*. Again, nothing to cause concern, yet my gut said *pay attention*.

At least I had a good hour before Roger's plane was now due. That provided lots of time to observe and run his face through my mental suspect book. Perhaps I'd seen his photo in one of the NISRA files I'd studied for the last week or so. Whatever the case, a few minutes' watching was a good use of my time.

My observation was cut short fifteen minutes later when he heard a boarding call for a Miami-bound flight. He finished his beer and left a few bucks on the table to cover the tip. I did the same, as something was telling me to watch this guy a bit longer.

He headed straight to his gate, but when he got there he met with another guy. This one was younger, mid-twenties, Hispanic, clean shaven, with short dark hair. He had a weightlifter build with a large chest and slim waist. He seemed to be taking orders from the guy I now thought of as 'DN,' standing for David Niven. The new guy was logged into my mind as 'SM,' since he looked like the actor Sal Mineo.

SM's head nodded up and down a lot as DN gave the orders. DN then took the carry-on bag that SM had been carrying and briskly walked to the plane. SM watched him approach the plane, then turned to leave the airport.

There was an arrival–departure board next to that gate so it'd been easy to stand there, studying the flights, while keeping an eye on those two gents. I also noted that Roger's flight was now due to arrive in fifteen minutes, so I still had a little free time. I let SM get ahead of me and started a simple tail.

He was heading to the short-term parking lot, so I went up to the second floor and found a view of that area. SM showed up and went to a black Pontiac, probably a late 1960s model. Might be a GTO, but it was too far away to tell from here. As he drove out of the lot, I could tell it wasn't a Virginia tag, but no way to see which state claimed it. More info to log into the brain—for what reason my gut failed to share.

I saw an airliner landing and figured it was the Chicago flight: the only incoming plane shown on the board for this hour. So I made my way to the gate to welcome Roger to the operation.

67

Spotting Roger as he entered the airport was easy; I'd studied his photo. Though actually a civilian special agent, he'd come in character in his dress blues, and a few folks were probably surprised to see an officer putting a seaman's seabag in the car. But if anyone is going to scratch the 'Cuda's paint, it'll be me. Chatting on the way home, I learned this would be his third undercover assignment, so I felt comfortable that he would be fine.

It was after 1700 hrs when we rounded the corner toward the house; it looked like a convention was underway. Cars were parked everywhere, save for a spot in my driveway for the 'Cuda. I'd given Roger a rundown on the plan for the evening, so we left his seabag in the car and went in to face the crowd.

Again, Kelly opened the door before I could and her smile told me a lot. She was entertaining our company and loving every moment of it. I introduced her to Roger and as they were talking, I strolled into the living room where all the noise was being generated.

What a sight. In addition to Sam, six NISRA agents, and SEALS Bill and Joe, several other SEALs were present. HM1 Donald "Doc" Stevens saw me first and yelled "Attention on deck" as he, RM2 Andy "Sparks" Waterman, BM3 Kevin Brown, GMG1 Larry Hanes, and GMG2 Glenn Jensen popped to attention—all looking better than when I'd last seen them in the hospital. Joe and Bill also rose, but they were a bit slower; these chiefs are never known to act hastily. The NISRA agents just sat there smiling, so I knew this had been planned.

Seeing these guys again, and noting the honor they were showing me, caused a big lump to form in my throat. Damn glad I had put on the Trident. *Thank you again, Captain Miller!* I shook my head and said, "I would say 'as you were' but knowing you misfits, I'm afraid to think about what you were doing before an adult arrived on the scene. Ah, hell with it, as you were, and thank you so very much. Good to see you all again!"

Bill was the first to speak as I came over for handshakes and man hugs. "Mr. Colt, I must say that third stripe looks good on you. As does that Trident. Congratulations, sir, well deserved!"

The next half hour was filled with welcoming and catching up with the old teams. I was finally able to go upstairs for a few minutes to change, which gave Roger a chance to meet and get to know everyone. Kelly, coming up the back way from the kitchen, met me as I entered my bedroom.

She closed the door behind her and walked over to me. After a huge hug and kiss, she said, "Welcome home, sailor. I really like your friends, Marcus." Then she paused, a thoughtful look coming over her face. "Any reason you never mentioned being a SEAL or spending time in Vietnam?"

As I pulled off my tie, Kelly started unbuttoning my shirt. "It's complicated. We'll have a long talk about all that later tonight. It's just something I've had trouble discussing with anyone."

I placed my hand on the back of her head and added, "And knowing you lost Richard over there, I didn't want to reopen any wounds for you." As she pulled my shirt off and unbuckled my belt, I continued, "You do know that what you are doing is making any further discussion very difficult and we do have guests waiting."

"Oh, you betcha, I know exactly what I am doing, and yes, you had better change faster." And with that, she smiled, pinched my butt, turned and headed out the door. First thought in my head was something I'd said earlier in the day: *No, Captain, she will not be a distraction.* Nope, not much at all.

After getting into my standard jeans and plaid shirt, I went downstairs to face the crew. Kelly had tossed a salad and had that, several different dressings, and the pizza set up on the kitchen counter. Somewhere she'd found the two leafs for the dining room table. With it extended and the smaller kitchen table in use, everyone had a place. Crowded, but workable.

Where she'd found the extra chairs was anyone's guess. Maybe they were in the basement. She was an amazing hostess, and I suspect she learned that from watching her mother, the Admiral's lady, all these years.

We decided it would be best to eat first and then talk about the surveillance. After we were seated, I led a prayer of thanks for the food and asked for the Lord's guidance and protection as we went forward. Those of us who were together last year understood the power of prayer.

I took the time, as we ate, to set one important ground rule. From that moment forward, my name was Mark Williams and I was a YN3. With most everyone calling me something else, even I was getting confused.

It was great to catch up with the guys I hadn't seen since last summer. Their lives had been interesting since then; I was so glad they were here working with us. It gave me a sense of calm knowing they were watching our backs.

After the food was cleared and fresh rounds of beer or coffee were in place, Sam started the official part of the evening. He outlined the operation to get the new guys up to speed, and then turned the meeting over to Bill. He and Joe had spent most of the day working on the parameters of the protection detail.

Between the two of them, they presented the things Roger and I needed to do to help them do a better job of keeping us alive. They had set up a schedule so that there would always be two members of their teams near us at all time. I could see the agents nodding in agreement, so I knew we were all on the same page and there wouldn't be any territorial issues.

After we'd beaten the operation parameters to death and everyone had given their input, there was nothing left to say, so the NISRA agents headed out the door. Sam had offered to take Roger to the barracks, so I transferred his seabag from the 'Cuda to Sam's car.

As Sam was closing his trunk, I told him I was taking Thursday off to get my mind into the new role in supply. I'd be in the office early Friday morning to pick up my modified service record and the fake set of orders the Chief had set up for this operation. He agreed that a day off would do me good, since I'd been pushing it lately.

I'd already given Roger my cubicle number and suggested he ask the guy on the duty desk to put him there. Tell him we were high school friends. That would help make the protection job a bit easier.

After the agents left, the rest of us retired to the living room for some friendly talk instead of business. The guys wanted to know more about Kelly. She beamed at their attention and it was obvious they were as enamored with her as I was. If this situation were a newspaper headline, it would read "Small Blonde Girl Easily Overpowers Two SEAL Teams Without Using Weapons." The first question was the standard 'tell us how you met.'

I started to answer, "Guess it would be easier to give you the entire time line of our relationship in reverse. We got engaged right at forty-eight hours ago and we ..."

Doc about dropped his beer and interrupted, "Excuse me?"

Kelly started laughing and said, "Oh, yea, he asked me at the jewelry store on Monday night. You must remember we've only known each other a short time. How many days now, Hon?" She looked at me for the info.

"I met Kelly at her uncle's house a week ago this past Friday, so that makes it right at thirteen days ago. It just seems like a lot longer since it's been so hectic," I said, smiling at the slack-jaw looks we were getting. "Of course, during this time, Kelly has been busy working on her master's degree, and I had to date a redhead to rule her out as being a suspect, but we managed to find time for each other."

Joe was the first to regain his composure, asking "So let me get this straight, Marcus—sorry, Mark. You have been here in Norfolk for less than three weeks. During that time, you figured out who is probably killing the CIs, you helped uncover a drug ring on the base, you dated a redhead who was also a suspect, you set up an undercover op, and you found time to meet and talk this beauty into marrying you? Did I miss anything?" He sat there shaking his head.

"That's almost right, Joe," I responded with a chuckle. "You left out that I also improved the quality of the coffee at the NISO. It was just another couple of weeks of boredom in the life of an NIS agent. But to be honest, Kelly has done the bulk of the pursuing. I am just a very happy victim."

"Oh, honey, I am so glad you're happy," Kelly quipped, "Now tell them the part about my family that shocked you." She was enjoying this way too much.

Bill asked before anyone else could, "What, your dad is a crown prince of some European country? Are you royalty?"

Again, I had to laugh, not at my friends, but at how crazy all this must sound to them. "Well, Bill and Joe, you met her uncle today. Captain

Miller, the NISO CO, is her uncle." They both shook their heads slightly as their jaws dropped open a bit.

Larry said, "Gutsy move dating your CO's niece, even if he's just a temporary CO for this op. Always knew you were either brave or crazy and I'm leaning more toward crazy right now."

"True, Larry, crazy can probably be found in my family tree," I responded. "And you have all heard of her father and a couple of you have already met the man. I called him at the Pentagon on Monday to ask permission to marry Kelly. Her dad, Admiral Gallagher, was happy to give me that permission. It is always best to keep the CNO happy." All I could do after that was put a silly grin on my face.

Larry looked at Kelly and asked, "You're the CNO's daughter?" She gave him the left-hook grin and nodded. He looked at me and continued. "Crazy it is, for sure."

Bill interjected, "Being the CNO's daughter is royalty as far as I am concerned. After all, Princess Kelly sounds good, right?"

"So, will the wedding wait until we catch the bad guys on this operation, or do we need to work it in around them this next week?" asked Doc with a huge sigh. That caused everyone to break up.

Kelly just gave them that cute smile again and told them to keep Labor Day weekend open. First I'd heard about that, but as I was constantly learning, this lady was full of surprises.

68

As much as I loved the guys and enjoyed visiting with them, the quiet of the house was oh so nice after everyone left. Entertaining can really drain your energy. So can planning an operation that could become dangerous. As they walked out I told them I'd see them on Friday, and to a man, they said "No, you won't, but we will see you."

Kelly had been busy cleaning up while we had the op overview, so when I locked the door and turned off the porch light, all we had to do was head to the sofa: our favorite spot to talk and be close. She turned off most of the lights, leaving on just the small lamp on the other side of the room behind the sofa. I turned on an oldies radio station and kept the volume low. And for the first time that day, we sat down to relax and enjoy each other.

She started off, "Those men have really missed you. I'm surprised you haven't kept in contact with them."

"After working closely together for nearly four months, we were separated at the base hospital in Saigon when the mission was over. Some of the guys were fine and came straight home. The rest had various levels of wounds, and they were sent to different medical facilities. I spent nearly a month in the hospital in Saigon, and by the time I was released, they all were in different places, either recovering or working back at their units. They had their work to do and I had mine."

Kelly nodded her understanding. "Before you got here, the guys were so excited to tell me about working with you, your awards, and how you earned them. And while you were changing out of your uniform, they mentioned how happy they were to see the Trident on your jacket. It wasn't there yesterday, was it?"

"No, it wasn't. Being a SEAL is another long story. I have to thank your uncle for the Trident being on my coat today. He and I recently had a chat about those awards and he put things in a different light. Yea, I'm glad I had it on my jacket too."

"Marcus, they gave me the 'Reader's Digest Condensed' version of what happened over there, but no details or the reason for the operation, which they say is still classified. I just can't understand why I haven't heard anything about it from you. Care to enlighten me?"

"There are still more than a few things you don't know about me yet. We will get to them all, I promise. As for this one, it's hard to explain."

"Most horrible memories are, but you have to get them out to let me in."

Silence and introspect. "Okay. On that mission, several men followed my orders and died. Couple of others who followed my orders came home with horrific wounds. Doc was one of those severely wounded and he just returned to full duty last month after a seven month recovery."

I paused to let that sink in, then opened up more. "Because of those men you met tonight and the rest of the two SEAL teams, my mission was successfully completed and I came home alive. I just don't feel I should've been given those awards. I didn't deserve them. Call it survivor's guilt, if you like."

She leaned against me and wrapped her arms around my neck. Looking at the side of my face from a few inches away, she whispered, "That is exactly what it is. Textbook variety and I know because I have included that in my master's thesis. And I can say a thousand times that it's not your fault, but that won't help you. You have to accept that reality."

She continued, "Your friends told me about all you did for them. They made it clear that without your leadership and courage probably none of them would have made it home. The men who were here tonight likewise followed your orders and they survived. So do you feel guilty that they are still alive?"

"Of course not."

"Then let go of the guilt that you carry about the others and yourself. Your brothers were clear that nothing you did led to the deaths and injuries. Nothing. The enemy did that. Not you. They still feel sad for the losses too. You all should remember those men and the good things about them."

Kelly kissed my cheek and continued, "And things must be kept in perspective, Marcus. Just like you, all the men on those teams were doing what they signed up to do. And sadly, not everyone going off to war is able to come home. You don't have any guilt to carry for what happened over there. You have to get a grip on the truth of that revelation and accept it. I can only offer you support and love."

"I'll work on it. Promise." I closed my eyes and leaned back, resting my head against the arm of the sofa. Kelly moved over a bit and pulled my legs up on her lap. I was fighting the fatigue that was taking over. Fatigue from the physical activities of the day as well as from the emotions running through my head. Quiet and dark helped the fatigue win.

I woke up from a dream where I was having trouble breathing due to pressure on my chest from something. I was nearly awake and the pressure remained. When I got my eyes open, I saw a mass of blonde hair just below my chin.

Kelly's head was lying on my chest. She was sound asleep. Soft light was coming in through the window blinds, so I knew morning had arrived. The radio was still softly playing, with an Elvis song wrapping up.

Rubbing her head gently, I softly said, "Good morning, beautiful lady. Guess it's time to face the day."

"Noooo. It's too early," she moaned.

"At least we know the sofa sleeps well. Move over so I can go put on the coffee." She moved enough for me to get up, then curled back up for more sleep.

In a few minutes, I had the coffee brewing. It was a little before 0700 hrs, so there was a lot of day left. Sam would let the Chief know where I was, and Dexter would have all the morning tasks under control, so I wasn't worried about the office. Sam had planned to update the Captain that morning, so that meant everyone in the op would be on the same page.

Roger had planned on spending the next two days in the office with the NISRA agents so he'd know the plans and the key people as well as I did. He would then spend time with them over the weekend, surveilling the Logistics Center. That would give him a much better understanding of the physical area.

Kelly had dashed upstairs after completely waking a few minutes ago. I admit seeing her sleeping in the morning was a wonderful thing. I laid out the ingredients for a couple of omelets and sat down to enjoy a cup in the quiet. And to think about what I needed to do, starting the following day.

But first, it was time to decide what I wanted to do with the rest of the day. Well, that statement needed to be immediately and permanently modified. From then on, I'd need to consult with Kelly and then *we* would decide what we'd do with the rest of our day.

69

FRIDAY MORNING THROUGH AFTERNOON

26 MARCH 1971

With Thursday having been the best day of my life so far, getting up on Friday was not enjoyable, but had to be done. After putting on my enlisted dress blue uniform, I added a couple of things a sailor was not normally allowed to carry on a Navy base: my 1911 .45 pistol tucked into a waistband holster under my jumper, two extra magazines in an ankle pouch on my left calf, and a Fairbairn-Sykes knife on the right calf. Nice thing about bell-bottom trousers is that a lot can be easily hidden there.

I also added my officer's ID card and the get-out-of-jail-free card to a pouch in the leather, money-belt-like thing I wear on assignments. It stays well hidden under my uniform and provides extra secure room for important things.

After a quick breakfast, I got the last hug and kiss for a while from Kelly. She would secure the house later and then head back to the base to stay with the Millers until this mess was over. Saying goodbye was difficult, but military families go through this all the time. At least I'd be nearby while I was out of touch. And hopefully not for long.

And with that, I proceeded back through the looking glass to another world—this one as a Yeoman in supply. The Blue Beast and I proceeded to the Naval Station, where I picked up my dummy paperwork from the NISO office. Now I faced the task of catching the vipers. The Fleet Logistics Center was just ahead. I didn't see any of the men assigned to keep me safe, but I trusted they were there.

The first two floors of the huge logistics building are filled with shelving and areas secured behind locked chain-link fence. Freight elevators are in several strategic locations, and a ramp for the forklift is on one side of the floor. There are two sets of stairs and one elevator for the staff to use. The third floor holds the storekeepers' office space and rows upon rows of shelving. The fourth floor has the command office spaces, and more shelving. I took the elevator to the fourth floor and found the man I needed.

"Good morning, Senior Chief. Williams, Mark, reporting for duty." And I handed over my records and orders to YNSC Don Pierce, who ran the office of Fleet Logistics Center Norfolk.

"Take a seat, Williams," he responded as he opened my records and started the look-through. "Great scores at 'A' School," Pierce mumbled along with a few other things as he perused my record. He kept nodding, so I assumed all was well as far as he was concerned. Perhaps he was putting on a show for the rest of the crew since he and the CO were both aware of my undercover assignment. Whatever worked for him was fine with me.

A glance around the area revealed the standard Navy office. There was a lot of gray—in several shades—on the desks, chairs, desk lamps, and filing cabinets. Makes you wonder if the Navy ever thought about using a light gray paper instead of white. About half the desks in this area were empty, but the rest were filled with yeomen and personnelmen who seemed busy. A quick count added up to seven male and four female enlisted staff.

The area against the windowed wall was divided into offices, with glass on the upper part of the wall facing the open area of the office, where I was sitting. Some efficiency expert probably felt an open-looking space would generate more work. One office was empty, and I guessed that had belonged to Ensign Appleton, who had yet to be replaced. The other five offices held officers, most of whom were busy on the phone.

Senior Chief Pierce finally finished with my record and laid it in his 'out' basket. He steepled his fingers and pressed his index fingers against his mouth, maintaining a look of contemplation. "Okay, Williams, let's get you settled in and busy."

And with that we did a walk around the office complex doing the meet and greet. Then he showed me to the desk that would be my new home, and provided a quick overview of my assignment. My task was to handle paperwork that the two lieutenants, who were in the two offices at the right end of the row, generated as they did their job.

The Chief also showed me around the rest of the complex and introduced me to the storekeepers, who manned an office one floor down from ours. While the rating name makes one think of a nice old fellow standing behind a counter in a general store, the storekeeper rating is for the sailors who do everything with supplies, including ordering, storage, dispersing, and inventory control. Their rating badge shows crossed keys, indicating they have tight control on everything the Navy needs to operate.

The CPO in charge of the enlisted storekeepers was a gruff old gent named Robert Lansing. His general appearance was rough around the edges, and his eyes were bloodshot. Must have been a bad night for the old guy. He didn't seem happy to meet me and went back to reading something on his desk right after Pierce did the introductions.

SKC Lansing was wearing stripes on his sleeve indicating over twenty years of service, yet he was still an E-7, the lowest level of chief petty officer. Actually nothing wrong with that, but usually everyone seeks a higher pay grade—for more money now and more later in retirement. So either he wasn't aggressive when it came to passing exams or he'd gotten into trouble early in his career.

I'd need to dig through the personnel file and BI of SKC Lansing, which David Bartow had sent the previous week. I admit I'd focused on the lower enlisted men as possible suspects, and had skimmed over the officers, senior, and female enlisted. I'd brought them to the NISRA offices, but if I could get over there the next day, I could read them in greater detail.

I felt eyes checking me out and turned to see two of the eight storekeepers on duty watching us, looking not happy. They saw me turn and quickly lowered their eyes back to their work. Okay, so these folks either don't like yeomen or don't like new guys. Either way, that was enough to put them on the new suspect list, right below their chief's name.

After meeting most of the SKs—a couple were not in the office—I headed back to my desk for several hours of real paperwork, trying to keep the Navy supplied with everything from paperclips to jet fuel. My main job right now was to sit there and be a target. Not one of my favorite things to do.

At least I had a few safe hours before Sam passed the info on to Royal that I was the new CI on the scene. Unless either the logistics' CO and/or the chief Yeoman were dirty. They'd gotten my info from Sam a couple of days ago, which was long enough for the vipers to have set up a plan to kill me. Okay, so there was no safe time. It would be full alert status from then on, with personal security a high priority.

The rest of the day was rather boring. I kept up with the office work, but having been in high gear for the last two weeks at the NISRA, average office work was not much of a load in comparison. It did give me a chance to get to know the rest of the enlisted office staff, though. The Chief departed at 1530 hrs, and after that everyone seemed to relax a bit.

I started getting the standard questions of where was I from, what was my last duty station, etc., and in return, I got to query them back. Great way to get to know one another and a great way to fill in the blanks that service records don't include. None had any flags in their records, but paper reports never tell all.

One of the WAVES, YN3 Rhonda Evans, looked familiar. "Were you in Bainbridge a couple of months ago? I feel sure I saw you there," I asked.

"Thought I recognized you too. You were in the class that started two weeks before I graduated, I think. Yea, that's right, you were in the same class as my friend Patricia Newton."

Smiling at that memory that seemed decades old already, I said, "Yes, that's true. Pat was a good friend and we helped each other get through the class." Another memory popped into my mind and I laughed. "You may not recall the first time I saw you. You were walking from the mess hall to class and we crossed paths. Trying to be polite, I said 'good morning,' to which you rudely asked if I was 'a blanky-blank weatherman' and gave me the finger."

Smiling and shaking her head, she replied. "Guess you caught me on a bad day. Sorry 'bout that. At least I didn't stomp your foot the way I did another guy."

"Glad you avoided physical damage. Otherwise, no harm done. My ego is strong enough to handle it. But I was going to mention the barometer was falling and a storm was on the way, but you walked by too fast," I said to a round of laughter from the rest of the staff. "By the way, what time do we get out of this place? And I didn't think to ask the Chief if there was a duty roster for the evenings."

YN2 Tom Brackin jumped in and answered, "No duty roster, weather guy, just a standard 0800–1700 day. Since the crews downstairs work twenty-four/seven, there's no need for fire watches, and they also provide building security. On the way out at the end of the day, either the Chief or I will lock the office spaces. So short answer for the first question: we all get out of here in about fifteen minutes."

Tom continued, "But there is a rotating duty roster for the coffee mess. You'll be added to that, but it will be a couple of weeks before your turn comes up. And in this office we work Monday through Friday, so have a good weekend off."

"Great! Thanks for the info, Tom."

"Naturally, in case of emergencies or all-out war, all that is subject to change."

"Well, let's all hope we can avoid that war thing!"

70

SAM'S MEETING WITH DETECTIVE ROYAL, meanwhile, went just as the previous ones had. According to what he told me about it later, things were cordial and relaxed. After all, they were just two professionals, working together for the good of the community. When they finished sharing information about current cases and discussing plans for working them together when appropriate, Sam set the trap.

"One more thing, Collin. We think there's a lot of drug activity at the base logistics building. Perhaps also some black market stuff going on. We've received some chatter about both, but nothing concrete."

"Hell, Sam, you know that stuff goes on all the time. Nothing new to see there."

"True, but all indicators are pointing to something bigger. Remember several military personnel from that place have died recently, and two of the cases are still unsolved."

"I'll let ya know if any of our people hear anything, Sam. Not much else we can do from outside the gates of the base."

"Good, have them keep their ears open as this might be a hot one. One of the tips we got mentioned a non-military contact. So you might have to get involved with this." Sam pulled out a small notebook from his jacket pocket and flipped a few pages.

He tore off a sheet containing two names and passed it to Royal, saying "What we're doing is putting these two men into the center to see what they can see and hear. They're not agents, just real sailors who volunteered to help as CIs. One started today as a Yeoman paper pusher in the office area and the other will start Monday as a laborer, helping move stuff around."

Collin's face seemed to form a momentary grimace before reassembling into his standard deadpan look. He replied, "So what do you need from me right now?"

"Simple—keep these names under your hat, but when you go over your people's cases, check to see if there is any mention of these two guys. If so, let me know ASAP. We need to make sure they stay safe, and if any of the scum discovers them, I'll pull them out immediately."

"Sure. Can do. Anything else?"

"No, Collin, that covers it for this week. I'll keep you in the loop on this one, but I don't really expect anything to pop from it for a week or three, maybe longer. If there is any dirty stuff underway there, it's buried deep."

Sam was happy with how things had progressed. Now the hard part of waiting and watching started. Afterwards, Sam stopped at a McDonald's for a cup of coffee. While sitting in his car thinking about all Royal had said, another sedan backed in beside him, putting driver's side next to driver's side. John Driscol rolled down his window and asked Sam if all went well. Sam gave him a thumbs up and John left to notify the rest of his team. As Sherlock would say, the game was afoot.

Getting back to the NISRA office after notifying the agents, through Driscol, that the trap was set, Sam next called the agents at the RB and RL and passed the word to them. He then walked to the CO's office to update Captain Miller. The bait had been dangled in front of the suspect. Now everyone needed to watch carefully and hope it worked.

71

IT WAS A SHORT WALK from the office to the mess hall, so I left the Blue Beast and started my stroll. Figured walking would make things easier for my security tail. There was nothing in the Beast I needed, so it could stay there overnight. Having been dubbed the "weather guy" earlier in the day, I looked at the clouds and, with complete lack of knowledge on the subject, decided that rain was coming. Maybe walking was not a good plan.

Being Friday night, the mess hall wasn't busy. Many sailors start their weekend early and head off base for more fun as soon as their duty is over. That was good news for me, as the line was short and the wait time was almost nonexistent. The main selection for the evening was broiled mackerel. I added a side of rice, asparagus, and hush puppies for a complete meal.

After I got my dinner, I started to head to a table near the back of the hall when I heard my name being called. Looking around, I saw Rhonda and two other WAVES motioning me over to their table. Needing to fit in with the crew and also gather as much info as possible, I headed over and sat, as directed, next to a girl with shining black hair.

"Mark, this is Cathy Easton and Ann Holt. We share a barracks room. They both work at the base hospital in the ER. Ladies, Mark is the newest

Yeoman in our supply office and we were in 'A' school at the same time earlier this year."

Cathy gave me a warm smile and a quick handshake. Her short brown hair framed and accented the heart-shape of her face and her brown eyes seemed to sparkle. While not a raving beauty, she had that girl-next-door cuteness about her. She was sitting across the table next to Rhonda.

On my right side, Ann turned toward me and softly said hello. Her black hair was slightly longer than Cathy's, and her blue eyes were bright and penetrating. Her face held a slightly elfish look with a small turned up nose and a slightly pointed chin. There was no handshake, but I got a slight smile. Based on the way she handled her greetings, she was probably the shyest of the three ladies.

"A pleasure to meet you both. Thanks for the invite to join you. Have y'all been in Norfolk long?" I asked.

That general question started an amicable, safe conversation, and an hour of building friendships. You can never have too many friends. And I was able to gather more information about all three. Granted, none were suspects, but more information is always a good thing.

They both got a good laugh when Rhonda told them about our first meeting in Bainbridge. And when I told them I was going to look to see if there is an 'A' school for meteorology, they laughingly all agreed I might have a future there. Laughter is great medicine when under stress. I'd tried not to look around too much, but still felt the need to watch my back.

After dinner, Cathy and Rhonda headed over to the enlisted men's club—or EM club—for a while, but Ann had duty early the next morning, so she started back toward her barracks. I asked Ann if I could walk with her since my barracks was in the same direction.

The walk was pleasant and we chatted about general things. Ann said she'd been dating a corpsman, but they had challenges getting together due to duty scheduling. I told her a bit about Kelly so she wouldn't think I was hitting on her by asking for the walk. We got to her barracks first. She went in with a wave goodbye and I walked on to mine.

Roger was not in our cube when I got there. He was probably at the club or was participating in my protection tail right now. Either way, he was a big boy and could take care of himself. I decided to head down to the common room on the first floor and check out the magazine selection. While there, I was able to spend time watching who was coming and going.

72

SLEEPING WITH ONE EYE OPEN is not the best way to get rest, but it is a good way to stay alive. I glanced over at the rack across the cube and saw a lump still under the blanket. The lump was snoring like the proverbial chain saw, so I figured it had to be Roger. He looked like one who snores loudly.

After hitting the head for the necessary morning ritual of the three Ss, with two of them being showering and shaving, I dressed in my standard plaid shirt and jeans. The previous night's late rain was the leading edge of a small cold front, at least according to the professional weather dudes on the 11 p.m. news program, so I grabbed a jacket and ball cap. And stuck a black watch cap in my jacket pocket.

Considering the parameters of the op, I added the 1911 to my waistband and the magazines and knife to my calves. Doing so covertly in an open cubical was a challenge, but I made it work. It's amazing how much a small locker door can block from view.

Roger had come alive by then and we followed the old high school buddy meeting-ritual of sharing the status of friends. Since it was all fake, it was difficult to keep a straight face, but that was a requirement. Roger said he would pass on the mess hall and we could catch up later. I understood him to mean we'd meet at the NISRA, and I headed out.

The mess hall was even deader than the night before, so wait time was not a problem. The breakfast was good and no one interrupted me. Missing my girl and the mornings we'd recently shared was frustrating, but I had to push Kelly to the back of my mind for now. *Focus, Marcus!*

After securing my tray in the cleaning station, I went into the head. There I stuck the fake glasses in my pocket, replaced the ball cap with the watch cap pulled down low, and turned up the collar of the jacket. Hunching over when I walked also helped change my look. Might be a waste of time, but I may as well make things challenging for the vipers.

Leaving the mess hall, I took a roundabout route to the NISRA offices. When I double checked to make sure I was not being followed, I did finally notice one individual who seemed interested in me. But another glance showed him to be one of the agents involved in my security. Good to know they were there.

My first task was to check the coffee mess. Urns were cold, so I put on the standard and my special brew. That done, I continued down the hall to the NISRA office space to review some of the personnel files of the storekeepers I'd met the previous day. Perhaps they were as white as snow, or maybe more like yellow snow: not something you wanted to be near. And if their records looked good, I'd leave a list of things to check that one of the agents could handle first of the week.

The crowd in the agents' area was a surprise. I planned to see Sam and perhaps a couple of others, but there were about a dozen people standing around talking, including the XO. I hadn't expected that. As I closed the door, CDR Peterson came over.

"Williams, the Captain read me in on this op. Since he cannot be here all the time, he wanted me and LT Kensey to share the duty—also so we'd have a NISO Norfolk officer here at all times. Is that okay with you?"

"Of course, Commander. Extra help is always appreciated. Glad the Captain made that decision, sir."

Sam came over and looked between the Commander and me with some concern on his face as he asked, "Everyone on the same page here?"

"All is good, Sam. Thanks," I answered while smiling at Peterson. "Fact is, it will be a great help to have several sets of fresh eyes looking over the records of a couple of storekeepers that caused my gut to cringe just a bit yesterday. Let me go pull their records." And with that I headed to the file room to pull out my stash of record copies.

As I laid the three personnel records and last BIs on my desk, I explained why I felt they needed more scrutiny. There was no need to explain any further as these professionals were used to looking for weird things.

Unexplained deposits or recent large ticket purchases are standardly looked at during a BI, which requires checking bank statements, talking with neighbors, and investigating other sources. Once these three were examined, the rest of the staff at the center would need a closer look. With over several hundred people assigned to the center, that was a lot of extra work.

"Commander, I suggest you talk with Lieutenant Colonel Tiller on Monday and get him to handle some of the BI work on these three. And please call the CO at the Logistics Center and tell him that security updates are underway for his unit. Explain it was a directive from the Pentagon and that should keep him happy. I'll have the CNO's office plant the cover story. We don't need anyone getting too concerned if they hear about someone asking questions. I hate to give these potential vipers any reason to think they might be suspect, but we need to have more info about them."

"Can do, Williams. Say, how about we get on a first name basis, Mark? Like I said, the skipper read Kensey and me in. And I mean completely in. By the way, congrats on your engagement, Lieutenant Commander."

Nodding, I said, "Thanks. I'll try to stick with Karl. Problem is I've been so deep in my YN3 persona for the last few months, I might slip back into it without thinking. Seeing you in civvies makes it much easier, for sure."

And with that, Karl and Sam each grabbed one of the remaining sets of files off my desk and walked away to do their analysis. I held onto the files for SKC Robert Lansing. My gut was telling me he was the resident viper. And if true, he was mine. But first, time for more coffee.

73

THE ONLY THING TO JUMP out of SKC Lansing's files was the trouble he'd gotten into as a young petty officer. He'd been caught stealing a small quantity of uniforms from his supply unit and selling them to friends at a big discount. A captain's mast resulted in him being reduced in rate and fined. Nothing there that could be considered a national security threat, but it was enough to slow his career. After that, he seemed to have been on the straight and narrow.

However, his wife had divorced him two years ago. There was nothing in his record about the reason for the divorce. Tiller would need to dig that up. It may have left him with a large amount of debt, so he might have had a need for extra money. With his current BI being three years old, there would be some new information that Tiller needed to uncover. Hated to say it, but for more info on this guy, it was time to wait a few days.

Neither Karl nor Sam found anything in the files of the other two storekeepers that had triggered my gut reaction. Here again, the age of their BIs could be hiding something, so Tiller had more work to do as well. And quickly, I hoped. The three of us prepared a list of people and things for Tiller to check.

Another nagging thought came to the front of my mind. Probably nothing, but sometimes "nothing" solves the cases. I called everyone over and told them about the two fellows I saw at the airport while waiting for Roger to show up. I used the same tags for them that I dreamed up then: 'DN' was standing for the David Niven doppelganger and 'SM' for the Sal Mineo facsimile. I also described the car that SM used to leave the airport. No one thought they were familiar.

I had to admit to everyone that there was absolutely nothing about their dress or actions that should send up a red flag, but hunches have been known to pay off. And like the old saying goes, just because you're paranoid doesn't mean the bad guys aren't out to get ya. Being suspicious had saved my butt several times in the past.

"Based on what I've seen from you, Mark, I want to arrest those two just based on your gut reaction," Sam offered.

"Thanks for the vote of confidence, but I prefer to have something a wee bit more concrete before I shoot them," I responded glibly. "Too bad we can't run them past the NPD. Wonder if the local FBI office has anything on them? With DN getting on a flight to Miami, how about we get with the NISRA that covers that area and have them ask around with their local police agencies?" Several of the other agents nodded in agreement.

Sam did a write up about each of the two new possible suspects, and with the info on the three storekeepers who might be people of interest, he sent copies to the agents manning RL and RB. They needed to keep a watch out for these guys. More work for the already overloaded staff, but it might pay off.

Darrell Tasker immediately got on the phone to a friend in NISRA Miami and chatted with him about DN. He didn't go into specifics, just that someone had mentioned something that might need to be looked at. Sam said he would call an agent at the local FBI office, whom he'd worked with in the past, on Monday. Not having any names was a challenge, but providing them with good descriptions was a decent place to start.

The surveillance of Detective Royal had not shown anything of interest yet. Friday afternoon after his meeting with Sam, he left his office and checked in with two other detectives working a case in downtown Norfolk. After talking with them for a few minutes, he went home for the night. Perhaps he'd called one of the vipers, but nothing was positive at this point. Or perhaps one of those other detectives was his bad guy contact.

And the group of agents and SEALs responsible for keeping Roger and me alive reported that no one had shown any special interest in either of us yet. Hoped it stayed that way for a while longer.

Saturday evening back at the barracks was calm, and Sunday after worship services was actually a bit fun. I convinced Roger to join me at the recreation center where we checked out a couple of recurve bows and practiced archery for a few hours. I figured if the vipers showed up we could always fill them full of arrows. Plus, being in an open field made the watching job easier for our bodyguards.

74

MONDAY CAME QUICKLY, AND WHEN I passed Roger as I headed out to lunch, he told me he was settled in and working on the first floor, moving boxes from one place to another. It was a job just a little more boring than the paperwork I was doing on the upper deck. He hadn't noticed anyone acting strange, but then he had no baseline to judge from yet. He did mention that SKC Lansing looked hung-over that morning.

A routine quickly formed. Mess hall for breakfast, work at the center, quick lunch, more work, mess hall for dinner, then an hour or so at the EM club for a beer, and back to the transient barracks for more magazine reading and TV watching. Tuesday became Wednesday, on and on, and then it was Friday afternoon again. Nothing had happened; no one was acting weird. I was beginning to think I'd dreamed up a wasteful, dead end operation.

Rather than continue the routine, I decided that Friday evening was a perfect time to shake things up by making a dash off base. Maybe that would excite the vipers into acting. I called the NISRA office and let them know my plans. Easier for the team to keep an eye on me if they knew where I was going. I didn't want to endanger Kelly by being with her, but

I could go to our favorite restaurant alone. Seafood—and mass quantities of it—were a poor substitute for being with Kelly, but I'd take what I could get.

The Blue Beast was ready for a drive and started right up even after sitting for a week. Speed limit on the base was a wild 15 mph. And they were serious about it, even to the point of placing speed bumps in several high-traffic locations. As I drove to the main gate, I had to traverse two of these obnoxious things.

The first bump went well. Going over it at about 5 mph, neither auto parts nor my teeth were jarred. However, the second one came faster than I'd planned and I hit it at the full 15 mph. The jarring was intense and I heard a nasty noise. Then I saw one of my hubcaps rolling off to the side of the road. I quickly pulled over and stopped to retrieve it. Hate to get a littering ticket from the SP.

Of course, my stopping on the side of the main drag got the attention of the SP gentlemen who frequently watched this area, and one pulled behind my car and flipped on his flashing lights. As I came walking back to the Beast with the runaway hubcap, the SP was looking down at the wheel that was missing it. He was shaking his head as I walked up.

"Looks like you are missing a few nuts, sailor. Is this how you normally maintain your vehicle?" he asked.

I looked down at the hubcap-less wheel and was shocked to see only one lug nut holding the wheel in place. The other four had been removed. "Petty Officer, that is definitely not normal." Before I could say anything else, another car pulled up behind the SP's vehicle and Agent Joe Mabry walked up. Joe had planned to tail me to the restaurant and keep watch while I was there.

"Glad you are here, Agent Mabry. I seem to be having a problem with my nuts, and you are just the guy to help me," I said as I pointed to the wheel.

Joe turned to the SP, showed his badge, and said. "I'll take care of this. Thanks for stopping, but nothing else for you to do here." After the SP had departed, he looked at me and said, "Well, most of us know you have a screw loose, Mark. Guess we should have been watching your car too."

We carefully drove the Beast over to a nearby parking lot and pulled the other hubcaps. The two front wheels had only one lug nut holding the wheel in place, and the one on the passenger side was not completely tight. The vipers had been there and this was a clear case of sabotage. All I'd have needed to do was get up to speed and take a curve—at least one wheel would have come off and a decent wreck would have ensued.

I put the hubcaps in the front floorboard so the team could check them for fingerprints. They were probably clean, but it never hurts to look. I removed two lug nuts from each back wheel and added them to the front wheels. That would hold the wheels in place, allowing me to safely limp back to the impound lot. There the agents could check the rest of the car exterior for prints. And see if anything else had been tampered with—like the brake lines.

After that, Joe ran me over to the barracks so I could brief Roger. The vipers were active and he too needed to be on higher alert. The rest of Friday night was uneventful. But one thing was now clear: this was no wasteful, dead-end operation.

75

COME SATURDAY MORNING, ROGER HAD duty at the Logistics Center starting at 0800 and I was vacillating between frustration and anger over the sabotage of the Blue Beast. Needing to do something as an outlet for those emotions, I headed into the NISRA office for more research. That would also give a couple of the guys watching my back a few hours of down time, since I'd be in a secured area. Or they could go help watch Roger; that decision was up to the Core Team leaders.

With the coffee brewing, I returned to my worktables in the NISRA file room. Granted it was 0930 hrs on a Saturday morning, but with the op underway and my near miss the previous night, I thought one or two guys would be around. Nope, the agents' room was empty and quiet, so at least I had some solitude in which to think. No messages were on my desk. However, there was a stack of folders sitting in the center with a handwritten note from Sam that read "interesting stuff—couple of red flags, but no smoking guns."

Opening the one on top of the stack, I saw it was the updated BI on SKC Lansing, courtesy of Colonel Tiller. Lansing's ex-wife, Kate, had divorced him due to his cheating. Research by J. Scott showed there was no proof of any affairs, but that information had not been brought up in the hearing. Kate got a good amount for alimony, including a portion of his eventual retirement. Lansing had not fought any of the allegations or the compensation she was awarded. Strange actions since he was probably not guilty … unless he was just tired of it all. The stress of divorce can make people reach a 'just get it over' attitude.

From what Tiller uncovered, his money problems started right after the divorce. That made sense: due to the large amount going to the ex, he was not left with much to live on. Then late that past summer, the money issues suddenly cleared up. He was able to get up to date on his overdue payments. And there were even a few bucks in his bank account. No record of a second job, but perhaps he was selling off some personal items. Or maybe he did some gambling at the Chief's club over the pool table.

But his drinking problem only started late last fall, well over a year and a half after the divorce. Had the money issues finally pushed him over the edge, or was something else to blame? A failed love interest perhaps? I made a note for Sam to check into that.

The remaining two folders were BIs on the other storekeepers of interest. They both seemed to have a little more money in their accounts than the usual sailor, but then they could just be frugal. Or they might be gamblers or drug pushers, but nothing about those possibilities was in the BIs. Once you got past the extra cash, no other issues jumped out about them. Looked like it was time to get to know them face to face and try to determine if either of them enjoyed taking lug nuts off my Chevy.

After reading the updated BIs, I added a response to Sam's note stating I concurred with his findings and planned to get to know them all better real soon. I moved the stack of files back to his desk, then headed into the file room. Okay, that's not exactly true. First I filled my coffee mug with my special brew, and *then* I headed into the file room. Priorities are important.

The cards I'd laid out the previous week listing specific pieces of evidence were still there, and I gave them another read. Even after a week of the info being in the back of my mind for the subconscious to work on, I was not seeing anything linking one case to another. My gut was saying there were links, but the brain had not yet got the message.

But I kept going back to the bird pin. There was something there. So using my time-honored and highly tested methodology of starting at the beginning, I pulled Ensign Appleton's case file and started reading every page one more time. It was a depressing job. This lovely young lady was just starting her career and her life, and both were brutally cut short. And her family in Ohio had not received the closure they so deserved.

There was only one ROI—Report of Investigation—from the Columbus-based NISRA agent who interviewed her parents. And there was one line in that report that caught my attention this time through. She was expected home for Thanksgiving, a known fact, but one thing not mentioned elsewhere in the file was that her folks had expected to meet her boyfriend for the first time.

According to the ROI, her parents did not know his name, just that he was a pilot and Joan was terribly in love with him. Nothing else was mentioned about the boyfriend. The boyfriend was a link and possible witness, but he had not been found. And from the look of the file, no one had looked for him. Someone missed that.

76

A QUICK LOOK AT THE clock showed it was finally a decent enough hour to call a probably still-grieving family, so I picked up the phone. After only three rings, a man answered.

"Hello, is this Mr. Appleton?"

"Yes. Who's calling?"

"Sir, please forgive the interruption. This is Lieutenant Commander Colt with the Naval Investigative Service Office Norfolk, and I am working on your daughter's case. I hate to bother you, but I do have a couple of questions if I may, sir."

His voice got cold and hard as he responded, "We thought you people had closed the case and written Joan off after handing her mother a folded flag last November."

"Sir, nothing could be further from the truth. Her case will remain open and active until you get the justice you deserve. Until you get the answers you need. I admit progress has been slow, but if I may ask a couple of questions, that might help things change." I closed my eyes to help my mind form a picture of Joan's family in my mind. It made it easier to talk to them on the phone when I knew they were hurting so much.

"Sorry, Lieutenant Commander. I allowed my frustration to show. We told your agent all that we knew back in November, but ask away and I'll do my best for you."

"No apologies needed, Mr. Appleton. I am so sorry for your loss. And I greatly appreciate your time. Our agent noted in his report that you had expected to meet Joan's boyfriend. Is there anything, even something small and thought to be insignificant, that you can tell me about him or his relationship with Joan?"

"Hold on," he said, and called his wife over to the phone. I could hear him quickly tell her who I was and why I was calling. Then he asked her the same question I gave him. Some background talk happened, then he came back on the line. "Lieutenant Commander, Doris said that Joan had only told her that he was a pilot and they had met at the officers' club on base. Joan always liked being dramatic and mysterious, so she was going to keep everything about him secret until they arrived."

"Thank you. That really is a help. Now the second question is a lot easier. Did Joan have any special hobbies that included birds? Painting birds, photographing birds, or just bird watching, perhaps?"

"No, why?"

"It's probably nothing. I'm just trying to tie up all the loose ends, sir. At this point, everything is important to me and I promise to follow each lead no matter how small. I am sorry to open wounds that may be starting to heal, but the information you provided today is critical. I'll let you know when there is any progress. Please call me if you think of anything else or if you just need to talk. We share your loss, Mr. Appleton."

"Thank you. Your call is greatly appreciated. Goodbye."

I hung up the phone and rubbed my closed eyes. Calls such as this one were part of the job, but never easy to do. Grieving family members deserved every courtesy we could offer. And they needed to know what happened. I kept my eyes closed, let out a deep sigh, and leaned back in thought. Then I heard the sound of a chair moving. Opening my eyes, I saw LT Greg Kensey standing at attention in front of my desk.

"Sorry to eavesdrop, Mr. Colt. When I came in, I didn't want to bother you during your call so I just remained quiet. Forgive me if I overstepped, I probably should have gone back to my office."

"Good morning, Greg, good to see you here. Nothing to apologize for as we are all working on these same cases. Grab a chair and I'll catch you up. I was surprised that no one was around here."

"Thank you, sir. Sorry, but I've been in my office trying to wrap up a case that needs to get to JAG on Monday. There were others here earlier, sir, but I don't know where they went."

I shook my head slightly and said, "Greg, drop the 'sir' stuff. Call me Mark, Petty Officer, or Yeoman Williams, but not by my rank or real name while this operation is underway. The skipper should have made that clear when he read you in on this." I put on my best smile to help reduce the pain of the rebuff and continued, "Besides, we are in civvies, so we are just a couple of guys working on a special project. Okay?"

"Yes, ssss … Mark. Can do. By the way, you handled that call well. I don't have that level of empathy."

"A lot comes with practice, which I'm sorry to say I've had more than enough of for this lifetime. As a lawyer, you probably have already put yourself into your client's frame of mind, which is the first step of sharing their emotions and developing empathy."

I paused and then continued, "When I was an ROTC midshipmen on my first summer cruise, I was selected to accompany our CO on a next-of-kin death notification. A young seaman had fallen off his carrier while traversing the Atlantic. Facing his parents at that moment was the hardest thing I'd ever done until about a week later when I was his pallbearer and helped fold the flag at that dead sailor's funeral."

I took a sip of coffee and continued, "His body had been found after a week in the water so it had to be a closed casket funeral. That news was almost as rough on his mother as the initial death notice. No last look at the face of her baby. She didn't need to know he no longer had a face."

"That had to be rough on his family. And you," Greg said through a grimace.

"Greg, the opportunity to share the grief of the military families and participate in such a sad event stays with you even though you never knew the guy. But he was a brother in arms, a member of our family in navy blue, and he and his family deserve our respect. I suppose that event helps me when I talk to others who are likewise suffering. It's never easy though."

Greg just nodded his understanding. But I knew that if you haven't gone through it, you really don't understand.

"Here, read this, then I'll share what I just discovered. But first," I held up my empty coffee mug as I passed him Joan's case file, "this needs a refill. Can I bring you one?" He shook his head and I left Greg reading Joan's file so he would be up to speed for my update when I returned, pleasantly caffeinated. Finally, a potential link had exposed itself—if we could only connect a few more little dots.

77

As I came back down the hall to the NISRA spaces with a fresh, steaming mug, I saw Sam coming up the back stairs. We reached the door at the same time, and since I had coffee, I let him handle the keypad.

"I think I have some good news, Sam," I said. Then I noticed he didn't look happy.

"What's wrong, Sam?" I asked as he held the door open. Greg looked up from the file as we came in.

Sam nodded toward Greg then took a deep breath. "Guess filling you in slipped through the cracks. Roger is in the hospital. At 0830 hrs, an accident occurred at the Logistics Center when a load fell off a forklift and pinned Roger to the deck. He is alive. He's critical, but stable. Surgery is underway to stop some internal bleeding, and then after that, they will take care of several broken bones. Most of the agents are at the Logistics Center now."

"Oh, crap. The vipers must be getting desperate to try something in their nest. Unless it actually was just an accident. Any update on that yet?"

"No accident: it was clearly intentional. With the failed attack on you with the car sabotage, we moved a couple of undercover personnel into the center to keep a closer watch on you guys. One of your SEAL buddies saw the driver turn toward Roger and dump the load. He was not close enough to stop it, but he was able to catch the driver as he tried to get out of the center."

Sam took a breath and continued, "John and Darrell are sitting on the driver now at the base hospital; he should not have tried to fight a SEAL. The nurses are patching up a few cuts he received for his failed escape efforts. Nothing very serious. Figured we'd let him recover some and also sweat a little over there before moving him here for interrogation."

"What's his name?" I asked, probably a bit too harshly.

"SK3 Donald Harker. Yea, he is one of the two guys you had bad feelings about. We are now looking for SK2 John Baker, the other guy you thought was a bad apple. He wasn't scheduled to work today and isn't in his barracks."

I sipped my now-cooling coffee as I ran the new info around inside my mind. Now was the time to move. "Sam, we need to bring in SKC Lansing for questioning about Harker; avoid anything that would make the Chief think we are on to him. Move Harker over here only when you can time it so Lansing can see him brought in wearing cuffs. We also need to bring in Baker as soon as we find him. Leave enough agents at the center to do the proper investigation, and get the rest of the crew finding these other two gents."

With that decision made, Sam picked up the phone to start the process rolling. After his call, he turned back to me and said, "You know picking up those other two will get back to Royal. And soon. That might make it harder to generate a case against him."

"Yea, maybe. But with Harker caught red-handed, I think we now have leverage against Lansing. I can't help but believe he's in on it all. And I do think Lansing will lead us to Royal. And since both Roger and I are burned, we might as well pull out and try to salvage as much as possible."

Greg looked as though he wanted to say something, but was holding back. I gave him the 'come on' hand signal and said, "Okay, Greg, what ya thinking? We need all the help we can get, so let it out."

"Well, sir, uh, Mark, if you pull out now, aren't you assuming the three people you initially tagged as guilty are the only dirty ones? What if there are other vipers there? What if the Chief was keeping your identities to himself and just sending out one of his people at a time to do the dirty work?"

Sam nodded in agreement and gave Greg a thumbs up. And I had to admit Greg was right. Assuming these three were the only dirty ones was a dangerous thing to do. And I realized I was striking out at those three in anger over Roger's injuries.

"Very true, Greg. I'm glad someone is thinking clearly around here. I let my anger over Roger's attack take control. Not good. Okay, Sam, call your guys and have them just quietly surveil John Baker, but not pick him up. Continue with the plan to bring Harker and the Chief here. I need to head to the hospital."

Sam made the call and then turned back to me. "And before you run out, what is the good news you were going to share when I got here? We could use something good right now."

I told them both about my finding in Appleton's file about the pilot boyfriend who should have been with her for the holiday, and the family's verbal comment about the boyfriend being a pilot who she met at the O club. And then I started the explanation about how it all tied together and where it could lead.

"And that brings me to this bird pin that was found with her body. Joan didn't care about birds in general according to her parents, yet we assume she had this pin. Perhaps it was a gift. Military pilots have squadron insignias. Could her boyfriend be a pilot from a squadron that uses the Gannet as an insignia and he 'pinned' his girlfriend like the fraternities do? And if so, could this bird's characteristics point to a specific squadron?" I tossed a photo of the pin on the desk in front of them.

I could see the gears were turning in Sam's head and Greg was keeping up with him. So I continued, "According to the Captain's wife, who is a bird enthusiast, the Gannet is a big sea bird that spots prey underwater and dives down to get it. My first thought is the Gannet is a perfect insignia for an anti-submarine warfare squadron since ASW aircraft spot subs from on high, then drop torpedoes that dive after them."

"Makes sense, Mark," replied Sam.

"So, Greg, do you feel up to some field work?"

"Whatever you need, Mark."

Sam was nodding in agreement since I knew he was already thinking the same thing I was. "Greg, get into your dress blues and go show this photo of the pin to every squadron at NAS Norfolk and NAS Oceana. Start with the ASW units. I am confident that one of them knows who uses the Gannet, and when you find that unit, talk with every member of the unit and find the boyfriend of Ensign Joan Appleton. It just might put us closer to her killer."

And with that, Sam and I headed to the hospital and Greg to the squadron offices.

78

WITH THE BLUE BEAST IN lockup for fingerprint checks and the 'Cuda stashed at the house, I was stuck being a passenger with Sam. I appreciated the ride, but was not used to taking corners on two wheels as he did getting across the base. I supposed the shore patrol officers knew his car and left him alone.

By the time we got to the hospital, Roger was sleeping soundly in ICU recovery. A talk with his doctor filled in the blanks: he had a ruptured spleen from a box impact, a couple of broken ribs, a broken left arm and right leg. The leg break was a compound fracture, so it was repaired while he was in surgery for the spleen. They were working on setting the left arm now, and would be done shortly.

We asked the standard questions on prognosis—when he would be awake, etc., and got the standard answers back: 'He will be awake later— check back tomorrow—and a full recovery looks pretty good; it will just take time.' And with that, the doc went on to other patients.

We crossed into the ICU for a look at Roger. Sam had already altered the unit's schedule to include at least two armed guards to watch Roger. My SEAL buddies, Larry and Glenn, were already on duty in the ICU.

Roger looked rough, but at least he was alive. Too many tubes and wires to count were connected to him, and the typical hospital noises of beeping and air flow hissing were in the background. Bruises were starting to show on his hands and face. His right leg was in a huge cast and wires held it up off the bed. His broken arm had already been put into a cast and was suspended to give the docs easier access to his torso for bandage changes. It brought back too many bad memories from last summer.

Leaving Glenn to watch Roger breathe, the three of us found an empty room in which to talk in private. Larry apologized for not stopping the attack, since he'd witnessed the whole thing. He went over all that happened and what he'd seen right before and directly after the attack. He was the one who "gently" convinced SK3 Harker to surrender and go with him quietly.

After hearing firsthand about the attack, I think I convinced Larry there was no way he could have stopped it from happening. If anything, his yelling "stop" at Harker at the last minute probably threw off his aim, most likely saving Roger's life. Quickly catching Harker was the icing on the cake.

I brought Larry up to date on the plans we developed for the three SKs and let him know that, come Monday, I'd be back at the Logistics Center as a Yeoman. I asked him to pass the word to the rest of the security team.

As we headed back into ICU, we got the attention of a pair of nurses just inside the door. Larry mentioned that the taller ICU nurse, a lieutenant, wasn't happy about the added security. When she realized that Sam and I were somewhat in charge, she pulled us out of the ICU into an office and proceeded to read us the riot act about how disruptive our presence and our guards were to her important operation.

My apology and words of explanation about the seriousness of the situation didn't do much to calm her down, but she got over all her issues when I showed her my get-out-of-jail-free card. After she read both sides, I asked if she would like to express her complaints directly to the CNO. She quickly decided that wouldn't be necessary. I told her to forget ever seeing this card and to forget seeing us. I think she was in awe of us by then.

As she quietly walked away, Sam chuckled and said, "That thing does come in handy."

"True, but I hate to have to use it. When I pull it out, that proves that I haven't been able to use reason, logic, common sense, or my devilishly handsome face to solve a problem. I really hate to fail."

Sam smiled and said, "Seems to me you don't fail too often. But one thing we've both failed to do is eat. It's way past lunch time. How about we go find some?"

"Hold that thought," I said as I walked toward the nurse's station and asked for a phone. A quick call solved two problems. "Okay, let's head over to Captain Miller's house. Dorothy is putting together a couple of sandwiches and we can use the time to bring the skipper up to date."

"Excellent planning and procurement on your part, Mark, and if it must be said, a very proper use of time. And who knows, you just might get lucky and see Kelly, right?" he said with a wink.

"Hell, Sam, it has been a long nine days! Go easy on me."

79

WE HADN'T QUITE REACHED THE Captain's door when it flew open and Kelly jumped out into my arms. Sam couldn't stop his laugh, and I just stood there and enjoyed the moment.

"Welcome home, sailor. It has been a long voyage," she whispered in my ear as I carried her inside. Her warmth, smell, touch, and voice filled my heart, and most of my problems went to the back burner.

Sam followed and closed the door. Dorothy came from the kitchen and gave an approving smile before motioning Sam to follow her back to the kitchen. Dorothy touched Sam's arm and said, "Thank you for bringing Marcus. Kelly has been so miserable this past week and it's driving us both nuts!"

"Mark must have a thick wall around his emotions. What little I've seen of him this week, he has been one hundred and ten percent into the operation. But it's good to see him with Kelly. He needs her just as much as she needs him. I don't think I have ever seen a couple like those two. I'll take credit from driving him over, Dorothy, but it was his idea to get over here and brief the Captain. Where is he, by the way?"

"Humphrey is hiding in his study to give those two a few minutes alone. I'll ring the dinner bell shortly and disturb them," she snickered.

A few moments later, Kelly and I entered the kitchen. I went over and gave Dorothy a hug and kiss, thanked her for letting us impose, then asked about the Captain.

"Right behind you, Marcus. I just got off the phone with LT Kensey and it seems you and I both have information to share. Let's go to the study." And with that, the skipper turned and headed out of the kitchen. Sam, Kelly, Dorothy, and I followed obediently right behind.

Sam took the lead briefing the skipper on the day's attack and Roger's health status. As he described the injuries, Kelly kept squeezing my hand harder, so I knew it affected her—she was thinking it could be me lying there. Dorothy was leaning against the door casing, listening, and just kept whispering, "Oh, dear."

We explained the plan with the three storekeepers, two of whom should be at the NISRA by now, ready to start undergoing interrogation as soon as Sam got back there. It was going to be a long night for Sam and a few of the others.

I then related to the Captain my call with Ensign Appleton's family, and the things I'd put together from her case file. And why we had Greg out chasing birds across the base.

The Captain leaned back in his chair and said, "Marcus, you hit a home run on that. After Greg said to thank Dorothy for her bird knowledge, he said you were one hundred percent right that the bird pin was a squadron insignia and it belonged to an ASW unit flying the P2V Neptune from here down the coast to Cuba. It is Patrol Squadron VP-3, nicknamed the Gannets. And a very interesting thing is that unit had a pilot killed last November under unusual circumstances."

"Was that pilot LT Jason Thomas?" I asked. I was suddenly sickened that I'd missed a connection when I read his file two weeks ago.

"How did you know?" asked the skipper.

I explained that I had read his still-open case file and had set it aside for more study. There were several things about his death that just didn't add up and it felt like we were missing something. I hadn't considered it might be linked to the Ensign's case. I should have seen it.

"And Greg also found out that, a few months before his death, he'd started dating someone from supply. None of his friends knew anything about her. He never said her name and no photos were anywhere to be seen. So they speculated he might be seeing an enlisted person. And that is why none of them mentioned a relationship to the agents when they did their investigation; they were protecting his reputation," the Captain finished.

Sam just shook his head, "That is the link we should have had last November. Crap, we might have closed both of those cases by now."

Now it was the Captain's turn to shake his head side to side. "Sam, neither you nor Marcus have anything to regret on this one. If you aren't given the information, you can't accurately handle the case. And Marcus, you can't link to something that doesn't exist. Thankfully, your persistence with that bird pin paid off. Enjoy your victories, no matter how small."

Dorothy vanished for a moment, returned, and stuck her head into the office asking, "Anyone care to join me for some food?"

80

DINNER WAS MUCH MORE THAN the promised sandwich. Dorothy had pulled out and heated some leftover baked ham. She served it with mashed potatoes, broccoli, and apple sauce. Sam and I were on the edge of starvation, so we greatly appreciated the excellent meal and especially all her extra efforts on such short notice. Sam and I made sure Dorothy knew how much we appreciated her work.

After that great meal, Sam was ready to head back to the office and start on Harker's interrogation. And I wanted to do some comparisons with the Appleton and Thomas case files to see what else I'd missed. But my plans were sidelined when the Captain suggested that I hang around a bit. I agreed, of course, since a suggestion from the CO is tantamount to a direct order. Sam said his good nights and left without me.

The Captain, Kelly and I returned to his study and got comfortable. "Any reason you failed to mention the problems you had with your car yesterday?" asked the Captain.

I had not wanted to get into that in front of Kelly. After her reaction to Roger's injuries, I didn't want to put the attempted sabotage on her shoulders just yet. Figured it could wait a day or three—it might not seem so bad by then.

"I didn't want to stress someone out any more than she is already, sir."

"Well, she heard about some of it when I got an update call last night. Any time the phone rings she is hovering around like a gnat just in case it's you calling. So if you want to reduce stress and maintain domestic tranquility, I suggest you tell her all about it. And do it right now."

The skipper stood and assumed his command stance and continued, "After that, plan on sleeping in our guestroom tonight; that was not a suggestion, Mr. Colt. Whatever you need to do at the office will wait until I drive you over there tomorrow morning. Those two cases have been open for months, and a few more hours delay will not cause any problems. But you not getting enough rest will. Now if you will excuse me, good night to you both."

And with that, the Captain walked out of his study, closed the door, and left Kelly and me sitting on the sofa. I smiled at Kelly and said, "Guess the skipper has an agenda, don't ya think?"

"Oh, you betcha, he does. The agenda is called 'Keeping Kelly Happy' and you had better get with the program, sailor." And then she got that sad look I hate and softly asked, "What really happened yesterday, Marcus?"

"I didn't want to get you concerned, and since nothing happened, I figured it was best to not mention it."

"Not the correct answer, Marcus. I need to know everything and I can handle it. And I'll be happier knowing what is actually going on rather than letting my vivid imagination come up with whatever scenarios it dreams up."

And with that, I gave her the complete rundown on the sabotage of the Blue Beast, what could have happened if the vipers' evil plans had worked, and what actually happened when they failed. Then I told her what I'd planned to do that next week and that if all went well, this mess would be over soon.

We talked for another hour or so and I got caught up on how well her master's thesis was progressing, and what all she did this past week without me being around. I told her how boring my week had been until the car incident. And what I'd hoped to dig out of the files while in the NISRA office the next day.

Roger was also on both of our minds. Kelly promised to visit with him the next afternoon. I needed to talk with him about the incident, but was not sure how the next day's schedule would go. If things went well, we'd meet at the hospital. Otherwise, that night was our last night together for a while longer.

As we talked, it was great to see the light reflecting off her engagement ring. And the combined birthstone bracelet looked wonderful on her right arm. Although we were sitting in the Captain's house, having her beside me made it feel like home. It was true; home is where the heart is.

Then faster than either of us wanted, the evening was over and it was time to get some much-needed rest. I got a marvelous good night kiss at my door, and with the pleasure of that on my mind, I quickly drifted off into a deep sleep.

81

"... SUDDENLY THERE CAME A TAPPING, as of some one gently rapping, rapping at my chamber door." As the night fog slowly cleared from my brain, my first thought was why the hell am I quoting Edgar A. Poe? Then the tapping started again. I realized where I was, and why, and immediately recognized it was not a dream. There really was someone gently tapping on my door. I made sure my near-naked body was covered and said, "Enter."

I had expected the skipper to provide a wake-up since there were no alarm clocks in his guestroom and we were heading into the office that morning. So it was a most pleasant surprise to see Kelly enter, and even better that she was carrying two mugs of coffee.

"Got a minute to share with your fiancée before you rush out to save the world from evil vipers?" she asked as she passed a mug to me and sat on the edge of the bed.

"If I may borrow a phrase: 'Oh, you betcha!'" I leaned over and was rewarded with a kiss. "Nice way to wake up."

She ran her hand down from my left shoulder across my chest. "What caused this scar?" she asked, her hand moving across a rough area on my right side.

"Just a memento from the fun with my SEAL buddies. They play rough." I smiled and pulled her hand from my chest. "There are a few more scars you can play with later. Right now though, I need to get moving." And I leaned forward into a sitting position.

"Not yet," she replied as she returned her hand to my chest and pushed me back against the pillow. "I still claim a few uninterrupted moments with you to call mine. Aunt Dorothy is just starting to prepare breakfast, so we have some time."

I so wanted to just be here with Kelly for the rest of the day, but that couldn't be, so I'd take what I could get, even if just a few minutes. We sipped our coffee, shared some general morning talk, and just savored being in the same place together.

Kelly ran her fingers through my hair and whispered softly, "I can't wait for my Mom to meet you. One look at you and she'll know I hit the jackpot, for sure. At least Dad knows you and what you look like."

"Call your Mom later today and ask her if I pass muster. I have not had the chance to mention it, but when I picked up your bracelet last week, the jeweler gave me several copies of the two photos he shot that night we got engaged. And earlier this week I took time to write your Mom, thanking her for raising such a wonderful daughter, and I wrote my folks about us. And I sent both families one each of the photos."

'You are the best and think of everything." Then she purred, ran her tongue into my ear and whispered, "I think ahead too. Check the closet and the top dresser drawer before you shower. Now get moving and come on down for some food before you dash off to save the world. Love ya!" And with that, she jumped up and went out the door before I could say anything else.

Checking the places she mentioned, I found that Kelly had moved some of my clothing from our house to the guest room in anticipation that I'd be staying here at some time in the near future. What a girl!

Heading into the guest bath, I found the medicine cabinet included packaged toothbrushes, traveler-sized tubes of paste, and razors, so I made good use of them. It only took a couple of minutes to shower and get myself presentable.

After dressing in fresh attire—my standard dress casual look of dark jeans, button-down pale yellow Oxford, and navy blue sports coat to cover the shoulder holster, I felt totally renewed. I grabbed my now-empty mug and headed down to the kitchen to officially start the day.

"Good morning," I said to all as I entered the kitchen. Dorothy was at the stove, and I gave her a quick kiss on the cheek. The Captain and Kelly were sitting at the table. Before I could react, she jumped up, grabbed my mug, and prepared another dose of caffeine to help get me going. The Captain chuckled and said, "Seems you have her well trained already, Marcus."

In response to that, Kelly stuck her tongue out at the skipper. I just smiled and gratefully accepted the mug from my darling. "Captain, I think you described her perfectly when you told me she is a 'force of nature.' I don't think I want to anger that force by insinuating any training is needed. My goal is to always stay on her good side. Therefore, I accept this beautiful woman just as she is." The skipper returned the smile and shook his head in agreement.

"Right answer, sailor," said Kelly as I got a kiss as a reward.

"Humphrey, unless you have a problem with it, Kelly and I will go visit your agent in the hospital later this afternoon," Dorothy interjected as she handed a full plate to the Captain and placed one at her seat. Kelly did the same for me and put her plate next to mine.

"Shouldn't be a problem. I suspect he will appreciate seeing you both. We might be flying his mother in from Chicago tomorrow. His father died a few years ago and he's an only child, so she's the extent of his next-of-kin. Marcus and I might be there later today. A lot depends on how things go this morning. Some important things might be happening, or at least we hope."

"Sir, I really appreciate staying here last night. That was the deepest sleep I've had since this operation started. I have been keeping one eye open every night at the barracks. And I know the men who are watching my back appreciate having the night off." I winked at Kelly and continued, "And the wake-up service here is excellent."

"Dorothy told me she thought it was clear that this house is always open to you. And that was before you became a part of the family. In addition to family, we take good care of our friends, and you have been in that group since that first Friday night."

"Thanks, Captain. That means a lot to me, and ..."

Before I could continue with my thought, the phone rang. The skipper quickly answered it. He didn't say much, but his face told the story. Something had happened and it wasn't a good thing. He hung up the phone and just stood there for a moment or two. He turned to me and said, "Eat fast, we need to go. The SPs found Harker hanging in his cell a little bit ago."

82

THE CAPTAIN'S DRIVING SKILLS WHEN angry were much better than Sam's, so the trip to the office wasn't stressful because of the driving. However, both of us were stressed as we considered the ramifications of the news. Suicide or murder was the unspoken question in our minds. And where did this leave us with the operation?

We both kept our thoughts silent as we stopped at the coffee mess for a mug of brew. Our brains were going to need all the jolts it could give. And with that done, we proceeded down the hallway.

Upon entering the agents' area, we saw a lot of 'just standing around' going on. Several men were on the phones. Sam and two other agents were in a huddle with the Shore Patrol Commanding Officer, Captain Simon Lavella. Sam motioned the SP CO and us into his office. Closing the door, Sam had barely started the update brief when the skipper jumped in.

"Before we get into all the details, Sam, I want to know how the hell the SP let this happen. Captain Lavella, you run the brig. Care to explain?" Captain Miller demanded in a harsh voice as he stared Lavella down.

"Excuse me, sir, but I have a more pressing question. Where is Chief Lansing?" I interrupted softly in hopes my tone would help the skipper to calm down. We needed Lavella's help and not his resentment.

Sam picked up on my tone and responded in kind, "Mark, since we told him last night that we had Harker under arrest, Lansing has refused to talk and even refused to leave the interrogation room. He is still there right now with two agents watching him."

I nodded my approval, gave him a thumbs up, and asked, "And SK2 Baker? Have we found him yet?"

"No, but we have people watching his barracks and office. It's only a matter of time," responded Sam.

Nodding in agreement, I motioned for the SP CO that it was his turn. Lavella looked a little confused, but he also looked like he'd been caught with his pants down in the middle of the O club: embarrassed and sickened. "Captain Miller, we are looking into that right now. All the men who were on duty last night and this morning have been sequestered and are under guard. Your agents are there now. Dr. Wentworth has Harker's body and is doing an autopsy to confirm if the death is really a suicide."

Captain Miller had gotten our message. He shook his head in approval of Lavella's comments and quietly said, "Sorry, Simon, to be so short with you. This was our first solid lead on a string of unsolved murders and we needed that bastard alive."

"No problem, Hump, I understand. I'm also extremely pissed. But we'll figure it out. And soon."

Sam took over and gave a full briefing to the skipper and me on the events from the previous night. He wrapped it up nicely. "The best news is that we have a signed confession from Harker, and he stated he got all his orders directly from Lansing. In addition, he implicated Baker as another one of the vipers. And you are really going to love this: he said one of our unsolved overdoses from January, SK3 Peter Rodriquez, was also taking kill orders from Lansing. He didn't say why, but Lansing ordered Baker to kill Rodriquez and make it look like an overdose."

"Excellent news, Sam. Now please tell me that Lansing does not know Harker is dead," I said.

"No, we have kept that quiet. How do you want to handle it, Mark?"

Lavella gave me a strange look and asked, "Excuse me, Captain, but why is your Yeoman calling the shots here?"

"Sorry, Simon. This operation has been a strange one from the start that needed more subterfuge than usual between NIS and our sister organizations, and even with many people in these NIS offices." And with that intro, the skipper proceeded to quickly inform Lavella about my real identity and reason for being here.

Lavella didn't look fully convinced after the skipper had finished, but he looked at me and asked, "So, what's next, Mr. Colt?"

As I've always done when put on the spot, I went with what my gut was telling me. "As long as Lansing thinks Harker is still talking, we have leverage. Sam, make sure no one talks to Lansing about anything. I hope the four of us can come up with a strategy to get him to roll over on whoever is giving him the orders—and I still think it's Detective Royal—and to tell us who else he has been giving orders to."

They all nodded in agreement as I paused to drain my mug. "Based on his heavy involvement in the murders and attacks, I now suspect his drinking problems might be due to guilt. Think about it—he spent his adult life mentoring young sailors and now he has to order them killed, and for what reason? Money. That has got to weigh on his conscience. And that might be another lever we can use. Run that around in your minds and I'll be right back because it's time for more coffee. Anyone need some?" With three heads shaking "no," my empty mug and I headed out the door.

In the coffee mess, I noticed that the spice and teabag supply was starting to run low. I needed to leave a grocery list for Dexter to handle next week, or there would be some unhappy folks around the NIS offices. We couldn't run out of supplies. After I added a dash of cream to my mug, I started the list for Dex. Across the top, I wrote "Needed Coffee Mess Supplies" and gave specific info on each item on the list. I dropped it off on his desk after clipping a couple of twenty-dollar bills to the list. Don't want Dex stealing supplies, I chuckled to myself. With that done, I left the AUTOVON room.

Walking back down the hallway to the NISRA spaces, one of those eureka moments occurred when *stealing supplies* jumped back into my forethought. We'd been so wrapped up in the murders and drugs that we overlooked another important thing. Ensign Appleton was going to be a CI because she believed there was fraud going on. Perhaps it was monetary, but it could have included stealing supplies. And CPO Lansing had a history of theft. As short-handed as we were, we now had another thing to throw in the mix. Rest is so overrated.

83

GETTING BACK INTO THE AGENTS' area, I saw that Sam and the two captains were briefing the rest of the agents. Everyone got quiet when I entered the office. Sam turned to me as I closed the door and said, "Mark, we felt we needed everyone's input on the best interrogation method to use on Lansing. Anything you want to add before we start brainstorming?" I gave him a big smile, and Sam said, "Oh, no, what now?"

It didn't take long to explain Joan Appleton's concerns, and the justification for considering fraud and theft when dealing with the storekeepers, including Lansing's history of theft. It might all tie together. Or it might not. But we needed all the ammo we could find to use against Lansing.

And then the fun started as everyone had an idea or two on the best way to break Lansing. Fortunately, when I jotted them down and looked over the final group, the list of ideas was mostly duplication, just phrased differently. I quickly summarized it in my notes for the group.

I got their attention and gave my observations. "Y'all are basically saying the same thing. First, we do not accuse him of anything. We mention looking into fraud and theft at the center, but give no specific details, letting him worry. Then we try to pull information from him about Harker's attack. And maybe he'll implicate himself if we listen carefully."

At the nodding of a bunch of heads, I continued, "Then if after all that he's still not talking, bring up the fact we already have a signed confession from Harker implicating him in the murder of Rodriquez and the attempted murder of Agent Robinson, and hint that more charges will be coming—and the investigation builds. So he can either talk now, which will hopefully implicate Royal, or he can shoulder the whole thing as the mastermind when we get more info from Harker and others. Did I miss anything?"

At the shaking of heads and a few mumbled no's, Sam asked, "Do you want to be in on the interrogation, Mark?"

"No, I am too pissed about Roger to be of any use in there. I'm ready to just shoot the bastard and call it a day." That generated a few chuckles and "right ons" from the agents. "I'll be more productive using my time to dig deeper into the Rodriquez–Appleton–Thomas connection. And I need to hit the hospital and check on Roger."

As the group broke apart and Doug Knox and John Driscol left to start on Lansing, I pulled Sam and both captains aside. "Gentlemen, I know we have a lot of balls in the air right now, but do we have any updates on the 'David Niven' or 'Sal Mineo' characters? I'd hoped to hear something positive yesterday, but that got lost with us all running in circles due to Roger's attack."

"Sorry, Mark, nothing received from either our friends at the FBI or our NISRA in Miami." Sam shrugged and continued, "I'll call Miami tomorrow and see if I can light a fire under them."

Captain Lavella looked at me like I'd lost my mind. The skipper came to his aid and said, "Simon, let's get some coffee before Mark drinks it all. I'll bring you up to date on those two gents; they are possible suspects and not the actors. Mark, we will be in my office if you need us." And with that, the two captains headed down the hall.

I took Sam into the file room and explained my method of using index cards to sort and evaluate the evidence and cause of death. He quickly saw the ease of seeing the entire case laid out in such a simple way. He promised to spend time going over them, in hopes of seeing something I hadn't.

As he studied the cases I'd already carded, I pulled the case file on LT Jason Thomas. His bludgeoned body was dumped and his car torched the same weekend his girlfriend, Ensign Joan Appleton, was strangled and dumped. Since there wasn't much evidence, I quickly generated a set of index cards for his case and lined them up next to Joan's column.

Then I did the same for SK3 Peter Rodriquez. Since he'd been implicated in the killing of Joan and Jason, there was a good chance of a link we had just not seen. Unlike the TV detective shows, real investigations are not solved within sixty minutes. A lot of time, effort, blood, sweat, and tears—and luck—goes into finding all the answers.

After an hour or so of looking again at all the evidence and discussing possible links, both Sam and I felt it was time to head to the hospital for two purposes: talk with Roger and see if Dr. Wentworth was close to issuing a cause of death on Harker. Both were important.

84

I'D PROMISED NOT TO LET Sam starve again, and to prevent that I said we'd visit the hospital cafeteria after checking on Roger. Entering ICU, I noticed he didn't look any better. Perhaps worse, actually, as the bruises had darkened.

Roger was still sleeping, and the SEALs on security told us the doc had been positive about Roger's status when he'd made his morning rounds. Roger had been awake for a short while earlier, but extremely groggy. I told them we'd check back later, and we headed down to the cafeteria.

On the way down, Sam asked, "Sure you want to eat before visiting with the M.E.? He might be in the middle of the autopsy."

"Either way is fine with me, Sam. Your call." With that, Sam made his decision, and we descended another flight of stairs to the morgue, where we hoped to find Dr. Wentworth and maybe get some news. And we lucked out in two forms. The autopsy was over and the doc indeed had news.

As we walked into his office, Dr. Wentworth looked up and said, "Just getting ready to call you, Sam. The preliminary results for Petty Officer Harker are death by strangulation followed by a fake hanging. The kid was choked, then they put the noose around his neck and pulled hard to form bruising and skin abrasions from that. Externally a nice faked job, but for those of us who go inside the body, the telltale markers cannot be faked."

"Okay, Doctor. Any progress on the blood work? Anything out of place there?"

"Sorry, Sam. The difficult we do immediately, but the impossible, like blood screening, takes a wee bit longer. Probably have some answers for you tomorrow at the earliest. By the way, who is your new partner?"

"Hello Dr. Wentworth. My name is Marcus Colt. I'm on special assignment to help out here in Norfolk for a while. I have been impressed by your autopsy reports I've been seeing in many of the NIS case files. Your reports are complete, and you shoot some great photos. But I'd be very happy if you'd forget you ever saw me here."

"No problem, Mr. Colt. I only remember the dead. Nice to meet you even though I didn't. And I'll pass your compliment on the photography to my lab clerk, Gerhard. He does all that hard photography stuff for me," he said as he shook my hand and smiled.

We talked more about the deceased and received a copy of the preliminary report. After saying our goodbyes to the good doctor—he had declined our invitation to lunch—we made our way up to the cafeteria.

Lunch was nothing to write home about, but it filled the emptiness in our bellies. We planned our activities for the afternoon and how we were going to figure out who else was involved with the vipers. Obviously, there was someone in the SP unit that had ties. Hoped the agents were able to find a clue or two over there.

We left the cafeteria and headed back to the ICU. Roger was awake, yet still groggy. We told him about the progress we'd made so far, and he tried to tell us what happened the morning of the attack, but his mind kept fading out. I told him to get more rest and promised to check back later, right before he fell back asleep. We left him under the stoic watchful eyes of two of my buddies. I warned them that Kelly might be by later and that got them smiling in anticipation. I knew their feelings!

Leaving the hospital, I wanted to stop by the SP brig to see how things were going with the interrogations of those on duty at the time of Harker's death. But Sam decided it would be best to let the agents there do their work without us hovering, so instead we returned to the NISRA office. We needed to see how things were going with Lansing. And I needed to get back to the grind of reviewing evidence.

85

IT HAD BEEN DECIDED TO keep Lansing in the interrogation room overnight again. The brig was obviously compromised, and we could not just let him go home. A cot was brought in and food was provided. Some of the SEALs provided guard duty. He seemed content with that arrangement. SK2 Baker had yet to be seen, but perhaps he would show up for work on Monday morning.

So far, Lansing had not opened up the way we'd hoped. He knew he was being charged with several crimes, and had yet to demand a lawyer. He simply smiled when we asked who else worked with him. And so far he hadn't mentioned Royal. It was like he had a plan in mind and we had yet to accomplish what he expected from us.

The agents were still going strong at the brig. No one had been charged yet, but there were several men who were frustrating the agents because they wouldn't crack. But they kept working on them face to face while other agents dug into their files. LTCOL Tiller and LT Kensey had been called; they'd start the updated BI checks first thing in the morning on those specific men before progressing to others who'd been on duty be-fore, and during, the so-called hanging of Harker.

I'd spent the last few hours reviewing the case files, now that we knew the connections between at least three of them. Pieces were starting to look different since they'd been put in a totally different perspective. But with the clock pointing to 2330 hrs, it was past time to call it a day and head to the barracks.

Since Roger was in a somewhat safe place where two men could keep an eye on him properly, my security team was augmented with a couple more watchers per shift. The good news for me was that they were even more determined I wouldn't end up in the hospital like Roger, or on the slab in Dr. Wentworth's morgue.

Sam had finally driven over to the brig to help with the interrogations of the SP members. So with the Blue Beast still in lockup—dusting for prints had moved down the priority list since Roger was attacked—I was back to doing a lot of walking. At least it made it easy for my watchers to keep up with me. I rounded up the guys, told them my destination, and gave them a head start. Then I notified the crew at RB of my plans, and headed out toward the transient barracks.

Leaving the building by the front door, I turned right and walked up the main drag. Somewhere in the shadows I knew GMGC Bill McCoy, GMG2 Glenn Jensen, and BM3 Kevin Brown were keeping an eye on me. With that coverage, it was easy for my mind to foolishly drift a bit and my guard to drop just the smallest amount. It was a beautiful night for a stroll, and the only thing missing was Kelly hanging on my arm.

Turning left off the main drag put me within 200 yards of the transient barracks, but the buildings around the area provided a lot of hiding places and the street lights were farther apart, creating long shadows. And, of course, one light was out so there was a darker area to traverse. While my gut was telling me to watch out, my brain didn't get the message fast enough; my turn to look at a movement to the left was slower than it should have been.

A shadow quickly appeared next to me and a pain shot up my left arm. The knife bit deep into my forearm as I raised it to block what my gut told me was coming toward my neck. My right hand automatically pulled the Colt 1911 from my shoulder holster, thumbed off the safety, and quickly fired two rounds at the shadow under my raised arm. The shadow flew backwards a few feet and went down.

Another shadow appeared on the right, but before I could turn to fire on it, a third shadow merged upon it. I recognized Chief McCoy as the merging shadow as the two struggled. The Chief jumped back and failed to stay on his feet. The attacker started to close the gap on the Chief; light reflections showed he had a knife extended. I fired a single round at the attacker and he went down.

By then, Glenn and Kevin had caught up with us. Using their flashlights, we saw that Chief McCoy was wounded in the left side. Glenn applied pressure to his wound. Bill was loudly complaining so we knew he would probably live.

I looked at the attacker that had gone after the Chief. My shot had hit him in the right side of his lower chest. Too low for a heart shot, but enough damage to put him on the deck. He was still breathing, but blood was flowing. I told Kevin to secure him and give first aid; we needed him alive. Then it hit me that I had just shot 'Sal Mineo.'

I took one of the flashlights and moved back to where the attack started. My left hand had trouble maintaining hold on the light, so I wedged the flashlight in my left armpit and held it there with arm pressure. The shadow that had come after me ended up being the body of SK2 Baker. Two rounds had hit him in the center chest and his eyes were still wide open, giving him a look of surprise, even in death. His hand still held the Ka-bar knife that had hit my arm. I sighed and muttered a soft "damn it" as I wished I had just wounded him. We needed more info from these vipers.

By then, the noise of the three .45 caliber rounds had attracted the attention of the roving SP units, and several vehicles arrived. We were suddenly facing the business ends of their weapons, but just as quickly another vehicle arrived and Sam Maker took charge of the scene. He'd been returning to the office from the brig when he saw all the lights. The SP, meanwhile, had radioed for ambulances and I heard several approaching.

The arriving SP vehicles had illuminated the scene nicely. When Sam walked over to where I was still standing over Baker, he took one look at my arm and said, "Oh, shit." He immediately used his handkerchief to apply pressure and called the SPs to help with a tourniquet.

My system was so full of adrenaline that I didn't feel the pain of the slash wound that had laid open part of my left arm, allowing blood to flow freely down my arm and off my hand. I pressed the thumb safety on and holstered my weapon. Then I was quickly surrounded by unknown hands pulling me down. Panicking, I started to resist and tried to pull my weapon again, but hands were holding my right arm as my body was lowered to the ground. I suddenly didn't have much energy to fight back.

I saw Sam standing over me, so I realized good guys surrounded me. No need to fight. Two people were working on my left arm as I lay there.

Cutting open the sleeve, they started wrapping up the wound. One gave me an injection in my left upper arm, right through the jacket sleeve; the burning pain that had just started was now fading. A sharp pain filled my right hand as they stuck something in there. It looked like an IV bag, but I didn't understand why. I was carried to one of the ambulances and quickly transported to the hospital.

Bill McCoy was already in the ER when I was wheeled in to the area next to him. Several doctors and nurses clustered around him. My head was spinning and it was hard to focus. I just wanted to go to sleep. I really hoped 'Sal' would arrive alive and the docs would get him well soon so I could kill him. He hurt my friend Bill. Why was I here? And where was I?

Someone was cutting the rest of my jacket and shirt off my body. Damn, it was my favorite jacket and a fairly new shirt. Someone else was holding my right arm. I heard someone yell about getting a second IV started STAT.

I tried to raise my head, but was pushed back down. Looking into the eyes of the pusher, I said, "Well, hello beautiful Ann. We have to quit meeting like this. People might start to talk." And I weakly smiled at Ann Holt, whom I'd met the previous week.

Then a panic memory hit me. Bill was wounded. I tried to look for him but couldn't move my head. I asked Ann. "How's the Chief doing? Is he okay? Where is Kelly? I need Kelly."

Something caused a pain in my right arm, and the room quickly became black as I heard her soft sweet voice say, "Time to relax, Mark, we got you."

86

WHEN SAM, GLENN, AND KEVIN finally got to the hospital to see me, they immediately went to the surgical area. The way Sam rehashed it for me later on, it seemed to take hours to get the SPs to secure the area and get some NIS agents over there. In reality, it was less than ten minutes, since there were several agents at RB and they came immediately upon hearing the gun shots. It only took a minute or two to relate the situation to them and race to the hospital.

Arriving on the second floor where the surgical area was located, he was told that GMGC Bill McCoy had already been moved to an OR. A quick check of his status with the head nurse proved worthless. No one knew anything except that doctors were working on him. "*Check back later.*"

The unknown assailant, code named SM, was also in surgery and his status was the same as Bill's. "No idea on his condition either, and check back later." No one knew about anyone with an arm injury. "Check with the people in the emergency room." Sam left the two SEALs there to guard both Bill and SM.

Heading to the ER, as he recounted it to me, Sam found me being tended to by two doctors and several nurses. He reached over and secured the pistol and money belt they'd taken off me when removing my jacket and shirt, to provide access to my arms and check for other wounds. I was out of it, Sam said, and there were a couple of IVs running into my hand and right arm.

A small nurse came over and asked who Sam was and why he was there. After he identified himself as an NIS agent and briefly explained the situation, the nurse said I should be fine. I'd lost a large amount of blood and the wound needed some heavy-duty surgical work to get it closed properly and prevent muscle damage. They were securing a couple of cut blood vessels now before moving me to the OR.

Sam told me he asked her how she knew to call me Mark. She responded that she'd met me at the chow hall the previous week; her roommate worked with me at the Logistics Center. She was surprised I had weapons, since I was a Yeoman. She also said that before I went under the sedative, I'd been asking about the status of someone I called "the Chief," and was asking for Kelly. If Sam knew Kelly, Ann suggested, he should probably give her a call.

Behind her, Sam watched them moving me from the curtained area toward the elevator that went up to the OR. I looked extremely pale, according to Sam. Ann excused herself and went to secure my clothing and other personal effects, like my extra pistol magazines and knife. She placed it all in a bag and handed it to Sam.

At the nurse's station, Sam found a phone and made a call he'd been dreading. While my wound wasn't life threatening, he still hated to be the one to share the news. This is how the conversation went, according to Sam:

"Captain Miller's residence. Miller speaking."

"Captain, Sam here. I am at the base hospital. Marcus was jumped and knifed as he walked back to the barracks about a half hour ago. He was wounded and is in surgery. Not life threatening—it was a deep cut on his left forearm. Lots of blood loss and some muscles needing repair. Chief McCoy is in surgery for a knife wound to his lower left side. No info was available on his status. Two vipers are down. Marcus killed the one who knifed him and wounded the second who had knifed the Chief. Number two is in surgery for a GSW to the lower right side. I have two of Marcus's SEALs guarding the OR to watch over Marcus, the Chief, and the number two viper. We had three SEALs watching him, but they could not move fast enough. Sorry, sir."

"Okay, Sam. Head back to the scene and take charge there. I'll be at the hospital in about ten minutes. Nothing more you can do there." And the line went dead.

Knowing the scene was under control with other agents, Sam still had work to do at the hospital. He returned to the OR area and briefed the SEALs. They'd seen me being moved into surgery and were keeping a sharp eye on all three of the surgical suites. Sam headed down the hall to the ICU. There he briefed the two men keeping an eye on Roger. One of them left to join the two at the OR area.

As Sam was getting off the elevator on the way out, he saw Captain Miller, Dorothy, and Kelly rushing in the door. He pulled them aside and gave them a quick update on my status. Kelly, he told me, had a look that clearly said get the hell out of my way or suffer dearly. She needed to be with me.

87

MARCUS

BEEP, BEEP. BEEP, BEEP. AND over and over and over again. Whatever was making that horrid noise was making sleep difficult. Sounded like a hospital. I tried to open my eyes to confirm, but the lids refused to cooperate; I was too tired and needed more sleep. I could not move my arms either. I needed coffee, but that could wait as I needed sleep even more.

Then it hit me that I needed to check on Chief McCoy. Memories from the encounter with the vipers came flooding back. The Chief was stabbed. I was cut. Baker was dead. It was time to make sure the Chief was doing okay. With some effort, my eyes opened, and a quick look around confirmed my suspicions that I was in a hospital.

Glancing to my left, I saw Doc standing by the bed looking at a monitor, the source of all those evil sounds. He turned his attention to me and whispered, "Good to see you back with us, Marcus. How are you feeling?"

"How's the Chief?" Talking was difficult with a dry mouth and a fuzzy brain. I saw that my left arm was heavily bandaged and hanging from some wires above my body. "Where's my weapon?"

As he spooned an ice chip into my mouth, he responded, "Chief is doing well. Right now, he's sharing a cozy spot in ICU with Roger. Both will be moved to a regular room later today. Sam took your Colt and IDs back to the office last night for safekeeping. Oh, and you are doing fine as well. But you might want to stop talking or you might wake up your snuggle buddy," Doc whispered with a smile and pointed to my bed.

Kelly had found a way to join me in the hospital bed. She was spooned against my lower right side sleeping soundly, and that was why I couldn't move my right arm. Her arm had been draped over it, between the IV lines. If I remembered later, I'd tease her about her light snoring. It was cute.

In addition to being a SEAL, Doc was also a Hospital Corpsman, First Class. Before joining the Navy he was in his third year of college, wanting to be a doctor. But chasing girls and failing calculus had put his GPA below the 2-S draft deferment level, so he joined the Navy and pushed to become a medic. Due to his rating choice and excellent scores in training, the SEALs had recruited him to be one of them.

Doc did not fit the standard image conjured up when hearing the term SEAL. He didn't have rippling muscles or a square jaw, or even the body bulk expected. At twenty-nine years of age, he stood five-foot-ten and weighed in around 175 lbs. His rather common-looking face was topped off with a 1950s flattop haircut. That was the first thing you noticed about him. Second thing you noticed was his sense of humor; Doc always had a comeback. And he could lighten the darkest mood since he was so easy going. But you couldn't let his persona fool you: he was a fighter who could take down men twice his size. And even though he was a healer, he could harm just as fast. He was a true warrior and could be a dangerous man to his enemies.

I completely trusted him and was reassured as he checked things on the monitor, took my temp, and inspected my bandage. He looked at something under the bed, and verified the IVs on my right arm were flowing properly. Lastly, he carefully moved my right arm out from under Kelly's arm. He gave me a thumbs up and returned to his chair where he could watch me and the door at the same time. I noticed Doc was wearing his sidearm. Doc verified that things were good, so I relaxed; sleep quickly overtook me once more.

When I came alive again, Kelly was gone. Bummer. Doc was quietly talking with a guy who looked like a real doctor, complete with standard lab coat and stethoscope. They were pointing to something on a chart that I assumed was mine. The sun was up and bright light was coming in through the blinds. Captain Miller was sitting in a chair listening to the medical guys discuss my problems.

I tried to speak, but only a croak came from my extremely dry mouth. Doc looked over at me and nudged the doctor. "Good morning, Lieutenant Commander. I'm your surgeon, Lieutenant Jack Ambrose. Talking will be difficult, so just nod your head if you can feel this." He touched each finger on my left hand with the end of his pin. I gave him positive acknowledgements as he stimulated each one. Ambrose seemed happy with that and went on to the next test: "Now try to gently close your fist."

That one was much harder, but I at least got all the digits moving in the right direction. It did cause pain to shoot up my arm, and I must have shown that in my face. The doctor said I did fine and ordered me to stop and rest. Doc was again shoveling ice chips into my dry mouth.

Captain Miller was now standing on the right side of my bed and it was he who asked the question my foggy brain had failed to form. "So what is the prognosis, Doctor?"

"Sir, the surgery went very well. We were able to take care of all the muscle and vein damage. And this small test showed that the primary nerves are in good shape. There may be some numbness in the area around the wound that may or may not improve over time. But he should have full use of his arm after a month or so of rehab. The scarring will be minimal. We'll need to wait a little longer before setting up that rehab schedule. Rest and arm stability is critical right now for the healing process." And with a positive head nod from the skipper, the doctor passed the chart back to Doc and left.

"How's the Chief?" I asked Doc.

"Doing well, and getting ready to send a thank you letter to his favorite Milwaukee brewer. Without them, he wouldn't have had a good layer of fat that slowed the knife blade from the viper. He'll be okay soon."

"And what is the status of the viper?" I asked. "We really need that guy alive to push the case forward. I think he is our SM."

Doc chuckled and replied. "Guess your blood loss affected your aim, Marcus. He still lives. He is in ICU after successful surgery to remove your slug and repair a lot of damage it did. Nice that you use hollow points. Kevin's first aid saved his life, just as that cute little girl, Ann, saved yours in the ER with that second IV she immediately put in when she saw you crashing due to blood loss. Sam told me you left several pints at the crime scene. You are such a damn litterbug."

Doc was on a roll: "By the way, Ann must be a member of your local fan club. She stopped by to check on you a few hours ago when she got off duty. She told me that she and two other ladies, named Cathy and Rhonda if I recall correctly, would be by to see you later this afternoon. How do you meet so many good-looking gals in such a short period of time? Especially being as ugly as you are. Anyway, unless she's an official member of your local harem number 245, I might have to ask her out on a date. She is adorable."

I tried to laugh, but not enough liquid had gone down the throat to moisten things properly, so it sounded like a dying frog trying to croak. "Knock yourself out, Doc. No harems are established anywhere. Just be prepared for disappointment—since Ann seems so nice, she might not like you too much." Doc laughed for us both.

The skipper laughed at our exchange and said, "I suppose this level of strange humor is one of the ways you warriors keep your sanity. Considering all that has transpired over the last twenty-four hours, it is a challenge to keep up with it all. And to help do that, Marcus, I am heading back to the office to see how things are going. Your orders are simple. Stay in bed. Rest and heal. Got it? I'll talk with you later."

"Aye, aye, sir. Thanks for being here, Captain."

As the Captain moved away from the bed toward the door, I saw Kelly leaning against the doorframe, listening to all that was being said. The skipper kissed her cheek as he left and patted her shoulder. Her face held that sad look that I hate so much. But when she saw I was trying to smile and wave, she lit up and came to my side with the smile I needed right then. Doc winked and headed out the door, pulling it closed behind him.

"Harems? Sounds like we have issues to discuss, sailor," she said as she gave me a kiss.

88

THE SUN WAS GETTING LOWER as I came back to a state of semi-awake. All day I'd been going in and out. Doc said I was getting a constant medium level of painkillers through the IV so I wouldn't thrash around too much. They were enough to keep me groggy and frequently push me over the edge into sleep.

Soft laughter was working its way into my brain. Someone was having fun, but it was not me. There was too much pain in my left arm to consider anything fun. I finally mustered enough energy to open my eyes and see the source. Ann, Cathy, and Rhonda had arrived and were in conversation with Kelly.

Ann was reading my chart and checking the monitor while the other three chatted and giggled softly. Seeing I was coming awake, Ann shoved the thermometer in my mouth and laughingly asked, "So Mark, tell me how you feel right now." The laughter got louder.

Kelly beamed at me and said, "Babe, I do like your friends. They even said I can join the harem!" With that, the laughter got even louder. I just shook my head in resignation, not completely sure what was going on around me.

Kelly filled in the blanks. Seems when the ladies arrived I was totally out, so Doc and Kelly told them what had happened the previous night, using the cover story that the Chief and I were attacked by muggers. They also told them what the doctors had said about my recovery earlier in the day. Nothing was mentioned about the shootings. And Doc, introduced as a friend of the family, of course had to share the harem story with them.

Now that I was awake, Rhonda told us that the CO of the Logistics Center had announced I was in the hospital, but hadn't gone into more detail. She continued that it was a weird day. There were a bunch of NIS agents all over the lower floors of the building, so everyone was wondering what's up. She also said there were five people missing from the storekeeper section that day, including their CPO. And some people were talking about a guy who was injured over the weekend by a forklift, but she hadn't heard his name.

"Rhonda, do you remember the names of those UA?" I asked.

"Sure, Mark, I had to do the UA report. In addition to Chief Lansing, the other guys are Donald Harker, John Baker, Dennis Moore, and Jesus Martinez. It's strange, since those guys have never been UA before. Wonder if they all went fishing and the boat sank?"

"Could be, or maybe they all flew to Vegas for the weekend and didn't make it back. Whatever happened, they'd better have a good excuse," I said. In the back of my mind, I knew that two of them were in the morgue downstairs. One was in custody at the NISRA office. Now I knew two more we needed to find ASAP.

Just then, Doc came back into the room, dragging Glenn and Kevin, the other SEALs who'd come to my aid on Sunday, with him. Neither looked like they'd seen sleep since sometime Saturday. And I was confused by their presence. But as always, I was happy to see them.

Kelly offered an explanation. "Mark, when Doc was here earlier, he offered to buy Ann a dinner for saving your life. He decided to make a party of it and he's bringing Glenn and Kevin as escorts for Cathy and Rhonda. Just too bad we can't go with them." After all the introductions, Cathy, Rhonda, Glenn, and Kevin looked happy to meet each other, and went into the hall to reduce the crowd and noise in my room.

Ann came over to the side of my bed and stood next to Doc. She had a questioning look on her face as she softly said, "Mark, last night I was the one who talked with that NIS Agent Maker, who was extremely concerned about you. He grabbed your pistol as soon as he got here, and I gave him the rest of your weapons: the extra magazines and knife from around your calf. Normal sailors don't carry such stuff on base, so I suspect you're more than you let on. And I've just seen your real name and rank on your chart."

She looked up at Doc as if for support or confirmation and continued, "Just know that I won't be discussing this with anyone, and definitely not Rhonda or Cathy. Your secrets are safe with me as long as you promise to behave and get better. Maybe someday you can tell me all about it, but I understand how 'need to know' works. Come on, Doc, I'm starving!" She grabbed Doc's arm and pulled him toward the door.

"Thanks, Ann. Greatly appreciated," I responded.

Doc put a big grin on his face and said, "Adorable and intelligent. This could be the start of a great friendship." And with that they left, closing the door behind them.

Kelly let out a big sigh after everyone had gone. She looked at me and said, "Wow. I'm not used to being so secretive. That stuff is hard work. You're a superman for being able to do all that undercover stuff day in and day out and keep all the stories straight. But one thing that was not a fake: I do like your friends. You seem to attract the nicest ones around … well, except for the ones trying to kill you."

I agreed, "Yea, undercover work is such a challenge. At least I'm fairly good at it, and that helps get the job done. Now where is everyone? We have some info to get to them." I asked Kelly to pass the phone, and I called the NISRA office to get them looking for Dennis Moore and Jesus Martinez.

And suddenly after that call, I was tired again and needed to close my eyes for a few minutes. Kelly snuggled down beside me and that felt so good.

89

THERE'S ALWAYS TOO MUCH NOISE in hospitals, especially when trying to sleep. Voices worked their way into my slumber and pulled me back to a wake state. And that wasn't exactly where I wanted to be right then. Opening my eyes, I saw my small room was holding a convention of NIS personnel and friends.

"Can anyone join the discussion?" I rasped. The skipper, Sam, and Joe looked over at me. "What day is this?" Two SEALs, Andy and Larry, were talking with Kelly over by the door.

"It's still Monday, Marcus. And no, you cannot join the conversation as you are still on very restricted duty until I say otherwise," answered the Captain. "We are here just for a medical update, and then we'll leave you alone to rest."

Kelly handed me a cup of water to help lubricate my dry throat. I had to agree with the skipper: rest was all my body wanted right then, as it fought against all the painkillers and the letdown from the overdose of adrenaline the previous night. But the operation pressed on my mind whenever I was awake.

"At least give me a quick brief, sir. Any change with Lansing? Have we found the other two storekeepers yet? SM wake up from surgery? How are Bill and Roger? Any of the SPs roll over yet? Come on, Captain, I'll rest better knowing how things are going."

Sam came over to the side of my bed and softly said, "Here, slide this under your pillow, Marcus." He reached under his jacket and handed me my Colt and a spare magazine. "All cleaned and lubed from your last excursion. Cocked and locked." I nodded thanks.

Sam glanced over at the skipper, shrugged, and said, "Sorry, Captain, but I agree with Marcus. He will rest better knowing." Getting no pushback, Sam turned back to me. "SM is awake and talking. He is actually SK2 Jesus Martinez, one of the missing storekeepers. We're looking for the other guy, but since he is still running around, I thought you might want your weapon. Bill and Roger are doing much better. We have the SP who killed Harker. And Lansing is starting to talk to cover his butt."

The Captain interrupted and added, "Tomorrow morning, all three of you will be moved to a private suite on the fifth floor. It is usually reserved for dignitaries and such, and has limited access and a private elevator. After talking with the CO of the hospital about our situation, we figured that would be the best place to stash you all for safe keeping, and to reduce the impact we are having on the hospital with all the security people coming and going to multiple rooms."

"But for tonight, Larry will be sitting outside your room, and you are stuck with me watching you from that chair," said Joe as he pointed to a chair in the corner.

"Thank you all. I appreciate it." I looked over at Kelly, then back to the Captain. "Sir, please take Kelly home for a good night's sleep. She is about to fall over, and this small bed does not have sufficient room for us both to rest properly if she does."

"But I want to stay," Kelly whined. But fatigue was taking over and she really knew heading home was the best thing for us both.

"Besides, you need a shower," I said through my laughter.

"You're a good one to talk, Lieutenant Commander Stinker," she responded as she giggled and kissed me.

"Well, I am looking forward to my sponge bath from future harem members. Now y'all get out of here. I need more sleep," I said as I held Kelly's hand and kissed it softly.

90

WITH THE CROWD GONE, I was finally able to talk seriously with Joe. "What is Bill's status, Joe, how's he doing?"

Joe came over and took Kelly's chair by the bed. "Doc called it with his funny beer comment. According to the surgeon, the damage done was limited to skin and fat. The blade did not get deep enough to hit muscle, and there were just a few minor vessels damaged. He needed about fifteen to twenty stitches to pull the incision closed. Nice scar to give him more bragging rights. Technically, he should be out of here tomorrow, but Sam decided that keeping all three of you in one spot a while longer would make things easier for the security teams as well as for any brain storming sessions. As the current SEAL group leader since Bill is down, I concurred with that assessment."

"Well, that is good news and relieves my mind a lot. I was afraid I'd let him down again."

"Bull crap. You did what you had to do the other night, and also last summer. Neither times did you fail; hell, even with your nasty arm wound, you stopped the bastard before he could stab Bill again. So stop your damn pity party right now. If anyone is to take the blame, it's him and me. We are getting too old to be chasing you young punks around at night."

A knock on the door announced the arrival of a nurse to check on my vitals. She checked the monitor, looked under the bed to make sure my kidneys and bladder were doing their job, and took my temp again. I asked her to turn down the pain meds and she promised to ask the doctor. She informed me a dressing change was coming in the morning when the doctors made their rounds. Since I was still doing okay, she marked the chart and left.

Joe started to give a detailed briefing on all that was going on with the operation. I was surprised so much had happened since my attack just twenty-four hours ago. And I was ticked I was missing out on it all.

I suppose I went into overload mode while Joe was talking; the next thing I knew, sunlight was coming in the room. Sleep overcame me during his review.

I awoke to find LT Kensey had replaced Joe sometime in the early morning hours. "Good to see you alive and awake, Mark. How's the arm?" he asked.

"Morning, Greg. The pain is telling me it's still there. And the itching might mean it's healing. But my body really needs coffee. Any way to get some?"

"I'll check." He headed to the door and spoke softly to whoever had hall duty then.

While waiting to see if coffee was in my immediate future, the door opened and three nurses came in. Time for a room change, the head of the trio announced. They started unhooking lines and tubes from the wall, and in a matter of moments, I was rolling out the door and toward the elevator. Greg followed and motioned for the hall guard to come too. Coffee would have to wait.

I was the first one moved into what I considered the executive suite. Nice place, it was. There were four bed positions against the back wall, each with various oxygen connections and other strange plugs. My bed was placed in the slot next to the window and all the dangling lines were plugged back into place. My moving crew left and things had barely settled down when the door opened.

My surgeon and two nurses arrived, with one nurse pushing a cart full of what could be considered torture devices. Dressing change suddenly had a whole new meaning and it looked painful. After releasing my arm from the suspension cables, they carefully cut off the existing bandage and exposed the bare arm. My arm was laid on a movable tray that helped keep it from shifting during the dressing change.

Once you got past the general gross post-surgery look of it all, the wound wasn't really that bad. It ran from an inch below the elbow on the inside, across the forearm at an angle, to where my watch band had stopped it on the outside of my arm. That made it about a six-to-seven inch cut that was being held together by about fifty black stitches on the outside. The wound was deep and there were a lot more stitches on the inside, I was told.

One of the nurses wiped the area to clean it up a bit, and the doctor looked and poked around the wound. He again checked for nerve problems; none were found. Overall, everyone seemed pleased. Except Greg, who looked a little pale. He'd taken one look at the wound and decided he needed to be on the other side of the room. Well, he is an attorney and not a warrior, so for him, a paper cut is a big deal.

The doc said he was concerned about infection since the knife had cut through two layers of cloth to get to my arm. Who knows how many germs were on the blade and clothing, he muttered. I suggested a total of forty-two, but he didn't appreciate my attempt at humor.

Per my request the previous evening, he told the nurse to stop the IV pain meds and switch to oral meds as needed. After removing all the IVs and taping up the various holes they'd left, they gave me another injection to fight off any potential infection. Finally, the bladder catheter was removed, which would allow me to leave the bed and let the body parts do what they do best. Oh, happy days!

A lighter dressing was to be applied once they finished with the wound cleanup; the nurse doing that was slow but very cautious. The nurse continued to wipe and clean areas around the wound, and it did start to look less gruesome.

And rather than placing my arm back in the suspension system, the doc opted to use a thin metal splint on the bottom of my arm, which extended out for my hand to wrap around the end. With lots of elastic bandages to hold it in place, it would be near impossible for me to move any muscle in that lower arm. Of course, it would be in a sling for the next few weeks; using my arm was forbidden during that time.

As all this was going on, the door opened again and Chief Bill McCoy was rolled into the slot farther down the wall from mine. Not that he was being antisocial; the next position to mine was taken up by the doc, two nurses, and their cart of torture tools.

McCoy was followed in by Roger Robinson and his moving crew. Roger was moved into position on the other side of the Chief. It was a bit of a circus, watching all the activities of the staff as they got the two new guys settled into place. On the other side of the room, their security detail was meeting with Greg Kensey to discuss the best scheduling.

The two moving crews had just left the room when the door opened again. Expecting more doctors, I paid no attention to who entered, but Bill McCoy did. He announced "Attention on deck" when he saw a sleeve covered in massive amounts of gold entering the room. Before anyone could comply, a gruff voice announced, "As you were."

91

ADMIRAL WILLIAM GALLAGHER'S PARTY CONSISTED of his wife, Elaine, Kelly, one of his aides, Commander Troy Montclare, and Master Chief Yeoman David Bartow. Following right behind them came Captain Miller, Dorothy, and Sam. The CNO knew how to make a grand entrance.

Seeing the men in their dress blues and the ladies in dresses on the edge of what I'd call semi-formal, I felt totally underdressed in my ugly hospital gown with two days' beard growth. Hardest part was trying to keep the laughter from erupting. Laughter is a great way to reduce stress, especially when under the influence of pain meds. And my pain meds and my stress had built up in me nicely.

By the time the Admiral crossed from the door to my bed, I'd started to get out of bed and stand, all while keeping my arm stationary on the tray. He looked me up and down and asked, "Colt, did they hit you on the head?"

"No, sir. I just received a small stab wound in the arm, Admiral," I replied.

"Well then, since you are not brain damaged, what part of 'as you were' do you not comprehend? Get back in bed."

Captain Miller started laughing and said, "Hell, Admiral. Give him a break. Marcus was trying to stand in honor of meeting his future mother-in-law, not you." And with that, the Admiral and everyone else in the Admiral's party broke into laugher as Kelly and her father helped lower me back in bed and under the covers.

The doctor and a nurse were standing there looking totally confused. The other nurse kept a hold on my arm to keep me from doing any damage to their fine work as I climbed back into bed.

The skipper turned to them and said, "Doctor, ladies, if the subject of the Admiral's wrath can survive without you continuing whatever you were doing for a few minutes, would you please excuse us?"

The doctor said, "Certainly, Captain. We will be in the sitting room. Mr. Colt, do not move that arm." And they started to leave by a side door.

However, Admiral Gallagher called the doctor back over. "Doctor, please give us an update on this man's condition before you leave. I'm not sure in his current mental state that he'll be honest with us if we ask him," he asked with a grin.

As the doctor gave great detail about my injury, surgery, and recovery plans, I noticed that Greg Kensey had the deer-in-the-headlights stare. It hit me that while he had been read into the operation, he did not know I was dating, much less engaged to, the CNO's daughter. Yea, that could mess your mind up quickly. It had mine, time and time again.

And now that the doctor and a couple of nurses knew, I suspected I'd be getting two servings of Jell-o at dinner instead of one, and maybe even pudding! Rank has its privileges, or in my case, rank-in-law. Pain meds must've been wearing off, as my arm was starting to hurt a lot more and my mental sarcasm had returned. The doctor finished his dissertation and his crew vanished into the other room of the suite.

I looked back at Kelly and found her focused on my arm. She gently rubbed the area around the wound, and her face had that sad look I totally hate. I reached over with my good hand and held hers. "It will be fine, Kelly," I said softly.

"It just looks so terrible. And so many stitches," she said, on the verge of tears.

The Admiral decided it was time to change the subject and said, "I should have asked your doctor if you were free to leave this place under adult supervision, Marcus. If so, you could join us for lunch before we have to head back to D.C. in a few hours."

"I appreciate that, Admiral, but with the pain meds still flowing through my system, I'd probably drool all over the place and keep dropping my fork. That would not be a pretty sight. Please excuse me from lunch today." I winked at Kelly. Through her laughter, she gave a small nod of understanding.

"Understood." He turned to his aide and gently ordered, "Troy, you are excused from the insanity of this sloppy family gathering. Give us an hour here. Before you find a place to hide for that hour, please call the O Club and have them set up a private lunch for eight in seventy-five minutes."

The Commander started to nod and turn, when Kelly interrupted and said, "Make it seven. I'll stay here with Marcus."

I squeezed her hand and offered, "Commander, keep it for eight. The way this crazy lady has been talking about weddings, this might be the last chance the Admiral and his wife can enjoy a nice lunch with 'just' their daughter. Next time, she might also be my wife." I leaned over and whispered something to Kelly and again she nodded and smiled.

"So be it, Troy. See you in an hour," responded the Admiral, and Troy departed after nodding 'thanks' in my direction.

Elaine asked, "Is it finally my turn to greet Marcus, or is there other really important stuff to do first?"

"Mrs. Gallagher, it is a great pleasure and honor to finally meet you. Thank you so much for making the trip down for a visit. Just wish it was under happier circumstances without hospitals, doctors and bandages, and next time I promise to dress a little bit better."

"Call me either Elaine or Mom. Your choice," she said as she leaned over and kissed my cheek.

"I'll stick with Elaine for now. After you get to know me you might not want me to use the Mom title."

She laughed. "If you were the one who wrote that beautiful letter, then I know the Mom title will never be revoked. So happy to see you in person, Marcus, and welcome to the family."

While the family chatter continued, the doctor and nurses were allowed to return and redress my wound. Kelly kept a close eye on them as they did it. It felt much better when they finished and my arm was resting in the sling. The ointment they put on the wound must have contained a painkiller. I noticed that one of the nurses placed a vial of pain pills on the table next to the bed; I'd try to avoid those as I needed to think more clearly.

I finally had a chance to talk with David. I'd missed his counsel these last couple of months and it was good to have him nearby, if only for an hour. He said it was probably time for Lieutenant Commander Colt to come out of hiding since my days of undercover work were over for this operation during the healing process. As expected, I agreed with his input.

It was great to see Kelly beaming as she, Elaine, and Dorothy started talking wedding plans. Hopefully they'd continue that over lunch and keep my girl's mind off my arm.

With my arm safely wrapped and in the sling, Kelly helped me out of bed and into my robe. Actually, not into it per se—the right arm went into the sleeve and she draped the left side around my shoulder and tied the belt. I carefully walked over and introduced everyone to Bill, Roger, and Greg.

The Admiral, the Captain, David, and Sam clustered around us as we discussed the latest developments and gave the Admiral a personal re-hash of the attacks. I could see that being involved with a brief to the CNO made both Bill and Greg's day. Roger was happy to be included, but as a civilian, he didn't have the same level of awe.

Faster than I wanted, Troy returned and announced it was time to head to lunch. Handshakes and careful hugs marked their departure and I got a knowing thumbs up from David as he closed the door on the way out. Greg set off to find out what we were doing for our own lunch, and I returned to bed for some much-needed rest. Entertaining is so tiring.

92

THOUGH I WASN'T AT THE lunch, the whole scene was eventually re-played for me. After everyone was seated in the private dining area of the club and orders had been taken, Elaine said, "I do wish that Marcus could have joined us. He deserves more than just hospital food."

The Admiral snorted and responded, "You know full well why he re-fused the invitation. He had three of his men there that he didn't want to leave behind. Sign of a true leader."

"So true, Dad. That's one of two things he whispered to me when he insisted that I come with you. And don't worry Mom, I'll bring him and the rest of the guys some decent food later."

"What was the other thing, Kelly?"

"He wanted me to have more time with you and Mom. He puts every-one ahead of himself. Just one of the many reasons I love him."

Waiters brought in the dishes and everyone was quiet as the eating started. Glasses were refilled and the wait staff exited the room.

Bartow, as he said in the retelling, had been uncommonly silent during most of the visit, the ride over to the club, and the start of lunch. Those who knew him recognized he was deep in thought. He finally cleared his throat and asked, "Admiral, if I may make a strong suggestion. Marcus will be operating with a big physical handicap for a while. Even driving will be nearly impossible since both of his cars have standard transmissions. He will also need a lot of medical attention. And on top of that, he needs someone watching his back. But I have an easy fix."

He took a sip of his beer and continued, "One of the SEALs on his security team, specifically HM1 Donald 'Doc' Stevens, should be assigned as a permanent bodyguard–driver–medical assistant to Marcus for at least the duration of this operation and probably until his arm completely heals. He can move into Marcus's house and be by his side twenty-four/seven to help in any way needed."

As David received positive nods, he went further. "Set him up with NIS agent credentials and that will help open doors for him. I know about his relationship with Marcus, after their time in Nam they are closer than just friends—more like brothers—and Doc will not take offense to the assignment of being an over-qualified babysitter. Fact is, he will probably be extremely honored, especially if you personally asked him to do it."

The Admiral looked at Kelly who nodded in agreement, then shifted his attention to the Captain and asked, "Hump, do you see any problem with that?"

"None, Bill. Good idea, David. Since Kelly still has work on her degree to finish, this will also give her time to wrap it up without the added stress of worrying about Marcus all the time. A winning plan all around. You talk to Doc and, if he agrees, I'll make the arrangements for a TAD assignment with the SEAL CO."

"Troy, when you finish eating, track down HM1 Stevens and have him—no, scratch that, ask him to meet us at the airport at 1500." As Troy laid down his fork and started to stand, the Admiral continued, "What is it with commanders today who do not pay attention to orders? First Marcus and now you. Sit. Finish eating first. Please, Troy."

Troy nodded and said, "Yes, sir," and picked up his fork again.

Kelly leaned over to David and softly said, "Thank you so much, David. You are the best."

"I try, darling, especially for you," David whispered to his goddaughter.

Sam had also been unusually quiet, as if part of him wanted to keep quiet but he knew he had to say something. "Admiral, not counting the attacks on these three men, this operation is going well and may be over soon. That's all due to Marcus. In addition to leading this operation, Marcus has provided a unique perspective on how we should look at investigating both our normal and our cold cases. His input has given us a leg up on several difficult cases in a short period of time."

"Well, that high level of thought process and leadership is why he's in charge of the internal affairs division of the entire NIS. He sees things differently and can spot bad from a distance," offered the Captain. "He has a lot of work there to do also, Sam, and Admiral Chance is looking forward to his return."

"I understand, sir. I guess, like David, I'm looking for a win–win solution. Face it, Marcus will need at least a couple of month's therapy on his arm and that is after waiting three to five weeks for the healing process to knit it back together. Granted he can get that done in D.C., but if he stays here, he will maintain continuity with his surgeon and his medical care. Then still have his surgeon handy later as he goes through his therapy. On top of all that, he will have Doc and Kelly taking care of him. All that is a win for Marcus."

Seeing a lot of heads again nodding in agreement, Sam continued. "In addition, having him here during that time will give us a chance to incorporate his extremely sharp mental processes into our standard investigating methods. More solved cases for NISO Norfolk. Hell—excuse me, ladies—we might even end up rewriting the book on how NIS investigates. That would be an incredible positive win for NIS."

As it was described to me, the Admiral steepled his fingers in front of his jaw and squinted in contemplation, a posture I was now familiar with. After a moment, he said, "Hump, your thoughts, please."

"I will hate to be the one telling Admiral Chance he can't have him back yet, but Sam has hit upon a great idea that's good for most everyone. Having seen Marcus and Sam working together these last three weeks—they're so alike they complete each other's sentences—I know Marcus will agree with the plan," responded the skipper. "Only one thing is lacking."

"Which is what?" asked the Admiral.

"Financial support. Marcus is buying a townhouse in Alexandria. And he is footing the bills for his rental house here and all the other expenses he has faced since day one of this operation. He probably expected to be here for a few weeks or so, but if we extend his time here to an additional three or four months, then rent and utilities here will add up quickly."

"That is true," offered Sam. "Norfolk rent is not cheap."

Nodding in agreement, the Captain continued, "He told me he is saving receipts in hopes of reimbursement, but I could tell he doesn't believe that will happen. Granted, he's not destitute, and Kelly won't need to take a job flipping burgers to help him out, but the right thing is for that reimbursement to happen. And going forward, he needs an operating budget to cover expenses he will continue to face while he's here."

"Interesting. He hasn't said a thing about any of that, has he, David?"

"No, sir, he has not. But I agree with the Captain. That is the right thing to do. Shall I take care of it when we get back to D.C.?"

"Work with Chance on fixing that problem, David. If it all came from our office, it might not look right, considering his engagement to Kelly."

"Aye, aye, sir. We should and can easily cover expenses to date under the TAD orders from our office. Kelly, help Marcus pull the receipts together and get them to me soon." She nodded that she would. "As for the future expenses, Admiral Chance can probably set it up as an educational budget line item under NISHQ since Marcus will be teaching agents different methods of investigation. We can use his past receipts to form a workable budget."

"If Chance balks, I'll have a chat with him. Perhaps the accounting staff in the Pentagon can find a few bucks laying around to move over to NIS."

Everyone was in agreement with these plans, especially Kelly, who, I was assured by my source, was smiling more than she had in the last two days.

93

THE LUNCH CONVERSATION WASN'T THE only scene I missed that day. Doc Stevens, as he told me later, thought the Admiral was up to something, but he couldn't figure out what. Being asked to meet with the CNO seemed a bit strange, but he knew anything dealing with me, Marcus Colt, was usually strange. So he just ran with it and would take what came. He was glad he had the opportunity to change into his dress blues before traveling to the airport for his first meeting with the CNO.

He told me he'd been allowed access to the Admiral's aircraft and was standing beside the stairs when the cars arrived. Most of the entourage stayed around the cars, sharing their goodbyes. Commander Montclair returned his salute and nodded at him as he boarded the aircraft to coordinate the departure.

Admiral Gallagher walked up to Doc and returned his salute before extending his hand. "At ease. I appreciate you coming here, Stevens. It is a true pleasure to meet you. May I call you 'Doc' or is that nickname reserved just for your fellow warriors?"

"Sir, it is an honor to have you address me as 'Doc' and you are most welcome to use it anytime. How may I be of assistance, sir?"

The Admiral smiled. Doc told me he had the impression the Admiral realized he was speaking with another man of integrity: the type that I find and keep close. "Assuming you are willing to volunteer, Doc, I have an assignment for you that I would consider a personal favor. Come inside and I'll run it down for you." And with that they entered the aircraft.

With the meeting underway inside the plane, according to what Kelly told me in her recounting of the day, those left outside finished their hugs and were discussing the rest of the day. Working out the logistics took a few minutes. While an army, or in this case Navy, moves on its stomach, detailed logistics are needed to direct those post-lunch movements.

The Captain would drop Dorothy and Kelly off at his house before heading to the NISO offices to call the SEAL CO.

Sam and Doc, if he accepted the assignment, would meet back at the NISRA to update the agents and generate a set of NIS credentials for Doc. It was time for Sam to check on the re-evaluation of all the surveillance options and see if there were any more needed changes. Then after getting the rest of the agents up to speed, Doc would head to the hospital to become my shadow.

After the Admiral's plane left for D.C., the logistics plan that had been devised worked perfectly. And as had been expected, Doc was now thought of as being my executive assistant; he would be wearing the attire and carrying the official ID and badge of an NIS Special Agent.

After Kelly returned to the Captain's house, she told me, she changed into a more relaxed outfit. She raided the stash of clothing she'd brought there for me, grabbed some important hygiene items from the bathroom, and returned to the hospital to make sure I was doing well and to keep me from doing anything that would hurt my recovery.

94

ACCORDING TO OTHER UPDATES I was getting from my hospital bed, the Captain had squared everything with the SEAL CO for Doc's TAD to NIS by the time Sam and Doc made it back to the NISRA office. Doc had opted to change out of his uniform into civvies, and Sam stopped at RL to check on things there.

RB had already been shut down, and the staff at RL had switched their mission from watching over me and Roger to finding the missing store-keeper, Dennis Moore. In addition, they were keeping a general watch on things there at the Logistics Center since drugs were still moving.

Sam introduced Doc to those who hadn't met him yet, and explained how I needed Doc to be my "just about everything" until I healed. And from that moment forward, Doc actually was an official NIS agent, though he hadn't gone through the official training. His SEAL training, and the fact that he'd always be under my watchful eyes, was a good substitute.

Things were coming together on the case. CPO Lansing had signed a confession that admitted his role in the murder of at least fifteen people over the last six months. He implicated Detective Royal as his handler for some unknown drug kingpin. He had no clues about the ID of the drug guy. The way he understood it, the drug guy told Royal who to kill and when, and that order was passed to Lansing. So all he ever knew was the who and when, but never the why.

And on top of that, he tagged several more people guilty of various crimes, ranging from drug pushing up to murder. I'd been right. Lansing had gotten into all this for the money, but the guilt had pushed him over the edge into full-blown alcoholism.

Earlier that day, agent John Driscol had contacted the Norfolk district attorney about how to proceed. Royal had not set foot on Navy property, but had been responsible for multiple crimes against the Navy, and NIS had the confessions. The DA decided that the confessions were strong, and a warrant for Royal's arrest had been issued.

I was happy to receive the news that he'd been picked up by NPD, and was now sitting in isolation lock up. The NPD had asked Sam Maker to participate in the interrogation, set to start sometime the next morning. The DA would call later with more information.

And Sam instructed the agents that in addition to the confessions, there had to be some mighty strong physical evidence to go with it. He did not want Royal to walk, so the case had to be stronger than what usually went to the lawyers in JAG.

He needed me and my analytical brain, he told me, to keep looking over and linking the evidence. At least with the confessions they knew the cases were linked. Just a matter of tying things together.

Sam gave the marching order to his agents, who now include Doc, and motioned for Doc to follow him. Since he was now an agent, he needed the standard tour of the office space and introductions to the other people in both NISRA and NISO Norfolk. Sam knew I did not need to spend my time telling Doc where to go and who to see, so this was step one of Doc's indoctrination.

They started in the CO's office. Captain Miller had met Doc at the hospital and had been impressed by his medical expertise. Seeing him dressed as an agent caused the skipper to admit—again—that the Admiral's right hand man, David, was right on the money. Doc would fit in well with the office.

Sam told the Captain why he was doing the "meet and greet" with Doc, and the skipper approved of that decision. In addition, Sam gave him a quick brief about the status of the case, and related how much they really needed me to help tie the evidence together.

The Captain, as Doc characterized him to me, assumed his standard position of contemplation: steepled fingers in front of his lower jaw. After a moment or two, he leaned back and offered a suggestion. "Doc, talk with Marcus ASAP and determine how he is feeling. If you think he can handle being here in the office for some part time work, then bring him in. But that decision is strictly yours based upon your evaluation of his condition."

"Can do, Captain."

"And when he is ready to come back, he will come as LCDR Colt, in uniform. Time for hiding is over and he deserves proper recognition."

"Yes, sir." And with that, they left the Captain and continued on the tour.

95

SAM AND DOC ARRIVED BACK at the hospital and entered my suite just in time to hear Kelly say, "Okay, before I call the restaurant, let me verify the order. We need ... oh, Sam, Doc, you're just in time. Hungry? I'm calling in an order for seafood dinners."

"Damn, Marcus, you look almost human again. Guess that visit from the CNO perked you up, eh?" ask Sam with a wink toward Kelly.

"Sam, I gotta admit, it was the sponge bath from the two potential harem members right before Kelly got here with my clothes that did the trick. Best medicine there is," I responded right before getting a gentle punch in my right arm from Kelly.

Kelly said with a laugh in her voice, "Sam, I got here soon enough to make sure they did not take any liberties with my guy. At least he smells a lot better now, and we have permanently ditched the hospital gowns."

Doc walked over to where I was sitting on a sofa and looked me over top to bottom. He placed the back of his hand against my forehead and checked the tension on the sling. He took my pulse, and nodding satisfaction, asked the most popular question of the hour: "How is the pain level, Marcus?"

"Worse than hitting my thumb with a hammer but a lot better than meeting my future mother-in-law while wearing just a ratty hospital gown. Seriously, not bad. I haven't taken any of the pain pills and the pain level is tolerable."

Bill McCoy asked, "What are you dressed for, Doc? Got a hot date lined up?"

And with that intro into the changed situation, Sam started to lay out the events of the afternoon. Kelly had not shared any of the decisions that had been reached over lunch since she felt it was Sam's job to do it, or perhaps her uncle's; but no matter who broke the news, she was thrilled about it all and had been holding in all her excitement.

"Sam, can you hold off for a couple of minutes. We were getting ready to call a food order into Kelly's favorite seafood place, and some of us are starving!" asked Roger. He was looking and feeling better, and it was good to see his appetite improve.

We got the food order called in and they promised to deliver in about an hour. That gave us plenty of time to go over the changes that the Admiral and Captain had put in place earlier in the day. Frankly, I had to admit it all made sense, which is always a scary situation with things that involve me. And I could see Kelly was over the moon with it all. I'd be in Norfolk for another couple of months or longer.

"Sam, since I now have a gentleman's gentleman and chauffeur in the form of a newly-minted NIS agent, when will it be okay for me to head back to my house?"

"Please wait until tomorrow at the earliest, Marcus. We need to pick up the last of the vipers first. Besides, you need to be here early in the morning for another one of those exciting dressing changes. Doc can observe to make sure he has the procedure down pat so he can do it going forward."

I nodded in agreement and hid that it didn't make me happy. I wanted out of the hospital. But hanging around another night would not be the end of the world. Bill was being released the next day and would finish healing at home, under Penny's watchful eyes. I should be there with him.

And the doctors were talking about letting Roger head home to Chicago in another day or so. His surgery went well, and the broken bones could heal anywhere. If it meant another night in the hospital to be able to spend quality time with men who put it all on the line for you, that was a very small price to pay.

Sam looked at Doc with a question on his face. Doc nodded in approval. Sam turned to me and asked, "Marcus, after the dressing change and checkup in the morning, do you think you will feel good enough to come into the office for a few hours?"

"Sure. I can go in later tonight if you need me."

Kelly stood up quickly and in a stern voice said, "No, you will not, Marcus. You are just starting your road to recovery and need more rest. Get that silly idea out of your head."

I grimaced knowing that she was right and I was letting my excitement for catching all the bastards overpower my common sense. "You're right, Kelly. Sorry I got carried away."

Then Sam jumped in with more information. "No one is going anywhere tonight, Marcus. But I do need your eyes on those evidence cards soon so we can build some solid evidence against Royal. And perhaps find some leads for uncovering his controller. I get to help with Royal's interrogation starting sometime tomorrow, so time is not our friend."

Sam paused to let that sink in before broaching another point from that day's decisions by the powers at NISO. "And by the way, the Captain has decided that Lieutenant Commander Colt will now appear in the correct uniform the next time you're at the office. YN3 Mark Williams has been retired. So get your officer's uniforms dusted off and try to remember how to return salutes instead of giving them."

As I was digesting that info, the dinners arrived. And for the next hour, conversation between bites of great seafood was restricted to family, hobbies, and friends; we talked about anything except our wounds and the problems with the case. We had to put the bad stuff out of our minds for at least a few minutes to help keep our mental balance good.

And I mentioned I was open to suggestions on how to get into my uniform with my arm in a sling. Another new experience that would teach me much before I could put it in the past. Fortunately, I'd have Kelly and Doc beside me, so I knew I was in good hands.

Sam left for his home right after dinner. He half joked that he might need a name tag to get into his house since his wife had not seen him in several days. While I'd been passed out in a hospital bed, he'd been catching cat naps in his office. He needed true rest just as much as I did. But he also needed to get into the office early, so his rest would be limited.

Doc also headed back to his place for the night. Since we had security watching our suite, and I had my weapon, he felt comfortable taking the remainder of the night off. And that would give him the opportunity to get some clothing and things together to move into my house the next day. He said he would be back early in the morning.

Bill and Roger were still tied to their beds by various tubes and lines, so to give them some quiet and privacy, Kelly and I adjourned to the attached sitting room and started to stretch out on the large sofa. We then discovered it was a fold-out bed, so Kelly did the honors and got us more room.

We kicked off our shoes and enjoyed the quiet moments of just being next to each other. I teased Kelly, asking if she was still going to take that vow about sickness and health since she was getting some firsthand experience. Good thing I was wounded or she might have hit me harder.

96

A SOFT SNORT FROM KELLY brought me awake. She had her back to me and was pulled up into a near fetal position. Her photo should have been in the dictionary under the word "cute."

I carefully got up and headed out the door. True to his word of being there early, Doc was waiting in the hospital bedroom talking softly with Bill. Roger was still snoring.

Doc had brought in a rolling cart with coffee, tea, and donuts. Bill already had his mug, and as I poured one, I mentioned to Doc, "You're getting the hang of this butler thing. Maybe the Navy should follow the British lead where every officer has a batman to handle important things like this." I smiled at Doc and received a middle finger salute in return.

I had barely gotten a couple of sips down when the door opened and my doctor and his nurse, complete with their cart load of tools, entered and pointed me over to my bed. While he'd met the surgeon earlier in the week, Doc explained his new role in the care of my health, and that he wanted to participate in the dressing change.

Again, the surgeon was pleased with his work on my arm. No sign of infection. No drainage. All was good, he said. I do think he was disappointed the CNO was not present that morning. He'd been in awe, the day before, I thought he was going to ask for the Admiral's autograph. Of course, I felt the same way the first day I met the Admiral.

The nurse let Doc handle the application of ointment and the gauze dressing. Then she showed him how to wind the elastic bandages around the arm and splint to her satisfaction. The nurse told Doc to stop by her station on the way out and pick up a supply of ointment and bandages that she'd have ready in about fifteen minutes.

After all that, the doctor granted me permission to leave the hospital as long as I promised to come right back if I started a fever. Or had severe pain in my arm. Or started leaking. The list went on and on. And I had to be in his office in a week for a follow-up exam. Then he took his leave, and it got quieter again.

Knowing our little band was breaking up that day, I spent some time thanking Bill for keeping me alive again. And I told him I'd be visiting him as soon as things calmed down on this case. Just rest and recover soon.

Roger was finally awake. I took him a cup of coffee and we talked a few minutes. He had performed well in his undercover assignment and I'd been impressed. Assuming all went well with his doctor's visit, he would be heading back to Chicago later in the day. Well, he'd actually be heading to the base hospital at NTC Great Lakes. He jokingly said the next time I needed help not to call him. Least I hope he was joking. He was another good guy in my book.

Doc and I grabbed more coffee and sat together to figure out the way to attack the day. I needed to be at the NISRA, but I also needed to be there dressed properly. That entailed a trip to my house for a clothing change.

We also tackled another transportation logistics problem. Doc's Corvette, a beautiful 1963 model in dashing red, was near impossible for a tall guy with an arm in a sling to enter and exit. And while not as bad as the Corvette, my Barracuda and Kelly's Mustang had similar disadvantages. Sports cars are designed for healthy people, not people who forget to duck out of harm's way.

I mentioned my Blue Beast was much better for carrying the infirmed since it had big doors and big roomy seats. Doc called the impound lot and found that they'd gotten all the finger prints they could find from the car and the crew had installed the lug nuts. They also checked over the brake system and other parts to ensure no tampering had gone on. So the car was ready to be released.

We didn't want the 'Vette sitting around outside my house. The garage would be full with my 'Cude and Kelly's Mustang. So we decided to stash the 'Vette in the Captain's garage, where the Mustang usually sat.

To accomplish this Chinese Fire Drill, Kelly would follow Doc to the Captain's house to drop off his 'Vette, then drive him over to the impound lot to pick up the Beast. She would then drive alone to the house to prepare my uniform of the day, and Doc would come back to the hospital to pick me up. Then he and I would head to my house for a uniform change. Yea, I told Doc to take notes since it was a confusing mess.

"Damn, I've missed that," Bill said as he chuckled.

"Missed what, Chief?" I asked.

"Watching and listening to you glance at a problem then come up with several complex solutions, give multiple people orders, and solve a couple of other non-related issues, all while sipping on a cup of coffee. Of course, over there things were a bit more hairy, but considering the number of wounded we have here, not much more," and he laughed at his own joke.

I had to agree with him. He was right. I'm in my element when doing things I believe need to be done. But he never saw that I was also praying the decisions I made were the right ones.

Before I could think of a good comeback, the sitting room door opened and Kelly emerged with the "I need coffee now" look on her face. I quickly poured her a mug-full as everyone bid her a good morning, and everyone laughed at Bill's comment about Princess Kelly looking so regal in her sleep-wrinkled sweatshirt. She stuck her tongue out at him for that one.

The five of us shared a few more minutes of friendship banter before the next round of doctors and nurses arrived to tend to Bill and Roger. Doc gave Kelly the rundown on the morning events and plans, and I sat back to enjoy a few more minutes of sanity while watching people I loved.

97

ONE OF THE ROTC INSTRUCTORS I knew in Georgia was an old Army master sergeant named Barney. He told us, whenever we were ready to head out for training, that it was time to sound *Boots and Saddles*. It's an old military bugle call for the troops to mount up. It seemed right for this adventure, so I sat my empty coffee mug down on the cart and said, "Lady and gentlemen, sound *Boots and Saddles*."

I knew I'd have to explain it to Kelly and Roger, but Bill and Doc knew exactly what I meant. And just like Barney used to do, Doc put his closed hand to his mouth and tooted out the right bugle call. He was ready to go. The Chief just sat there laughing at the insanity of the situation. Or perhaps the insanity of just me: it was hard to say which.

Doc and Kelly left the room. Doc would call me there in the room when he got back with the Beast. Bill's doctor and nurse had unhooked all the lines and tubes and redressed his wound. He was waiting for Penny to come pick him up. And Roger had gotten the seal of approval for his transfer to Illinois. He'd be out of here in a couple of hours.

In these precious few moments of down time, I decided to shave. It was a task I could safely do with one hand without adult supervision, and for the first time in three months, the upper lip was clean. It felt somewhat strange, but at least a familiar face was now staring back at me from the mirror. And when the hair was combed in the former, pre-yeoman way, I saw what I really needed was a haircut. Oh, well, couldn't worry about that now, it was time to pack up the few things Kelly had brought over for me and await Doc's call.

Heading down to the first floor after getting Doc's call, I made a quick detour to the ER. It was blissfully calm in there that morning, and a fast look around found my target. "Good morning, Petty Officer Holt. How are you today?"

Ann did a quick double take before recognition came across her face. "I almost didn't recognize you, Mark, without the mustache and glasses. How are you feeling?" The nurse in her started checking my sling tension.

"Ann, thanks to you and your quick actions, I'm still breathing and feeling, and getting better by the minute. I've been discharged, but before heading out, in addition to another big personal thank you, I wanted to give you this."

I passed her an envelope containing a folded sheet of paper. "That is my home address, where Kelly and Doc will be living with me for the next few months. The house and our office phone numbers are there too. Doc is now officially an NIS agent who's also my chauffeur, bodyguard, and medical staff while this silly arm heals. I think you two look good together, and seem to work well together, and who knows, I might need two medics to help keep me alive through this mess. Kelly and I hope to see you soon, Ann. You are always welcome in our home."

She gently gave me a hug and slipped the envelope into her pocket. "Thank you so much for this, Mark. It's a promise, I'll see you soon," she said. "And yea, I really like hanging out with Doc." I gave her a wink, a nod, and a quick salute, and then headed out to find Doc before the SP had the Beast towed away for illegal parking.

Never one to pull punches, Doc agreed I needed a trim. Compared to his standard flattop hairstyle, my hair would almost qualify for hippy rock star status. We hit the base barbershop and were fortunate to find two empty chairs. Doc figured he might as well get clipped while he had the time. My standard cut is high and tight on the sides and back, and medium-short on top. It felt good to get my head back under control.

As we walked to the door of my house, it hit me that I didn't have any keys. I thought I'd left them in the locker at the transient barracks, but wasn't sure. Seems I'd lost track of more than one thing over the last few days. Of course, having some of my clothing cut off before surgery—and being on pain meds for a couple of days— will interrupt many thought processes.

Doc had his suitcase in the trunk. I had no idea when he'd moved it to the Blue Beast. But as usual, Doc was ready for just about anything. He pulled it out and carried it to the house.

Fortunately, the lady of the house was there. Kelly opened the door when we walked up the porch stairs. And for once, I caught her by surprise. A shave and a haircut were not what she expected to find. She looked me up one side and then down the other, and stared closely at my upper lip. Her mouth twisted over to the right and formed an 'I'm not sure about this' look that caused me some concern. Then she smiled and gave me a huge kiss, followed by two or three more.

"I like this smooth face, Marcus. And you look so much younger, if that is even possible," she purred. "And that shorter hair gives you more of a warrior look. Come on in, I have your uniform ready."

Doc chimed in, "Yea, long haired hippy freaks are not warriors. Welcome back, Marcus!"

As one who hates to admit I need help, the non-functioning left arm had convinced me that I did need help, and a lot of it. After I got out of my civvies, Doc helped me get into a tee-shirt and my trousers. He had to tie my shoes for me since that isn't something one can do single handedly. I needed to check the regs and see if loafers were acceptable in cases such as this.

Kelly brought in my shirt. It took both of them to thread it over the bandage of my left arm and work it around to my right arm, but it was finally in place. At least I could handle some of the shirt buttons, but more help was needed on the collar buttons. Kelly devised a way to pin my left sleeve to the bandages in a way that looked nice.

Doc took care of my tie, and Kelly returned the sling to its place to hold my arm in position. She then helped get my right arm into my jacket sleeve and draped the left side of the jacket over the sling and arm. A check in the mirror showed a look that wasn't too bad for a guy with only one good arm.

The worst thing was getting used to an inside waistband holster on my right hip, for my 1911. I needed a new shoulder holster since the ER staff had cut mine off the other night. And it seemed the sling would be in the way anyhow. So I needed to hit the range for some practice real soon, to get used to the new draw position.

Doc noticed that my ribbons now included the Navy Cross and Purple Heart ribbons. He nodded an approval and smiled. He dusted off the SEAL trident and smiled even more.

So with the uniform challenge over, I put my cover in place, got a couple more warm kisses from Kelly, and Doc and I left for NISRA Norfolk for some real work again. As we drove away from the house, Kelly was on the phone delivering a brief message.

98

I'D HOPED TO USE THE back stairs and avoid many of the people coming and going from the HQ building, but that wasn't to be. Doc said there was maintenance going on, so we had to use the front entrance. It did take a minute to get used to returning salutes from all the sailors coming and going. At least with our arrival being after the 0800 hrs official start time, the number of people was smaller.

As we entered the NISO spaces through the security area, it was strange that GM2 Jimmy Kincade was not on duty at the gate. The gate was blocked open, so we walked on in. As we got to the hall and turned the corner to head to the skipper's office to check in, a voice yelled "attention on deck."

I was taken back to see the hall filled with the entire NISO and NISRA staff, officers, enlisted, and civilian personnel, all standing at attention. Even our token Air Force officer was present. Doc had a truly silly grin on his face, so obviously he knew what was coming. The Captain was near the center of the group and he nodded in my direction. I got the hint and responded, "As you were."

The Captain stepped forward and extended his hand as he announced, "Lieutenant Commander Marcus James Colt, we are happy to welcome you to your temporary duty station here at NISO Norfolk. The entire crew has been briefed and they all understand why we have known you as Mark Williams in the recent past. They all have been made aware of why you had to do that and we are now looking forward to getting to know the real you soon. Care to say a few words?"

With emotions running high and me still in a bit of shock seeing everyone, I did believe this to be harder than briefing the CNO the day before, but you do what you have to do. "Thank you, Captain. Ladies and gentlemen, everything about the last few weeks has made me believe I have followed Alice through her looking glass. It has been most interesting, and recently somewhat painful." Pointing to my bandaged arm got the expected chuckles.

"While I'm sorry for the initial subterfuge, I am extremely grateful for the friendships and working relationships that developed while I was here as Mark, and I look forward to building them stronger as you get to know me as Marcus. I am honored by your presence this morning and the smiles that greet me. Thank you so very much. And I sure hope Dex has a fresh pot of special brew going; after all this excitement, I can really use a cup or two." That last comment got a good laugh, which helped me relax. The applause that followed, though, was embarrassing.

The skipper nodded his approval and turned to face the group. "Dismissed. Thank you, people. We have a lot of work to do, so let's get it done. Sam, Marcus, please join me in my conference room. You too, Doc."

As everyone dispersed, I got a big smile and wave from Laura. But then I noticed Dexter didn't look happy and had quickly ducked back into his office. I told Doc I'd be in the conference room in a minute and to tell them to start without me.

Entering the AUTOVON room for the first time as an officer, it felt familiar and yet, at the same time, strange. Changing status will do that. Per protocol, Dex stood when I walked in and rather harshly said, "How may I help the Commander, sir?"

"If I have to say 'as you were' to you every damn time I walk in here, there might be bloodshed." With that, I walked around his desk and extended my hand. "Dex, unless the skipper is nearby, you'd better continue to treat me just like you did last week. Whichever uniform I wear does not change our friendship. As for keeping you in the dark, everyone was initially, including the Captain. If doing my job pissed you off, sorry, but you'll get over that. And I still need my friend." I gave him my best smile.

"Thank you, sir, uh Mark, or do you prefer Marcus? Oh, hell, what should I call you?" he asked in a nicer, but confused voice as he shook my hand.

I shrugged, "Just as before, Dex, go with whatever feels good to you, but you might want to clean it up just a bit. Using vulgarity toward an officer is a violation of something somewhere in the UCMJ. And make sure you keep the coffee pots full, please." And with that we shared a good laugh.

Dex nodded and looked down at my arm, "Really, man, how is that arm doing? The Captain told us a bit about what happened, but didn't go into details on the wound or your recovery or frankly much of anything."

"It will take a couple of months for the huge gash to heal, then there'll be rehab. My personal satisfaction comes from the fact I killed the bastard right after he cut me." I used my good hand to point to the location of the cut on the bandages, and his eyes got big when he realized just how huge it was.

And I continued, "Things have been worked out with HQ so I can stay in Norfolk during the recovery time and work out of the NISRA office. It's hectic right now, but we'll find time to go into all the gory details soon. Shoot, you probably know more than me since you send all the traffic out. Question is, are you doing okay? Sorry I left you shorthanded."

He laughed when he said he'd get by without me since he didn't have to waste all that time redoing my sloppy work. It was good to be back on kidding terms with him. Then he told me that things were going great with Karen. He was grateful I had pushed that opportunity. Life is good when sharing great news.

With too many things to do, I told him I had to run to the meeting, but since I would be around for a long while, we'd talk later. As I closed the door behind me, I thought again that true friendships are hard to find, and are so worth the effort to keep.

When I got to the conference room, it was easy to see everyone was waiting for my arrival. Taking my seat I said, "Sorry for the delay, Captain, there was a fence that needed mending immediately."

The skipper chuckled and said, "Only one?"

"The day is young, sir."

99

IT WAS AMAZING HOW QUICKLY the morning vanished. We wrapped up the "get everyone on the same page" meeting in about an hour. Sam was heading to NPD to start the interrogation of Royal at around 1300 hrs. Another cup of coffee after the meeting helped perk me up a small amount. But I found chatting with Greg, Karl, and "call me Scott" Tiller post-meeting in the coffee mess sapped a lot of energy.

The skipper asked us to join him and the XO at the officers' club for lunch, but I begged off. I told him the hard truth: eating in public with one hand was a skill I had yet to master. For now, I'd just run to the cafeteria and pick up a sandwich to eat in the quiet privacy of the agents' area. Life was much less stressful and embarrassing that way.

He said he understood, but was looking forward to introducing me around. He mentioned that there were a good number of officers I needed to get to know, as they may be important to my future military career. I promised to work on my eating skills and let him know when I wouldn't be an embarrassment.

With another full mug in hand, Doc and I headed to the NISRA office spaces. Sam offered to let me use the office next to his, but I told him my old desk next to the radiator would still be just fine. No need for any changes. And Doc could use the desk that butts against mine, so he would always have me in his sights, just as he promised the CNO.

I spent a good amount of time instructing Doc on my index card method of evidence analysis. We had the list of murders Chief Lansing admitted to ordering, and compared that list to the odd cases and dead CIs that I'd pulled. There were several more cases I hadn't pulled, since nothing in them waved the red flag during my initial analysis. Doc pulled those cases and I asked him to generate the index cards, as we'd discussed.

I sat at my desk, working on the mug of coffee, thinking about the entire operation, and jotting down some things to bring up with Sam. We'd picked up so many of the vipers, and still there was at least one more running around. And the kingpin of the operation was still unknown. While hoping Sam would pull something about him, or her, from Royal, I knew we couldn't hang everything on that. We had to continue to investigate.

It hit me that one thing not mentioned in the morning meeting was whether or not we had more information on the airport stranger I thought of as DN. I wondered what we'd heard from NISRA Miami and the local FBI about the guy. Granted it was a long shot, but we knew SK2 Jesus Martinez knew him, so maybe he had talked about DN. Naturally, when you needed them, the agents were all out in the field; evil continues all day, every day.

And I took the time to call the CNO's office and give David Bartow an update on my condition. He was glad to hear I was doing better but concerned I was already back to work. Rest is important, he said. I agreed as I stifled yet another yawn. I also let him know Kelly would be at my house with me and Doc if he needed to reach any of us. He said he'd pass the info on to the Admiral, who naturally was in another meeting.

David also reminded me he'd sent another package of my personal mail to the PO Box the previous week, and not to forget about that in my pressure to capture all the bad guys in the Tidewater area. We finished up the call with him challenging me to another non-dominant hand shooting contest real soon. He thought with my arm in the sling he might have an even chance to beat me. It's always good to hang up on a happy note.

A call to the folks in Florida got me off my mother's bad list. They were happy to hear about my progress, and like David, delivered many warnings about resting properly. They were thrilled about Kelly. It had been all Kelly could do to keep them from flying up on Monday morning when she'd called them about surgery. But Kelly had briefly explained the security issues and that, since my injury was not life-threatening, it would be best for them to stay home. She also promised that we'd be visiting them soon.

Next I gave Kelly a call to let her know I was behaving as best I could, and had checked in with my parents and her dad via David. I didn't want to get on her bad list either. I mentioned she might want to call her mother with an update. She claimed innocence when I accused her of setting up my welcome, but her laughter gave her away as one of the primary culprits. I reminded her that paybacks are hell.

Since she was heading to the campus for a meeting with her professor later that day, I asked her to swing by the post office and get my mail David had mentioned. "The key is on the table in the foyer," I told her. After a few loving comments, I hung up and sat back to savor the sweet sound of her voice for a moment.

Doc interrupted that reverie when he called me to come back into the file room. He'd finished with the new files and had all the index cards laid out properly. Watching him grasp the concept so quickly was not surprising. Doc was probably the smartest man on the team, but used humor to hide much of it. I expected him to excel no matter the challenge, and again he had not let me down.

I asked him to read the cards aloud. Trust me, I told him. That's another trick that does two things for me. One, saying something out loud helps lock it into long-term memory. It also helps create a better visual image in your mind. And that "picture worth a thousand words" in my mind is easier to connect to other things, because of that.

We went down the new lists backwards and forwards, but right this minute nothing was popping out at me. We needed to get a strong case built from this mess, but it wasn't happening yet. I stifled another yawn and wished for more coffee. And a nap. I really wished I could take a nap.

"Doc, I'm frustrated. I'm not taking any of the pain pills, and I did get a decent night's sleep last night, but I am so damn tired. All I want to do is nap. What is wrong with me?"

"Nothing. Absolutely nothing. Here's the deal, Marcus, you were given IV pain meds from Sunday night until Tuesday morning. And you were under anesthesia late Sunday night for your surgery. It takes about five days for the effects of the anesthesia to leave your body. And a similar amount of time is needed for your body to flush out all the doping effects of the pain meds."

"Marcus, on top of all that, the attack gave you a massive adrenalin dump, and the adrenal glands, which have yet to recover from that, are also still pumping out adrenalin to compensate for the pain you're having from the wound. And don't sit there and tell me you are not in pain. It's all over your face. Hell, with that deep a cut—you do know that it was only the bone that stopped the knife—most people would still be in a hospital bed. At least take a few aspirin several times a day to help your body handle the pain. Taking them isn't a sign of weakness, it's the smart thing to do for your body."

He continued in his best doctor voice, "You need to realize that your body is reacting just as it should, Marcus. You have to go easy on yourself. Have patience. Let your body heal and let it clean itself up the way God designed. Bottom line, if you need to close your eyes and nap, do so."

"I'll work on that patience thing, Doc, but don't hold your breath. What say we head down to the cafeteria and grab some lunch? Perhaps some walking and food will help perk me up. I'll even buy," I said as I stifled yet another yawn.

"As always, boss, your leadership and decision-making skills are outstanding! Let's go. I'll get the door for ya, gimpy."

IOO

It didn't work. Lunch consisted of a tuna melt sandwich—an easy thing to eat with only one hand—and a soda, but it failed to perk me up and the yawns kept coming. Again, it looked like Doc was right about the slow return of my energy. Perhaps a glass of wine later with Kelly and snuggling against her side might help me get more rest that night. I was glad Doc would be driving us home, because yawning while driving might be dangerous.

Sam finally got back from his time at NPD a little after 1600 hrs, and we received an update on Royal. There was nothing exciting about his report. So far, Royal was not talking; he just sat there. He and Lansing must have gone to the same anti-interrogation school. It didn't matter who asked what question, the jerk was using his Fifth Amendment rights to the fullest.

We needed some solid evidence, to go with Lansing's confession, to nail Royal. Right now, it was just the word of a well-liked senior detective against a Navy CPO with an old theft record, and in a jury's eyes, the detective probably had more credibility. Only consolation we had was that, so far, he was off the street.

I took the time to tell Sam some of the things I'd been pondering while he was having fun with the NPD. When asked about DN, Sam admitted he'd forgotten to follow up on our airport guy with his FBI friend. He'd planned to get back with him, but it fell through the cracks. It was easy for things like that to happen with so much going on. And with Sam being the leader of all this chaos, he had more on his mind than the average agent.

Darrell had been tasked with checking NISRA Miami to see if they had any info on DN. Sam hadn't heard anything from him about any results. Darrell had been busy on surveillance, too, and again, Sam forgot to ask. So it was time for both Sam and Darrell to get on the phones and follow up on their requests.

Sam said that Jesus Martinez was still in the hospital and still under the watchful eyes of several SEALs and SP members. No one would get to him. He was talking about the things he did, but no one had asked him about DN. So it seemed all the excitement, with several of us in the hospital, had resulted in some holes in the investigation. Time to fix that.

"Sam, feel up to a visit to the hospital? We have SM, our knife-wielding 'Sal Mineo' stand-in, AKA Martinez, in our custody. We need to talk with him about DN. He's our only lead to him right now. And who knows, he might be able to tie DN back to Royal. Want to go with me?" I asked.

'Hold on," Sam said as he picked up the phone. He placed a call to the hospital and asked for the head nurse on the floor where Martinez was under guard. After asking for a status report on Martinez, he was told he was awake and doing well. He looked back at me and said, "Okay, he is awake. Therefore it won't be a wasted trip. Let's roll."

We agreed it would be a quick visit to Martinez, and I outlined how I wanted things to progress. We were all tired and needed to call it a day, so we'd hit him hard and fast and make our getaway. As we went to the door, Sam's phone rang. "Probably Marie wanting to know if I'm ever coming home. Hold on, guys."

He walked out of his office with a big smile on his face. "Anyone wish to guess who extremely Special Agent Joe Mabry and a couple of SPs just picked up? How about our missing storekeeper, Dennis Moore. He was hiding out with a buddy who works on the first floor of the Logistics Center. Joe also picked him up for aiding and abetting. Considering the Harker problem with the main brig, we've made arrangements to keep these guys, and Lansing, in the brig on the USS Forrestal. Joe is there with them now and starting the interrogation."

"Wonderful news, Sam. Now we have another card to play with both Royal and SM. Let the fun begin," I said as we closed the NISRA door.

On the drive over, I gave Doc some direction on how I thought he should act. Naturally, he could adlib all he wanted, and he was very good at that. We knew Sam understood his job was to basically stand there and look intimidating. If all went well, we would plant seeds that would grow overnight.

It was good to see the SPs on duty, both outside and inside Martinez's room, as well as one of our SEALs. Our bad guy was still hooked up to a monitor and a couple of IVs, so if he decided to move, the SP on duty would have plenty of notice. He did not look happy ... perhaps his pain meds weren't working well.

Sam stood against the back wall with his hands together in front of his jacket. That's the standard position for secret service-type personnel when they're ready to draw their weapons. Doc pulled Martinez's chart and walked over to the monitor as he read. I walked to the other side of the bed and stared down at our wounded viper.

"Who are you and what do you want?" he asked, switching his gaze between the three of us. Standard nervous reaction of licking his lips followed.

Doc snickered. Sam just stared. I smiled.

"What is this? Who are you guys?" he asked again.

I started, "Jesus." I pronounced it with the word spread out like Hayyy-sooooossss and spoke softly and slowly. "We are all special agents of the Naval Investigative Service. You might remember me as the guy you tried to kill on Sunday night."

"It was not me, I swear," Martinez said nervously.

I smiled again.

"And I want my lawyer, man, I know my rights."

I increased my smile and responded, "Of course you do. But first off, you do not need a lawyer as you haven't been charged with a crime. At least, not yet. Second, and most important, you are being held as a material witness. Think of it as being for your safety because there are people out there who will kill you if they can."

Doc came in right on cue and started chuckling. Sam maintained his professional 'I will just kill you' stare. Jesus kept looking between the three of us.

Keeping my smile, I continued the push. "Your problem is there are other people we've already arrested who are telling us, in great detail

I might add, that you're one of the leaders of a gang we call the *vipers*. And you were the reason I was attacked and almost killed the other night."

"No, man, Baker told me we were just going to rob a guy, then the shooting started and I got hit. That's all I know. I'm not in charge of anything, I swear."

Doc chuckled again and added, "Commander, did you ever notice how all the guilty people swear they are innocent. It's almost a 'tell,' like gamblers use to spot liars."

"Yea, Doc, I have noticed that. And we're seeing it again right here with Jesus. I suggest we head back to the office and start writing up his charges. By now, Lansing, Harker, and Moore have spilled their guts and we have all we need to get this guy hung."

Jesus was sweating now, and Doc pointed to his increasing heart rate on the monitor.

Looking back down at Jesus, I hit him with my last thought for the night. "Did you notice I didn't mention Baker talking to us? Good reason for that—he's in the morgue downstairs. My two .45 rounds caused his heart to explode right after he cut my arm."

I pulled my jacket open and exposed the Colt on my side. "And the one slug I put into you with this same weapon took out a nice chunk out of your liver and wiped out your right kidney. While my poor shooting is causing the US Government a lot of money to put you back together, it's not a long-term issue for you. Tell him, Doc."

"Yes, sir. Jesus, when we finish writing up all the charges and push them through the courts martial—by then you'll be healthy enough to meet some new close friends in the prison shower—you'll spend just a short period of time in Portsmouth Naval Prison. It'll be short because we will hang your sorry ass for all the evil you've done."

Jesus was sweating now and his heart rate was still climbing. "But I didn't do it all."

"Thanks, Doc, good synopsis of what is facing Jesus. Of course, we'd like to tell the JAG staff that Jesus cooperated just as the others are doing, and that might reduce the sentence to life or maybe as low as twenty years. Just depends on how much help he offers."

Doc looked down at Jesus while he continued to talk with me. "So true, Commander. Jesus here wants help to save his worthless shot-up butt, and we need information about things like that Miami-bound guy you saw him with at the airport."

"And his other friends who helped with the thefts, drugs and murders. Think of it as a share the blame opportunity," I added. "Ponder on it overnight, Jesus. If we're not too busy listening to the other guys telling us how evil you are, we'll try to see you in the morning. Take care and get a good night's rest."

We waited until we were out of the hospital before saying anything. Sam broke the silence first. "Have you guys practiced that routine before? If not, I'm truly impressed."

"Think it worked?" I asked.

Sam shrugged and offered, "I'll let you know in the morning. I'll stop by here on my way into the office and see if the overnight fermentation has generated anything good. As for now, I'm heading home. Good night, gentlemen."

"Doc, what say we head to the ranch and see what Miss Kelly has been up to without our much-needed adult supervision?"

"Again, boss, your decision making skills are second to none. The car is this way."

"I still think you'll make a great batman. Tally ho!"

IOI

IT WAS ONLY 1745 HRS when Doc drove the Blue Beast into my drive-way, which meant we were not running too late. Kelly already had the porch light on for us, just in case we ran later than expected. Climbing the porch steps, it again hit me I still needed to find my keys.

I mentioned that to Doc and he said my transient barracks locker had been cleaned out and my seabag was now in the truck. Keys were either there or in my clothing that was removed at the hospital and was now re-siding in evidence. Doc said he'd make it a high priority item for tomorrow.

As I started to push the doorbell, Kelly opened the door and waved us inside. Her normal smile had been replaced with the 'left hook,' so I knew something was up.

"Hello, Angel. You look great. Things go well for you today?" I asked.

"Oh, yea, things are marvelous," she purred softly. Wearing blue jeans, white sneakers, and a bright red blouse, she had the look of an all-Ameri-can beauty pageant winner heading to a picnic. She pulled me into a gen-tle hug and said, "Doc, you need to go into the living room. Right now."

"Yes, ma'am," he said, and went that way. And with him gone, I finally got my welcome home kiss.

In the background I heard Doc saying something. I pulled Kelly over toward the door and saw him holding Ann's hand; both of them were smiling and chatting away. Now that was a wonderful surprise. With my jacket and cover on the hall tree for the night, Kelly and I vanished upstairs so I could get out of the rest of this uniform and relax.

It turned out to be a great night. Seems Ann had called earlier to chat with Kelly, and after some discussion about Ann's lack of plans for the afternoon and evening, Kelly ran to the base to pick her up. Ann needed a lift since she'd decided a car was something she could do without for a while; saving money was a higher priority.

Together, they cooked a great dinner of tomato and onion salad, cornbread, and beef stew. While digging into that, the four of us enjoyed the company of good friends. After dinner we retired to the living room and continued talking about everything except work, until Doc said it was time to check my wound since I'd been more active that day than I should have been. Okay, back to reality.

Since he had an assistant with Ann being there, my dressing change went quickly. The professionals stated my wound was healing nicely, and reminded me not to try to use that arm. It was fun to watch the two of them working in sync, like they'd worked together for years, as they applied a new dressing and did the elastic bandage wrapping. They made a good team.

With that finished, I received another lecture on the importance of taking at least a few aspirin for my pain, this time from Ann. When that was over, Doc took Ann back to the base so she could get some sleep before her next shift. Kelly had two more sets of house keys made while out that day, and gave one set to Doc. She gave me the other set to use until I found my originals.

Kelly and I enjoyed some quiet time on our sofa while Doc was gone. As sleep started to take over, it hit me we hadn't addressed the sleeping arrangements. The third bedroom was still decked out as an office. And Doc deserved better than a sofa. When in doubt about any situation, it's best to ask a professional. So I did. I asked Kelly.

"Not a problem, sailor. You sleep in your bed. Doc sleeps in the guest room—I've moved my things out."

"And where will you be?" I asked.

"Sleeping right next to you. There's no other place I'll ever be from this moment forward for the rest of my life, so you had better get used to it. And even if you weren't wounded, I trust you to be the perfect gentleman. Let's turn in."

102

WE LEFT A NOTE FOR Doc on the door telling him where to sleep. I had no idea when he came in. As soon as my head touched the pillow I was out. The aspirins I took after dinner took the edge off the pain in my arm, and that helped me get a very solid night's sleep. Sunlight was coming in around the edges of the shades on the eastern side of the room, so I figured it was early morning.

Kelly was on her side, with her back against me and her legs pulled up. A soft snore was coming from under a mass of blonde hair. When she'd explained the sleeping arrangements the previous night, I was afraid I'd have problems keeping control after seeing her undressed for bed.

But again she was ahead of me, and now I saw her chosen sleepwear was a one-piece flannel pajama-thingy … I suppose there's an official term for it, but I have no idea what. It fell into the 'really cute' category and not 'ultra-sexy,' as I had imagined. Guess I can't win them all.

Moving slowly to prevent waking her, and to keep the pain in my arm down to a tolerable level, I left the bed and grabbed my jeans and sling. As quietly as possible, I finally got them both on and went down to the kitchen to start the coffee. And just like Kelly, Doc was ahead of me. He was sipping on a cup as I stumbled into the kitchen.

"Rough night, Mr. Colt?" he asked with a grin.

"Did you even go to bed last night, Doc?" I responded. "You seem too damn perky for this early."

"Yes, I got plenty of sleep, and if you had grabbed your watch, you would know it ain't early. It's just past 0900 hours. Officially, we could be considered late for work, but Ann and I discussed your health last night on the way back to the base, and we decided you needed to sleep in today."

"You and Ann made that decision, did you now?"

"Yep. That was part of my agreement with the CNO when I took this job. I can make medical decisions for you. Buddy, you are pushing it too much too soon. I've already notified Sam and the Captain, so they won't list you as UA. We'll try to get into the office just before lunch if your wound looks the same this morning; otherwise we head to the hospital. Or better yet, we hang out here resting and goofing off until after lunch. You need your rest, Marcus. It really is important."

"Ugh. Okay, thanks, 'Mom.' Glad to know my medical team is on top of things. And I do like your choice for backup on the team. Ann is so cool," I answered as I poured a much-needed cup of coffee.

"Yes, Ann is very cool. But the question of the day is did your sleep-in nurse take good care of you last night?" This time, Doc had a grin that would have made Alice's Cheshire Cat jealous.

"Sorry, nothing decadent to report. I passed out as soon as I got horizontal. You'll need to ask my nurse for a status report when she wakes up; she may have taken advantage of me while I was passed out."

"And some reports are classified above even the doctor's level," said Kelly as she entered the room and gave me a kiss. "Good morning, Marcus. Hi, Doc."

"Guess my quiet departure wasn't. Sorry, Hun, I tried. And I suspect you already know that I was allowed to sleep in this morning, right?"

Kelly chuckled and replied, "Of course. After watching you pass out right after lying down, I waited up until Doc got home and we talked about it all. You're still drained, energy-wise. So yes, I'm completely in the loop with Doc and Ann on the 'trying to keep Marcus healthy plan,' even when he fights us constantly."

Doc was smiling, as he enjoyed this banter between Kelly and me way too much. Then he added, "And Marcus, another plan to keep you healthy is to eliminate the challenges of naval dress codes. I explained to the Captain how difficult and uncomfortable it is wearing a uniform with your injury, so you're now authorized to wear civilian clothing similar to that of us lowly NIS agents. Loafers are acceptable. And you do not need to wear a tie. Naturally, the jacket is required to hide your hardware, but at least you're off the hook on the full uniform thing."

"Thanks, Doc. That is great news!"

"No big deal since the Captain got what he needed yesterday with you being fully decked out upon arrival."

"Guess I'm slow due to my pain. What did the skipper get?"

"Blame it on the lack of coffee 'cause I know you ain't slow. In one brief moment, he got the entire NISO and NISRA to be in total awe of LCDR Marcus James Colt. They saw that you actually are a Lieutenant Commander, that you have the Navy Cross and multiple clusters on your Purple Heart, you were wounded again just a couple of days ago doing NISRA undercover work, and you even wear a SEAL trident. That showed the staff that you really are the extremely impressive creature—the true badass warrior—even if you still don't think you are," Doc added with a sarcastic grin on his face.

He continued on while I shook my head in disbelief. "And in a few days, they'll all know about your shooting skills. Things like that can never be kept quiet. So you will have earned even more respect from the agents. I bet at least half, if not all of them, have only fired their weapons on the range. Never against a bad guy."

"Yea, I can see now that the uniform established my credentials faster and stronger than any speech or memo could. And that's why he scheduled the dog and pony show in the corridor to drive the point home. The Captain is a genius."

"Yes, he is the perfect combination of a sharp military mind and a crafty politician. He knows how to get the best from everyone. Enjoy the freedom of civvies because in a few weeks the splint and bandages will be gone, and you'll probably be back in uniform again unless you can sweet talk the skipper."

Kelly added with a touch of pride, "Uncle Humphrey learned a lot of that genius routine from my Dad. He is even better at it."

"Agreed. So on a different note, what do we do with our extra hour or so of freedom this morning? Any suggestions from my handlers?" I asked sheepishly.

Kelly walked across the kitchen to the cabinet mumbling, "More coffee—right now—is high on my list, then breakfast. You can flip pancakes with one hand, right?"

103

THURSDAY MORNING

08 APRIL 1971

MEANWHILE, AS WAS REPORTED TO me later, the agents were using a heck of a lot of notepaper that morning. SK2 Martinez was awake and talking pretty much non-stop at the hospital. He had a lot he needed to get off his chest, it seemed. He'd been offered a JAG attorney, but decided that talking straight to the agents was the best thing for him.

Sam and Darrell Tasker were doing the honors of committing his confession to paper, ready for his signature. Actually, Darrell was taking all the notes and Sam had assumed his position from the previous night: just an angry man ready to shoot. Intimidation. Interrogation. They sounded a lot alike and often generated the proper results when combined.

Joe Mabry was on the USS *Forrestal* with John Driscol and Douglas Knox. With Chief Lansing still adding information to his confession against his lawyer's advice, and with the two new arrivals—SK3 Dennis Moore and his hideout buddy BM3 Chet Peterson—now needing interrogation, these three agents were going to be too busy. Sam had called in SA Bill Collins from NISRA Oceana to help with this, and he was due to arrive on the carrier before noon.

Peterson had demanded an attorney, and the JAG folks agreed to send one over when they had a chance. Joe had asked that they not hurry. Naturally, Peterson had the standard answers; he didn't do anything, didn't know anything, etc. But he still wanted his attorney. Since he wasn't cooperating, Mabry decided to just start listing and reading aloud the charges against him. Perhaps that would give him a few things to consider before the lawyer arrived. Worth a shot, it seemed.

Moore, like Martinez, had been informed that there were several other SKs all talking and it would be in his best interest to do the same. But he, however, was not talking. Moore demanded an attorney, so they left him alone for most of the morning to consider his fate without cooperation. Of course, as they left they reminded him the other SKs were chatting up a storm and said they were off to start his list of charges.

Clyde London and Steve Crosser were busy searching the rental apartment where Moore lived. He wasn't the best housekeeper, so their search was going slow. For a low-end enlisted man, Moore had enough money for a lot of toys, clothes, and other junk that filled his small one-bedroom apartment. Only after a full hour of looking did the special agents find their first solid piece of evidence.

It was the old hollow book trick. They discovered a unique book on a shelf full of books, mostly spy novels, that a normal sailor would read. This book, *Great Expectations*, had been gutted and now contained at least $30,000 in fairly new $100 bills. Not something a normal third class petty Officer would have—neither that classic book nor that amount of money. After calling the info in to Joe, Clyde and Steve realized it was time for a lot more digging.

And their persistence paid off when they found a pocket-sized notebook hidden in a cut on the bottom of his mattress. While some entries were obviously names and numbers of women, there were several that grabbed their attention. Specifically, the names of two CIs who had been murdered: GM2 Roger Mobley, and SK3 Walter King. Dates and times were listed beside each, as well as a note about payment of $10,000 for each.

Now they wondered what the other $10,000 was from, or more specifically, who he'd killed to earn it.

104

KELLY AND DOC HAD WRAPPED my arm and its old dressing in kitchen plastic wrap, even rigging a sling with it, so I could take a careful shower. They figured at worst, the dressing would get damp, and Doc was going to remove it soon anyway.

"Kelly, you do know I can't wash my back properly. Care to get in the shower and help me?" I queried with a smile and bouncing eyebrow.

She smiled, "You betcha, sailor, we will shower together every day after September fourth. But not until then." And with that, she slapped my butt and left the bedroom.

"Well, Doc, it looks like we now know the wedding date. Keep your social calendar clear."

Kelly had escaped downstairs to check our lunch options while Doc was upstairs changing my dressing, post shower. After choosing New England clam chowder and grilled cheese sandwiches, Kelly used the time it took for the soup to get hot to sort my mail. David Bartow had sent a rather large package from D.C.

She quickly created three stacks: obvious bills, junk mail, and personal stuff. The last envelope going into the personal stack was intriguing. A

344

cream-colored square envelope, it had to be some sort of formal invitation from a couple in Florida.

The soup was ready and served into large mugs. The grilled cheese sandwiches were crispy and light brown. In addition to the standard American cheese, Kelly added a slice of Monterey Jack and thinly sliced red onion to each one. A couple of sliced dill pickles and a handful of chips finished off the sandwich plate. Kelly made the 'lunch is ready' call and smiled, she later admitted to me, at the warm feeling she got from cooking for her guy. *Life is good*, she thought.

Doc and I were appreciative of the hot lunch. As we ate, Doc told Kelly about the status of the healing arm wound. Things were going well, and better news was, I was not running any fever. Having been given the all-clear, I planned to get into the office for a few hours to go over the evidence one more time. There had to be something there.

As I carried my dishes to the sink, I noticed the three stacks of mail. Kelly saw my stare and offered an explanation. "That's the first sort from the package David sent from D.C. last week. There's an interesting square envelope on the personal stack on the left. Looks like an invitation."

I picked it up and saw the return address. I chuckled and replied, "Well, yea, this is interesting. Ugh."

"Honey, you haven't mentioned that family before. Who are they?"

"Doc, you know most all of this, so sorry for the rerun. Kelly, these are the parents of my ex-fiancée, Sandy."

Doc moaned and said, "Not good. Let's not tempt the fates. Toss it out. Or do you have a burn bag handy? Can't we set it aside and open it in a few weeks or months? Even saying that name is bad juju, Buddy."

"Well, open it, Marcus. My interest is totally piqued right now," Kelly laughed as she punched Doc in the arm.

"Here, Doc, you know pretty much all about her anyway, except the ending, so you read the damn thing," I said as I tossed the envelope to him.

Shaking his head in disgust, Doc extracted the inner envelope and started reading. "Mr. and Mrs. Jacob Cane request the pleasure of your company at the wedding of their daughter Sandy Marie Cane to Lucas John Jamison, son of Mildred Jamison, on Saturday, May Eighth, Nineteen Hundred and Seventy-One at Half Past Three o'clock in the afternoon at the Sacred Heart Catholic Church, etc. etc. Oh, by the way, reception to follow. Now can we toss this piece of crap? Nothing else in the envelope like an apology or two."

Doc was still shaking his head when he added, "And I guess you'll want to show up in dress whites with all your medals. That ought to mess with her mind, even as small as it is."

"Be nice, Doc," I begged. I turned to face Kelly and quietly said, "I haven't told you all the stuff that happened with her. Doc knows much of it, but even he doesn't know the ending. So rather than have you start putting your great imagination to work, here are the facts of it all."

And as quickly as possible, I filled them both in on the entire two-plus years of my life that had Sandy in it. I laid my history on the table to the lady I trusted completely. As I spoke, Kelly's expression kept bouncing between shock and anger.

Doc spoke first. "Marcus, I'm damn glad you were the one to end it, because she had been lying to you for a very long time. And it looks like the invitation proves it. Y'all broke up on February twenty-eighth and the postmark shows her parents mailed the invitation on March twenty-second. On top of that, I hear it takes a couple of weeks to get these fancy things printed. So she had to meet a guy, fall in love, make all the wedding plans, and reserve the church within a week? Come on."

I couldn't help but chuckle at Doc's logic, "Doc, I met Kelly on March twelfth, and ten days later we were engaged. Her dad thought she would convince me to elope the weekend before I gave her the ring. Some things happen fast. Maybe it did for Sandy as well." Doc just snorted hearing that.

Kelly just sat there without saying anything. "Okay, Kelly, your comments?" I asked.

She turned her mouth up to the right, which was not the good direction, and just sat there. Finally, she leaned back, smiled and said, "Well, dearest, I'm torn between extreme anger and total happiness. Angry that anyone would treat you the way she did. There's no excuse for torturing the person you supposedly love like that, and especially a member of our military, off doing their duty."

"Right on, Kelly," interjected Doc. "See, Sandy is evil."

She shifted her smile to the left side and continued, "And I am thrilled beyond belief with her actions. Because that probable-but-not-proven deceit, and her absolutely despicable treatment of you, provided you the opportunity to see the real person she is. That knowledge gave you the determination to dump her on her sorry ass. And said dumping on her sorry ass put you in the right frame of mind to accept me into your life. So, I'm thrilled. Okay now, babe, the only remaining question is will our RSVP for this shindig include Doc?"

The laughter from the three of us lasted for a long time. Reality was that none of us were heading to Florida to that wedding, especially since both Doc and I were always armed and Doc still carried a big grudge. Me, not so much a grudge as a massive regret that I'd put so much into a relationship filled with dishonesty. That really hurt. It was obvious now that one of her dance partners had been much closer to her than I was. So much for the 'just a dance' excuse, I thought.

Doc wanted to send a broken toaster as a wedding gift, but I think we talked him out of it. He also wanted to send a sympathy card to "poor old Lucas," and that got the laughter going again. Our laughter was the best medicine any of us had enjoyed in many days, but that too was cut short by the phone.

Kelly answered, frowned, and passed it to me. "What's up, Sam?" Sam laid out his request in concise terms, and it was time for Doc and me to get back to work. After a quick kiss from Kelly—for me, not Doc—we were out the door heading toward the base.

105

ACTIVITY AT THE LOGISTICS CENTER was calm that afternoon, upon our arrival. We took the stairs and paused on the second floor. With five storekeepers now out of work, there were a lot of empty desks on the second floor and a lot less noise. Doc and I climbed to the third floor and entered the main office area.

Rhonda was over by the desk of YN2 Tom Brackin, the one who'd explained the rotating coffee duty on my first day undercover. They seemed to be discussing a report as we walked in. Rhonda reacted first, and after doing a double take said, "Mark? What are you doing here? You should still be in the hospital."

While the plan had been to brief the CO upon arrival, Brackin was acting like he was ready to bolt. Plans changed quickly and I approached his desk. I knew Doc was behind me a couple of feet, to my left.

"Thomas Brackin, please stand and place your hands behind your head. I am Lieutenant Commander Colt, Naval Investigative Service, and you need to come with us." Doc held out his credentials so Brackin could see them.

Rhonda was just looking between us, baffled. "Commander who? What's going on?" she asked. She was trying to understand it all when

Brackin jumped up and grabbed her around the throat with his left arm. He pulled her in front of him, and suddenly his right hand held a small pistol, now pointed toward Rhonda's head.

By the time he had his arm around Rhonda, both Doc and I had our weapons drawn and pointed at Brackin. "Drop the weapon and let Petty Officer Evans go right now," I said firmly. Rhonda looked panicked and confused.

"No way!" he yelled. "Back off and let me get out of here!"

I smiled and lowered my voice. "Not going to happen, Tom. Let her go now before things get worse for you. And they will get much worse for you, I promise." I was hoping Rhonda was not too shocked to remember something important. "Rhonda, you did tell me that this jerk thinks he's a weatherman, right?"

After a tense and silent couple of seconds, her face perked up and she winked. "For sure!" she yelled as she drove the heel of her right shoe into Brackin's instep. Her movement threw her body over to her left, away from the front of Brackin's body.

The intense pain in his foot caused Brackin to release his grip on Rhonda and lose directional control of his weapon. It was now pointed toward the overhead. With the right side of his body fully exposed, Doc and I took the opportunity to each discharge a round into his right shoulder. As promised, things quickly got much worse for Brackin.

I started to get all the screaming and yelling under control while Doc went to give Brackin first aid. The CO came running out of his office, and I ordered him to call for an ambulance. When I finally got everyone calmed down, I herded them into Ensign Appleton's old office. There I quickly introduced us, explained why they'd known me as a yeoman with a different name the previous week, and told them we were here to arrest Brackin on multiple charges.

Rhonda just kept looking at me with glazed-over eyes and shaking her head in disbelief. I brought her back to reality when I said, "Still want to be part of my harem? It might be too exciting for ya." That got her laughing enough for me to know she wasn't too deeply in shock and should eventually be fine. Doc needed to check on her soon. I told her we'd talk later.

Calling the hospital, I connected with Joe. I asked that he and at least one other SEAL meet the ambulance when it got to the hospital, and not to let Brackin out of his sight. Sam had been with Joe when my call came in, so he immediately came over to help us. YNSC Don Pierce started setting up two areas for interviewing the witnesses of the confrontation. As always, paperwork must be done.

Doc helped get Brackin into the ambulance and updated the medics on what he had done so far. Without proper supplies, all Doc could do was get the bleeding under control. Brackin was still alive as the ambulance pulled away. And we needed him alive.

Now Doc needed to get cleaned up, as his hands and face were covered with blood. Judging by his grumbling, his blood-soaked dress shirt and tie were total losses. When he came out of the head, his hands were much cleaner and he'd dumped the bloody shirt. I told him the tee-shirt and sports coat combo look was a good one on him and might set a fashion trend. We finally shared a smile in the midst of a FUBAR situation.

I took the time to brief the CO, XO, and Chief on who I really was, and why we were here to arrest Brackin. My gut, and lots of time studying his records, was telling me the Chief was clean, so nothing was lost giving him more details. I explained that SK3 Martinez had told us that Brackin was involved with supply theft and was responsible for the murder of PN3 Elliott Abbott. And more investigations were coming their way.

On the way out, I pulled Rhonda aside. She was looking a little pale. "You okay?" I asked. "Do you need to talk to someone?" She probably hadn't seen the blood splattered on her uniform or the side of her face.

"No, sir, I'll be fine. Just quite a shocking day. And seeing you shoot Tom is just hard to believe. You work for NIS? As an officer?" she stammered.

"Yea, I do and have for years. Long story. You need time to decompress." I walked her to her desk and told her to sit. I sat down in the chair next to it, picked up the phone, and called home. It only took a few minutes to brief Kelly and tell her what I needed from her. She was probably out the door by the time I hung up the phone.

"Rhonda, as you heard, I gave Kelly a heads-up about what happened here, and told her you're invited for dinner. I will not accept 'no' as your answer. Consider it an order, petty officer. You should not be alone while you settle down from all this. Kelly is on the way to pick you up from your barracks, which is where Doc and I are taking you right now. I've told the CO you need the rest of the day off, and tomorrow too. He understands. Let's move."

"Yes, Mark, yes, sir."

Doc overheard our conversation and quickly called Ann at the hospital. She was getting off in fifteen minutes and would hurry to the barracks to help with Rhonda.

Overall, it had been a bad couple of weeks for the Logistics Center. I doubted things would get any better in the near future.

As we waited for Rhonda to catch up with us on our way out the door, Doc pulled me aside. With a melancholy grin he said, "See, I told you that invitation was a bad omen. But ya just had to open it, didn't ya."

All I could do was offer a sad grin and shrug.

106

DOC AND I DELIVERED RHONDA to the barracks right after Kelly arrived; we found her waiting by the main door. She was so cool dealing with all the excitement, adventures, and challenges that came with my job.

"You're the best, Kelly."

"I know, babe. Just keep remembering that!" After a quick kiss for me, she took control of Rhonda and steered her to her room for a cleanup and a change of clothes.

Ann was coming down the sidewalk at that time. She told us Brackin was in surgery when she left. No updates on his condition. We filled her in and told her to ride to the house with Kelly and Rhonda. She nodded and hurried after Rhonda. And suddenly we'd have a group for dinner in a couple of hours; never a dull moment in the Tidewater area.

Doc and I dropped off Brackin's pistol at the lab so they could do the ballistics check against the slug used to kill Abbott. While the confession from Jesus Martinez was strong evidence against Brackin, solid physical evidence—like matching slugs—was the best way to get a conviction. His resisting arrest and threatening to shoot a petty officer would also stack up against him nicely. And there were plenty of witnesses for that stupid move.

Finally getting back at the NISRA offices a few hours later than expected, we now faced a debriefing from both John Driscol and the Captain. We were individually debriefed, and then together. Our stories matched, and they both seemed satisfied with our reports. I didn't let on, but shooting another viper was bothering me. I kept going back over the events, trying to see if there had been another way to resolve the situation. No luck.

Sam finally got there and said he was sorry he'd asked us to pick up Brackin. We didn't need all that stress, he said, and with one arm in a sling, it was a miracle I wasn't shot. But Doc replied he was glad it was us. If any other agent had been there, he said, they wouldn't have known that 'foot stomping' trick that got Rhonda out of the firing line, so things could have been much worse.

The general consensus listed it as a justifiable shooting. All the witnesses had agreed we tried to talk Brackin down, and only shot as a last resort. No innocents were injured and we stopped the bad guy.

Doc pulled rank as my medic and told everyone it was time to get me home for another dressing change, and more rest. They all agreed. The skipper suggested I sleep in later in the morning; the hospital was running out of room for my targets. At least he winked and smiled when he said it. But it still hurt.

Before running out the door, I checked with Kelly to see if we needed to pick up anything for dinner. A couple of bottles of wine were a high priority, and a few other things would be nice, so we had our orders and left.

107

DOC SAID HE HAD A plan to help Rhonda, and to follow his lead. I told him I was too tired to argue and planned to just sit there and nod in agreement to whatever he said. "Excellent plan," he replied.

Kelly met us at the door before I could try my new key. She must have had x-ray vision and been able to see through walls. Or she correctly estimated the time we needed in the Giant to pick up her supplies. She grabbed some of the groceries from Doc, and motioned us back onto the porch.

"Rhonda is doing okay now, I think. She lost it when she saw the blood on her face and uniform, but with Ann's help, we got her calmed back down. I'm not sure what she needs right now, but I suspect a bit more wine and small talk with good friends might help," Kelly offered.

I just shrugged. Between Kelly, Ann and Doc we had three excellent resources and they'd know what professional to call when and if needed. "Doc has a plan, so just run with it."

Doc nodded and said, "Let's get inside. The wine needs chilling."

Ann smiled when we came in and gave Doc a playful slug to his arm. Rhonda got up and came into the kitchen with her. Rhonda just stood there for a minute while we unloaded, then turned to me and said, "Lieutenant Commander, I appreciate what you did for me today. I still can't believe it all. I was so scared. But thank you again, sir."

Doc winked at me and nodded. He placed his hands on her shoulders and smiled while looking her directly in the eyes. In a light, cheerful voice, he said, "Rhonda, pay close attention. Inside this house, the rules are a bit different from the rest of the world. You can drop the 'sirs' and any reference to rank. Unless you're being sarcastic or making a joke, then it's okay. But the joke had better be a good one."

Doc continued, "Oh, and one other caveat. If Kelly's uncle or her dad is here, they always get called by their rank. But aside from those two, we're all just friends on a first name basis inside this house. Got it?"

She nodded and then started to tear up. Doc pulled her into his arms. Nothing at all sexual about the hug, just needed emotional support between warriors. Rhonda had seen the enemy, been on the wrong end of a weapon, and performed well. She was a warrior. Kelly and Ann quickly joined the hug and then I did, too.

After a moment, we pulled back. Rhonda looked around and smiled, then said, "I got it and will try to follow the house rules. Thanks, Doc. You, too, Kelly and um, Marcus, right? I'll probably call you Mark too many times before I get it right. But who is Kelly's uncle and dad?"

With that, I broke into a laugh. "Well, her uncle is Captain Miller, the head of the local Naval Investigative Service Office, who you'll meet if you keep hanging around this strange crowd. Besides him, Kelly gets to call the Chief of Naval Operations, Admiral Gallagher, Papa. Her dad isn't here too often since he keeps busy in D.C. Let's grab a seat in the living room. I'm tired of standing."

The girls were very impressed with that information; after all, to most personnel the CNO is as reachable as the Greek gods on Mt. Olympus were to the average Greek. And those facts opened the floodgates of questions, as Ann and Rhonda were both interested in all that was going on. Ann already knew some things, but Rhonda had been completely in the dark and was still getting over the surprise of finding out I wasn't a yeoman.

Doc answered many of their questions, but was hesitant to get too deep. I came to his rescue with a thought. "How would it be to recruit both Ann and Rhonda as CIs?" I wondered out loud, "Face it, Doc. We need another set of eyes and ears in the Logistics Center since we're not sure we have all the vipers."

Rhonda perked up on that word, "Who or what are vipers? I hate snakes. And what is a CI?"

Doc chuckled, "Viper is the nickname we hung on the bad guys like CPO Lansing and your good buddy, Brackin. Saying 'worthless evil bastards from hell' got old really quick. CI stands for confidential informant."

I sighed, "And if I may continue, children, we know Rhonda can handle herself under pressure. And with Ann already involved to a degree, and her being in the ER, she can be on the lookout for any strange ODs or other things. There is a possible deal breaker: are these two ladies willing to do it."

"How about following this for a plan, boss? Put all that work stuff on the back burner for tonight; I'm just too damn tired to think about it. In addition, we have some important info to share with our guests about what happened today and why, and the best news is that we have wine to drink. Why don't you head into the kitchen with Kelly, grab a kiss or two while out from under our watchful eyes, pour us some of that wine, and work on dinner together. We'll call if we need ya."

I couldn't help but smile. Doc had stopped me from getting too heavy into work junk and gently reminded me that we were here that night to help Rhonda. I never went wrong when following Doc's lead.

108

ANN AND DOC DID A great job getting Rhonda to talk through the events of the day. Since he'd been on both sides of such events—as a victim in the past, and as one of the shooters at that day's mess—he was able to provide Rhonda with an explanation of the emotions that she was now experiencing, from completely different views. Ann was learning about a new side of Doc, as a counselor as well as a medic. She looked impressed.

Dinner was easy even with only one working arm. I guided sous-chef Kelly through preparing paprika chicken, a wonderful Austrian dish, which we served with mushroom risotto and roasted asparagus. She did all the hard work, and I spent most of my time stirring the risotto and listening to Doc counsel Rhonda more. She was doing well, considering the day she had. Kelly went in there several times to inject a thought or two, since her master's degree was based on helping overcome stress like this.

By the time dinner was over, everyone was full and basically talked out. We'd all mellowed nicely. Good food always helps make life better. So we retired to the living room and just talked about family, dreams of the future, and other non-stressful stuff.

Rhonda said she was feeling okay and greatly appreciated the opportunity to talk about the day with people who understood. Then Doc had another suggestion, and Ann agreed it was a good one. The ladies would spend the night with us. *Welcome to Hotel Tidewater*, I thought. I should have rented a bigger house.

Our favorite sofa folded out to make a queen-sized bed. We had several extra new toothbrushes in the cabinet, Kelly had a couple of large sweatshirts that could double as their sleepwear, and neither one had duty in the morning. So there was no need to head back to the barracks that night.

Unknown to Rhonda, right after dinner Doc and Ann had a couple of moments alone. Ann was concerned that Rhonda might have a nightmare about the shooting, and if so, it would be best to have Doc nearby. Not something he could do at the female barracks. They cooked up the sleep-over plan and he told her he'd leave his bedroom door open listening for the call to help. He would be there quickly if needed.

When the yawns outnumbered the words spoken, Kelly and I said our "goodnights" and headed off to bed. Doc said he'd follow us up shortly, but first wanted to talk a bit more with Rhonda about how to cope if emotions started to build up tomorrow. Emotional overload is nasty.

I was totally drained from my own emotional overload earlier in the day, but had put on a good show for our guests. We'd been so concerned about Rhonda that Doc and I had pushed our own issues to the backs of our minds. Over time, we had learned how to handle most of it. Most people don't understand, but it doesn't matter how many people you shoot: each one is a human that you're either killing or wounding. And every one you shoot creates a memory that stays with you forever.

Each shooting memory is nearly the same, just with different faces and locations. In slow motion, you see the moment you pull the weapon up, the exact moment of pulling the trigger, the loud noise of the weapon firing, the recoil flowing up your arm, the surprised look on the face of the bad guy, the smell of the smoke from the weapon, and the wetness and smell of the bad guy's body fluids following a bullet ripping through him.

All of that comes back to you much too vividly and all too frequently. And no matter how bad a person they are, no matter how much they deserved it, each shooting takes away a piece of your soul. And in my case, I had another three incidents that week. At least with the first two, I was under sedation for a couple days afterwards. That helped me not to think about it all.

Now that I had my own personal live-in head shrinker, I took some time to talk with Kelly about the shooting as we snuggled together. After a while, I drifted off to sleep. Our chat had helped. I had earlier decided to let Doc take full control of my schedule for tomorrow, so the alarm clock wasn't set.

109

EVEN WITHOUT THE ALARM, MY body decided it was time for coffee. Ann was sitting at the table nursing a cup when I walked into the kitchen. She smiled and held a finger to her lips, indicating quiet. I figured Doc and Rhonda were still sleeping, as Kelly was softly snoring when I strolled out of our bedroom.

After getting my cup filled, I joined Ann at the table. She told me about Rhonda's nightmare and how easily Doc had gotten her settled down in a short period of time. She was impressed with Doc's skills, and to me it looked like he had a groupie. Excellent news, I thought—he deserves someone like Ann in his life; they complement each other.

A quick glance into the living room showed a lump under the sofa covers and Doc about to fall out of a chair, sound asleep. Ann wasn't sure of the time they finished talking as she'd gone back to sleep while those two were still going.

"Doc called one of your guys at the hospital after initially dealing with Rhonda. The report is Brackin is out of surgery and stable. He may never have the use of his right arm due to the damage from two bullets. He should be awake any time now," Ann reported quietly.

"Well, it was nice to have a night off without all this mess. Guess it's time to get back to work."

"So, Marcus, what's on your schedule for the day? Any more bad guys to shoot?" she asked with a soft chuckle.

"Dear Lord, I hope not. While it has to be done at times, it isn't pleasant," I responded sorrowfully. Then I perked up, since Ann didn't need to carry any part of my burden. "As for the day, that's up to Doc. He, with your help I hope, will check on my healing and change the dressing, and then he'll make a decision on what I can do."

Ann grimaced as she shook her head and asked, "But you're an officer, and Doc is enlisted. How does that work with him giving the orders?"

I had to chuckle at that one. "Doc has been assigned directly, and personally, by the CNO to have control over me—as my shadow and personal medic. If he says 'stand down,' then I don't do anything and he has the CNO to back him up. But fortunately, he understands the importance of the operation, and knows we have bad guys to catch."

I took a sip of coffee to help clean the brain and continued, "In addition, he and I are much closer than the normal officer–enlisted relationship. We think of each other as true brothers. We've been through things together that form a bond much closer than blood." I got lost in my memories for a second and quietly added, "I'd forgotten how much I need Doc around until this operation started, and that was even before I was wounded."

"Why is that? Don't you normally work together?"

"Oh, no. I work out of an office in D.C. as an internal affairs investigator for NIS, and he is a medic on a SEAL team operating from here. Normally, our paths wouldn't cross, but we met and worked together much of last year in Nam in an unusual situation. We have been apart for about seven months now while he healed from injuries he suffered on a mission I ran in Vietnam. Sadly, his injuries were the result of my decisions. Guess our relationship is hard to grasp unless you've been there."

Ann nodded and placed her hand over mine. "I can see that relationship is a strong one. Doc has talked about it some, but not very much. He's extremely protective of his feelings and makes it really hard to get inside his shell. He tries not to let on, but I believe he needs you more than you need him. It's funny now that I think about it, no disrespect intended, but neither one of you fit the image of what most of us conjure up when the word SEAL is used."

"Doc is a true warrior who, unlike me, actually survived SEAL training. Yea, he is skinny, but tough, and also one hell of a mean fighter." I gave a small grin and continued, "Trust me, I don't think of myself as one either. The two teams who helped me last year on a mission pushed their admiral to make me one of them. It's a great honor that I still don't believe I deserve."

"Well, that is just too damn much bullshit to hear first thing in the morning. And what the hell are you doing up this early, anyway? You need your damn rest," Doc said rather unpleasantly from the kitchen doorway, where he was leaning against the casing. He looked rough from lack of sleep. It looked to me that the door casing was holding him up.

"Good morning, sunshine. It is oh-so-pleasant to hear such vulgarity from you so early in the day," I replied rather sarcastically.

"Okay then, try horse hockey, Marcus, if it makes you feel more civilized. But you know you are just as much one of us as any other member of the team, official training or not. And we probably ought to hurt ya if you continue to disagree. Got it? And quit holding hands with my girl."

Ann pulled her hand back from mine as her jaw dropped, "Your girl? Do I have any input on that decision?"

Now that got a good laugh from both Doc and me. "Probably not," I said as I stood and walked to the coffeepot, poured and prepared a cup for Kelly, and quickly left the kitchen. "Play nice, you two. See ya later." I winked at Doc as I departed.

110

THE DRESSING CHANGE WENT FAST, and my personal medical team pronounced the healing to be going better than expected. I told them it was due to clean living, and Ann lost control of her giggling on that one. Doc just snorted; at least he wasn't so bitchy after coffee. Feeling was getting better in my fingertips, but the area around the wound was still numb. Doc said I was expecting too much too soon.

Rhonda finally came alive from her slumber and seemed, to me at least, almost back to normal. Doc had convinced her that she should talk with one of the professional crisis counselors at the hospital. He'd be calling in later to set things up.

For now, she and Ann would spend the day goofing off with Kelly. The three ladies were deep in conversation at the table. When asked, Kelly said they hadn't made any definite plans beyond having a third cup of coffee, and of course, pancakes.

Now that Doc had pronounced me fit for a partial day of work, hopefully a bit more, we headed into the NISRA a little before 0900 hrs. As I was getting my goodbye kiss from Kelly, I noticed that Ann quickly kissed Doc on the cheek. *Progress, it seems.* Maybe if this investigator gig doesn't work out, I should consider matchmaking. Always keep the options open, I thought.

Hated to pull the two new potential lovebirds apart, but I needed to look at all that evidence again, hopefully to find the links we needed. In addition, it would be interesting to hear what Brackin had said or what the agents had found in his place. I had to get to the office, and Doc was critical for moving me around, so like Ruth in the Bible, wherever I went, Doc went. Or to be more precise, since he was the one doing the driving, I went with him.

Sam Maker was holding court with several of the agents—Darrell Tasker, Joe Mabry, Clyde London, Bill Collins, and Steve Crosser—as we tried to quietly enter the agents' area. Too bad the door keypad made so much noise that wiped out the quiet. When we entered, the agents got to their feet and started applauding.

Sam faked a bow. After restoring quiet, he smiled at us and said, "Gentlemen, after a complete analysis of the events surrounding yesterday's arrest of YN2 Brackin, it has been determined that you both performed better than the above-average agent in a stressful, radically changing, and potentially disastrous event. We were trying to determine if sticking a gold star to your foreheads was an adequate reward. Or perhaps I should just take you to lunch at my favorite seafood place." And with that, we all broke up in laughter.

Darrell chimed in, "And the surgical team at the hospital sends their thanks for so many interesting cases."

"Ouch," I muttered to myself. "Well, we try to please all departments," I said louder through a grimace, probably a little too harshly. Doc just laid his arm around my neck and pushed my head into a nod. He knew that while their humor was all in fun, he and I viewed things differently than the rest of the world. Something the agents would probably never understand. Time to move on.

"Where are John Driscol and Douglas Knox?" I asked, in a voice that still sounded too harsh.

Sam was the first to answer. "They're at the hospital. Checking to see if Martinez has anything else to say while they wait for Brackin to wake up. When I talked with them at 0800, he was still out. Why?"

Doc responded before I could be more snarky with the guys. "Just trying to change the direction of the conversation. Shooting people is never as much fun as some people think. And someone is staying too far away from his pain meds, so he's even less fun to be around. So unless there's anything else, Gimpy the Grouch and I will hide in the quiet of the file room for a while."

"No offense was intended, Marcus, Doc. We're just thrilled you stopped the guy before he shot that poor woman or hurt either of you. You handled yourselves like the professionals you are," offered Joe.

"Thanks, guys," I said as I made my way into the file room to get started. "It's been a rough week."

III

WE LATER AGREED WITH SAM that the gold star on the forehead was a bit over the top, so we decided to let him buy us lunch. Doc handled the driving of the Blue Beast and insisted that Sam and I sit in the back like royalty.

I wanted to stop at the hospital to see how things were going with Brackin, but Sam refused for two reasons: he didn't want to be looking over the shoulders of his agents too much, and he felt I needed the rest. Of course, Doc concurred. With that decision made, we headed to the restaurant.

Even with us coming in later than normal, it had been a long "short" morning. Doc and I had been in the file room for nearly three hours straight. Well, at least I had. Doc had done the honors of making the multiple coffee runs I required, since a second working hand is needed to open the keypadded door while the other holds coffee. And he did the chore of updating the skipper on how things went the previous night. The Captain got a chuckle out of the Hotel Tidewater name.

But the primary reason I stayed put in the file room was I didn't want to interrupt my train of thought. Going with Doc, and probably running into others who wanted to chat or ask how I was doing, would destroy it. I needed to focus. But after looking back over the files and cards another few times, it seemed there was something right on the edge we weren't seeing. Lunch was needed.

Following Sam's directions, Doc drove us to the same seafood restaurant where I first opened up to Sam. While that was only a couple of weeks ago, it sure seemed like months. Time gets distorted when stress, undercover work, and hospital stays are mixed.

Doc and Sam finished their meal before this one-armed slow eater, so they were chatting about the case while I cleaned my platter of fried shrimp and oysters. Some things, like fresh Chesapeake Bay Oysters, need to be savored slowly. Doc asked Sam if there had been any new information from the medical examiner after he received the lab work on Baker and Harker.

"No, Doc. Nothing new showed up. No strange drugs or other medical issues were found. Why do you ask?"

"Sam, sometimes small points in the doctor's finding can lead to something bigger. But not this time, I guess," Doc answered.

My last delicious oyster was gone, and I drained the last of my beer. Per doctor's orders—well, at least Doc's orders, which as far as I was concerned was about the same—I'd considered a beer at lunch beneficial. It might not have helped my healing process, but it helped take the edge off the pain from the wound and reduced my negative attitude created by the shootings. As I sat there listening to them discuss autopsy and lab analysis results, it hit me.

"Doc, Sam, we need to get back to the office right now," I said as I stood and reached for my wallet.

"Now that you're finally finished, of course, your majesty, we shall depart posthaste," quipped Doc. "But pray tell me, sire, what this hellish rush is all about?"

"Sorry, gents, I got hit with a mental explosion," I stammered in excitement. "Doc, you need to closely read all the autopsy reports for the victims over the last nine months. My gut is screaming that there's something there we haven't seen. Let me rephrase that. It's my fault. There is something there. I know it. And I haven't seen it since I didn't even look at the damn reports! I took the agents' comments about the autopsies as the total information. And with my lack of medical knowledge, I probably wouldn't have seen it anyway. But I bet it's there."

"You're rambling, Marcus. But I think I follow you, which scares me a little," said Doc.

Sam nodded at me and ordered, "Put your wallet away, Marcus. Remember lunch is on me. Let's roll."

112

ON THE DRIVE BACK TO the NISRA, Sam had one of his standard brilliant ideas. Before we started reading more files, we needed to have a meeting with the agents to recap and make sure everyone was up to speed. So much had happened over the last six days, there was a good chance for overlooking something. And that something was usually the important something.

Only three of the agents were still in the office: Darrell Tasker, Clyde London, and Steve Crosser. Joe Mabry and Bill Collins were back at the brig on the USS *Forrestal*, waiting for Moore to break his silence. John Driscol and Douglas Knox were still at the hospital. Brackin was awake, but extremely groggy and not talking. More waiting was needed.

Sam called the short meeting to order and started, "We all know it's been one hell of a week. Three of our guys were wounded. Two vipers are dead, two are in the hospital recovering from wounds, and four are in the brig on the USS *Forrestal*. Add to that, Detective—I really should say ex-detective—Royal is in the NPD jail."

Darrell jumped in with more information. "And we have signed confessions from both Harker and Lansing. With Lansing still being alive, his confession has more impact and it covers many more crimes. So that's a good thing."

"And where are we on the NISRA Miami and FBI checks on our buddy DN?" I asked.

Sam shrugged and said, "My buddy at the FBI didn't have any clues about him. He said if we had a name that might help, but without it not much to go on. Darrell, what about NISRA Miami?"

Shaking his head, Darrell added, "Naturally, when you really need a friend, that friend has been on vacation for over a week; his wife just had another baby. Anyway, my buddy Martin just got back to work yesterday and returned my many calls. The airline has been a pain and won't release the passenger list of that flight to him without a warrant. And we don't have enough info to get one. So no names to start with there."

"Well, that stinks," said Clyde.

"But it's not all bad," Darrell added with a smile. "As for the description, Martin was a bit better than our friends at the FBI. He said it might be an ex-Navy flyer who was court-marshalled a few years ago for selling drugs. Martin was working the fringes of the case, with NISRA Charleston agents taking the lead. The suspect has houses in both Norfolk and Miami and is into various things that border on illegal, but he seems to always stay clean. Paul Raffe is his name. Our good friends in South Carolina are sending us a copy of his files. That should be here tonight or tomorrow."

Sam beamed with that news. "Well, that's better than what we had."

"Sam, call Joe and have him mention that name to the three guys we have locked up over there, and ..." I started.

"Then Darrell and I will head to NPD and confront Royal with that name ..." Sam interjected.

"While Doc and I head to the hospital to run the name past Martinez and Brackin. They won't know if we have Raffe in custody, and that just might push them over the edge to spill their guts," I concluded.

Sam shook his head at that last part. "John and Doug are at the hospital now. They can handle that while you and Doc do your magic we discussed at lunch. None of us can do what you do, so no need to waste your valuable time at the hospital."

"Okay, agreed. My excitement got the best of me. But while Doc is going over the autopsy records, rather than waiting for the delivery, I'll call NISRA Charleston and get some specifics from Raffe's record. There might be something there."

With that conclusion, Sam and Darrell left for NPD, Clyde and Steve headed out to investigate a just-reported sex crime, Doc went to the file room, and I got on the phone. And that was when I had to fight another level of frustration, as the junior agent left in the Charleston office refused to give me any information without the authority of his SSA, who was out of the office on a case. He would leave him a message with both my office and home phone numbers. Ugh.

Doc had a good start on the M.E.'s reports by the time I finished with my phone call and got the coffee mug filled. Starting with the most current and working back in time, he was creating a stack of index cards with the important features.

I hovered over the original index cards, looking at them as Doc mumbled things that grabbed his attention in the reports. Sure, it was a slow process, but we needed to find something. And this might give us what we need.

After about an hour—a very frustrating hour, I had to admit—a few pieces of the puzzle finally came together. Doc found that the analysis of the drugs that killed SK3 Peter Rodriquez, AD3 David Nelson, SN Lee Chris, and SN Paul Wayne were all from the same batch of cocaine. And the tests showed the cocaine matched some that had originated in Venezuela.

We knew from the confessions of Lansing and Martinez that Rodriquez, also a member of the viper gang run by Lansing, was murdered on orders from the big boss—who might be DN, the guy we now thought was Raffe. And that Rodriquez was the one who killed the other three. So we now knew who done it, and we knew how he done it, but we still didn't know why he done it.

113

OUR ENERGY LEVELS HAD DEPLETED to zilch by the time Doc got through the autopsies from the last nine months. I knew the pain meds were still trying to get out of my system, but I complained anyway. Doc again told me I'd feel better tomorrow. With this depth of wound, he kept saying, most people would still be hospitalized. Ugh.

I knew I shouldn't be short with Doc. Poor guy was probably working on pure adrenaline by then. He didn't get much sleep the previous night due to taking care of Rhonda. I knew that being my shadow as well as my medic, and an investigator on top of all that, was rough. Adding Rhonda to care for just made it more so. With our combined lack of energy, we made a great pair of near-worthless grouchy investigators.

Even with lots of coffee, we were yawning more and both of us were having trouble focusing. The drug link was the only one we'd seen thus far, but considering how tired we both were, it was understandable we probably overlooked some things. I wanted to wait for Sam to return and hear how things went with Royal; however, it was past time for us to get some rest. Hopefully, we'd be able to return with fresh eyes in the morning. We left a note for Sam.

A quick call to Kelly before leaving the office resulted in our stopping at the Giant. Hotel Tidewater was still going strong; Rhonda was staying until she went back to work on Monday, and Ann would be there likewise until she left for duty late Sunday night. Kelly had taken our guests back to their barracks for some fresh clothing and other essentials. The ladies had chosen pizza and beer as the top selections for the dinner menu. Of course, since we were already out, it just made sense that we were assigned the pickup task.

While waiting for the pizzas to bake, I had the guy at the deli counter make five of my pseudo Cuban sandwiches. Figured if the pizza wasn't good, we had backup, or at least a great midnight snack. Of course, they would work as lunch for tomorrow, with a quick reheat.

We were nearly to the house when a thought flashed through my mind. The bag of Cuban sandwiches sitting on the seat beside me had triggered it. Cuba! Something was pulling at me about Cuba. Well, drugs could move relatively easily from Venezuela to Cuba, then to the USA by Navy aircraft, if someone on the crew was corrupt. Add to that the fact Raffe was an ex-naval aviator. Ding, ding, ding. Bells were going off inside my head.

"Doc, start thinking back to the bird pin in Appleton's file. Do you recall where Greg said LT Thomas's squadron flew? What areas of operation they covered?" We came to a stop in my driveway.

"Sorry, Marcus. I'm not sure I even heard him talk about that. Why?"

"That's right. He and I talked about it before my attack; you were probably on a security team at that time. It had to be last Saturday, which right now seems like a month ago, not just six days. No problem, I'll give him a call shortly," I responded as I climbed out of the car into the waiting arms of Kelly.

"Welcome home, sailor." After an extremely erotic kiss, she asked, while looking in the backseat, "Where's the food?"

"Well here I thought you rushing up to the car meant you missed me. But alas, I come in second to chow," I said through a fake frown.

"If you weren't wounded, I would slug you for that, Marcus. You know you're always first in my life, but we have two female guests who cannot have you, so they want food as a consolation prize. Hey, Doc, you get the beer and I'll get the pizzas."

114

DINNER WAS A GOOD TIME, providing the needed change from the operational issues. Pizza was an excellent choice that I could eat with one hand. Since only a few slices were left, the obvious conclusion was that Doc had selected the perfect toppings. The Cuban sandwiches went into the fridge for later. Conversation was light and filled with laughter.

Rhonda was acting fairly normal that night and wanted to talk more about the incident. Doc said that was a good sign. So we discussed it from the viewpoints of both the good guys and the bad guy. We did a full analysis on what we did, should have done differently, and must never do in that situation. I provided the analysis from Brackin's view.

Ann was surprised that things could turn bad so quickly. I explained that in most situations, you have about three seconds to react. That is not a lot of time for in-depth analysis. Rhonda again expressed her thanks for saving her from Brackin, which, we reminded her, was due to her courage and action.

We had just about worn out all aspects of Thursday's event when the phone rang. "Lieutenant Commander Colt's residence. Colt speaking," I answered.

"Sir, this is SSA Brian O'Malley, NISRA Charleston, returning your call. I hope it is not too late in the evening."

"Not a bit. Great to hear from you, O'Malley. Hold on while I put you on speakerphone, as there's another agent here who needs to be up to speed on what I hope you'll be able to tell me." I pushed the correct button and replaced the handset.

"Okay," I said. "I hope your agent explained why I called."

"Yes, sir, he did. And first, let me apologize for him not cooperating with you fully. He is new and was too cautious. I explained to him that the Director of NIS Internal Affairs gets whatever he wants when he calls, sir."

"Brian, I hope we can be on a first name basis here; please call me Marcus. No apologies needed. Your agent didn't know if I was on the level so his caution is appropriate. If I'd been thinking clearly, I should have gone to the AUTOVON room and first sent a message letting your office officially know that I'd be calling. So, no harm done. I know you shipped us a copy of the complete file that might be here tomorrow, but time is critical. What can you quickly tell us about Raffe? Got a five minute overview, Brian?"

Doc was taking notes as Brian gave us what ended up being a ten minute overview of Raffe. One key point jumped out: before he was arrested in Miami while visiting a relative, he'd been assigned to NAS Norfolk flying Neptunes to Guantanamo, Cuba, and back. Brian provided the squadron number. Lots of bells were now ringing in my head. Brian said the most frustrating part of the case was they could never prove his source for the drugs.

"Thanks, Brian, for all that info. That really helps. Can I get you to issue a 'locate, but do not detain' order on him? We might need to pull him in if this leads where I'm thinking it will."

"Certainly, sir, uh, Marcus. I'll get that right out and keep you updated on the status. Anything else?"

"I hate to be a pest, but we might need to call you tomorrow or Sunday with more questions, so please keep that file handy. May I have your home number?"

Brian provided his home phone number just in case. And again offered his apology for the mix up earlier. He said he planned on being in the office over the weekend, doing more digging on Raffe and other possible connections. After a little more chat, we concluded the call, again thanking him for his help.

"Damn, Marcus, I knew about the promotion to Lieutenant Commander, but never heard you're now a director. Way to go, brother!" Doc nodded appreciatively. Kelly just gave a wink over her knowing smile while Ann added the thumbs up sign.

Rhonda was a bit bug-eyed and said, "Wow. I was impressed with you as a yeoman, more so as an NIS investigator who can shoot, and now this. Extremely impressive stuff, Lieutenant Commander. Yet you act like such a normal guy."

"Uh, thanks, I think," I replied with a smile and a chuckle.

The remainder of Friday night was relaxing. At least it was after I called Sam and filled him in about Raffe. His excitement was building to the point I had to tell him I was too tired to think anymore tonight. He started to tell me something, but held back. I think he finally understood my fatigue was getting the better of me. So he agreed that an early Saturday meeting was in order with all hands on deck, including the NISO officers. He volunteered to call everyone; I let him.

Doc jumped into the conversation by telling Sam that 0900 hrs was early enough for the walking wounded. We'd see him no earlier than that time but we promised to bring donuts. Sam concurred on both the schedule and the snacks. He promised to have the coffee ready when we arrived.

115

THE MORNING STARTED SMOOTHLY. EVERYONE was already there when Doc and I drifted in at 0850 with boxes of treats. Seventeen of us were crammed in the skipper's conference room. In addition to Sam, his seven agents, the CO, XO, and Greg, Doc and I were pleased to see BMC Joe Devland representing the SEAL teams. I was really surprised to see Master Chief David Bartow sitting next to the Captain. The Admiral's rep was on board.

Sam chuckled and got things rolling. "Marcus, now that you've *finally* arrived ten minutes early, would you care to say a few words to get us going? And make it very few, as we have a lot to discuss."

My big grin was hard to hide. "Can do, Sam. Great to see you here, David. When did you get in?"

"Last night. When I called the Captain to let him know I was heading down and would probably be staying at your house, he let me know about all the guests at Hotel Tidewater, and was kind enough to put me up at his place for the weekend. The Admiral and I figured my presence would save you time and energy keeping him updated. So here I am."

"Well, I'm happy to have your counsel and you know Kelly will be thrilled to see you at dinner tonight. And your input is always welcome."

And there were two new guys sitting next to Sam. When I looked their way with a quizzical look, the biggest new guy introduced himself as the Norfolk Police Department Chief of Police, Michael Epps. I walked over and did the introductions for Doc and me. Epps stood about six-foot-two and weighed in the neighborhood of 220 lbs, most of it muscle. Red hair rapidly going gray topped a head that held the intelligent face of a man in his mid-fifties. Not the kind of guy you wanted to box. We exchanged handshakes as we sized each other up.

"Mr. Colt, I apologize for the entire department for the actions of that bastard Royal. I'm here to offer the help of the entire NPD. We are ready to assist any way you need us."

"Thanks, Chief Epps. While none of you are responsible for the actions of that jerk, we will gladly accept your help wrapping up this case. I suspect it will be a big benefit for our city as well as the Navy. It's good to have you here with us this morning. And you are?" I asked the slender, younger fellow sitting next to the Chief.

"Deputy Chief of Police Darren Cobb, sir. I'm here as backup for the Chief."

"Welcome, Deputy Chief Darren Cobb. Don't be surprised if we tag you with the nickname DC-squared before the meeting is over."

After some laughs at my joke, and a few more hellos and good mornings, Sam took charge and updated everyone on what had been discovered over the last couple of days. The info on Raffe and the number of deaths attributed to the same batch of cocaine created a lot of interest. Chief Epps promised to send over his files on unsolved drug-related deaths for Doc to analyze. It didn't seem like a long shot that others had died from the same batch of drugs.

John Driscol had been at the hospital, and he reported that Martinez had tried not show any reaction when Raffe's name was dropped in conversation—but he failed. Brackin may not have been talking yet, but his facial reaction to Raffe being mentioned showed that he at least knew who he was. After this meeting, John and Doug would head back to the hospital for more work on them both.

Bill Collins had been working the vipers in the brig on the USS Forrestal. He said that SK3 Dennis Moore was still not talking, but at the mention of Raffe's name, he also had a facial reaction he failed to hide. He knew him.

However, it was the info Sam shared from his discussion with ex-detective Royal that got the most attention. "It's amazing how a simple name can turn a stone wall into jelly," Sam said through a chuckle. "All I had to do was say 'Raffe' and Royal opened right up."

Sam proceeded to share with us the info he'd received. NPD Detective Collin Royal was caught in a honey trap with a prostitute in early spring 1970. This trap had been set by Raffe, in hopes of enlisting the help of several members of the NPD. Raffe had one of his girls come on to Royal at a local bar, then entice him back to her bedroom. It was an easy task, since Royal's wife had not been satisfying him lately. The bedroom was set up with cameras and sound recorders.

Raffe used the photos and tapes from the trap to blackmail Royal into helping Raffe's drug gang. He had to do whatever was requested, or he'd be exposed, ending both his marriage and career. Not long after, Royal was promoted to captain of detectives, in late summer 1970.

It was then that Raffe had insisted Royal initiate the frequent meetings with SSA Sam Maker, under the pretense of "working together" to keep Norfolk safe. Royal used the meeting to gather info on NISRA investigations, including names of CIs, and passed the info on to the drug gang leader. Raffe, in turn, made the decisions and sent the kill orders to Lansing. He usually called Lansing rather than trusting a face-to-face meeting.

The Captain, having been quiet during Sam's presentation, was the first to ask the question all of us were thinking. "So do we have any idea where Raffe is right now?"

"Sorry, Captain," responded Sam. "We do not. However, NISO Charleston has issued a 'locate, do not detain' order, since we know Raffe has a house in Miami."

"Since he also has a house here in Norfolk, I issued one late yesterday from the NPD," interjected Chief Epps.

"From all we have heard here, seems we need to turn those 'locate orders' into arrest orders," offered Darrell Tasker.

Shaking my head, I asked the group, "And aside from the confession of a disgraced detective, do we have any firm evidence to back up that confession? I don't think so. How about you, Chief Epps?"

"Hell, no. But I think I have enough to get a warrant to search his house and business locations. Hopefully that will uncover at least the blackmail tapes."

"So as it sits right now, an arrest today will probably put him back on the street tomorrow. Not a good plan," I responded. "Chief Epps ..."

"Call me Mike, please."

"Thanks, Mike—can your warrant be for the ability to search the airline records? When I first saw him, he was flying from here down to Miami. Perhaps he's had other destinations and other houses we don't know about right now. We should hold off on the warrant for any physical location searches until we check the airline data. That might uncover more locations to add to the search. Or it might point to his current location. And since you're now part of this crazy group, call me Marcus."

"Can do, Marcus. I'll try to track down the judge just as soon as this meeting is over. If it's okay with you, DC will hang around here."

DC was smiling as he nodded his head in resignation. The nickname had been applied and would be around the NPD precinct before Monday.

116

BEFORE NOON, WE HAD BEATEN the subject to death, coming up with too many possible scenarios. Once the donuts were gone, I decided we'd done all we could do for now. It was time to do the hard part of any investigation and sit on our butts, waiting for a nibble on the lines we'd thrown out. More info was needed before we could actually do anything positive.

Chief Mike departed to do his magic with the warrant. He mumbled that the judge might be on the golf course. The agents headed back to their office with DC in tow. They would share with him the evidence we had, in hopes he might spot something overlooked or be able to connect something to cases that NPD was pursuing. And it was time for lunch anyway.

Lunch with Sam, the Captain, Doc, Joe, and David at Sam's favorite seafood restaurant turned into another discussion of the problems we faced with this investigation. Even with all the challenges, David shared that he was impressed with the case progress. Furthermore, he was happy to see that Doc and I were working well together, handling the medical and physical limitation issues.

I used this opportunity to bring up a possible use of YN3 Rhonda Evans. I'd tried to address it the other night at the house with Rhonda, but Doc shut that conversation down. I approached it again now that one of the key people, the skipper, was involved. My plan got mixed, but mostly positive reactions, and Doc said he'd look into it from the mental health side. The Captain had no objections to my plan, but he and David both agreed that Doc had the final approval.

Quickly changing the subject, Doc and Joe got caught up on things with the SEAL teams. Joe had visited with Bill on Friday; his recovery was "going good." At the end of the meal, it was fun to watch the skipper and Sam argue over the check. As usual, the skipper won that argument.

Too quickly, we had to get back to the problems at hand. Signing back in with security at the main building entrance, we were informed by the duty officer that the overnight delivery service actually worked. The package waiting for us from NISO Charleston was a thick one. Doc carried it up the stairs with the anticipation of a kid at Christmas, based on the smile he was wearing. He was enjoying this agent work.

We spread the file out on the conference table in the NISRA area and dug into the details. Several agents came over to get the info first hand. There was a lot more there than we'd learned in the ten-minute brief from SSA Brian O'Malley. The case went back three years to a time when then-Lieutenant Paul Raffe was a pilot in a Neptune squadron out of Norfolk that flew to the Navy base at Guantanamo Bay, Cuba. He'd been in Norfolk for just over a year.

Prior to his assignment in Norfolk, he was stationed in Guantanamo for about eight months after being commissioned as an ensign in January 1966. He excelled in flight school and quickly transitioned to multi-engine aircraft. His post-school assignment in the late summer of 1966 was at a small squadron in Gitmo. Raffe hated it.

He considered himself basically a flying taxi driver. He was assigned the task of flying personnel from Cuba to the mainland and back in an R4D. Granted, flying the R4D Skytrain, the Navy's nomenclature for the ubiquitous Douglas DC-3, was not as exciting as flying bomb-laden jets off an aircraft carrier, but the old beast did its job well.

For Raffe, however, this type of flying was not the warrior position he signed up to fill. He wanted action, and many times tried for a transfer to the south Pacific. All requests were turned down and frustration become the norm for Raffe. He hid the fact that using drugs diminished that frustration.

As a Cuban-American—his parents moved to the US in the early 1940s—his CO in Gitmo found his dual language skills extremely helpful for working with the local civilian contractors around the air station. It was later believed by the agents that he'd used those civilians to establish a drug trafficking scheme, but they had no proof. Since the number of locals working on base had diminished since the 1959 revolution, his services were deemed not critical, and due to his constant bitching, he finally received a transfer to Norfolk in the early spring of 1967.

His Norfolk duty station was a squadron of P2V Neptunes. Transitioning from the R4D to the P2V was an easy task for Lieutenant Junior Grade Raffe, who was what some called a natural pilot. In a relatively short period of time, he became the aircraft commander, moving from the right seat to the left. Being pilot was much better than being copilot. And the flight schedule took him to Gitmo a couple of times a month.

Things went smoothly for Raffe until he took a week's worth of leave to visit friends in his hometown of Miami. His decision to pick up a little extra cash on the trip ended up costing him dearly when the NIS arrested him. The drug case against him was based upon the testimony of a NIS confidential informant that succeeded in buying cocaine from Raffe at a topless nightclub in Miami. When Raffe was picked up by the agents later that night, he had in his possession over $5,000 worth of drugs. Between the hard evidence and the CI, it was an easy case for the JAG folks to handle.

It seems the court went easy on him, though: he was only sentenced to one year and then dismissed from the Navy. But for an officer, a dismissal is similar to a dishonorable discharge for enlisted personnel. So Raffe's dream of eventually working for an airline, after his time in the Navy, was destroyed.

Despite the conviction and jail time, there was one big problem with the case as far as NIS was concerned. The agents had a theory that while stationed in Gitmo, he'd set up a drug pipeline with the Cuban civilians that continued after he transferred to Norfolk. And that the flow of drugs had continued long after he was sentenced to prison and served that sentence. It was a good theory and probably true, but the investigators couldn't find hard data to prove it.

One small but interesting point in the file was that Raffe had been overheard saying he was going to kill the informant who got him arrested. His hatred correlated with Royal's comments that Raffe wanted to kill all CIs working for NIS. And with the help of Royal and Lansing, he had succeeded remarkably.

David called his friend in BUPERS to help locate the CI from that case. He might already be another victim. Master Chief Beaumonte was not thrilled about being called on a Saturday, but since it was a request from David, he was on the way to the office by the time David hung up the phone. Nice to have high-placed friends.

Dead CIs were a problem for NISO Norfolk that had only come to light because of the large number, in a small geographical area, over a short period of time. However, I started wondering if there were other dead CIs, maybe one or two, here or there, that wouldn't have waved a red flag. Were more people dead because Raffe had ordered it? Time to get back on the phone.

"NISRA Charleston. This is SSA O'Malley. How may I help you?" asked Brian from his office in Charleston, SC.

"Brian, I warned ya that I might have to call. This is Marcus, and I have a request."

"Didn't the package arrive?"

"Yes, it did. Thank you. It's just what we needed. We saw a comment in there that triggered this call. Over the last couple of years, specifically since Raffe was arrested, have you lost many CIs?"

"Not sure, I'll have to check. I think I see where you're going, Marcus. There was one OD I do recall but we didn't associate it with Raffe. We missed that possible connection. Call ya back shortly."

"Thanks, Brian. You have the NISRA number." As I hung up, I turned and looked at David.

David must have felt my eyes, as he quickly looked up from the file. "And you want 'what' from me?"

"How about a full search of the HQ files for CIs that have died over the last five years? Get us names, locations, cause and date of deaths."

"Why five? Raffe has only been on the warpath for the last three."

"We need to set a baseline. If the numbers are flat, except for Norfolk, then we might see that his reach is limited."

David again turned to the phone and placed the call to Admiral Chance. The guys who run the computer system at NIS HQ would be setting up a program to pull that data from the system. Computers are fast, but programmers need time to set up the program, key the punch cards, and get it going. Now it was time to sit on our butts again and wait.

Before too much of the afternoon passed, I took the time to call Kelly and let her know David was in town and would be joining us for dinner. She was excited and immediately did some dinner planning over the phone. I was surprised I didn't have to stop at the store. She and Rhonda would take care of the quick shopping, and I was not to worry about a thing. Ann would be handling some of the prep work, so all was under control by the staff and guests of Hotel Tidewater. Worked for me, since I had enough on my plate already.

After another hour of discussion, the Captain and David returned to the skipper's house. I gave David instructions to my place and he said he'd be there no later than 1900 hrs. The agents, and their new associate DC, had called it a day. After all, it was more fun to wait at home than there in the office on a Saturday afternoon.

Brian called back from Charleston. He did see a couple additional deaths of CIs for NISRA Miami, but no other areas under their jurisdiction were affected. I shared with him our plans to pull nationwide data from HQ, and he was anxious to hear the results of that. I suggested he go on home and wait like the rest of us were doing. He agreed, but said he, and his agents, were ready to do whatever we needed. Just call, he said.

Sam, Doc, Joe, and I sat around the NISRA conference table coming up with scenarios on how this case might progress. And as we did so, we were jotting down questions that really needed answers. Things like why was Lieutenant Thomas killed? Had he seen something at the squadron? Or just wrong place, wrong time?

Then we had Brackin and Martinez showing recognition to Raffe's name. And we had Harker's signed confession that both of them took kill orders from Lansing. What was their connection to the drug ring? More interrogation needed.

Where did Moore fit into all this? Moore probably knew of Raffe, but did he just know the name after hearing it from Lansing or Harker, or was he getting orders and pay directly from Raffe?

And perhaps the most baffling question thus far was why was SK3 Rodriquez, a man successfully doing dirty work for Lansing, killed. The why questions for most of the other dead CIs were explained by Raffe's hate, but not Rodriquez and Thomas. Baker killed Rodriquez and tried to kill me. Since Baker was in the morgue, no confession would be coming from him. And nothing had turned up in his personal gear.

As with all cases, the questions would have to wait until we got more information. Like I said before, waiting is the hard part. I need to write that on the back of my hand.

117

It didn't matter that David was almost old enough to be father of any of them; he fit in well with Doc, Ann, and Rhonda. Hanging around the Admiral for all those years had provided him the ability to blend in and feel at home with most any group. That night was no exception. He blended so well that Ann and Rhonda had trouble believing he was a master chief, working directly for the CNO.

After a superb dinner of country-style steak and gravy served with garlic-mashed potatoes and dilled peas, we sat around the table chatting and sipping glasses of wine. Rather than having a sweet dessert, Kelly and I prepared an assorted cheese and cracker tray to go with several bowls of chips. I laid out the crackers single handedly while she sliced the different cheeses. Snacks always make relaxed conversation easier.

On the way to the house, Doc offered a suggestion to David that might help Rhonda. And it could lead into a discussion on my earlier plans for her. David agreed it was worth a shot. With David taking the lead talking with Rhonda, Doc could sit back and quietly observe her actions and reactions. As the second round of wine was poured, David signaled Doc with a small nod and got started.

"Rhonda, we need to talk. Marcus and Doc have given me their versions of Thursday's events in great detail. Before I make my final report to the boss, I'd like to hear your version. But only if you're up to it."

Smiling shyly and feeling a bit uneasy, she said, "Sure, if you think it will help your report." Seeing David nod, she gave him a very thorough overview of the events leading up to, and through, the shooting of Brackin. Her statement was mostly accurate. David asked a few questions to pull out specific pieces of information, to which she responded clearly and with great detail.

Granted, her description of Brackin's weapon had exaggerated its size. When a gun is pointed at you, it gets much bigger in your mind. However, it was impressive that she remembered so much and in the proper order. Most people get their facts all jumbled up due to the stress and emotions of such an event.

Hearing her talk about the shooting in a calm voice was a good thing, and Doc was pleased. Seemed his plan was working, and we all could see that Rhonda was most likely over the worst part of the trauma. Sadly, the incident would stay with her forever. And most likely pop back into her mind when she least expected it.

Finishing up her review, Rhonda asked "Sir, is there anything else?"

David looked over to Doc, who nodded. Then he asked. "There are a couple more things we should address. And I want honest answers and not what you think I want to hear. Okay?"

"Okay. Ask away."

"How are you feeling emotionally?"

Her face gave a slight grimace before she answered. "I know this weekend has to end. And I'm grateful to Kelly and Marcus for letting Ann and me stay here. And of course, I'm grateful to Doc and Ann for their support. I know it's only been two days, but I feel so much more relaxed and at ease."

"And how do you feel about going back to the Logistics Center on Monday?"

"I guess I've tried not to think about Monday. I know things will be different after what happened. But I think I can handle it all right."

David rubbed his chin as he pondered her answer. "And what about knowing there are probably still some additional bad guys working around there? Are you worried for your safety?"

Rhonda audibly inhaled hearing that. "Guess I had not gotten that far in my thinking. Yea, that's scary. Especially since I helped stop one of their buddies, I'll be on their hate list, for sure."

David nodded, and looked over at me. It was my turn to lead the conversation. "Rhonda," I asked, "how attached are you to doing supply work? Would you consider a change of duty stations?"

"Thinking about more evil people being there, I am definitely ready to move on. I can be a yeoman anywhere."

I smiled at her and asked one more question. "How would you like a permanent transfer to Naval Investigative Service here in Norfolk? No moving involved and a much more secure work environment."

"Can you do that?"

"Yea, we can make it happen. We already have the approval of the NISO's skipper, Captain Miller. Is this something you might want to do?"

"Hell, yes! Oh, Marcus, thank you so much."

"Okay, consider it done. Come Monday morning, YN2 Dexter Wilson has a new trainee for the AUTOVON room. Kelly can run you over to the barracks tomorrow to pick up your uniform if you want to spend another night at Hotel Tidewater, and you'll ride in with Doc and me on Monday. Then perhaps you can get your life back to some level of normal."

Judging by the number of smiles I saw in the room, a good thing had just happened. And the hug and kiss on the cheek I was getting from Rhonda, under the watchful eyes of Kelly of course, confirmed it. Nice way to end a traumatic week.

118

IT WAS STILL DARK AND everyone else was sleeping as I quietly entered the kitchen to start the coffee. It was nice to have friends around, but also very nice to have a quiet moment or two alone to reflect on things. Life ahead of me with Kelly would probably always be this exciting—she seemed to attract excitement—so I needed to learn to enjoy the quiet time whenever possible. Sounded like a good plan that I hoped would work.

The previous night had been a blast, due to Rhonda's excitement about her transfer. There were a couple of toasts to her future success in the intelligence field. I believed she'd be a great asset for NIS, and it seemed the change would be a good thing for her. The chatter went on for hours. But my energy level bottomed out around 2200 hrs, so Kelly and I said our "goodnights" and left Doc and the ladies to carry on without us.

Before he left at 2130 hrs to head back to the skipper's house for the night, David had called Master Chief Beaumonte, his buddy at BUPERS, again. He cashed in a few more favors and told him that Sunday would be a good day for him to get his butt into the office and generate the orders for YN3 Rhonda Evans's immediate transfer from Fleet Logistics Center Norfolk to NISO Norfolk. David gave him her service number and particulars, and he provided some details about why the transfer was needed ASAP.

And David continued by telling him he'd also better start looking for at least two YNs, second and third class petty officers, five SKs, two third, one second, a striker, and a chief petty officer, for the Fleet Logistics Center Norfolk. Due to a nasty run-in with NIS this past week they were suddenly shorthanded with two in the morgue, two in the hospital, and two in the brig. Obviously, they needed more people soon.

The details and the request surprised Beaumonte, but knowing David was always on the level, he'd start digging for replacements in the morning. The official request had to come through channels, and would take about a week. By then the Chief would have all the right people selected and would look like a genius. That helped offset the favors David had requested.

I decided, as the ranking officer of the Hotel Tidewater, as well as the guy paying all the bills, that I deserved a solitary cup of coffee in the dark quiet of the kitchen before taking one up to Kelly. Besides, she needed more rest. It had been a challenging couple of days for her helping with Rhonda. At least she got to practice her psychology skills on someone besides me.

In the quiet, it was easy to think back on the week. And again, it was hard to believe it had been only a week since I was attacked. What a mess it had been. I silently chuckled, wondering what else we could have squeezed into such a short period of time. We really needed to wrap up the mess soon.

With my first cup empty, I fixed a second cup and one for the adorable woman sleeping in my bed upstairs. At least with a pair of covered travel mugs with huge handles, I could easily and safely carry two upstairs with my one working hand.

Doc was coming down the stairs as I started up. He looked like he started to say something to me then stopped, so I paused and just came out with it. "Morning, Doc. What do you need besides coffee?"

"We need to talk, Marcus."

"Fine. Allow me time to deliver this to the princess"—I raised the two mugs in my hand—"and I will be right with ya. Kitchen in about five minutes okay?"

He nodded and continued on to the kitchen.

Princess Kelly was still softly snoring when I kissed her ear and roused her gently from her sleep. She rolled over on her stomach, moaning and pulling her face deep into the pillow. I started gently rubbing her shoulders, then her back and worked all the way down her adorable body. I look forward to the day I could use both hands for this pleasure and without all the clothing in the way. The massage of her feet finally brought her to a state of wakefulness where she took a deep breath and understood that coffee was nearby.

"Good morning, future husband. That is a wonderful way to start the morning," she purred softly. "I really hope you keep touching me like that for the next hour or so."

"Well, future wife, if you liked that, you will really enjoy September fifth, won't you now," I responded with a big grin as I gently swatted her perfect butt.

"I see you've got the right date memorized. Good plan, sailor."

"And I hope I can hold out until then. But sorry, that's all the touching you get this morning. Enjoy your coffee, sweetie. Doc needs to talk about something, so I'll be in the kitchen with him."

"Do you need me?" she asked with concern as she rolled onto her back.

"Always and forever, but probably not for the chat with Doc. Take your time before heading down in case it's something private for him."

I gave, and received, a superb kiss—actually several, but who's counting—and headed back downstairs. I was so looking forward to the day when climbing back in bed with Kelly for more than a back rub would have the highest priority in my life. My calendar was cleared for all of September and beyond.

"Okay, Doc, what is on your mind?" I asked as I poured another cup and joined him at the table.

"Marcus, I've been doing a lot of thinking lately." Doc chuckled and continued, "Yea, all of my free time between hospitals, shootouts, investigations, bandaging, chauffeuring, and therapy sessions has been used for thinking. Probably should say soul searching. But seriously, maybe it's time for me to make a career change."

"Really?"

Doc nodded, took another sip of coffee, and sighed, "I hate to admit it, but it took a while to bounce back from our last adventure together, and no, sir, you are not to blame, so shut the hell up before you start your guilty crap again, sir."

I opened my mouth to say something, but Doc's look said 'do not mess with me' in no uncertain terms. As did his respectful use of 'sir' in place of my name. He was being extremely serious. So I sat there in silence, but mostly in respect.

"Look, I know my body is not one hundred percent, probably will never be. And I also know as a corpsman that I'll never lead a team. I might make chief in the next year or two, but beyond that I have my doubts about future advancement. And I gotta admit being an NIS agent, even a fake one, has been an interesting adventure so far. I think with time and some training, I can be pretty good at it. Can you pull out your magic wand and get me assigned as an agent permanently?" He gave a slight grimace as he said the last sentence.

Wow. That came from left field. I knew it took a lot for him to open up like that, and to even ask for a favor. Doc does not ask for favors. He's always the one granting them, with never a thought of calling them in later. Truly, Doc is a rare man in today's world. Sipping coffee gave me a moment to think before I had to put my mouth in gear.

"You have a lot of faith in me, Doc. Not sure if I can live up to that. I need to throw out some questions, but I don't want your answers; keep them to yourself and think about them. Okay?"

Doc nodded an affirmative.

"Guess the first question is critical: are you ready to give up the teams? That is a big step for you. Are you ready to give up being a corpsman? What about your plans for med school after the Navy? Are you willing to be the 'old man' at NISHQ as you go through five weeks of agent training with kids right out of college? After being the second highest rate on the team, can you handle going back to being a rookie for a year or so when assigned to a NISRA? And speaking of college, are you willing to go back part time to finish your degree while working full time?" I stopped there to get more coffee.

I could see that Doc was taking all this seriously and the gears were turning in his head. Good. This life-changing decision would require a lot of consideration and hard thought.

I continued, "That's probably enough for you to think about for a bit. My wand's power is pretty limited, Doc. I can recommend moving a yeoman from one yeoman slot to another yeoman slot—that quickly got the CNO's approval. Well, at least David's approval, which is just about the same thing. But pulling a SEAL without a degree off active duty to go through agent training is quite another task."

"I understand, Marcus, but I had to ask." Doc was looking down at his coffee cup like a kid who didn't get the puppy he wanted for Christmas.

Doc's look hurt me worse than the slice in my arm. As I was rolling out the questions, a thought started growing in the back of my mind.

And as we sat there in silence for a moment, it quickly grew. As with most problems I face, I started with the facts. It didn't take long to run through them in my mind.

With Doc on TAD from the SEALs as my executive assistant/medic/bodyguard for about five months, the SEAL skipper would have to get a new corpsman to fill his slot; he probably already had. Therefore, Doc didn't have a 'home' to return to right away. And with Doc involved with helping me develop this new agent training routine, he'd be a least as knowledgeable about it as I was. Since I'd been neglecting my job with internal affairs, I wouldn't have time to incorporate the new training into the system.

So, with all these facts quickly laid out on the mental table, my solution just might work. In this solution, I would recommend that Doc stay on active duty and get transferred to NISHQ to work with the NIS training division. There he'd incorporate the new methods into the manual and help with actual agent training. He could also work on finishing his degree at nights, which would prepare him for an agent's position. Perhaps Ann could transfer to Walter Reed Medical Center to be close to Doc if their relationship grew over the next few months. When this case was over, and if Doc was still serious, I needed to talk with Admiral Chance.

"First thing a good agent learns is to listen carefully to what is said and what is not said. Both are very important. And nowhere did you hear me say a definitive 'hell, no' or 'not going to happen.' Take some more time and mull over the questions I gave you. This is a big decision. Only you can answer those questions and formulate the correct answer for yourself. After you do, if you still want to head in that direction, then we can sit down with Sam and later Admiral Chance for some good talks. But first, let's get this case over with quickly."

Doc perked up and smiled, "Yes, sir. That is an excellent plan. Thank you, sir."

Kelly walked in right then waving an empty coffee cup and asked, "So, what's the good plan? Pancakes, I hope, and lots of bacon!"

119

BEFORE DOC AND I CAME back to the office to hopefully get some answers to our many case-related questions, Kelly had a meeting with the ladies. Their meeting was held after pancakes, of course, served with a generous amount of crisp bacon, just as Princess Kelly desired. I could still prepare both with just one hand.

Her plan of attack for the day included taking Ann back to her barracks later so she could get ready for her night shift at the ER. At the same time, Rhonda would ride over with them and pickup her uniform for Monday's duty at NIS. So we had one less guest for the night at Hotel Tidewater. But first, after breakfast, they were going to convert my office back into a real guestroom. Works for me, I told them.

Doc and Ann were pleased with my arm's healing progress. More feeling was coming back to the incision area, and still no sign of any infection. The surgical team did a great job of cleanup, they both said. The new bandages were in place, and Kelly helped me get my shirt buttoned. She made that simple task so sensual that it was easy to get sidetracked.

We finally got away from the house a bit after 0920 hrs. Driving to the NISRA office, Doc asked what our mission was going to be that day. A logical question, I had to admit.

"Doc, today is one of those days where we just wait and see what comes to us. We have so many irons in the fire it's anyone's guess which one gets hottest first. Personally, I hope Brackin and Moore start talking. We need more confessions, unless we uncover a ton of hard evidence soon. Evidence which has not been found thus far."

"I was afraid you were going to say that. You know I hate waiting, unless bourbon and a sexy woman are the end results."

That got a laugh from me. "Better not let Ann hear you say that, Agent Stevens. Unless I'm mistaken, which we know rarely ever happens, you two fall into the 'made for each other' category. I can see that you have a great future with that girl. She helps keep you grounded. Don't mess it up, my brother."

"Yea, you are so right, Marcus. We're looking forward to spending more time together, in a much less stressful and less crowded environment than your house, real soon. No offense intended, but it is rather hectic around you. I have never said these words before, but she might be the one."

"I think that might be true. Best of luck, Doc."

We arrived at the office a little before 1000 hrs only to discover we were the first ones there. We already knew that Clyde London and Steve Crosser would be on the *Forrestal* that morning in hopes of hearing Brackin or Moore talk. Or maybe Peterson would open up and surprise us all.

The duty officer handed me a couple of notes of calls he'd received earlier, as we signed the log. First one was documenting a call from Sam: he decided to visit the vipers in the hospital and those in the brig on the USS *Forrestal* before heading into the office. Second was from the Captain: he and David would be in before noon—no other information was provided. And the last call was from Darrell Tasker: the shore patrol had called, and he and Joe were responding to a wife abuse case. Even with vipers all around, evil in life goes on.

Doug Knox and John Driscol were taking the day off. They'd been on the USS Forrestal for nearly a week straight and needed to rest and recuperate for a day. I could fully understand that need. And Bill Collins had to be back at Oceana NISRA to catch up on paperwork there. He might be back with us tomorrow, but a lot depended on what he found awaiting him at his office.

The first thing to do was an obvious standard, but not for this one-armed guy. Doc put on the coffee under my supervision, and with that critical task accomplished, we headed to the file room for more study of the index cards. We often use the term 'fresh eyes' to mean someone new can see something we have been looking at, yet overlooking. It also applies to getting away from something for a while and coming back later only to see the obvious that had been overlooked.

When I walked up to the table where the evidence cards were laid out, I saw it. Lieutenant Thomas had been hit in the head with something like a round metal bar, and that blow killed him. His girlfriend, Ensign Appleton, had been stabbed in the abdomen; her wound was not what killed her, but the small round wound had done some damage. And the agents had found a tire iron with blood on it in the trunk of SK3 Peter Rodriquez's Chevy, while investigating his own murder.

"Doc, look at this. We have a tire iron from this case with blood on it in two different places. It's round, like the rod that took out Lieutenant Thomas, and has a pointy end about the size of the hole in Ensign Appleton's abdomen. Do we have any analysis on the blood samples from that iron?"

"Let me check."

I decided to let Doc follow this lead on his own, and just sat back to enjoy my coffee. If my guess was true, Doc would get a kick out of tying this link together. We all need victories no matter how small, and it was a great learning experience for him. With his efficiency, it only took a few minutes for him to pull the info from the three files.

"Okay, Marcus, the tire iron has type B on the pointy end and AB negative, a really rare blood type, on the other end, near the lug nut wrench. I know there are probably official terms for each end of a tire iron. Guess I need to research that before we submit our written report. And Ensign Appleton has a blood type of B in her record, and our Lieutenant Thomas is AB neg," said Doc with a big smile. "Can we now assume that this tire iron was involved with both their injuries?"

"That, my dear Doctor, is a most elementary and logical assumption as you look at the three files. However, looking at the tire iron as a stand-alone item as part of the Rodriquez case, no, we cannot. It was not found at the scene of the murders, and does not have any victims' fingerprints on it. And neither of the victims is missing a tire iron. Therefore, there is no way to tie it to either of them."

I finished my coffee and continued, "However, it's a logical assumption that will have weight in the trial after you add to it the fact that the two victims were dating and they both were murdered the same weekend. Now their blood types on the tire iron have greater importance. When we add on more pieces of evidence, then there are way too many points to be coincidences."

Doc had that look that said 'I think I'm getting there' when he offered, "So we can start to believe that SK3 Peter Rodriquez, the guy that owns ... scratch that, *may own* the tire iron, is the person who might have killed Appleton and Thomas. Guess my question now is how do we get to a point where we can say definitively that's true?"

I gave Doc a smile and said, "Okay, time to go back to the index cards. Good news is that we can narrow down the analysis, at least for now, to just these three files. While I get more coffee, look for additional links." I'd just seen one more link and hoped that by the time I returned, Doc would also find it. And perhaps one or two others I hadn't seen.

A surprise awaited me in the coffee mess. "Good morning, Scott. What brings you in today?" Lieutenant Colonel J. Scott Tiller had just finished fixing his coffee and was dropping a buck in the money can. Coffee is only a quarter, but it was easier to pay for several cups at a time. I did the same and poured a cup of my special blend.

"How's the arm, Marcus? I read the report on your attack and on Thursday's event. Quite a week you had. Impressive the way you handled yourself even after being wounded. The Captain told me you were a warrior, and your actions prove it."

I shrugged. "I got lucky, and the bad guys didn't. As for the arm, my personal medic says the arm is healing well. I just know that a week in this sling has been way too long, and sadly they keep telling me I have about five more weeks to go."

"Well, that stinks. Sorry I haven't had the chance to talk with you since the attack. Sam has been keeping me hopping with his demand for new BIs on most of the personnel at the Logistics Center. It was a damn good thing I could borrow a couple of agents from NISRAs Charlottesville and Camp Lejeune to help out this past week. I'm trying to finish up the final paperwork on a few today to have on Sam's desk in the morning."

"No apologies needed, Scott. There will be time for socializing soon, I hope. Anything worthwhile in the BIs?"

"Only with the ones for the bad guys you have already uncovered. Everyone else we have done looks clean, but there are still about twenty more people to wrap up. The agents should have them finished no later than Tuesday."

I thanked him for his hard work, and asked that he pass my compliments on to the agents, and went down the hall to the NISRA. Then that silly lightning bolt hit and I turned around. The Colonel was heading in the opposite direction toward his office down near the skipper's. I walked fast to catch up.

"Scott, one more thing if you don't mind."

"Whatever you need, Marcus. The Captain has put your needs above just about everything else, so your wish is my command, as the old, tired, and greatly overused saying goes. And aside from the Captain's wishes, I value your friendship and expertise, and would put anything you need at the highest priority anyway."

It took a moment to get my emotions under control and find my voice. Guess the meds were still messing with me since I never used to get choked up like this. Or perhaps it was the thought of working with people I respected and getting that same respect back from them, like with the SEAL teams.

"Colonel, sir, thank you. That means a lot to me," I finally said. "Look, I know you're slammed with work, but could you also check into the enlisted personnel of a specific Neptune squadron? Greg has already talked with most of them about the death of one of their pilots. So he can narrow down the starting place to the ones he thinks might be hiding something. I'll call him and ask him to work with you on the BIs."

"Anything specific bugging you about those guys? And by the way, I thought we were on a first name basis."

"We are, Scott, but showing you more respect just felt right at that moment. Your friendship and support are greatly appreciated and I'm honored." I paused a moment to let that sink in. "And sorry, but there is nothing specific; it's just one of my gut feelings. We're seeing a link between a dead pilot from that unit, his dead girlfriend who was working at the Logistics Center, and one of the vipers from there who probably killed them both. So there could be someone in the squadron who has ties to the vipers."

"No problem, Marcus. I'll call Greg as soon as I get to my office and ask him to come on in; you have enough to do with one hand. Hope to have some prelim data for you in a couple of days, okay?"

"Perfect, Scott. Thanks, my friend."

120

DOC WAS GRINNING LIKE HE just got a date with a porn star as I came back into the file room. He waved an index card and exclaimed, "Got another link, Marcus! Appleton's body was missing a white tennis shoe and an exact match to the missing one was found in Rodriquez's truck with several drops of type B blood on it."

"Excellent," I responded, "Glad you saw that. Now what else do we need?"

Doc frowned and started nodding his head, "Okay, I understand now. You already knew that. You are now in training mode and I'm the trainee, right?"

"You broke the code, Doc. Now answer my question. What else do we need right now to go with that shoe?"

Doc's face twisted into a look of concentration mixed with frustration. I let him stew on the question as I sipped more coffee. My attention was pulled from Doc as the office door opened. Sam wandered in wearing his standard 'I am not happy' look. Hate it when he does that.

"Afternoon, Marcus. What ya up to?"

"Before I answer that question, what is bugging you, Sam? I don't see a happy look."

"Just a bit frustrated with the lack of progress on this mess. The vipers in the brig are not offering anything, and the two guys in the hospital are about the same. We need a big break and it ain't happenin' bubba."

"Patience is needed, Sam. This mess is so damn complicated that the normal 'find bad guy, arrest bad guy, convict bad guy' routine is not going to happen."

"Yea, I know it. But that still does not relieve the frustration. And we have nothing back from the NPD chief yet either. We need to find Raffe."

I agreed and then told him about asking Scott to do BIs on Thomas' squadron based on not much more than a gut feeling. Sam thought that was probably a good idea. Then he said he'd call the squadron's CO first thing tomorrow to give him a heads-up on the BIs. Like we did with the Logistics Center, their CO would be told it was just a routine thing, in hopes of not causing anyone to panic.

"Marcus, remember Raffe was part of that squadron a few years ago, so he might have associates there too. Extremely good idea on the BIs. And I'll call my FBI contact now that we know a name to go with the description. Maybe they have something on him that will help with our case."

"Good plan, Sam," I said. I motioned him to follow me and we stepped out into the hallway for privacy. "Doc let me know that he's thinking he has a future as an NIS agent. I agree with him, but want to make sure he really wants it. I told him I would talk with you after this case is over, but I decided to give him more responsibility while I look over his shoulder. Sort of force him into training mode to see if he likes the work."

"Okay, so what do you want from me?"

"Go into the file room and talk with Doc. He's found a couple of links that help tie up a few loose ends, and it will boost his ego to brief you on them. While they're small links, they are much better than no links. And don't mention our chat."

Sam smiled and said he understood and would work with Doc. He returned to the agents' area and I decided to leave the two of them alone for a bit. Doc needed the practice of presenting evidence and associated links to a senior agent on his own, and this was a perfect opportunity. I headed back down the hall toward the coffee mess in hopes of finding a snack and another cup of my special brew. Doc and I had decided to skip lunch and call it an early day, around 1600 hrs, so the hunger pangs were getting strong.

Again, the coffee mess provided a surprise in the form of Captain Miller and Master Chief Yeoman David Bartow. Both were filling their mugs, and they nodded when I entered.

"Good afternoon, gentlemen. Hope all is well with the leadership of this circus," I joked.

The Captain put on a fake frown and replied, "Your circus and your monkeys, Marcus. How goes your progress keeping them in the proper ring?"

David broke up at our comments and promised to share them with the CNO in the morning. We took a moment to enjoy the humor and finish preparing our coffees. I grabbed a candy bar to keep the stomach growls under control.

The three of us headed down the hall to the Captain's office so I could update him and the CNO's representative. David wanted a quick update, as he was heading back to D.C. in about an hour. Before heading out, he also wanted an update from Sam, and would stop by my house on the way out of town for a hug from Kelly. Hugging Kelly was always a high priority, as far as I was concerned.

Since the day's progress had been limited, the update didn't take long. Both of them seemed pleased with things Doc had discovered. I took that opportunity to share Doc's request to become an agent and my plan on how to make that happen. Both the skipper and David agreed with my logic and plan. And they agreed that letting Doc ponder my questions was the right direction for now.

With the sharing time over, the skipper dug into the pile of paperwork on his desk and David and I returned to the NISRA office to talk with Sam. David huddled with Sam in his office and I went back into the file room to face Doc.

"Okay, Doc, figure it out yet? What else do we need?"

Looking dejected, Doc quietly replied, "I don't have a damn clue, sir. My head hurts from thinking so much. And Sam told me I was on my own and left."

I gave a soft chuckle to lighten the mood and replied, "Doc, this thinking process is one of the many things taught in the agents' class. It's a unique process and it is radically different from anything you have done as a corpsman or a SEAL. So don't feel bad, okay?"

"Yea, right. I feel like crap for not figuring it out by myself. So tell me."

I punched him in the upper arm, and said, "Quit whining, shipmate. Remember, the only easy day was yesterday."

That got a laugh out of him. And I received a nod of understanding.

"Doc, here is where you stop being an investigator and put on a lawyer's hat. What will the trial council need to convict? We have the missing shoe in the trunk. The question that will come up is why did he keep her shoe? Logic tells us he didn't intentionally, because that would be ridiculously foolish. Again, logic comes into play and we can theorize that the shoe fell off either as she was put into the Chevy's trunk or when he pulled her out. And he never noticed it."

"Well, hell, that makes sense."

"Sense, yes. However, proof is needed. Does the evidence file mention anything about hair, fibers, blood, or anything that would indicate she was in the trunk at any time?"

"No, Marcus, but the car is still in the impound facility. Can we take a look at it right now?"

Sam and David were standing at the door during the latter part of our conversation. Both were smiling. Sam winked and said, "Doc, no offense, but you might not know what to look for in that trunk. However, we have trained people who do. Try this plan on for size: tomorrow morning, after you drop off Marcus here, head over to the impound area and they'll give you a quick overview of what they do. Who knows, you might even find a hair or two."

"Sounds good, Sam," I said. "Heading out, David?"

"Yea, it's time to hit the road. Doc, keep our boy on track for quick healing. Sam, you and your team are extremely impressive. And Marcus, do take care. I'd hate having to brief the CNO that you stupidly got yourself injured again or killed. Happy trails, gents."

121

Doc and Rhonda were whispering and giggling like children as we walked out of the house to head to work at 0715 hrs. I figured they were up to something, but I didn't have a clue until we got to the car. Rhonda opened the passenger side rear door and indicated I was to enter. She got into the passenger front seat and Doc drove us down the road.

When Doc pulled to the curb in front of the 5th Naval District Headquarters building, Rhonda jumped out, opened my door, and came to attention. I did my best to keep a straight face as she closed both car doors and quickly walked to the building ahead of me. There, she opened and held the door for me again at attention. Her actions got a lot of looks from those coming and going at that time. I'm just glad the Admiral was not around to see it; he might have been jealous of the royal treatment I was getting.

On the way up the stairs to the NISO offices, she winked and whispered, "Just one of the benefits of having a harem, Mr. Colt."

"Petty Office Evans, I appreciated that courtesy," I grinned back at her and replied. "And you probably don't want Kelly to hear that harem comment used too often. You might want to make a note of that for future reference." I returned her wink.

That got both of us laughing as we approached the NISO security desk. After introducing GM2 Jimmy Kincade to Rhonda, and explaining the entrance security protocols, I took her to meet Chief Giatano. I explained to him the reason behind the quick transfer and promised to have her service record to him before tomorrow. I left her with the Chief so he could do his standard introduction and get her settled in properly.

The agents were all in attendance that morning, and we were happy to have DC there as well. No sign of the NPD chief, but his deputy would do. Sam had called a quick meeting to find out if there was anything new and to make sure everyone was on the same page.

Sam started off. "Morning. I've called my buddy in the FBI and passed on Raffe's name. Perhaps they have something. He promised to call back soon." He then looked at DC and gave a 'come on' hand signal.

"Gentlemen, the Chief was able to find the judge—he was on the four-teenth green—and we got the warrant we need for the airline data. The Chief is at the airport this morning with two other detectives, combing over their data. Like Sam, I'm waiting to hear back."

I went next and told them about the links we'd found the day before. And that Doc was checking the car for more evidence at that moment. It was time to also explain the new yeoman assigned to NISO Norfolk. I concluded my statement with a similar refrain: "Like Sam and DC, I'm waiting to hear back. There's a lot of that 'waiting stuff' going around this morning."

That got the expected chuckle, and we continued sharing info until one of the phones rang. The call did not provide any of the info we needed, but Doug and John left to handle a breaking and entering issue at an officer's house on base. Since we were done anyway, four agents headed out to continue working on the vipers in the hospital and in the brig. Sam and DC met in Sam's office for some heavy conversation. That left SA Bill Collins standing there.

"Bill, let's get some coffee," I said as I ushered him to the door and we headed down the hall. "I'm sorry we haven't had much time working together these last couple of weeks. But I've looked over your work and it is impressive."

"Thank you, sir."

"Please, just call me Marcus," I replied as I poured another cup of my special brew. Bill was going for a cup of tea. "Do you have anything pressing right now?"

"No, I was hoping to get back to the *Forrestal*, but Darrell and Joe said they had it under control. Is there something I can do for you?"

I smiled as I stirred the sugar and cream into my coffee. "I love your enthusiasm, Bill! As a matter of fact, there is."

We walked back down the hall and went into the file room. I explained my index card method to Bill and could see he was picking up on all the parameters quickly. He had never considered that approach and was enthusiastic to learn about it.

"Bill, fresh eyes are critical. Doc and I have gone over these dead CI records and a couple of unsolved deaths too many times. I hope you can look them over and perhaps spot something we've missed. Up to it?"

"Certainly. I'll call you when I find something."

I showed him what we'd pieced together and suggested the best way to search and compare the index cards. With Bill left to his analysis, I stuck my head into Sam's office and gave an update on what I was having Bill do. He and DC were still waiting on their calls, so I left them to it. Then I headed down the hall to the AUTOVON room.

As I pushed the door closed, Dexter looked up from his Teletype and stood. Rhonda was typing on her machine and failed to notice my arrival due to the noise level. I motioned Dex back down and walked over to stand behind them.

"Everything under control, Wilson?" I asked in my best officer voice. "How's the rookie doing?"

Rhonda jumped up when she heard my voice, "Sorry, sir, I didn't hear you enter."

"As you were, Rhonda, not a problem. How is it going?"

Dex gave me a thumbs up and nodded his approval. "Marcus, she is a sharp one. Thank you, thank you, and thank you!"

"Dex, I know you have been lonely since I left, so I figured you needed the best replacement I could find. And Rhonda, I know it's early, but what ya think about this place?"

"So far, sir, it's great. Dexter is doing a good job with my indoctrination, and the rest of the crew has been most welcoming. I like Captain Miller."

"Good to hear. Dex, whatever you do, don't make any comments that could be considered weather related. It will be painful for ya. Fill him in later, Rhonda," I said chuckling. "By the way, Rhonda, will you be okay going back to your barracks for the night, or do you need a lift to Hotel Tidewater?"

She chuckled at both those comments and said, "Mr. Colt, I'll be fine on my own at the barracks from now on. But thanks so much for all your help."

"Rhonda, it will be all right for you to fill Dex in about what happened last Thursday and over the weekend. In this job, he has already, or will soon, read all the reports anyway, so there aren't too many secrets inside this office. Just make sure they stay in the office. And don't you be a stranger at the house; that would really upset Kelly and me. Gotta run." And I walked out the door.

Dex looked a bit shocked when he heard that and turned to Rhonda. "House? Kelly? Weekend? What is going on?"

122

RIGHT BEFORE LUNCH, DOC CALLED to tell me he was finally leaving the impound lot. They had found some hair and blood in the trunk, and he'd be dropping the samples off at the lab before heading to the office. I asked that he run by the Logistics Center and pick up Rhonda's service record before coming in. Gotta keep the Chief happy, I told him.

Lunch time ran late that day. Bill left with Sam, Doc, and DC to get a bite off base just after 1300 hrs. I wasn't feeling very social so I begged off joining them. I planned to grab a sandwich and soda to go, from the cafeteria. Not wanting to meet anyone, I held back to let the noon crowd get through.

Succeeding in my leave-me-alone mission, I ended up hiding in the file room, which gave me the opportunity to eat without having to talk with anyone. The solitude and quiet gave me a chance to clear my head and go over the high points of this case. I don't do it often, but every now and then I stop to reevaluate my decisions. This was one of those times.

Back when we figured out that Royal was involved with the CIs murders, I'd asked the agents to hold their plans to arrest as many pushers as possible based on the data we'd gathered. The thought was to avoid spooking Royal and whoever he was working with selling drugs. However, we now had Royal and a bunch of vipers off the streets. Could making a massive quantity of arrests help pull Raffe out of hiding? Or could any of the pushers we might arrest have a lead on Raffe? I needed to talk with Sam and the Captain after thinking on this a bit longer.

Sam's FBI buddy called him right after he got back from lunch. Yea, their records showed that they knew Raffe well: he had been a person of interest in several cases. But right then, there were no current investigations involving him underway. He seemed to bend the law frequently, but stopped short of actually breaking it. The FBI offices in select cities would cooperate with the "locate, but do not detain" order.

NPD Chief of Police Mike Epps finally showed up around 1500 hrs. Mike had the travel records for Raffe showing that besides frequent travel to Miami, he spent an equal amount of time in Brownsville, Texas. The data the warrant provided showed him flying into the South Padre Island Airport about once a month for a week, similar to the schedule for his Miami trips.

Mike had already called the Brownsville police chief to explain the situation. The Texas chief had issued a 'locate, but do not detain' order on Raffe, and had found that he owned a home right next to the Mexican border. Mighty convenient for moving drugs north. They promised to keep a watch on the place.

There were no other travel destinations for him, so we had to assume these three cities—Norfolk, Miami, and Brownsville—were the key points. Granted, he could fly to one and drive elsewhere, but he didn't seem the type to waste time driving. And the last flight showed him coming back to Norfolk from Miami over the weekend. So this head viper might be in our area—and could be for the next two weeks, as suggested by his previous travel schedules.

Mike headed back to his office to prepare the search warrants for Raffe's houses and offices. He knew those warrants had to be held back for now, but he wanted to be ready when the time came; he would leave the dates blank. He asked Sam if DC was free to head back with him. Sam agreed and the two NPD reps departed for the day. The chief was proving to be an outstanding officer who had things under control and was willing to cooperate with sister agencies.

"Sam, we need to talk. Bill, you and Doc should also sit in."

Doc started shaking his head, "What the hell is wrong now, Marcus?" He looked over at Sam and Bill, giving them a shrug. "I hate it when he starts a conversation that way."

"Doc, keep cool, nothing is wrong for a change. But I had a rethink of one of our—actually my—plans." And with that intro, I laid out my thinking from earlier. Saying it out loud made it sound even more logical. Then I looked to Sam for his input.

"Only one damn thing wrong with it: I didn't think of it first. It will probably take a day to get the SP troops lined up and ready, but we should be ready for the roundup on Wednesday afternoon. You have any thoughts, Bill?"

Bill shook his head, "Makes sense, but do we have enough manpower for a big sweep?"

Doc jumped up and hurried to the door. "Excuse me while I go ask the Captain to call in our SEAL friends again. As of yesterday, they didn't have an assignment, and this will be fun for them."

When I nodded in agreement, Doc left to talk with the skipper. I didn't mention it, but it was strange to hear Doc refer to the team members as *they* and *them* not *we* or *us*. Interesting word choices. Perhaps subconsciously he'd already moved on from the teams to a new role in NIS.

Sam and Bill started calling the agents to give them overnight to start thinking of this new direction before the 0800 hr meeting tomorrow. I called LTCOL Tiller to see if the remaining BIs on the Logistics Center had been finalized. He asked that I come to his office.

I gave a quick knock and opened his door. "What ya got, Scott?"

"Marcus, we have one more potential viper at the Logistics Center. Seaman Carlos Menendez is working as a laborer. He is a second-generation Cuban who was raised in Miami. And the clincher is that he's a cousin of your friend, SM, a.k.a. SK2 Jesus Martinez. While we don't have any solid proof, I'm willing to wager a lot that he's involved in this mess, since we found nearly $5,000 in his bank account, all from recent cash deposits."

"Yea, all that points to him being involved in some way. My guess is that he's on the drug side of the business and not the murder side. Murder would get him much more money. I'll ask Sam to pick him up first thing in the morning. Maybe that will shake him up enough to talk. How about the other guys you mentioned yesterday?"

"I just finished going over all the reports. The rest of them look clean from my perspective. Granted, some of them might be hiding stuff better, but usually they're not that smart. So, like I said, they look clean."

"And as if you don't have enough on your plate, has Greg given you any pointers on where to start with the people at that Neptune squadron, Patrol Squadron VP-3, nicknamed the Gannets?"

Scott smiled and answered, "Oh, yea. He and my borrowed agents are hot on that project right now while I'm stuck here doing paperwork. Greg did point to several possible bad guys and they're doing their BIs first. I hope to have something for you in the next day or two. Sooner, if possible."

"Thank you, sir!" I said. "That will be perfect. We'll be rounding up the drug sellers either tomorrow or Wednesday so that might spook anyone involved with the squadron. Pass that info on to Greg so he can be alert to the possibility."

"Can do, boss," said Scott with a big smile.

123

KELLY ANNOUNCED EARLY THAT MORNING that she'd be at college all afternoon and into the night, catching up on her schoolwork. No idea when she would be home. Graduation was about a month off and she wanted to get that degree. Doc and I picked up some Chinese food on the way to the house. I was too tired to even think about cooking.

On the kitchen counter where it could not be overlooked lay a note from Kelly.

> *Hi, Sailor!*
> *Since without my supervision you will probably want to goof off tonight ... don't. There is a minor task that needs to be done. Pull together all of your receipts from this operation before you and Doc finish off all the beer. I want to send them, and the proposed budget, to David ASAP.*
> *Love you so much, K.*

I passed the note to Doc. "Okay, Doc, do you know what she's talking about with this budget thing?"

He snickered and passed it back to me. "This is just another case of the skipper, and the future Mrs. Colt, taking good care of you. Last week when the CNO and Mrs. CNO dropped by for a visit, you passed on joining them for lunch. David filled me in the other day on all their discussions about you."

"Well, that'll teach me to skip a free lunch. Got some details you can share?"

"Over lunch, the CNO, Captain Miller, and Sam were planning your future for the next six months—you know, the decision to keep you here in Norfolk for your health, etc. and getting me to watch over you. When the plan was finalized, the CNO asked Captain Miller's opinion. He liked it, and then he mentioned finances, and continued on to explain that in addition to paying for your house in D.C., you were footing all the bills for this operation."

"Yea, I do recall mentioning that to him the first time he came here for a planning session."

"So the brass put their heads together and decided that the CNO's office would cover the bills until you close this case. Then, using a budget based on an average of what you've already spent, the NISHQ, under a training TAD order to Norfolk, will send you a monthly expense check while you're here. David is to coordinate all the funding details and smooth over any rough spots with Admiral Chance. David wanted the existing bills so he could get you a check quickly. Kelly was there and probably remembers more of the exact details."

I chuckled. "Well, then, next time we buy the premium beer from Germany! No more Rolling Rock in the pony bottles for us, my good man."

After a quick dinner, and only one beer each, I showed Doc the safe in what was now back to being a guest room, and gave him the combination. I needed to remember to give it to Kelly, too. We grabbed all the receipts and the check book, then headed down to the kitchen table to sort them out.

Doc suggested that the food used during several planning sessions, and the extra used while the ladies were here for emotional support, should be considered an operational expense. Ditto for a portion of the normal food bill that was used to feed Doc. The cost of the Blue Beast would not be a reimbursement item, but I had no regrets on buying that car.

We were just wrapping up all the documentation to go with the receipts when Kelly made it home. As she walked into the kitchen, I expected to see her in the standard jeans and ODU sweatshirt, but that was not what walked in and got our full attention.

She was wearing a dark blue dress that came to just below her knees. This dress was on the edge of what I'd consider semi-formal attire, for better lack of proper terms—knowing fashion terms has never been a big need in my life. A wide black belt accented her outstanding figure by showing off her petite waist. Her hair was down and had a small, flipped up curl at the bottom. Simple makeup, black high heels, and a simple gold necklace finished the look.

"Wow," I stammered. "Princess Kelly is home. And you look every bit like a princess."

Doc just stared and blinked.

Kelly smiled at the compliment and did a quick twirl along with what some would consider a Rebel Yell. After I got over the shock of that, we pulled together in a hug and kiss, and she purred, "I hope you saved me a beer. It has been quite a day! This is a day for celebration, sailor!"

Doc made the 'out with it' hand sign and said, "Hurry up and kiss her. I need to know the details of whatever caused all this!"

She gave me a big kiss and pulled back from my embrace for another twirl. "Boys, keep the evening of May twenty-fifth open. I don't care if the entire Navy base is on fire and you're the only ones with extinguishers, you both will be at my graduation ceremony that night. Today I successfully defended my thesis, and I passed with a 3.85 GPA. Work on my master's degree is completely done." And with that, she twirled again while letting out yet another scream.

For the first time in my life, I was so happy that tears were rolling down my cheeks. I grabbed her with my good arm and swung her around the kitchen. Doc kept out of the way and grabbed three beers from the fridge. Time to celebrate!

124

A LOT HAD GONE ON the previous night. We'd stayed up late, between Kelly calling her parents and the Millers with the great news, to letting out her emotions while describing the day's events and faculty reactions. Not to mention that we probably had one more beer than we should have. Because of all that, Doc and I were moving a bit slowly that morning. My appointment for the check up with the surgeon was at 0800 hrs and we were almost running late.

As Doc and I entered the hospital just a few minutes before 0800 and started to scan the directory board in hopes of quickly finding his office, a familiar voice asked "You gentlemen look lost. Need some help?"

We turned to see the smiling face of Ann. Her shift was over and she was about to leave when we were spotted. She led us to the surgeon's office and asked me if it was okay for her to sit in on the checkup. Doc was vigorously nodding behind her back.

"Sure, Ann, you've been involved with this arm trauma since day one, so you earned a spot on the team. Maybe between you and Doc translating, I'll understand what the guy tells me."

The nurse called us in and started unwrapping the bandages Doc had just put on an hour ago. She was nearly finished when the surgeon, Lieutenant Jack Ambrose, strolled in to join us.

"Looks like a party in here, Mr. Colt. I see you brought not only your personal corpsman but have confiscated one of ours as well. Good morning, Petty Officer Holt."

She glanced down and softly said, "Hello, Doctor."

"Doctor, Ann is here at my request. She was the first one to work on me in the OR, and due to her swift actions, I owe her my life. Since then, she's been working off and on with Corpsman Stevens here to try to keep me out of trouble and off your 'bad patient' list, assuming you have one of those. I figured she deserved to hear whatever wisdom you share with us this morning."

As he looked down at my sad-looking arm lying on the exam table's elevated tray, he started gently poking. "Fine with me, sir. Looks like the healing process is going well. Very little redness around the wound is positive. These two corpsmen have done a good job keeping the wound clean and properly reapplying the splint." He tested the area for feeling, and as he did the previous week, checked each of my fingers for feeling. All was looking good, he said.

"And when can I get out of this sling and splint?"

"You're stuck with that for at least another three to five weeks, sir. Any sooner and you risk the chance of causing permanent damage. Granted, your rehab will be more painful and a bit longer due to the atrophy of the muscles, but that was a deep laceration and your muscles need time to heal properly. Your strength and full use of the arm will return. Unlike the poor guy I worked on last Thursday. A couple of overaggressive SPs put two bullets into his right shoulder and it will never be the same."

Behind Ambrose, Doc was slowly shaking his head at me. I knew he saw my face cloud over as the anger built, so I tried to let it pass like he wanted. However, I was surprised to see Ann's face get red and her fists clench.

"Excuse me, Doctor Ambrose. Do you know why that guy was shot?" she asked with just a touch of anger in her voice.

"No, Holt, I did not get any further details about the guy. I just know he suffered needless extensive damage. Why?"

"Sir, with all due respect, he was holding a gun to the head of my best friend and roommate, Yeoman Rhonda Evans, and he was verbally threatening to shoot her and others. And the two men who shot him did so to protect her, the other sailors in the office, and themselves, as a last resort. I have no sympathy for that piece of trash. And neither of the gentlemen was overaggressive in their actions as they could easily have shot to kill." Ann was getting more hostile and louder with each word.

The doctor did not appreciate being spoken to in that manner, especially by a young enlisted person, and was about to jump down Ann's throat. She just stood there with her arms crossed tightly across her chest, and it seemed she got madder by the second as the doctor started his response, "Holt, I don't appreciate ..."

"Lieutenant, stop right there," I ordered sharply.

"Sir, I will not be talked to in that tone and manner."

"Okay, Lieutenant, try my manner and tone on for size," I offered softly and slowly. "Doctor, I greatly appreciate your surgical skills, but find major flaws with your lame inaccurate assumptions on the actions of others. Petty Officer Holt is totally correct in her evaluation of the incident except she left out that the 'piece of trash' was being arrested at the time for theft and at least one murder."

I paused a moment to let that sink in. "And I suspect her tone and manner are due to her still being stressed and damn tired from spending Thursday afternoon through Sunday night offering emotional support to her friend. A good friend who was greatly traumatized by having the bastard's gun stuck in her right ear. Holt worked round the clock with Agent Stevens, with and under the watchful eyes of a psychologist, to help Evans understand and handle all the emotions that were crashing through her head. So cut Ann some damn slack, mister."

Hearing my voice get a bit louder and harsher, I toned it back down and continued, "That's not an assumption, Doctor, or a wild guess, or hearsay. I know all this for a fact because my fiancée, a psychologist, and I hosted both of these ladies, and Agent Stevens, at our house through the end of the weekend. All three of them were with us from about an hour after Agent Stevens and I each shot the bastard 'piece of trash' in question until Ann's work shift started late Sunday night."

The old adage about seeing someone's jaw drop came true with both the doctor and his nurse. I had never seen that happen and if I weren't so angry, I probably would have broken out in laughter. I finished up giving the doctor one last thought, "And as Navy SEALs as well as NIS Special Agents, Stevens and I fully understand the difference between our reasonable actions and being overly aggressive."

It took the doctor more than a moment to reply, "Sir, if an apology is necessary, please consider it offered."

"Doctor, we have a situation here with multiple wrongs involving multiple people mixed with some wild emotions, and rather than waste time apologizing back and forth, we need to learn from it. None of us should make wild assumptions. And we all need to work on controlling our emotions and tempers, which is often hard to do. Best thing is to move on and forget the last few minutes ever happened. Okay?"

Both the doctor and Ann nodded in approval and each mumbled a quick "Yes, sir." Doc gave me a thumbs up from his position behind their backs. The nurse gave a quick nod and smile.

"Good. I would tell you and Ann to kiss and make up, but since Agent Stevens is her boyfriend that might result in another shooting. And none of us have time for that! So can you please wrap me back up, give us our orders for the next stage of proper care, and tell me when you want to see me again. There are more bad guys out there we need to catch."

The doctor smiled and quickly said, "Aye, aye, sir, and thank you."

125

AS WE LEFT THE HOSPITAL, Doc stopped us when we were near the car. "Marcus, I keep thinking of you as just my brother who crawled through the jungle with me and saved my butt. And it isn't until times like now, with that jerk doctor, that you show me you're the totally cool, ass kicking, super-intimidating, take no prisoners, outstanding leader, professional Navy officer, sir. I gotta say you handled that situation better than I would have. I wanted to shoot him in the knees."

"Thanks, Doc. I considered the assassination route also," I chuckled.

Ann looked like she was going to throw up. She started to get tears in her eyes and said, "Sir, I am so sorry for that outburst. I don't know what came over me. I guess I should go apologize to Doctor Ambrose. I'm so sorry, sir."

I shook my head and placed my hand on her shoulder, "Ann, pay close attention as we have a two-sided situation here. As an officer, Petty Officer Holt, hereby consider yourself admonished for speaking rather harshly to a naval officer. Granted, he deserved it for making such wild ass and totally foolish assumptions, but there are less confrontational ways of straightening his sorry butt out. Work on your diplomacy skills, Holt."

That got a slight giggle out of her. I continued with my counseling, "Now as your friend, and one of the guys who you were so eloquently defending, I was so proud of you I could just bust and so honored to know you have our backs no matter what the consequences. Thank you, Ann that means a lot to me and Doc."

"Thank you, sir," she said as she wiped her eyes and smiled at me.

"And by the way, in case you're wondering, we do not go around shooting or assassinating people, even if they so richly deserve it. That's just more of our strange humor. And on the serious side, there is one other part of the learning experience: I just did something wrong in there. As you each grow in your leadership positions, do not dress down someone in front of others. Take them aside in private. I'm sorry that I let my anger get the best of me. No excuse. Learn from that, people."

They both nodded their understanding. Doc came over and put his arm around Ann's shoulder and led her to the car. I stood there and enjoyed seeing two of my good friends sharing a tender moment. Sometimes they are rare things.

We dropped Ann off at her barracks and headed to the NISRA offices. We had missed much of Sam's meeting, but we would not be out there picking up the trash, so to speak, as they rounded up the druggies. We'd be hunkered down in the NISRA since they didn't need a one-armed guy getting in the way. Besides, someone had to answer the phones, and it was our turn.

It was good to see CPO Joe Devland in attendance. That meant the SEALs were on board for this shindig, along with the SP contingency. The Shore Patrol Commanding Officer, Captain Simon Lavella, was there with a commander who I assumed was his XO. We had the manpower we needed to clean up the place.

We got there just in time to hear about the arrest of Seaman Carlos Menendez. The original plan was to just bring him in for questioning, but since he decided to run when the agents identified themselves to him in his barracks, earlier, he'd been arrested. Too bad for him that his sprint to freedom didn't have much endurance. The two agents caught him before he got down the stairs to the first floor. His immediate claim that he "didn't do nothing" was considered gospel by the agents since the use of a double negative became a positive.

Bill Collins was in the process of searching the seaman's gear in hopes of finding some solid evidence of what he did do. That evidence hopefully would firm up the financial concerns that Scott had uncovered. Darrell

Tasker and Joe Mabry would be handling his interrogation as soon as the meeting was over.

The operation, now dubbed "Street Sweeper," was scheduled to kick off on Thursday morning. It would take the rest of the day to finalize the plan of attack and establish the areas where the SP and SEALs would be deployed. Captain Miller and Lieutenant Greg Kensey would be talking with JAG that day to get sufficient attorneys in place to handle the influx of bad guys, and the XO was working to set up the base gym as a processing center.

Then Wednesday, while the agents finalized the list of suspects and helped get the admin staff in place at the gym, Devland and Lavella would use the day to bring the SEALs and SP teams up to speed on their specific tasks. The hardest part of it all would be keeping it a secret as more people were brought into the loop.

With the meeting over, and the crew dispersed to do their jobs, I made my way to the coffee mess for my first cup. The visit with the surgeon messed up my caffeine schedule. Heading down the hall, I took a minute to say hello to the ladies in the office across the hall. I noticed that Laura had a new photo on her wall. Karen and Dexter were standing in front of her fireplace. It was a nice addition to her collection.

I also stuck my head in the AUTOVON room and chatted with Rhonda and Dexter. Dex said he expected a report from me on the quality of the coffee, since this was the first pot that Rhonda had made without his guidance. Keep the antacids handy, he offered. She just shook her head at the friendly jab from Dex. I left them to work it out.

LTCOL J. Scott Tiller was in his office when I paused at the open door. I knocked on the door casing and asked, "Got a minute?"

"Sure, Marcus, come on in. What's on your mind?"

"I need to talk about some thoughts. And I need the opinion of someone that knows what is going on around here, yet doesn't have the locked-in mindset of an agent. No disrespect intended, but you're about the only one around here that fits that group."

Scott laughed and replied, "I'm not offended because what you say it true. What's your theory?"

"More like random, somewhat connected thoughts than a theory. We've got drugs, Cubans, Gitmo, airplanes, local distribution, Mexico, Venezuela, Raffe, and his relatives, all pointing to a drug network that we believe Raffe set up when he was in Gitmo. We're working the local distribution issues, and we, well at least you, are looking into the squadron as possible mules. But so far, we haven't talked about how drugs get from Venezuela to Cuba or how they get on base at Gitmo. Or what the heck Mexico has to do with it."

"I can see we have a bunch of pieces of a puzzle that are all turned face down right this minute. I can see a couple of starting points. How about you?"

"Right now, my only thought is that we need to start digging into the aircraft maintenance people at Gitmo. And I need to figure out how to do that quietly."

"Right answer, Mr. Colt, and you came to the right office. Let me start doing some quiet BI digging. We'll use the same excuse we gave the CO at the Logistics Center. I'll make some calls to determine which unit does the maintenance down there and get started."

"Thanks, Scott. Let me know if you need any extra pull with the NISRA Gitmo staff. I can make a couple of calls."

"Not a problem, Marcus, since my future career is doing BIs, I'm getting pretty good at asking for help in such a way that they don't hate me. However, if I hit any roadblocks, I'll scream for help. I ain't proud as the saying goes."

"Well, life will be easier if we ever get our hands on Raffe. I'm surprised that snake hasn't raised his head."

"He is slippery, you gotta give him that. And second puzzle piece that I can help turn over for you is to make a call to a buddy in the Bureau of Narcotics and Dangerous Drugs, also known as the BNDD, even though it's awkward to say. Maybe they'll have some info on the movement of drugs from Venezuela to Cuba. And they also might have knowledge about what all is going on in the Brownsville, Texas area. Always a good thing to keep contacts with our sister agencies. Now get out of my office, boss, I have work to do."

I gave him a quick nod and closed the door on the way out.

126

AN EARLY LUNCH CONSISTED OF Doc running down to the cafeteria for grab-and-go sandwiches and sodas. We stayed in the file room to keep out of the way, and continued digging through evidence boxes looking for more links. Adding the Neptune squadron, Gitmo, and Texas into the mix forced another look at all the evidence, with those new group parameters in mind.

Sam came into the file room and he wasn't smiling. "Marcus, can you and Doc handle a quick investigation of an attempted suicide? Hate to ask, but I have all the other agents covered up with Street Sweeper."

"No problem, Sam, give Doc the address and we are on the way."

Suicides are horrible and I hated investigating them. Someone reaches a point in their life where ending the mental and emotional pain seems to be the lesser of two evils. In their way of thinking, it has become the only way to stop the hurt. Their reasons for the pains vary from victim to victim. No two reasons are identical.

But there are some constants in suicide: the victim controls the method, time, and place of death. And there's one other constant that the victims all seem to overlook: the extreme pain of family and friends left behind, which goes on forever. At least this one was an attempted; maybe it wouldn't be so bad.

We headed over to the BOQ. The caller who reported the incident had notified the SP office, saying he was a friend of the victim. The SP OOD had in turn called the hospital to dispatch an ambulance, and then called NISRA Norfolk. As we pulled the Blue Beast into the parking lot and stopped next to the SP jeeps, we saw two SPs talking with a Lieutenant Junior Grade (LTJG) who was extremely animated. No ambulance was around, so it must have already returned to the hospital.

"Like I said, it was horrible. Blood everywhere, sir. And Richard was just lying on his bed," said the LTJG to the SP Lieutenant as we walked up to them. Doc flashed his ID and introduced us. The LTJG seemed to calm down a bit, or maybe his adrenalin was exhausted from all the emotion. "Can I go now?" he asked.

"Sorry, no," I said. "Agent Stevens, please take this officer to his room and take his statement. Keep him there." They left and I turned to the SP Lieutenant, whose name tag identified him as Anderson. "Lieutenant Anderson, what is left to do around here? I assume you want NIS to take the lead."

"Yes, sir, Mr. Colt, you've got control. We've just started taking the caller's statement and have secured the victim's room. Not many people around right now, but I have two men checking each room in the BOQ. The victim was alive when transported, but his head is a mess. It looks like he meant to do a brain shot, but instead lowered the weapon and shot through the temple below the brain. That .38 round took out his eyes. Damn ugly mess with one eyeball hanging out on his cheek."

I shook my head and sighed. "Suicides are never pretty, Mr. Anderson. I suspect he added to whatever mental issues he has by blinding himself instead of dying. He'll probably be in psychiatric care for some time."

"By the way, sir, it's good to see you out and around so soon. I doubt that you remember me from the night you were stabbed last week, but I was one of the first people on the scene. I helped get you down so the medics could work on you. You are a fighter, that's for sure. How's the arm doing?"

"I appreciate your help that night. I don't remember much except you guys were quick to arrive and that helped save a few lives, mine included. Please express my appreciation to your crew. As for the arm, it was a really deep slash and I have a few more weeks in the sling, and then get to do rehab. So they tell me it will be months before I'm back to normal. But that's better than being dead."

Anderson smiled and nodded. "You reacted well considering your injury, Mr. Colt. Impressive control of your weapon in that situation. Don't know if they told you, sir, but you left a hell of a lot of blood behind. I'm just glad the medics got there when they did 'cause you were more than a quart low. And have fun in rehab. I had a few weeks there for a broken leg last year. It was the closest thing I seen to a medieval torture chamber."

We got a good laugh from that thought. He handed me a card with his name and phone numbers. "Give me a call if you ever need anything, sir, anything at all. My friends call me Clyde. Oh, yea, sir, I like your car; nice to see NIS has some class!"

"Thanks, Clyde. I appreciate that," I replied. Calling him 'Clyde' seemed to make his day. And I quickly added him to my growing list of friends in the Tidewater area. He and the other SPs departed after finding only one other officer in the building, who said he didn't hear anything.

With nothing else to do in the parking lot, I headed into the BOQ to check in with Doc. Doc was wrapping up the interview with the sole witness, so I left him to it and continued on to the victim's room.

Upon entering the victim's room, several things quickly became apparent. His name, based on the stack of mail on the dresser, was Ensign Richard E. Less. Easy to imagine the nickname he had to tolerate in OCS, and probably earlier in high school and college. What the hell was his parents' thinking? That might be part of his problem, but I let Kelly worry about mental things like that.

There was nothing here to indicate his unit, so I'd need to contact the housing officer to find out that information. But first, the scene needed to be handled.

Blood splatter on the bed and wall indicated he was sitting on the side of the bed facing the dresser when he shot himself. And the splatter showed he was right handed. A Colt Detective Special snub-nosed revolver was lying on the bed with blood also splattered on it.

Doc came in and looked around. "Yep, LTJG Coldman was right: there is blood everywhere."

"Oh, yea, and we have a suicide note. What did Coldman tell you?"

Looking around at the mess and shaking his head, Doc filled me in on the weak comments from Coldman. "I bet he knows more, but he ain't talking to me. Felt like I was a Gestapo agent in an old World War II movie and all I got was name, rank, and serial number. To be more useful, I'll go get the camera."

"And grab a handful of evidence bags because it looks like we may have found another Raffe link," I said.

His suicide note, found on the table near the window, was neatly printed and included his signature and that day's date. It was far away enough from the victim that no blood had hit it. And once I got past the standard "I cannot handle life anymore" crap, followed by "I am such a failure" bull, I found an interesting line that read he was "tired of the drugs and being forced to do things." The word *drugs* in the note raised a big red flag for me.

In just a few minutes, Doc returned and was busy shooting photos of everything in the room and from every different angle. I took a moment to step out of his way and find our favorite non-cooperative LTJG.

LTJG Ron Coldman was in his room, sitting next to the window, looking out in deep thought. His room was neat and there was no clutter anywhere. I knocked on the door casing since the door was open, and he quickly looked over.

"Got a minute, Coldman?" I asked quietly.

"Sure, sir, how can I help?"

"How close are you to Ensign Less?"

His face took on a concerned look as he answered, "Not very, sir. Ricky and I have talked a bit, and did spend an evening drinking at the O Club once a couple of months ago, but not much more than that. We just didn't have much in common."

"Does he use drugs?"

"Not that I have seen, sir."

"Do you?"

"Hell no, sir!"

"Will you submit to a blood test?"

"Of course, sir. Any time, any place. I don't use drugs. Search my room."

I expected the "hell, no" answer, but I was pleased to hear him agree to a test. If he were really using, he would've found a way to avoid an answer, while opening up to a search meant he had nothing to hide there in his room. Of course, he could have hidden it elsewhere. We would check his room, duty station, and vehicle.

"Okay, I believe you, Coldman." Not really, I thought as I continued, but I needed to put him at ease. "Did you know that Ensign Less was selling drugs?"

"No, but then, we didn't spend much time together, sir."

"Who are his close friends?"

"Sorry, sir, I have no idea. Like I said, we didn't spend much time together."

"Ever hear him talk about a guy named Raffe? Paul Raffe?"

"No, sir, but we don't spend …"

My voice got harsher and louder. "Yea, I know, you didn't spend time together. I've heard that too damn many times from you already." I quickly cut him off at the knees to throw him off balance a bit. "Who did he spent time with, Coldman? I need some names right now or you will face obstruction of justice charges, and I will make your life more miserable than it is right now."

"I don't know, sir. But I think Ensign Chuck Dawson might be a good friend of his. They're in the same squadron and always seemed to hang out together. He should be able to help you. You can find him on duty right now at one of the ASW squadrons over at the air station. He works in the maintenance department of, uh, well, I'm not sure of the squadron number, but I think they fly Neptunes."

Again, my lack of trust with coincidences holds firm.

127

A QUICK PHONE CALL GOT Sam up to date on our investigation. When I mentioned the victim's name, he paused while flipping through some papers. Ensign Less was part of Raffe's old squadron. Sam said he'd bring Scott up to speed and get him some help with the squadron BIs, starting with Ensigns Dawson and Less.

Sam and I talked it over and decided it was time to round up and sequester the entire squadron. As Doc and I drove over to start looking around, Sam coordinated with the SPs and a few agents to descend upon the squadron in full force, ASAP.

Sam also asked Captain Miller to call Commander Eric Zimmerman, CO of the Patrol Squadron VP-3, and let him know what was coming his way. He'd need to immediately call in all off-duty crews while saying nothing about why. Just get them there and hold them, isolated.

Our phone call to the hospital let us know that Ensign Less was still in surgery. We wouldn't have a chance to interrogate him for at least five more hours, and that was assuming he survived the surgery. A couple of SPs were dispatched to watch over him in case his suicide was a staged event. Not likely, but nothing could be assumed.

All the needed photos had been taken, and evidence had been bagged and tagged. The Ensign's room had been sealed and locked. Doc and I headed over to the NAS to find Ensign Chuck Dawson. So much for us investigating a simple attempted suicide.

For once, something in this investigation went rather well. As we opened the door of the squadron's building, we literally bumped into Ensign Chuck Dawson as he came rushing out.

"Ensign, where is the fire?" Doc asked as he held up his ID and we led him over to the side of the building out of public view. "We need to talk right now."

"Sorry, sir. I have a date waiting at the O Club. How can I help NIS?"

On the drive over, Doc had asked if he could lead the interview. I think he could see I was getting tired and more irritable as the day progressed. And he needed the practice. So I agreed. Now I'd just need to keep quiet—often a challenge for me.

"Mr. Dawson, tell us about your buddy, Ensign Less," said Doc with a serious look.

"Sorry, sir, what do you want to know?"

"Start with something simple like where is he right now?" Doc asked as he pulled out his note pad.

Dawson looked down and mumbled some profanity. Then he looked up at the sky and said, with a deep sigh, "Okay, I knew this would end up bad, but he asked—no, actually he begged me. Right now, he is about an hour south of here flying to Cuba at around 200 mph. He wanted to make today's flight, and I worked it out for him to go under the pretense of checking on an infrequent sonar glitch. Normally, he doesn't fly and calibrates all the equipment on the ground, but wanted the experience of seeing Gitmo. Why?"

"Did you talk with him here before he got on the craft?"

"No, sir, I saw him from a distance and he waved as he boarded. He was the last one to board right before takeoff."

"So you cannot be sure it was Ensign Less that boarded the aircraft. Right?"

Dawson held up his hands in a symbol of disbelief, "Well, who the hell else could it be, sir?"

Doc continued with the interrogation while I slipped away to find a phone. Sam answered, and I shared what we'd discovered already. And asked that he verify the guy in the hospital actually was Richard Less. Right now, there was doubt. Granted not much doubt, but enough to need verification. I shared with Sam my belief that Raffe was on the aircraft heading to Gitmo.

With the interrogation finished, Doc ordered Dawson to return to his office and remain there until we called for him. I told Doc about my request to Sam and then asked his opinion of Dawson's story.

"I think Dawson is a total idiot and got played by Richard Less, who is almost as stupid and probably under orders from his drug boss Raffe. Seems to me that Raffe took his uniform and boarded the flight in his place. If I were taking bets, my gut is telling me Raffe was armed and the aircraft has been hijacked. When it lands in Gitmo, Raffe will find a way to get off before anyone can stop him, and he'll vanish into Cuba. He is running, Marcus."

I smiled and enjoyed seeing Doc put the pieces together quickly. Now came the hard part. "Agreed, Doc. Now what the heck do we do next?"

128

WE SHARED OUR THEORY WITH the squadron CO, but he was not convinced. He wanted to contact the aircraft and talk with the pilot about the situation. I explained that since Raffe was a qualified P2V pilot, he may have taken full control of the aircraft. It was best not to let him know we were on to his plan. I was finally able to talk the CO down from making that call, and suggested we check on the position of the aircraft with the control tower. He made the call to the air traffic controllers.

Radar check showed the flight wasn't on course. It normally flew along the coast, fifteen to one hundred miles offshore. That meant a flight distance of nearly 1,500 miles, with flight time to Gitmo normally being eight hours. Since the takeoff had been just over an hour ago, in normal circumstances we'd have at least six hours before the landing in Cuba.

However, normal was not in vogue right then, and the course the aircraft was taking was more of a direct flight toward Cuba. But at least they were maintaining cruising speed of a little under 200 mph. The 'as the crow flies' distance is around 1,150 miles, so assuming they maintained that same speed, they'd land in Cuba just over four hours from now, instead of the usual six. Neither case allowed much time for planning, but Raffe's current beeline directly to Cuba was worse for us.

Sam arrived at the same time as the XO of the Gannets. The XO said that all ground and air crews had been secured in the maintenance hangar, except for those in the air. In addition to our potentially hijacked flight, there was a P2V and crew sitting in Cuba, getting ready to make a return flight to Norfolk later that day. Sam told us that several agents and a contingency of SPs were in route, and the agents would start interrogations upon arrival.

Sam also said he'd contacted NISRA Gitmo; they were in the process of sequestering the P2V personnel. The entire base had gone on lockdown and additional Marine patrols were in place.

The five of us moved to the briefing room, where we could see a large map of the east coast and Caribbean area and had a conference table. We didn't have much time, so we put hypotheticals into high gear. The CO thought a hijacking to a Cuban airport was possible: Raffe could get points from Castro's people for giving them a Navy aircraft. Sam discounted him landing at the Gitmo field, since he'd be immediately surrounded by SPs and armed Marines.

The XO thought Venezuela might be the destination, but immediately shot his own theory down due to distance. The P2V has a max range of 2,150 miles and it's around 2,200 to the closest Venezuelan airport, in Caracas. Even running the engines very lean, making it there would be a push.

Sam vocalized his idea about a possible landing at a remote civilian airport in Cuba. The CO thought that unlikely since most remote airports would be too small for the P2V. Then he suggested Raffe might do a parachute jump over Cuba and let the P2V land at Gitmo. I had to admit, that was the most likely thing so far.

The CO checked with air traffic control again on the P2V's location. Things had changed and it was now heading toward Puerto Rico. Same speed and altitude, which meant that arrival time over PR would be just under four hours. The theories brought up the same problems as with a landing in Gitmo: lots of local US Navy around PR.

While looking at the map during this Puerto Rico discussion, I glanced down to Venezuela. The drugs had been coming from there, and it would be logical for Raffe to run there to hide. But the aircraft didn't have the legs to make it. But a lot of small boats travel from Venezuela to the small resort island of Aruba. Where there was little military presence.

"Skipper, what is the flying distance to Aruba from here?" I asked.

"XO, look that up quickly," ordered the CO.

After a moment looking at a chart, the XO replied, "Aruba is just over 1,700 miles, skipper. It's doable in a P2V. Based on their current speed and location, they should be in Aruba in about six hours."

"And what aircraft do we have available that can put Doc and me on Aruba ahead of the P2V?"

"Not sure, Mr. Colt. I know we can get a SEAL team out of PR there in about three hours, or one out of Key West."

"And we need to do that. Actually, make it two teams if they're available. But skipper, none of them can identify Raffe. I'm the only one who can."

The CO leaned back and looked at the overhead for a moment. "If we had a P2V fueled and ready, it could make it, but we don't have one ready, and by the time we do, it will be too late."

The XO smiled and offered, "We can rustle an F-4 from Oceana and get Mr. Colt down there in time."

Doc jumped in, "We will need two of them. I go wherever Mr. Colt goes."

"Okay, skipper, who do we call to borrow two F-4 Phantoms?" I asked with a smile.

129

WHILE WE WERE RUNNING TO the car, the Gannets' skipper was on the phone to the CO of the VF-83, the Hooligans, giving him a heads-up that two aircraft would be needed ASAP for two NIS agents on their way over. The F-4 squadron skipper was not a happy person and proceeded to tell him, in no uncertain terms, that it was not possible.

Doc drove us over to Oceana with little regard to the posted speed limits. Sam had called in a favor from the NPD Chief, and a police escort was waiting outside the gate of the base as we left. We quickly entered the squadron offices and went to see the commanding officer, CDR Alexander Marcaise. We saw on the door that his call sign was "Claymore," so deducing a Scottish heritage was easy—especially after seeing his flaming red hair.

"Commander, I believe you are expecting us. I am Lieutenant Commander Marcus Colt and this is SA Donald Stevens. We're from NIS and are chasing an extremely bad guy who has hijacked a P2V. We need to get to Aruba ASAP and we understand you can help us do that."

"Not going to happen, Mr. Colt. We are not an aerial taxi service."

Expecting some form of negativity, I had my 'get out of jail free' card handy and passed it and my credentials to the CO. He looked the card over on both sides before passing them back to me. His snort when he read the card gave me a clue about his intentions.

"Sorry, Colt, but I don't believe a chair-warmer has that leverage," he responded with a slight sneer as he leaned back in his chair. "Delta Air Lines can probably get you there fast enough."

I held back my growing anger and picked up his phone without asking. For that I got a rather evil look, but I dialed a special number and pressed the speaker phone button. Even at this hour, I knew who would be there to answer.

"Office of the Chief of Naval Operations, Master Chief Bartow speaking, how may I be of assistance, sir?" barked David.

"SA268 for the Admiral ASAP."

"Hold on, sir."

"Marcus, what the hell did you injure this time?" asked the Admiral with a slight chuckle.

"Good afternoon, Admiral Gallagher. Physically, I'm doing well, or at least as good as can be expected. I have a problem with the case. Our prime suspect for the CI murders has probably hijacked a P2V and is heading out of the country. We don't believe the suspect knows that we know. We'll need one or two SEAL teams at the Aruba airport in about three hours. There are teams in either Puerto Rico or Key West right now. Ask their leader to call Sam Maker for instructions."

"Can do. David, make the call."

"Admiral, I'm on speaker phone here at the office of VF-83 trying to convince the CO, Commander Marcaise, to loan NIS, or rather me, a pair of F-4s so Sam and I can quickly fly to Aruba and catch the bastard when he lands there. The Commander is rather reluctant to do so, sir, and does not have faith in my special card." As I spoke, Marcaise was getting paler with each of my words.

"Marcaise, do you trust that I am who Marcus said I am?"

"Sir, yes, sir," Marcaise replied, standing almost at attention.

"Like his special card says, Lieutenant Commander Marcus Colt, the guy with his left arm in a sling, is working directly for me, and I do not appreciate this delay in his request. Can I feel comfortable that you will do as he asks now that we've had this little chat?"

"Sir, yes, sir. Sorry for the delay, sir," Marcaise stammered.

"Thank you, Commander. Marcus, take care of Doc and yourself, give my love to Kelly, and go get that damn bastard. Gallagher out."

I felt sorry for Marcaise, but sometimes we can be our own worst enemies. He pressed the off button on the phone to kill the dial tone and sat down behind his desk. His ruddy complexion was back and even redder, and I hoped he was not going to stroke out on me.

"Commander, I am sorry about that, but we need to get moving."

"Yes, sir, Mr. Colt. My apologies for doubting you. It just seemed so unreal, you know, like a joke another squadron would play, and I don't have time for fun right now." He picked up his phone and dialed a number. "Rooster, get Kooter to the ready room yesterday. Call down and have two 'up toys' ready to fly in thirty minutes. No RIOs. Full fuel. Have the Paraloft get ready to have two new guys fitted for torso harnesses, G suits, helmets and survival vests. And by the way, you're in charge until we get back."

He looked up at me and said, "We will need two mid-air refuelings to get down there quick. Am I authorized to set that up?"

"Sounds like a good plan. I can't swim well with only one arm. Call whoever you need to make it happen, skipper." That comment got a partial smile out of him.

I suspected the skids were already being greased by one excellent master chief who had stayed to listen on the line. He'd probably called the admirals in charge of air operations all down the Atlantic coast and told them to expect calls for assistance. Based on the quick affirmative responses that Marcaise got, I was right. I asked Marcaise to instruct them not to mention our destination over the radio since we didn't know if Raffe was monitoring. Our flight would be designated as a training flight from Norfolk down south and back.

As Doc and I were helped into the flight suits by the crew chiefs, the skipper introduced the other pilot, CDR Steve Koots, call sign Kooter, who was the XO of the squadron. Not being aware of the call to the CNO, Kooter was a lot friendlier than the CO and asked an important question.

"How much flight time have you two had?"

I smiled and said, "We have a lot of miles as passengers on Delta and United if that counts." I gave the skipper a wink.

Doc laughed and added, "We also have some C-130 passenger time to scenic spots around Nam last year. Marcus doesn't remember them all since he was in a coma from his head wound on one flight."

Marcaise frowned and said, "So you two really aren't the chair-warmers I pegged you for?"

I just shrugged and Doc decided to elaborate, "Sir, SEALs are never considered chair-warmers. Mr. Colt has ..."

I quickly cut him off, "That's enough, Doc. These gentlemen have enough on their minds right now. Maybe they'll let us buy them a beer when this mess is over and we can swap lies then. Until then, mind on the mission, please."

"Aye, aye, sir."

Knowing now that we were fighter virgins, they proceeded to explain too many things way too fast. But we did our best to keep up and even asked a few questions that seemed to make them happy. We were to use their call signs when in flight, and if we didn't vomit all over their toys, we might get our own call signs before the mission is over.

Entry into the F-4 cockpit usually requires two hands. In my case, the second hand was Doc's, as he shoved against my butt to help get me up there. The crew chief helped plug me in and showed me what not to touch and how to communicate with the pilot. Then he handed me two barf bags—just in case, he said. I thanked him for his forethought and consideration, and he laughed as he thanked me for flying Phantom Air.

After a takeoff acceleration which I wish my 'Cuda had, we leveled off at 30,000 feet and headed south. Claymore told me that the communications turned on now were strictly between our and Kooter's aircraft. He would be monitoring the ATC channel while we chatted amongst ourselves.

Then I heard Kooter ask Doc about my arm. I tried to tell Doc to be quiet, but it seemed my mic key wasn't working. I didn't know that Claymore had full control of the radio and wanted to hear the story. Naturally, Doc proceeded to describe the bad guy who tried to kill me with his knife last week, and how I dropped him with two .45 rounds to the chest while I was bleeding out, right before I shot the other guy trying to knife the Chief.

Then he went on to describe my wound and his role in keeping me alive. And oh, yea, the men shot worked for the guy we were trying to catch that day. And then he proceeded to describe the previous Thursday's shooting event. It was starting to sound like all I did was go around shooting people. *Damn it, Doc, shut the hell up.*

"Mr. Colt," said Claymore. "We're now talking just between you and me. Is what I just heard true?"

"Yes, sir, but Doc has a tendency to talk too much. Just forget about all that."

"Mr. Colt, I'm sorry for the way I treated you guys earlier. I would appreciate being on your 'good guy' list, or at least on the 'might be a good guy' list." Then he chuckled and continued, "And I sure as hell don't want to be on your 'bad guy' list. And please call me Alex when we're not flying."

"Only if you drop the Mr. and stick with Marcus, Claymore."

"I appreciate that, Marcus. I get you don't like to talk about yourself, but can I ask two questions?"

"Sure, you can ask, but I might not answer."

"Fair enough. Is your partner actually a SEAL? He doesn't seem to have enough meat on his bones for that role."

I chuckled at that one and replied, "Oh, yes, he has been one for most of his career. His nickname of Doc comes from him being a hospital corpsman for the team. He might be slight, but he could take you apart easily."

"Amazing. And who is the Kelly that the CNO mentioned?"

"Another long story, Claymore. Short version is I started working for the CNO in January on this special investigation and came to Norfolk the first part of last month, undercover as an enlisted man. After being here for just a week, I met and fell in love with an adorable lady. It was only after we both verbally expressed love to each other that she happened to mention her dad is the CNO. I didn't know she's his daughter, and she didn't know I was working for him undercover. After we stopped laughing about it all, we got engaged less than two weeks after meeting. And so far, my future father-in-law is happy with the situation. True story."

"No shit? Wow. Not too many dull moments in your life, are there. When you're ready to settle down to a calmer life, become a Radar Intercept Officer and we'll go do some Wild Weasel stuff in Nam. It will be relaxing for you," he said with a laugh.

130

THE SUN WAS HEADING DOWN as we heard the radio announce "Texaco. Angels fifteen." It was time for our mid-air refueling.

"Roger, Texaco, two thirsty F-4s on a training flight heading your way. Leaving angels thirty now," replied Claymore.

Two KA-6D tankers, A-6 Intruder attack bombers converted to carry four fuel tanks, came out of NAS Jacksonville and met us about 300 miles east of Jacksonville Beach. The radio came alive with their chatter.

"Double Ugly one and two, this is Texaco one and two. We forgot our window washer fluid, but happy to top off your tanks with high test whenever you're ready. Basket is extended."

"Roger, Texaco flight. 12:00 twenty miles." Claymore continued to chat with the pilot of the tanker as we closed the distance. "Coming in now. Prepare for contact." Time to get our tanks topped off.

I was glad there was enough light to watch the refueling. It was very interesting. My first thought was it looked like a drunken mating dance between two aircraft that eventually succeeded in making the connection. It's something I suspect takes a lot of practice. Claymore hit the basket immediately and topped off our tanks. I glanced over and saw that

Kooter was doing the same. After what seemed to be a short period of time, the probe pulled back from the basket and Claymore thanked the tanker pilots for great service.

As the tankers pulled away, Claymore got on the intercom. "Marcus, have you ever gone faster than the speed of sound?"

"My Barracuda is not that fast, sir."

"Well, let's make it happen. We have enough juice for a few minutes of fun. Kooter, try to keep up." And with that challenge, our F-4 got a swift kick in the butt as the afterburner pushed us past the sound barrier. I somewhat expected the rolls and hoped that Doc was ready for his when Kooter did his best to stay with us. I could tell Claymore was in his element and was happy.

After our few minutes of fun, Claymore checked in with NAS Norfolk ATC on a special channel and found we were now way ahead of the P2V, which had shifted its course firmly toward Aruba. I had guessed right—at least it looked that way so far. As things were going, we'd be in Aruba at least two hours before the P2V arrived. A SEAL team from Key West would be arriving about the same time as us. That should give us enough time to set our trap.

As soon as Doc and I were in the air, Sam had called the state department. Together they'd quickly worked with the government of the Netherlands and the US Consulate General in Aruba to allow armed US military aircraft to land. And more importantly, they'd agreed to allow the NIS agents, with the help of the SEALs, to carry weapons in their country and to arrest Raffe. They were happy to extradite him to the US on charges of murder and drug trafficking.

The Consulate General sent one of his diplomats, a commercial attaché—a.k.a. an undercover CIA agent—and several of the Marine guards to the airport, to work with the control tower staff and generally smooth over any rough spots the military created. Little things like our military aircraft needing to be hidden before the P2V arrived and our team needing access to the control tower. Fortunately, the Consulate General and the island's governor were in an office at the airport, just in case something needed their immediate attention.

Claymore had speculated that the P2V would declare an emergency, probably an onboard fire or drastic loss of fuel, which would require them to land in Aruba without prior agreement between the governments. Emergencies were always the best way to get easy access to any airport, he told me.

We had to hit the tankers again before we approached Aruba. Our two F-4s were allowed to land under the premise, supported by open radio communications, that they were Royal Netherlands Air Force aircraft, a common sight in Aruba. We responded accordingly and touched down shortly after 2100 hrs Eastern Standard Time.

Getting out of the F-4 was a bit more difficult than getting in, since I was tired and didn't have the crew chief there to help. Claymore helped get me unplugged and unhooked from everything. Again Doc was my 'other hand' as I carefully worked my way down the side of the aircraft.

Since the P2V wasn't due for another couple of hours, I sent Doc to confer with the SEAL team that had just arrived. I figured with him being a true SEAL he'd be able to work faster with them than I could. Claymore asked if he and Kooter could help. I asked him to get both F-4s fueled, ready to go, and out of sight. Raffe might just pull a fast one and head someplace else at the last minute. Claymore saluted and headed off with the commercial attaché to make that happen.

For a rare moment, I had nothing to do, so I went inside to find a phone. All the military had been updated and kept in the loop, but my most important personal connection was still in the dark back in Norfolk.

"Collect call from a Marcus Colt. Will you accept the charges?" asked the long-distance operator.

Kelly quickly responded, "Yes, of course, operator."

"Go ahead, Aruba." The connection was horrible. Communication from the moon was clearer than this.

"Hi Kelly. Wanted you to know Doc and I are running a bit late, as you probably noticed already. Sorry for the delay in calling, Babe, but we were out of normal phone service areas for a while at 30,000 feet," I said with a chuckle.

"Hey, sailor, great to hear your voice. Did that operator say Aruba? Like in the island near South America? Why did you fly there? Everything okay?"

"Oh, yea, we're here way down south. There is a long story to go with it, but I don't have time right now. Just wanted you to know we're safe and should be back home late tomorrow. Give Sam a call and he'll fill in all the details. Gotta run. Love ya so much."

"Good night, darling." I imagined that Kelly looked at the dead phone for a moment before hanging it up. She later told me she thought *Life is getting interesting with this man, since last week at this time he was in the hospital and this week flying down to a vacation island in the Caribbean.*

She dialed Sam's number to get the rest of the story, as that radio guy said every day at noon. The house suddenly felt lonely, but she smiled, she told me, knowing she was loved.

I went to the tower to check on things up there. There was a problem getting access, but the commercial attaché finally arrived and vouched for me. The P2V was coming straight in to Aruba, and should be on the ground in forty minutes. As Claymore had speculated, they declared a fuel emergency due to a leak in one of the wing tanks. Fire trucks were appropriately spaced along each side of the main runway, which happens to be the only one.

With the updates in my mind, I headed down to find the teams. I found Doc first, or rather he found me, since he was lurking in the shadows just outside the tower. He led me over and introduced me to the team leader, Lieutenant Jim Dockerty. "It is an honor to meet you, sir. I know some of the guys you were with last year. Bravo Zulu, sir. And thank you for including us on this." The Lieutenant looked like a weightlifter trying to hide in a tight Hawaiian print shirt.

"Mr. Dockerty, we greatly appreciate you being here. I assume Doc has laid out the situation and our plan which is, and will continue to be, very fluid because we're making it up as we go. Remember, we believe Raffe is armed, but I'd like to take him alive so I can watch him hang later—figuratively speaking, of course."

"Yes, sir, can do. We will be ready. Being this is a vacation spot, most of us have on casual clothing instead of our standard rigs. Six of our guys are now dressed as civilian ground crew so they can approach the aircraft without causing suspicion. But we're all heavily armed, of course, and Doc and I have placed three snipers at several locations. We got your back, sir."

With nothing else to do right this minute, Doc and I went inside the terminal building to quickly find the head and a cup of coffee … in that order based upon priorities. Then we needed to decide what to do next.

131

THE BLADDER BREAK AND TWO cups of coffee each helped get the creative juices flowing for both of us. Especially the much needed, long overdue bladder break. Doc suggested we just let the P2V land and, as would be expected in an emergency, immediately surround the plane with emergency vehicles, all with their headlights pointed toward the P2V. The extra light from the vehicles would allow us to see the crew better.

Our CIA "attaché" would be on one of the vehicles next to the actual airport fire chief. He would make sure the Chief said the right things. SEALs dressed as emergency workers would be on several vehicles, and those team members dressed as tourists would be casually strolling toward the vehicles once the fire equipment stopped in position.

Hard as I tried, I could not come up with any problems with Doc's plan. With my nod of approval, he left to talk with Dockerty to make sure we were all on the same page of the fluid plan. I decided to just sit there and run through all the plans in my mind. Perhaps I'd think of something that we overlooked before it ended up biting us on the buttocks.

The P2V was ten minutes out. Our F-4s and the SEAL's R4D were fueled and hidden. The teams were in position. Emergency vehicles were in place, ready to chase the plane to the end of the runway. And two fire trucks were positioned at the end of the runway to keep the P2V from accelerating and taking back off. Doc came back from his last-minute verification of plans, and we just looked at each other and shrugged. It would work or it wouldn't. No need to panic right then. There was always time for panic later.

Part of me wanted to be in front of the fire trucks ready to get Raffe. The other part of me felt there was going to be shooting, and I wanted to be far away from that. I had shot enough people lately. I didn't consider my thoughts cowardice. Just normal self-preservation, as I was afraid that one day the faces of those who had been in my sights, those faces that haunted my memories, would overpower the good that resided inside me. I wanted the good to win in the end.

Coming out of my deep thoughts, I saw landing lights in the distance. Doc was heading to the door, and I followed. The night air was still warm from the day's sun as we headed toward the jeep that would carry us to the runway. The P2V's wheels chirped as they hit the runway, and the roar of props reversing filled the quiet night. The P2V rolled toward the end of the runway and, with a small squeal of the brakes, stopped. Both engines were shut down as the emergency vehicles did their job of blocking the aircraft in place.

For a few moments, nothing happened, and then finally the fire chief used his bullhorn to tell the crew to leave the aircraft immediately and walk toward him. There should be eight men on that aircraft including Raffe. A hatch under the fuselage near the tail opened and five crew members came down. They moved out from under the aircraft and stood still in a group looking nervously over their shoulders at the aircraft. Two men climbed down from behind the nose wheel and walked toward the fire chief. A third man came down behind the nose wheel and just stood there.

Doc and I had been standing toward the rear of the truck, and the fire chief and the commercial attaché stood on a deck behind the truck's cab, where a spray nozzle stood ready. As the two men we assumed were the pilot and copilot walked toward the truck, we moved toward the front of the truck, while still remaining in the shadows. Vehicle headlights and spotlights on several of the trucks illuminated the aircraft and the crew members well. Raffe was not one of the two men approaching.

I could not see the face of the third man still standing by the nose landing gear. He had found a shadow and was using it well. All I could tell was that he was standing very still and seemed to be looking in our direction. His hands were in his flight suit pockets. I motioned to the CIA guy and gave him a specific order. He nodded and took the bullhorn from the Chief.

"Let's go, Doc. Time to do what they give us the big bucks to do." And with that, I started walking toward the aircraft and specifically to the man in the shadow.

"Attention American aircrew, get on your knees and put your hands behind your head immediately. Get on your knees and put your hands behind your head immediately. We will open fire if you do not comply," said the CIA guy through the bullhorn.

"Stop where you are. Get on your knees immediately!" Doc yelled at the man, who had started walking. "Stop or I'll shoot!"

The man stopped, about halfway between the aircraft and the ring of emergency vehicles. He quickly turned partially around and pulled his right hand from his pocket. He had a weapon. The weapon came up quickly and he fired.

Doc and I were already on the ground when the shot rang out. I have no idea where that bullet ended up. He fired again; this round sparked off the runway about ten feet from us. He then turned and bolted toward the ring of vehicles. We couldn't return fire since emergency vehicles and personnel were directly behind the shooter.

Doc, having both his hands to assist, was up and running immediately. With only one useful arm, and the hand on that arm holding my weapon, I was slower to rise and finally run after them. It had to be Raffe and he was getting away.

As with most things in life, Murphy's Law often takes control, and it did so again. There were more vehicles than there were SEALs dressed as airport staff, and Raffe ran between two vehicles that did not have one of our people on it. That meant that since Doc was about ten feet ahead of me, he was closer to Raffe than anyone else. So we were the tip of the spear and we would not let him get away.

Off the other side of the runway were several maintenance buildings; probably one or two held electrical components for the many landing lights. I saw a dark figure disappear behind a building on the right, with Doc about fifteen feet behind him. With my weapon ready, I headed around the other side in hopes of cutting Raffe off. Before I got to the back corner, though, another shot rang out, followed by a thud. Not a good thing.

Edging up to the corner, I looked around to find Lieutenant Jim Dockerty kneeling on Raffe's back, twisting his arms together and pulling the small pistol from his grip. Doc had his weapon trained on Raffe. Two other members of Jim's team appeared and helped him secure Raffe's hands. They pulled Raffe to his feet.

Jim handed me Raffe's weapon. He smiled and said, "Like I said, sir, can do."

Team members locked arms with Raffe, one on each side, and Jim fell in place behind Raffe. Together we walked the head viper toward the terminal building.

132

THE NEXT HOUR WAS ANOTHER hectic mess, which seemed to be my standard operating procedure. When we got into the lighted area around the terminal, we saw Dockerty was bleeding from his left bicep. Raffe's last shot had grazed his upper arm. In the excitement, Jim hadn't even noticed. Doc found a first aid kit and treated the wound as soon as we got into the conference room reserved for us by the Consulate General.

The SEAL teams hauled Raffe off to another room for a strip search and to keep him under tight control. Local police were happy to provide handcuffs and leg irons. They also provided external security around the airport and the terminal. Raffe was not going anywhere for a while.

Doc and I quickly interviewed each of the P2V crewmembers, and they all had the same tale. Raffe boarded last in Norfolk, and immediately pulled his weapon on the crew in the back of the craft. When they were about a half hour out of Norfolk and he had tied up the five men in the back, he went to the cockpit and informed the pilots he was now in charge. He secured the copilot and kept his weapon trained on the pilot during the entire trip.

He had untied the crew after landing. He kept their cooperation by threatening to blow up the aircraft if they tried to rat him out. He had carried on a metal toolbox in Norfolk and told the crew it contained a bomb. His lie—it contained normal tools—proved you cannot trust a bad guy.

The crew had been surprised at Raffe's openness about his plan. He told them all about it on the trip down. Perhaps he'd been boasting due to insecurities. Anyway, Raffe's plan was to use the confusion from the emergency landing as cover for his escape. After sneaking away from the scene, he'd join up with some of his associates from Venezuela. They'd promised to have a boat ready to haul him off the island once he was clear of the airport.

And frankly, it was a decent plan that would have worked had we not been there ahead of him, with force. And we would not have been there had Ensign Less not tried to kill himself. Some days, luck, at least for us and not for Richard Less, was just as important as investigative work.

I sent the P2V pilots, under the watchful eyes of Claymore, to ready their aircraft for departure and fuel it with sufficient gas to get us to Gitmo. The criminal facilities there in Aruba were not what I considered high security, and we were too close to Venezuela to keep me happy.

Claymore and Kooter were invited to join us in Gitmo for the rest of the night and probably much of the next day. As the operation leader, my request was more along the lines of an order, but I wanted to keep my new friends, so I was nicer than I needed to be. Now that the "fun" was over, we had at least a ton of paperwork to do, and they had their share. They were happy to continue the adventure with NIS, said Claymore.

I expressed our gratitude to the island's governor, police and emergency crews, airport staff, and members of our consulate—even our CIA buddy—for all their assistance with this arrest. I did my best impersonation of a diplomat as I smiled and shook way too many hands. With a wink and a nod, the governor promised that the only thing to appear in the local newspaper would be that a test of emergency procedures worked well at the airport.

That task finally over, I placed a quick call to Sam with an update. He promised to call Admiral Gallagher, Captain Miller, and Kelly, but not necessarily in that order since I suspected he knew my priorities. And he'd be immediately notifying NISRA Gitmo to expect us and have everything in place for our arrival.

I told Doc it was time to sound "Boots and Saddles" and head to Gitmo. Two SEAL team members joined the crew of the P2V to make sure no other 'issues' occurred, and they departed. Claymore and Kooter got back into their toys and decided to have some fun with a full afterburner takeoff. It was great to watch and hear the "sound of freedom" ring through the night as they roared into the sky like shooting stars. They would be sleeping soundly in the Gitmo transient BOQ long before our slow R4D arrived.

"Excuse me, Lieutenant Commander Colt. Thought it an appropriate time for this," said Lieutenant Dockerty as he handed me and Doc each a glass of brown liquid. "I pegged you as a bourbon man, sir. To a job well done." A simple toast was all that was needed to mark the end of a successful operation.

"Thanks, Lieutenant. A true pleasure to work with you and your team."

With our glasses drained, new friendships solidified, comrades saluted, aircraft engines warmed up, and Raffe under the control of his new SEAL friends, Doc and I climbed aboard the Navy R4D and finally left Aruba a little after 0300 hrs. Cuba was a few hours away, so with the SEALs alert and watching Raffe, Doc and I adjourned to the rear seats and promptly fell into a deep sleep with the combined help of exhaustion, the bourbon, and the sweet drone of the radial piston engines.

133

THE SUN SPARKLED OFF THE water, and its flashing against my closed eyelids pulled me from my sleep. As I slowly came back to consciousness, I nudged the snoring Doc to join me. The R4D was in a gentle descent and a shallow turn as we approached Cuba.

We were directed to a hangar where I could see our two F-4s being serviced on the right side, and the nose of a P2V visible inside. A rolling ladder was put in place and the door opened. I half expected a band to be playing, but instead I saw two civilians and three officers as I stepped down to the tarmac followed by Doc and LT Dockerty.

The short older civilian spoke first. "Good morning and welcome to Naval Station Guantanamo Bay, Agent Colt. I am SSA Troy Archer, and this is SA William Hawkins."

"Morning," I responded with a nod. Something bothered me about Archer, but it could just be fatigue. "Where is your third agent?"

"He is holding down the office, SA Colt, because normal work still has to be done."

Before Archer could continue, the Navy Captain walked over to me with his hand extended. "Marcus, I am John Frost, the base commander.

A mutual friend in the form of an ugly old master chief yeoman in D.C. called me very early this morning and asked that I take real good care of you and Doc. Another mutual friend in the same office said he thought it would be all right for me to call you Marcus. We are all at your disposal for this operation."

I shook his hand and smiled a knowing smile. Before I could reply, the Captain continued.

"Commander Wells," the Captain pointed to the officer on his left, "is the skipper of the P2V squadron that NIS has sequestered. And the other gentleman is Lieutenant Commander Priestly, who is in charge of base security. With your permission, he'll take charge of your prisoner."

"Thank you, Captain. It is a true pleasure to meet you, sir, and I appreciate all the help you have provided. We'll try not to be too much of a bother going forward. And I'll be happy to let the old ugly one know that you were here the moment we arrive. Neither of us want to get on his bad side, do we?" We shared a chuckle.

I turned to the officer on the far left. "No disrespect intended, Mr. Priestly, but several of the SEAL team members will be joining you as you move Raffe to a cell. They will also remain there until I tell them otherwise. Raffe has been a slick bastard, and we greatly suspect he has access to a tunnel here on the base that would allow him to make a one-way visit to Cuba. I want him to sit and worry before we interrogate him back in Norfolk. Doc, will you please 'volunteer' a couple of the team members and make that transfer happen."

Doc turned and went back into the R4D. I continued, "Commander Wells, I am sorry we've disrupted your command so much, but as soon as SA Stevens, LT Dockerty, and I finish a much-needed breakfast, where I hope all five of you will be my guests, we'll try to get things straightened out. Lunch yesterday was a long time ago in a faraway place." That got the expected laughter and nods of agreement.

The Captain motioned over one of the lieutenants who were standing near his car and whispered something to him. The Lieutenant vanished into the hangar. On the way to the officer's mess, the Captain mentioned that the "other guy" in the ugly chief's office had been a good friend for more than two decades. He also congratulated me on my engagement. I told him to keep Labor Day weekend open for a wedding.

We found Claymore and Kooter heading into the mess and I asked them to join us. As we proceeded in, a Marine Colonel drove up. He approached the Captain, who turned to me and said, "Lieutenant Commander Colt, this is Colonel Matt Janson. He is in charge of the Marine contingent here at Gitmo, and will want to hear about this tunnel theory you mentioned. I called him to join us." The party just got bigger.

Rank does have its privileges, and the Captain secured us a private dining room in the officer's mess. It took a few minutes to get all the introductions over with, then we finally sat down to eat. Nice thing about breakfast foods—eggs, sausage, toast, etc.—is they can usually be eaten with one hand, which helped eliminate any embarrassing moments like having Doc cut up a piece of steak for me.

Our private dining room allowed me the opportunity to start the briefing and bring the key players here in Gitmo up to speed on what was going on and why. As happens too often in the military, orders are passed on to do something and the justification behind the orders is overlooked. I find that the more people understand the why, the better they fulfill the order.

SSA Archer informed us that while they'd sequestered the entire P2V squadron personnel, they hadn't yet started interrogations. Archer felt he needed more information before getting started. I noticed that Agent Hawkins rolled his eyes a bit on that statement.

Pertinent questions were asked and answered to the best of our abilities. And I told Archer that I hoped we had provided the info he needed to proceed. He nodded that he did. But before I could go further, there was a knock at the door and the Captain's Lieutenant stuck his head in and said, "Excuse me, Captain, but there is a call for Mr. Colt. Shall I bring it in?"

The Captain looked to me with raised eyebrows and I nodded an okay. Seeing that, the Lieutenant brought in a phone and plugged it into the closest wall socket. I took the handset. "Lieutenant Commander Colt speaking. How may I be of assistance, sir?"

"Nice to know you're still alive, Colt."

"Good morning, Admiral Chance. How are things in Foggy Bottom?"

"Things here will be much better when you return to work here so I can kick your butt for getting wounded again, but until then, the CNO asked that I send you some help. Guess lounging on tropical islands takes a lot out of you." He laughed at his joke and continued, "Seriously, I have six agents from the Miami area in transit to you right now; they should be there well before noon. All of them speak a Cuban version of Spanish so that might help. Since there are currently three that are assigned to Gitmo those six will triple the manpower available to you. Do you want more?"

"Thank you, sir, but no more will be needed. Those six will be a big help with the interrogations we need to get done ASAP."

"Fine. Let me know if you need anything else. By the way, great job on outthinking that Raffe bastard, but don't let that go to your head. And get well soon! Chance out."

As I handed the phone back to the Lieutenant, the questions were showing on the faces around the table. I told them all except the kicking my butt part. Archer had a concerned look on his face while William Hawkins looked relieved. I'd need to talk with him privately. I asked the Captain if his lieutenant could make sure interrogation spaces were set up for the incoming agents. He agreed and sent the Lieutenant on his way to make it happen.

Colonel Janson suggested several options for finding the theoretical drug tunnel, and I told him I believed all options should be taken immediately. We needed to find and close this tunnel as soon as possible. Hopefully, the interrogations would give us a clue where we might find the tunnel.

Breakfast was over and Captain Frost insisted on virtually grabbing the check. He told the steward to put it on his mess tab before a real check was presented. He asked if we needed anything further from him. When we thanked him and told him we were good to go, he said he'd be back in his office working with the base facilities officer. This guy would know which buildings were currently unoccupied and would know where all the drains were located.

Doc stopped him and asked, "Captain, which way to the base hospital? We're a bit overdue for a dressing change on his bum arm." He smiled as he pointed to my sling.

"Ride with me," the Captain said as he pointed to his car.

"Thanks, sir. Greatly appreciated," I responded. Then I looked over at the rest of the team members, who were standing around looking to me for direction. "Okay, gentlemen, here is what we need. Dockerty, please go with Priestly to make sure your team is taken care of and that Raffe is secured—very secured. Archer, you and Commander Wells head over to the control tower and check on the arrival of the incoming agents. Be there to pick them up and take them to the Gannets' hangar."

Heads were nodding as I continued, "We will have a brief meeting before starting the interrogations. Hawkins, please ride with us to the hospital so I can get some info from you about the base. Colonel Janson, I'll do my best to keep out of your way, sir, as you try to find this tunnel ASAP.

I'll let you know if any of the suspects give us a clue or two. Claymore, you and Kooter need to rest up just in case another crazy flight is needed. And I appreciate you both writing up after-action reports to be included in this investigation. I'll be at the hangar as soon as this quack here finishes torturing my arm." That got the expected chuckles and my orders received the expected "yes, sir," "can do," and "you got it" responses as they all went to accomplish their tasks.

As everyone headed to do their tasks, the Captain chuckled, "Colt, you remind me of that man in D.C. the ugly old one works for. He also has the ability to juggle a hundred tasks at once when he's dead tired. But you forgot my orders. What can I do?"

"Sir, I would really appreciate it if you would stop me when you think I'm about to screw up."

134

ENTERING THE HOSPITAL NEARLY CAUSED a Chinese Fire Drill. I expected Doc would quietly ask for a room and some bandages, but that changed when the staff saw the base commander escorting us. People scurried in every direction and STAT announcements filled the air. Suddenly we had the head doctor and a senior nurse doing a dressing change under the watchful eyes of Doc.

I could tell the Captain was surprised by the extent of the slash, and Hawkins just shook his head when he saw it. But the doctor said it all looked great to him, and he watched as Doc handled the new bandages. Doc was happy to tell the doctor how it occurred when he asked, so now more people knew of my shooting skills, even when injured.

After the new bandage was in place and the doctor and his staff were thanked for their great care and ushered out, Doc asked the Captain to help him find us some coffee. He did that to give me the chance to privately talk with Hawkins. "Do you prefer William or Bill?" I asked him.

"Bill is fine, sir."

"Okay, Bill, what is it Archer isn't telling me that your rolling eyes want to reveal?"

His face screwed up into a frown and he said, "Mr. Colt, Troy Archer is a fine agent, but this past year he seems to be more concerned about not making waves and less concerned about solving cases. With this one, he decided to wait until a 'higher authority' arrived before starting the interrogations. We received what I consider sufficient information about the case from Norfolk yesterday and I think we've wasted a full day waiting."

I nodded my understanding. "Thanks for the straight answer. I appreciate your honesty and I won't say anything to Archer. Just know your concern has been shared with the right person and all information will be held in confidence."

After a quick jolt of coffee, we drove over to the hangar where the Gannets were waiting their interrogations. The Captain dropped us off and returned to his office to meet with the base facilitates officer about drains.

At the hangar we were pleased to see Archer, Commander Wells, and six agents from NISRA Miami standing by the door to the office area. After a round of introductions and an overview of the case to make sure everyone was on the same page, I called Archer aside. We moved about twenty feet away from the group.

"I probably should have asked this earlier, but have you interrogated Wells yet?"

"No, sir, I felt it would be better to wait for your arrival."

"It would have been nice to know that before we included him in the breakfast brief. That's info you should have shared immediately, Archer. And hell, you had plenty of time yesterday. Oh, well, we need to do that right now." I turned and yelled over to Doc, "Doc, please take Hawkins and the XO to his office and do the standard interrogation. Archer and I will take the CO to his office."

The six new agents started with the rest of the officers and senior enlisted. As expected, all of them seemed to be clean. By the time we finished with those interviews, Sam had called from Norfolk with the list of possible vipers based upon the BIs. Scott and his team had completed them in a hurry, and there were seven names on the list. I shared that info with the other agents and we started work.

The other sixty-five enlisted members of the air and ground crews were done and so far, all seemed to be clean. I'd decided to hold the seven potential vipers until the end. The longer they sat and worried might help us break through their firewall of innocence. And with the number of agents we had now, every one of the seven would be in interrogation at the same time. That meant no one would be able to confer with any of the others. This way, we could play them against each other.

Hawkins and the six Miami agents each took one of the possible vipers to a separate room and got started. We had worked out a story line that everyone would use. Doc, Archer and I would be moving from room to room observing. Sometimes we would enter individually, other times we'd come in pairs. Anything to throw the suspect off in hopes of getting more info. We needed to break at least one of these bastards and do it soon.

I left them to the interrogations and headed to the Captain's office. I needed to see where things were on the tunnel search, and I wanted the Captain's input on my next step. My timing was perfect, as I saw Colonel Janson heading into the HQ as I walked toward the building. I caught up with him as he approached the Captain's yeoman.

"Any news, Colt?" asked the Colonel as he shook my hand.

"We're down to interrogating the last few men right now, sir, and it looks promising that these seven are dirty. We are working them against each other and hope to have a breakthrough soon. But right this minute, we got zilch. You?"

"About the same. We have the entire Marine and SP contingency working on this, but nothing yet. I figured it was time to update the Captain."

"Gentlemen, the Captain will see you now," announced the YN1 who was the gatekeeper for the skipper. "Please go on in."

"Please tell me that both of you being here together is a good sign," stated the skipper as he came around his desk to greet us. He pointed to a sofa over to the side and we sat down. "What ya got, Colonel?"

The Colonel went first. "Nothing yet, Captain. We're about fifty percent done on the building checks, and will soon start on drains. I've doubled the crews checking the integrity of the fences. I just wanted to keep you in the loop."

The Captain nodded and looked at me, "How about you, Marcus?"

"Captain, we now feel sure that seventy plus people are not involved. And the agents are now digging into the last seven people. These are the ones who Norfolk tells me all have hinky BIs. With this case, we started looking to see if the possible suspects had excess money and any lavish lifestyles that do not fit their pay grades. The agents should be wrapping their interrogations in the next hour or so. I'm here to run my next step by you, and now that he is here, the Colonel."

"And what is that?"

Before I could lay out my thoughts, the Captain was notified by his yeoman that both Agent Stevens and the base facilities officer, Lieutenant Commander Tony Macon, needed to speak with him ASAP.

"Send them in," he replied. They entered and came to attention. "At ease, sit and tell us what deserves that ASAP. Macon, you go first."

"Captain, we just found our end of the tunnel. It comes up inside a deserted small building that once housed some of the electrical switching components from when we received power from Cuba. That building has not been used for the last few years."

The Colonel looked surprised and asked, "Where is this building located?"

After hearing the location, the Colonel nodded and said, "That is the area my team was working on when I came here. I must have just missed it. What is the condition of the tunnel?"

"Sir, the tunnel is about fifteen feet underground and looks impressive. It has a metal track for moving small carts, lots of shoring, and electrical lights. We backed off until you were notified."

I spoke up and asked, "Doc, what generated your ASAP?"

Smiling a Cheshire cat-like grin, Doc let us know, "Four of the seven possible have already confessed. And the other three will probably break when we finish telling them the others have rolled over on them."

There were smiles all around on the news. The Colonel explained that he wanted to take a group of armed Marines through the tunnel to secure the other end. The Captain was concerned about armed military on Cuban soil.

I spoke up again. "How about we call the local Cuban authorities and let them know we've found the tunnel and plan on exploring the portion that's on our property before we destroy it. Perhaps there's an honest man there who will want to work with us. Or at least be watching the buildings on his side to see where the dust cloud from the explosion comes out."

The Captain looked at the overhead for a moment, and then at me as he answered, "Sounds like a descent diplomatic compromise, Marcus. Any other suggestions?"

"One more, sir," I offered. "Have Lieutenant Commander Priestly, or better yet his XO, make the call to the local cops rather than you or the Colonel. That way it won't seem like too much of a big deal. Oh, and one more small thing: find out the names of the personnel who've been responsible for providing security for the area of that deserted building.

They might be dirty and have allowed things to go on. Give their names to Archer so he can run a quiet investigation on them."

The Captain nodded his approval and dismissed us with a simple order: "Make it happen, gentlemen."

135

THINGS HAPPENED FAST FOR THE rest of the morning and early afternoon. Phone calls were made to the right people in Norfolk and Washington D.C., providing them with updates. In return, they called back after decisions had been made on how we were to proceed. We finalized the plans and documented the case to date. Aircraft were serviced and investigation paperwork finalized. The JAG officers had already started their part of the investigation, laying out all the charges.

Doc and I finally had a couple of moments to just sit and not have to think, plan, or worry. It's difficult to turn off the brain, but it's occasionally needed to get things back in perspective. And right now, we both had that 'all the air has been let out of the balloon' feeling as the emotions drained from us.

Lieutenant Commander Priestly had passed the responsibility of contacting the local police to his XO, so he sought us out to see what else we needed. While it was only 1530 hrs, Doc proclaimed that the sun was over the yardarm, so we could officially splice the main brace in honor of our victory over the vipers. We left word with the others to join us when they could, and with Priestly's expert guidance, we found the officers' club in record time. It was time share a drink.

458

We talked about the tunnel and all we'd seen down there. Looked impressive, and it was amazing it was done in secret. I was still surprised the drug movement had gone on for so long. Looked like all the drug money bought silence, as did the killing of CIs who ratted on Raffe. Doc told Priestly that he needed to tighten his base security because there were probably more people involved in this mess. He agreed and promised to initiate work with the local NIS agents to start looking for them.

A few more key players drifted in to join us, and it was nice to share a moment of victory. But there were still tasks to be done, so after a bit of back slapping and congratulations, Doc and I went back to the Gannet's hangar, which had become our HQ for this part of the investigation.

The decision had been reached, at the highest level, that all legal proceedings would take place in Norfolk. The C-130 that had flown the agents from Miami was loaded with the suspects, including Raffe, who were guarded by the entire SEAL team from Key West. The Miami agents also boarded, and as we watched from the ground, the aircraft left for Norfolk.

Doc and I had decided that flying in the F-4s again, probably for the last time in our lives, was a wise, and especially fun, decision. Think of it as a bonus for a job well done, I told Doc. Claymore had worked out the flight plan and coordinated with the tankers, so we were ready to roll at any time.

We'd already paid our respects to Captain Frost and said our good-byes to the NISRA agents when we sought out Commander Wells. He was busy supervising the maintenance crews, who were sealing up the places in the wheel wells where the vipers had been hiding the drugs. We wished him well as he rebuilt his crew and continued to be more watchful for drug activities in the future.

A couple of the crew chiefs helped us into our gear. I noticed the helmets were not there, and the crew said the F-4 pilots had picked them up earlier. As we started to walk out of the hangar, the XO of the squadron ran out of the office area and told us to quickly come outside and take a look north. We felt the ground shake, saw a dust cloud rise, and then heard a deep boom. Our side of Raffe's tunnel had ceased to exist. My lingering concern, which I'd shared earlier with Colonel Janson, was what other tunnels or drug conduits had we not discovered. He promised it would be a main issue for him and he'd make sure base security also considered it that.

Claymore and Kooter were anxious to get home, and I was anxious for a shower. It had been a long time since early Tuesday morning. And with the exception of remembering that day's breakfast, I couldn't recall any other decent meals Doc and I had since Monday night. Suddenly I was feeling dirty, hungry, and dead tired.

Claymore was smiling a bit too much as Doc and I approached our rides home. Same for Kooter. Claymore cleared his throat, "Gentlemen, if you expect to fly with the Hooligans, you must be in the proper uniform. Kooter, please get these two Hooligans squared away."

"Aye, aye, sir," Kooter replied as he brought two new-looking helmets from behind his back and held them out to us. The one he gave Doc had "Bones" painted across the front in blood red. He handed me my helmet that was lettered "Bossman" in gold outlined in black. Both had "Hooligans" lettered across the back in blue and gold.

"Shall we head to the ranch, Bossman?" asked Claymore.

I could not get any words to come out. I just nodded and we shook hands.

The Neptune ground crew helped get me and Doc settled into our F-4 backseats, and after a brief chat with the tower, Claymore lined up on the runway and advanced the throttle past full military power to engage the afterburners. Claymore obviously wanted a bit of fun from this trip as well.

I was looking forward to watching the refueling again, but Claymore had seen the fatigue on my face. He had shut off my comms after he heard my snoring. He told me later that I fell asleep about three minutes after takeoff. I came back to life only when I felt the jolt of landing at NAS Oceana. After we taxied to the hangar, I noticed we had a reception committee awaiting our arrival inside the hangar.

Expecting only to see Sam and a few other NISRA Norfolk agents to help handle the arrival of the C-130, which was about an hour or so behind us, I was surprised to see a few others there. As I descended from the cockpit, again with the great help of Doc, I turned and found Kelly latching on to my neck and planting a welcome home kiss on my lips.

"I missed you, sailor. Welcome home." She smiled, kissed me again, and said, "I need to know, Marcus, how do you do it?" She gently ran her hand down the side of my face.

"Do what?" I asked in confusion.

She winked and replied, "How do you look so good all the time, either as an enlisted yeoman, a naval officer, a secret agent, and now a fighter pilot?"

That got a chuckle out of Claymore who had descended from his place of honor as true fighter pilot and was standing behind Kelly. After

I introduced him to Kelly, she gave him a hug and thanked him for keeping me safe. His look bounced between pride and embarrassment, and I could tell he was impressed with Kelly. We turned and walked into the hangar and caught up with Kooter as we entered through the main door. Doc and I carefully carried our special helmets under our arms.

The reception committee contained even more surprises. We headed over to where the group stood. As expected, Sam and the agents were there, but also Captain Miller and Captain Simon Lavella, commander of the SP contingent, and YNMC David Bartow. And as we approached them, both Admirals Chance and Gallagher emerged from behind an F-4. Seems they'd flown down from D.C. to make sure Raffe was handled correctly and to let all involved know their efforts were appreciated.

We popped to attention as the admirals approached. The CNO bellowed out the 'as you were' command and we relaxed a bit. I could see the CNO smiling as he viewed Kelly hanging on to my good arm.

"Colt," said Admiral Gallagher, "this is the first time I've seen you two standing together. You make a great looking couple and look overly happy." He turned to Admiral Chance and continued, "John, last week was the first time I saw these two since they met and Colt was in a hospital bed during the entire visit." Admiral Chance got a chuckle out of that. "Marcus, you and Doc have done a great job with this investigation."

I spoke up and said, "Admirals, Captains, everyone, these gentlemen are Commander Alexander Marcaise and Commander Steve Koots, the CO and XO respectively of this squadron, who were essential in the completion of this mission. And when the C-130 touches down shortly, you'll get to meet some of the others who helped get the job done, including a SEAL team and the Miami NIS agents. My final report will be sure to mention them, and those not present, who we relied on greatly during this assignment, sirs."

Marcaise smiled and offered his two cents worth. "Sirs, Koots and I have been honored to be under the excellent command of Mr. Colt and Agent Stevens, and appreciate the opportunity to participate. They can fly with us anytime, sirs."

Both admirals started to laugh. Admiral Chance spoke first. "Gentlemen, your humility is noted and appreciated. Trust me when I say that all of us here, and all of those involved with this effort elsewhere, understand and know who did what, and we are thankful to you all."

The CNO shook his head in agreement and said, "Kelly, I think it is time for you and Doc to get Marcus home. He looks like he is ready to fall over. We will hang around here to make sure all those aboard the C-130 are taken care of properly. Marcus, we will see you in the NIS offices no earlier than 1300 tomorrow. Dismissed."

136

DOC DROVE THE BLUE BEAST home as Kelly and I leaned against each other in the back seat. Holding hands was taking all the energy I had left. My sense of time must have been totally off—I knew I last saw Kelly less than forty-eight hours ago, but it seemed like a month since we were together. Love has a tendency to do that time-warping thing, I supposed.

Doc immediately went up to his room to fall over while Kelly and I headed to the kitchen. She pulled out some leftovers and two beers. The aroma of the food got my mouth watering, and I quickly devoured my late dinner. We adjourned to our sofa to finish off the beers in what had become our favorite spot. Low light, soft music on the radio, and Kelly leaning against my shoulder was the answer to all my problems.

She asked what all had happened and I gave her a quick synopsis of the events. She was amazed that so much occurred in such a short time and thrilled that Raffe was finally in custody. She hoped the entire case would be behind me soon. I explained that I still had a ton of paperwork to do and then there would be the testifying at the trials, but basically the hard and dangerous part was done.

For the first time in our quick and wonderful relationship, we talked about plans for the immediate future, plans that revolved around us and not around my job. Kelly wanted us to get away for a while. I suggested the three of us—after all, Doc was still under her father's orders to be my shadow—head up to D.C. for a few days. That would give us a chance to visit with her mom and dad, as an engaged couple should. And we could stay at my—scratch that—our townhouse. I could check in with NISHQ and introduce her around. She agreed that the trip was a wonderful idea and we should head that way on Friday. I promised to ask her uncle tomorrow for a few days off.

And I suggested that after the splint and sling come off, she and I head to Florida for a week to visit my folks. Again, my plan was well accepted and we jokingly argued about which car to drive down. I wanted to get the 'Cuda back on the road and she firmly believed her Mustang, top down and beach bound, was ideal for a Florida visit. Being a wise man, I quickly agreed with her. No matter the vehicle, a road trip with Kelly was bound to be nothing short of outstanding.

The beers were finished, and it was time for bed. But first, I desperately needed a shower. After heading upstairs, Kelly helped me out of my shirt and carefully wrapped my bandaged arm in the standard plastic wrap. I went in for a hot shower. I looked forward to the day when we could shower together, but for now, snuggling together and falling asleep in each other's arms was enough. But September was so damn far away!

She was asleep by the time I got into bed, but just having her close was nice. Enjoying her soft snore, I drifted off into dreams of our future together. Exhaustion had gotten the better of me and it was nearly 1000 hrs before I woke. Kelly's side of the bed was cold, so I knew she'd been up for a while. I headed into the bathroom and did the morning routine before heading downstairs to face the day.

Doc and Kelly were sipping coffee at the table when I came stumbling in. "What year is this?" I asked as I poured a cup of much needed coffee from a nearly empty pot.

Doc snickered and said, "Still 1971 and you're still in Norfolk. Kelly still loves ya, and I sort of like you—at least on good days when you buy the coffee and nobody is shooting at us."

"Be nice, Doc, and remember he is still considered walking wounded," said Kelly with a laugh. "You have about three hours before you have to face my dad again, Babe, feel in the mood for some bacon and eggs?"

"Oh, you betcha, sweet lady. I bet this means you want me to cook, right?"

She laughed and said, "Well, not by yourself, Ol' One Arm. I'll scramble the eggs and handle the toast while you tend the skillets."

This was a most wonderful way to start the day.

137

THE 5ᵀᴴ NAVAL DISTRICT HEADQUARTERS building was all a buzz when Doc and I arrived. Having the CNO in the house for a day had caused a bit of excitement. When we got to the NISRA office, the laughter coming from the agents' area hinted that he might be hiding out there.

Coming through the door, I was amazed so many people could fit into such a small space. In addition to the agents, the CNO, Captain Miller, and YNMC Bartow, we also had the district's admiral and much of his staff in attendance. Sam was holding court, regaling everyone with stories of how I'd been such a terrible yeoman but one hell of an investigator.

Doc and I entered to face a round of applause. And after that settled down, I jokingly reminded Sam that I had been first in my class at Yeoman A School and, while I thought I was a halfway decent investigator, I was damn proud of my crossed quills. That also resulted in another round of laughter, applause, and agreeing nods from the agents. I had to admit it was nice getting their approval.

After everyone settled down, Doc and I gave a briefing on all that had happened over the last few days, and what was coming in the immediate future. There were still many loose ends to tie up and that meant a ton of work ahead of us on this case, but the good news was that the vipers, or at least most of the worst ones, were off the street. The agents in Norfolk and Gitmo still had work to do, as did the sheriff in Brownsville, Texas, but at least some of the drugs would no longer be flowing. And hopefully the CI murders had been stopped.

After a few questions from the 5th ND admiral, he and his staff offered their congratulations and returned to their offices. The CNO, the skipper, David, Doc, and I retired to the skipper's office to go over some final details.

Actually, most of the details revolved around my request for a few days off so we could head to D.C. to visit my future in-laws. The skipper at first kidded that I'd just returned from a paid vacation to a Caribbean island and didn't need more time off. After the expected round of laughter, he said he understood and gave his approval. He also reminded me that I could still take at least ten days of recovery time and that wouldn't be charged as leave. He recommended we head to D.C. on Friday and take all of next week off. He felt we needed the rest.

The CNO was happy to hear and quickly approve my plans, and suggested that the Captain and Dorothy come up for a day or so too. David nodded his approval of the plans and asked that we reserve a night for him to take us to dinner. Life was good.

138

APRIL THROUGH AUGUST 1971

THE NEXT FOUR MONTHS FLEW by, with one activity after another filling the days and nights. Kelly and I realized our lives would probably never be sedate. There was always something to do, a place to go, or someone to see. But that was a good thing.

The search warrants against Raffe for his houses and businesses in Brownsville, Texas; Miami, Florida; and Norfolk, Virginia were all executed immediately after his arrest. Large quantities of drugs were discovered as well as a pile of notes about the CIs that were targeted. More than enough evidence was discovered to overcome the lack of confession. Some of it helped close other cold cases for both the Navy and civilian law enforcement. In addition, there were more arrests made as his minions were found.

Our first trip to D.C. together was great. Kelly loved our townhouse, and didn't plan on changing anything about it. Well, she wanted to add more furniture since I had purchased the bare minimum, and two of the three bedrooms were totally bare. Poor Doc had to sleep on the sofa the first couple of nights of that first trip. Kelly went furniture shopping to get him a bed as soon as she could.

Our time spent with her parents was interesting and filled with fun. At first, I had problems getting over the fact he was the CNO, but after a few hours hanging around together in civilian clothes, I started to feel more at ease. In just a few days, we fell into a comfortable and close relationship.

Operation 'Street Sweeper' went off without a hitch early that Thursday morning after Doc and I returned from Gitmo. I slept through most of it. Thirty-five drug pushers were removed from the streets of the base and dumped into the brig, waiting their turn at a court-martial. A large group of users was also pulled off the streets.

My parents and Elle came up for Kelly's graduation on May 25. Everyone was thrilled to finally meet her, and she them. Our families got along great. Kelly was so excited to finally have a little sister, and she spent a lot of time with Elle. Dad, Captain Miller, and the CNO hit the golf course together for several days after her graduation. Mom enjoyed spending time with Dorothy Miller and Elaine Gallagher as they helped work on the wedding plans and shared embarrassing stories about Kelly and me as kids.

Kelly started looking for a job in the D.C. area, all while planning our wedding. We made frequent extended weekend trips so she could interview and we could spend time with her folks. She also volunteered at the base hospital in Norfolk several days a week to get some practical experience. I planted the seed that perhaps she should continue her education and get a doctorate. She said she'd consider it.

Doc and I were surprised to be summoned to the NISHQ the first week of June, and told to make sure we reported in dress uniforms. With the CNO, Captain Miller, my parents and our families present, Doc was awarded the Meritorious Service Medal for his outstanding performance in the viper case. Admiral Chance presented me with the Legion of Merit, which he said he'd insist that I wear all the time along with other awards. As he phrased it, and made it clear to all present, my days of being out of uniform were over.

While we were at NISHQ, members of the NIS Internal Affairs division presented me with the 'Next Time, Duck Stupid' plaque in honor of my bandaged arm. It featured a painting of Daffy Duck with his left arm in a sling. Lieutenant Doty told me to hurry up and get back to D.C. as he was not having fun doing my job. Perhaps now he'd appreciate me a bit more.

With school out for the summer, Elle asked to stay in Norfolk for a while. It worked out well to have her stay with us. She and Kelly were inseparable and spent many hours at Captain Miller's house planning the wedding with Kelly's mother and aunt. Sam's wife was also a big help with the planning.

Doc and I kept out of trouble in May and June, wrapping up the viper case. There were tons of paperwork that had to be done, and on top of that, trial preparation was crucial to get a conviction. Doc's investigator skills were developing nicely, and he was really enjoying the work. Sam called on him several times a week to go out on local investigations.

My weekly checkups on the arm went well. The surgeon finally allowed me to drop the splint the second week of June. Then the torture of physical therapy began. Doc stayed by my side during it all and made sure I did the exercises while at home. My arm felt like so much dead weight that I knew it would take a while to get it close to normal strength. But I kept working it, and while overseeing my exercises, Doc forced me to do one more rep every day because, as he kept yelling, "the only easy day was yesterday." Finally, by the first week of July, enough strength had returned to my arm that I felt comfortable driving again.

Doc and Ann had become a regular item by the first of May and announced their engagement at our July fourth cookout. They'd been spending more and more time together as Doc felt more comfortable leaving me on my own. Well, on my own under the watchful eyes of Kelly.

I discussed it with Kelly, and with her enthusiastic approval we gave the Blue Beast to Ann. I could not bear to sell that car to a stranger, so giving the car to Ann kept the Beast in the family, so to speak. Through her tears of happiness, she promised to give it back if she ever wanted to get a newer car.

Our house became the location for friends and co-workers to come together and relax. Frequently, Commander Alex Marcaise and Commander Steve Koots and their families were guests for dinners or cookouts. The NISRA agents and families were always coming and going, as were other members of the NIS team, both military and civilian, including Rhonda and Dex, with Karen on his arm. Sam kidded that he and his wife needed to pay us rent or at least buy some groceries since they were there so much.

I finally got to meet many of Kelly's friends, professors, and classmates, and they also quickly became fixtures around the house. It was a wonderful time to build friendships and enjoy the company of good people.

Most of July was spent attending and testifying at too many court-martials and a couple of civilian trials. All of the vipers were convicted and sentenced to many years in the Portsmouth Naval Prison. Two civilian trials saw Raffe and Royal both convicted and sentenced to the death penalty. Ex-detective Royal never got his turn in the electric chair. There were too many convicts there in prison because of Royal. He was found dead in the prison shower the second week of August; he'd been stabbed. Not many tears were shed.

It was a bittersweet call that I made to the parents of Ensign Joan Appleton once the trials were all over. It felt like I might again be opening a wound that had started to heal, but I had promised Mr. Appleton that I would not give up on finding Joan's killer and would let him know how things went. He sounded happy to hear from me and I felt like I was talking with an old friend. I explained how Joan's killer had met a similar fate and that the ringleader who ordered her death was now himself facing the death penalty. I shared what I knew about LT Thomas and what little I could uncover about their relationship. Closure is important, and sharing facts is one part of the job I know helps people heal. Ensign Appleton's case was one of those that would stay with me forever.

After all the pieces of the puzzle came together, numerous phone calls and official visits were made to the families of the others killed by the vipers. Explanations and apologies were given as needed to help with their closure. The service records of the deceased were updated and any incorrect negative conclusions were removed.

News from NISRA Gitmo was not surprising. The week after we left with Raffe, SSA Troy Archer decided it was time to retire and move back home to Joplin, Missouri. He joined the local police force there as a senior detective. SA William Hawkins was promoted to Supervisory Special Agent and took over the leadership of the NISRA. Under his watch, several members of the base security team were arrested. They had been complicit in allowing the tunnel to be used for drug trafficking.

During the first week of August, we finally had time to drive the Mustang down to Florida to spend a week with my folks, and since this was Kelly's first visit to my area of Florida, we spent a lot of time doing the tourist thing. That Tuesday evening, we dined at Ted Peter's Famous Smoked Fish restaurant that specialized in smoked fish, hot German potato salad, and ice cold beer. A true gourmet meal served outside on picnic tables. It's located on beautiful Pass-A-Grille Beach in St. Petersburg.

After that superb meal, we drove back up to Clearwater to watch the waves come in around the pier in the cool and quiet of the evening. Kelly and I were walking arm in arm along Pier 60 in Clearwater when I heard a familiar voice. Glancing behind me, I saw a very pregnant Sandy saying some not-so-loving things to a fellow I could only assume was her husband Lucas. I nudged Kelly and whispered the info to her. She turned and watched the couple for a moment before turning back to me and quietly announcing that I'd dodged a bullet with that one. We held our laughter down until they'd left the pier.

Doc and I were able to finalize the documentation on my unique method of file card analysis before the end of August. Doc's input was critical in the process. He had a way of translating the complicated into everyday language. Creating the manual ended up being a lot of work, and my skills as a yeoman came in handy; I did much of the typing once I discovered that typing was also good therapy for my arm. So, I was killing two birds with one stone, as the saying goes—rebuilding muscles while getting my job done. After the wedding, Doc would be assigned TAD to NISHQ to handle the agent training on this new method. Step one of his transformation into a true special agent.

Kelly and I spent many hours on our sofa talking about our lives before we knew each other. She now knew almost all the things that haunted me from my time in Nam, and used her professional therapy skills to help me work through some of the issues. In turn, her stories of growing up all over the world as her father went from duty station to duty station were great to hear.

We planned our two-week honeymoon around a trip to Rome, beginning with signing up for an Italian class at ODU over the summer. We figured between immersion into the language and our love of history and food, we could find plenty of time to practice our Italian as we explored ancient Roman sites and restaurants during the day and excitingly explored each other all night. Italian is, after all, one of the world's most romantic languages.

My Hooligan's helmet found a place of honor in the living room inside a protective glass case. It wasn't sealed inside the glass box since I might need it again one day. Be prepared is always a good motto.

139

OUR WEDDING DAY WAS FINALLY here. We had decided on a late-morning wedding with a start time of 1100 hrs. The organ music came drifting into the room where I was pacing. Nerves were trying to take over my usually calm persona, and at a time like this, that's never a good thing. I looked into the full-length mirror and wasn't sure who I saw looking back. After spending so much time earlier that year as Petty Officer Mark Williams, then wearing civilian clothes for several months as an agent, seeing Lieutenant Commander Marcus Colt looking back, decked out in a white dress uniform, complete with sword and medals, gave me one of those *Twilight Zone* moments.

A sharp knock on the door brought me out of my mental fog and back to the moment. I announced "Enter," and was rewarded to see the Chief of Naval Operations, also in his dress uniform with enough medals to cause him to walk with a list, enter and close the door. "Shouldn't you be with Kelly right now, sir?"

"I just left her and she is more than ready. Chomping at the bit as the old saying goes. I came to check and make sure you were also," replied the Admiral with a small smile on his face. He held a couple of small boxes in his left hand, pulled in tight against his leg, as he looked me over from head to toe. "Kelly told me that you would probably be out of uniform, and we, especially she, will not allow that." He extended the boxes.

I knew what they held. The Navy Cross is the highest honor any sailor can receive, short of being awarded the Medal of Honor. I received mine after the mission in Vietnam just over a year ago. That same mission was the reason for the Purple Heart with an oak cluster. The job I did cost some men their lives, while others now carried life-changing wounds.

I initially refused to wear them because they caused me mental anguish. But a few months ago Captain Miller helped me understand the importance of wearing them and I now had the ribbons in place. But until that day, I had avoided the actual medals.

Still holding out the boxes, the Admiral put on his sternest face and said, "Marcus, I thought you and Captain Miller had worked out your issues with these."

"Yes, sir. We did. I should have picked them up at the house. Sorry, I was not thinking. Please do the honors of pinning them on in the right place, Admiral." I closed my eyes and was overcome with the memories of the men who sacrificed their lives and bodies.

With the medals pinned in place, the Admiral stepped back and saluted. I returned his salute sharply. We turned and headed out the door.

By the time we finished the guest list two months ago, we decided an outdoor service would be best. Lots of room for adding chairs as the number kept getting higher. Kelly and I have just the average number of friends. But it seemed since the father of the bride was also Chief of Naval Operations, and my boss was head of the Naval Investigative Service, there were many others that needed to be added to the invite list. And there were the new friends I'd picked up since being assigned to Norfolk.

I suspect there were several hundred white chairs filling this portion of the base golf course that the Admiral had sequestered for our wedding. He had two trailers brought in so we'd each have a convenient dressing room. The Admiral slapped me on the back and left for the trailer housing Kelly.

I walked to the back of the seating area and stood with the preacher. Well, he was an Admiral and also the chief of Navy chaplains, but I still thought of him as just the preacher. He looked at his watch and nodded.

"Aye, aye, sir, let's proceed into the valley of the shadow," I thought to myself. I still need to work on that sarcasm thing. At least I'm learning to keep most those things in my head. We turned and slowly marched to the front where the vows would be exchanged.

The preacher assumed his position facing the group of people, and I turned toward them as well. I have to admit it was overwhelming. On the front row on the groom's side sat my parents and little sister. Lots of expected grins were seen there. A few aunts, uncles, and cousins filled the next two rows.

Seated on the next row behind the family was a man I had not expected to see in person again ... the current Secretary of State and his wife. That was a shock, and just as shocking was seeing the Assistant Secretary of Defense and his wife sitting beside them. Looked like the wedding reception was going to be an impromptu reunion of last year's team, with those two gents there. To their left was the wife of Admiral Chance; I was honored they chose to sit on my side.

Filling out that row and several behind it were the wives and husbands of the men and women I'd had the honor to serve with these last few years, both here and elsewhere. I glanced over toward Kelly's trailer and saw a huge grouping of men and women in dress whites milling around her trailer door. At least they had not run off to the bar, I thought with a smile, well not yet. Behind the lonely military spouses, I saw the rest of the members of NISO and NISRA Norfolk.

On the bride's side, Kelly's mother, Elaine, had been seated on the front row along with the Captain's wife, Dorothy Miller. Behind them were too many spouses to count that I did not recognize, but knew them to be friends of the CNO and his family.

Standing alone at the front of this huge assembly of dignitaries, family, and friends was intimidating. The preacher was ready. I think I was ready. I felt lonely standing up there—lonely, but ready. Kelly and I had decided not to have any bridesmaids or groomsmen. There were just too many close friends and we didn't want to offend any of them by keeping them out of the selection.

But the lack of an official position in the wedding party did not stop the military attendees, both officers and enlisted, from forming an honor guard. They lined up, shoulder to shoulder, on both sides of the walkway to be used by Kelly and her father as they came from the trailer. Their positions made me think of the side boys piping someone onboard a ship. With a small chuckle, I wondered if they had a bosun's whistle. They all stood at attention as Kelly and her father passed. The way they were placed tightly together prevented me from seeing Kelly and her father, even though they had walked to the end of the gauntlet.

I could see the top of the Admiral's head and that he had stopped. One of them issued a 'be seated' command and the members of the honor guard marched down the aisle and took their seats. The array of military uniforms included every branch of the service, ranging from the lowest enlisted to four-star holders.

It just hit me that in addition to men and women I'd served with over the years, this impromptu escort contained many associates of the CNO, including Doc, Master Chief Bartow, Ann, Rhonda, Clyde Anderson, and even Petty Officer Cummings, as well as the rest of the Joint Chiefs of Staff. Talk about impressive.

It was only when the last of them left the back that I could clearly see Kelly hanging on to the arm of her father. The impressiveness of the members of the escort left my mind completely as I gazed upon Kelly. I know I'm expected to believe she was the most beautiful bride ever to walk down any aisle. But that description palled when looking at Kelly.

The organist started the standard wedding march, and the Admiral led Kelly down the aisle past the many rows of standing and smiling attendees. He stopped at the end of the row of chairs that contained his wife, gently kissed Kelly on the cheek, and passed her hand to me. He leaned toward me and gave me one last command as he gave his daughter to be my bride. I nodded to him in complete agreement and said a soft "aye, aye, sir." I believe a saw a glint of a tear in his eye as he went to sit by Elaine.

The ceremony went much quicker than I had expected. I remember reciting the vows and knowing in my heart that it was a monumental change in my life. Neither of us dropped the rings as we'd been dreading, and before we knew it the preacher said the "you may kiss your bride" part. My brain was saying *Aye, aye, sir. Can do.* And I did. A cheer and applause arose from the guests as we walked hand in hand back down the aisle and led them to the clubhouse for the reception.

I look forward to seeing the wedding photos, since the reception was such a huge event that I just vaguely remember our first dance, followed by socializing with more people that I'd ever seen in one place. The CNO told me it was going to be written up, with photos, in an upcoming issue of the Navy Times, since it turned out to be the social event of the year for Norfolk Naval Base. Guess I'll read all about it when that issue comes out.

Getting together with people that had become like family over the last few years was an outstanding time. Kelly was happy to finally meet the rest of the team that I had told her about from the events in Vietnam, and they were thrilled to meet her. The reunion went well and fallen comrades were remembered; remembering them didn't put a damper on the happiness of the wedding, but it did help those of us who are missing them.

We socialized for hours and danced with everyone who asked. One memorable sight was Dexter dancing with Karen; they made a good-looking couple and there is promise for that relationship growing into something special. Doc and Ann were inseparable, and Rhonda was spending a great amount of time dancing with Jimmy Kincade. Weddings seem to bring more people together than just the bride and groom.

When time came for us to leave the reception, I saw a large group of officers standing outside the door. I knew what was coming, and it was going to be great. The Arch of Swords is an old military tradition. The officers lined up on each side of the door facing each other, and as we got to the door, the command "Officers, Draw Swords" was issued. This was followed by "Invert Swords," leading to the sword tips touching at the top of the arch. It was an impressive display and a nice honor to receive. My boss, Admiral Chance, was on the door end, and he was the one to announce, "Ladies and gentlemen, I have the honor of presenting Lieutenant Commander and Mrs. Marcus James Colt."

We slowly walked arm in arm under the arch until we got to the end. The last two members of the arch lowered their swords as we approached, to prevent us from leaving. It was the Chairman of the Joint Chiefs of Staff, wearing his outstanding Marine dress uniform, who had the honor of ceremonially tapping Kelly on her exquisite behind with his sword. This was the traditional way of welcoming her to the military family as he boomed out, "Welcome to the Navy, Ma'am." Her look was hilarious and completely priceless. Hope the photographers got a good shot of that one.

As we walked to the waiting car, at least a half ton of rice was in the air heading in our direction. Commander Alexander Marcaise called out, "Eyes Up!" There was a diamond formation of F-4 Phantoms, all leaving a white trail of smoke behind them as they passed overhead. Another overwhelming event on a day that was filled with them. I gave Claymore a big smile and salute. Thank you, sir!

Not sure who closed the limo doors, but we were finally in a quiet place and, for the first time that day, alone together. We sat there for a moment, holding hands and just smiling at each other. After a sensual kiss, I looked into her wonderful gray eyes and said, "You know we are going to have a great life together, right?"

Kelly returned my smile and gently touched my cheek. Her mouth twisted up to the left and she whispered, "Oh, you betcha, sailor!"

GLOSSARY

ANGELS—Flight level, i.e., altitude given in thousands of feet.

ATC—Air Traffic Control.

ASW—Anti-Submarine Warfare.

AUTOVON—Automatic Voice Network. A worldwide American military telephone system with high-speed switching centers.

BI—Background Information Check. Used to determine eligibility for security clearances. Includes talking with friends, previous employers, and educators, looking into social memberships, and analyzing financials.

Bravo Zulu—International naval signal code for "well done."

BUD/S—Basic Underwater Demolition School. SEAL training.

Call Sign—Nickname for a pilot used for radio communication.

CNO—Chief of Naval Operations. The military head of the US Navy. Advisor and deputy of the Secretary of the Navy.

CO—Commanding Officer of a military unit.

CPO—Chief Petty Officer.

FUBAR—Navy version of SNAFU. Fouled Up Beyond All Recognition.

Gitmo—Guantanamo Bay Naval Station, Cuba.

M.E.—Medical Examiner.

NAS—Naval Air Station.

NIS—Naval Investigative Service.

NISHQ—Naval Investigative Service Headquarters located in Washington D.C.

NISO—Naval Investigative Service Office. Designation for the headquarters over a specific geographical area that contains multiple NISRAs. Staffed by both military and civilian personnel.

NISRA—Naval Investigative Service Resident Agency. Office that houses agents and staff that are responsible for a smaller portion of a NISO.

NTC—Naval Training Center.

Petty Officer—A noncommissioned officer that has shown skills and leadership, allowing them to advance over other enlisted personnel.

RIO—Radar Intercept Officer. Handles navigation and radar in a two-seat fighter/bomber.

SA—Special Agent.

SEALs—Special Warfare Operators. Acronym for Sea, Air, Land.

SP—Shore Patrol. The police force of the Navy.

SSA—Supervisory Special Agent.

TAD—Temporary Additional Duty.

UA—Unauthorized Absence, same as Army's AWOL (Absent WithOut Leave).

UCMJ—Uniform Code of Military Justice. The foundation of military law in the United States.

Wild Weasel—An aircraft equipped with anti-radar missiles and used to destroy radar and surface-to-air missile installation by first making themselves a target.

XO—Executive Officer of a military unit. Second in command.

ENS—Abbreviation for the Navy rank of Ensign. Lowest level commissioned officer in the Navy. Pay grade of O-1. Insignia is a single gold stripe around the jacket sleeve and on the shoulder board or a collar device of a single gold bar. This device is often referred to as a 'butter bar.'

LTJG—Abbreviation for the Navy rank of Lieutenant Junior Grade. Second lowest level commissioned officer in the Navy. Pay grade of O-2. Insignia is a wide gold stripe and a narrow gold stripe around the jacket sleeve and on the shoulder board, or a collar device of a single silver bar.

LT—Abbreviation for the Navy rank of Lieutenant. Third lowest commissioned officer in the Navy. Pay grade of O-3. Insignia is a pair of wide gold stripes around the jacket sleeve and on the shoulder board, or a collar device of a pair of gold bars. This device is often referred to as 'railroad tracks.'

LCDR—Abbreviation for the Navy rank of Lieutenant Commander. Fourth level commissioned officer in the Navy. Pay grade of O-4. Insignia is a single narrow gold stripe with a wide gold stripe above and below, around the jacket sleeve, and on the shoulder board, or a collar device of a gold leaf.

CDR—Abbreviation for the Navy rank of Commander. Fifth level commissioned officer in the Navy. Pay grade of O-5. Insignia is three wide gold stripes around the jacket sleeve and on the shoulder board, or a collar device of a silver leaf.

CAPT—Abbreviation for the Navy rank of Captain. Sixth level commissioned officer in the Navy. Pay grade of O-6. Insignia is four wide gold stripes around the jacket sleeve and on the shoulder board, or a collar device of a silver eagle.

RDML—Abbreviation for the Navy rank of Rear Admiral (lower half). Seventh level commissioned officer in the Navy. Pay grade of O-7. Insignia is a single, very wide gold stripe around the jacket sleeve. Shoulder board and collar device is a single silver star.

RDM—Abbreviation for the Navy rank of Rear Admiral. Eighth level commissioned officer in the Navy. Pay grade of O-8. Insignia is a single very wide gold stripe, below a narrower single gold stripe, around the jacket sleeve. Shoulder board and collar device is a pair of silver stars.

VADM—Abbreviation for the Navy rank of Vice Admiral. Ninth level commissioned officer in the Navy. Pay grade of O-9. Insignia is a single very wide gold stripe, below a pair of narrower single gold stripes, around the jacket sleeve. Shoulder board and collar device is a trio of silver stars.

ADM—Abbreviation for the Navy rank of Admiral. Tenth level commissioned officer in the Navy. Pay grade of O-10. Insignia is a single very wide gold stripe, below a trio of narrower single gold stripes, around the jacket sleeve. Shoulder board and collar device is a set of four silver stars.

F-4—McDonnell Douglas Phantom. Two-seat, twin-engine long-ranger supersonic jet interceptor and fighter-bomber. Often called 'Double Ugly,' 'Flying Brick,' 'Rhino,' 'Old Smokey,' and a few other names.

KA-6D—Grumman A-6 Intruder attack aircraft that has been outfitted with extra tanks and equipment for mid-air refueling.

P2V—Lockheed land-base maritime patrol aircraft. Features two Wright radial piston engines, two Westinghouse turbojet engines, and a range of ASW weapons.

R4D—Navy version of the Douglas DC-3 aircraft. Used as a passenger and cargo hauler.

B. R. WADE, JR. BIO

BILLY R. WADE, JR., though new to fiction writing, has been all too happy to add it to his list of life accomplishments. Born in Roanoke, Virginia, he spent his teen years and much of his adult life in the Tampa Bay area of Florida. While in Tampa, Bill worked in retail management before switching to a career as a computer systems analyst for the local school system. He changed careers again after nearly 20 years of working with mainframe computers and started a manu-facturing company. After this last change, he made his self-proclaimed escape to the mountains of West Virginia shortly after the turn of the century.

After enlisting in the U.S. Navy Reserve in 1969, he was called to active duty and graduated top of his class from both basic training at Naval Training Center (NTC) Orlando, Florida and Yeoman 'A' School at NTC Bainbridge, Maryland. Soon after, he was assigned to the Naval Investigative Service Office in Norfolk, Virginia for nearly two years. While there on active duty, he earned the Navy's Pistol Marksmanship Ribbon with ribbon device 'S' after qualifying as a Sharpshooter with the standard sidearm at that time: the 1911 .45 ACP semi-automatic pistol.

Eventually, Bill left active service as a Petty Officer Third Class, though he wasn't quite ready to hang up his Navy uniform just yet. He spent three additional years as a weekend reservist at his local Navy Reserve Center assisting with the clerical demands of the center, a Seabee unit, and a training course development unit. And, despite his busy schedule during and after his naval career, Bill also dedicated his time to obtaining degrees in Business Management and Computer Science. He also took his business training a step further and studied marketing at the University of South Florida.

Happily, all of Bill's business, educational and military pursuits have proved quite inspiring and provide him with plenty of writing material. He has written several technical "how-to" articles that were published in hobby magazines, and he is nearly finished with the next adventure for his *Fair Winds* NIS novel protagonist, Marcus Colt. Bill also attributes his new love of fiction writing to surviving brain surgery a few years ago. As he phrases it, some of the connections in his brain have found "new and definitely different pathways."

In addition to writing, Bill owns and operates a hobby kit manufacturing business on his property in rural West Virginia. He also devotes time to fostering rescue animals with special needs from his local volunteer animal shelter. When not working, writing, cutting firewood, or shoveling snow, he spends his little bit of remaining free time staying proficient with his Colt 1911 .45 pistol to better assist with security at his church.

CPSIA information can be obtained
at www.ICGtesting.com
Printed in the USA
BVHW071413180921
616993BV00002B/8